What the critics are saying...

SERAPHIM is a must-read for fans who love the idea of falling in love when least expected...Gia and Joachim are such a magnificent couple that I found myself rooting for their love to blossom. ~*Contessa Scion for Just Erotic Romance Reviews*

Reminiscent in some ways of Peretti's *This Present Darkness*, *SERAPHIM* is fast-paced and exciting. Readers will appreciate the creative license the author has taken in order to depict the battling factions of Heaven and Hell...the scorching scenes of denied lust between Gia and Joachim will keep you reaching for a glass of ice water. Attraction to the forbidden is the main theme in this novel, and readers will not be disappointed at the end result. *SERAPHIM* is a book I will most certainly read again. ~ *Angela Etheridge for The Romance Reader's Connection*

SHELBY REED

An Ellora's Cave Romantica Publication

www.ellorascave.com

Seraphim

ISBN # 1419953141

Edited by: Briana St. James
Cover art by: Syneca

Electronic book Publication: June, 2005
Trade paperback Publication: December, 2005

Warning:

The following material contains graphic sexual content meant for mature readers. *Seraphim* has been rated *S-ensuous* by a minimum of three independent reviewers.

Ellora's Cave Publishing offers three levels of Romantica™ reading entertainment: S (S-ensuous), E (E-rotic), and X (X-treme).

S-e*nsuous* love scenes are explicit and leave nothing to the imagination.

E-*rotic* love scenes are explicit, leave nothing to the imagination, and are high in volume per the overall word count. In addition, some E-rated titles might contain fantasy material that some readers find objectionable, such as bondage, submission, same sex encounters, forced seductions, etc. E-rated titles are the most graphic titles we carry; it is common, for instance, for an author to use words such as "fucking", "cock", "pussy", etc., within their work of literature.

X-*treme* titles differ from E-rated titles only in plot premise and storyline execution. Unlike E-rated titles, stories designated with the letter X tend to contain controversial subject matter not for the faint of heart.

Also by Shelby Reed:

A Fine Work of Art

The Fifth Favor

Midnight Rose

Seraphim

Dedication

To the talented ladies at Romance Writers Unlimited—I never would have written the first book without your friendship, skill and support. And to my mother, who taught me to believe in angels.

n. pl. ser·a·phim (-̇-fm)—Six-winged angels of the highest rank in the traditional hierarchy, flanking the throne of God.

Trademarks Acknowledgement

The author acknowledges the trademarked status and trademark owners of the following wordmarks mentioned in this work of fiction:

Candyland: Hasbro, Inc.

Glock: Glock, Inc.

Swamp Thing: Dc Comics composed of Warner Communications Inc.

BMW: Bayerische Motoren Werke Aktiengesellschaft

Levi's: Levi Strauss & Co.

StairMaster: StairMaster Sports/Medical Products, Inc.

Prologue

"The child is dangerously frail," Olivier said, his attention fixed on the small, dark-haired girl standing before a chipped mirror in a grimy tenement bathroom. "Her human form is undernourished. And her soul—starved not just now, but many lifetimes before. Love has been denied her again and again. In its absence, shadows dance. How is it possible that she holds the Medallion?"

Joachim, his mission leader, cast him a faint smile. "The Archangels don't err. Look at the Medallion. It shines like a beacon around her neck."

Neither spoke for a moment, just watched through the celestial transom as the girl alternately studied her reflection and the heavy, ornate chain around her pale neck. The Medallion dangled at her solar plexus, warmed by the energy radiating from her fragile body.

"She doesn't yet have the Sight," Olivier determined at last. "She's much too young."

"Yes." Joachim shifted his attention from her delicate face. "Too innocent. The wait will be lengthy before we can act, as the Archangel predicted."

Beyond the cracked panes of curtainless windows, leaden clouds roiled closer, fingers of hail and fire creeping across the sky.

The darkness was coming.

But there is one who holds the light, the Great Warrior Michael had told his seraphic operatives during the preliminary briefing.

This thin, love-hungry girl wore the Medallion, and what little sunlight that remained in the summer sky seeped into the bathroom's squalor and bounced off the pendant's surface, a blinding spark of certitude.

"Behold the Daughter of Longinus," Joachim said softly, more to himself than to his fellow angel. "Soon it begins."

Chapter One

Twenty years later

Gia Rossi rolled onto her back and adjusted her bikini top, releasing a sigh as the sun's heat drenched her muscles. It was unbearably hot for an Illinois summer. The air lay like a thick, sopping blanket over the suburbs, broken only by an occasional paltry breeze.

She didn't mind. The trickling sound of the pool filters and faint strains of rock music from the veranda lulled her into sensuous distraction, and she drifted in a heat-induced haze, floating in and out of consciousness.

Her personal assistant, Frank, would bring her a fresh pitcher of margaritas if she buzzed for him, but then she'd be morc than tipsy. For now, the simmering warmth of a little too much tequila and sunshine was enough to wipe out any anxiety remaining from Vincent's departure earlier that morning.

As usual, she didn't know where her husband had gone, only that he planned to return home to Chicago in a week.

"A long business trip," he'd told her with a brush of lips against her forehead. "Boring, my love. You'd be miserable."

Nevertheless, a sick knot of foreboding had tied itself in her stomach as she'd stood in the portico of their Barrington Hills mansion and watched him slide into his limousine. He wasn't himself lately. He looked pallid, terse, distracted. And in certain lighting, like a complete stranger. Nothing she could explain without sounding like the clingy wife she'd promised herself never to be.

A trickle of perspiration slid down her temple, and she squirmed on the chaise lounge, brusquely wiping her brow.

Maybe he was in some kind of trouble. Vincent's business

dealings were unquestionably shady and possibly even mob-connected. How else did the money just appear in his hands? Bundles of it. As though it grew in some secret, sprawling orchard for his benefit alone.

He would never tell her where it came from, of course, and she knew better than to ask. The one time she'd point-blank inquired about the nature of his mysterious business endeavors, he'd shut her up with a single chilled look. A look that filled her with the sickening suspicion she'd married a man she didn't know at all.

Still, Gia wasn't about to leave him. He'd played Henry Higgins to her Eliza Doolittle, taught her how to dress, to speak, to exist on a lofty level of fine food, fine wine, fine literature and culture. He loved her as only an artist can love his creation and pronounced it constantly, in words as well as in the tiny treasures he left hidden around the mansion.

As much as Gia appreciated the expensive trinkets, it was the symbolic meaning behind them she truly craved, and Vincent seemed to understand this. He understood *her*. Materially and emotionally, he showed her nothing but love and approval.

Except for that one bad moment in three years of blissful marriage, that icy look across the breakfast table that she shuddered to recall even now.

You're being silly, said the pushy little voice that served as her mental stage mother. *Silly Gia Torio, born in a bleak Chicago tenement to an alcoholic mother with no hope and no future. Look around you, Gia Torio. At this mansion. At these vast, lush grounds. Foolish girl. Sip your margarita and shut up.*

Out of nowhere, a cool breeze shivered over her naked torso, raising goose bumps on her skin. The sun drifted behind the clouds and daylight faded, as though dusk had swathed the estate six hours too early.

Someone was watching her.

Tiny prickles of awareness raised the hairs on the back of Gia's neck. Lifting her head, she slid on a pair of sunglasses and glanced around the yard.

Nothing appeared out of sync. A pair of golden butterflies chased each other among the ivy-filled urns lining the pool, until they caught a breeze and soared into the cornflower sky.

Her attention shifted across the lawn, where a gardener in a straw hat clipped topiaries with artistic precision. She didn't recognize him, but the estate retained so many employees, she only knew the immediate house staff.

The gardener was fully absorbed in his task, his back turned in her direction. It wasn't his gaze she'd felt a moment ago.

No one else was in sight. Still, she couldn't shake the creepy sense that her solitude had been shattered by someone's unwelcome observation.

Self-conscious of her skimpy bikini, she reached for her robe, then dropped it and bolted upright on the chaise lounge, heart pounding. Two men from the kitchen staff—since when did the cooks carry *guns*?—dashed across the gardens and disappeared into the woods surrounding the estate.

"What the hell…?" Before she could grab the intercom from beneath her chair, the snap of gunfire exploded through the air, followed by panicked shouting.

Fear clawed at her heart and she nearly tipped the chaise lounge as she leaped to her feet, her gaze wildly scanning the edge of the woods. *Where had the shots come from?*

Before she could make a mad dash for the veranda, Frank DeSalvo appeared and tackled her to the lawn, muffling her scream beneath his bulky weight. "Head down, Mrs. Rossi! Don't move!"

Pressed flat and breathless by the man she'd come to regard as her oversized executive assistant, Gia couldn't even cry out. The sweet scent of grass and suntan oil mixed with Frank's rich cologne and threatened to suffocate her. Her mind went numb with terror while some lovelorn diva sang out from the house stereo about craving the man who'd dumped her.

For a moment, all was still. Then two sets of black military boots appeared an inch before Gia's nose.

Materialized out of thin air.

Frank scrambled to his feet, his warmth and weight abandoning her, and she flung her arms over her head as the sound of scuffling and fists hitting flesh filled the air around her.

A male cry of agony tore through her paralysis—*Frank!*

"Frank! Oh, my God—what's happening?" Wild with panic, she glanced up, but the glare blinded her.

It wasn't the sun. Brighter than any solar glow, the preternatural radiance poured down on her, but she couldn't identify the source. All she saw was the shimmering outline of three figures…two hovering over her and one prostrate in the background, motionless.

Stars and floaters danced in front of her gaze. The grass scratched her bare legs and torso as she shielded her eyes from the mind-numbing brilliance.

Then, as if someone had thrown a switch, the light dimmed. Gia immediately regained her faculties and got to her knees, but she couldn't move fast enough. Strong hands hauled her to her feet and pushed her forward when she tried to whirl free.

Petrified, she managed to look back at two black-attired assailants dragging Frank's rag-doll body toward the mansion. It would have taken a bulldozer to bring down the giant of a man. *What had they done to him*?

A steely arm snaked around her bare waist from behind and pulled her in tight. Cold metal imprinted itself low on her spine.

"Walk," a male voice murmured against her ear.

The need to survive took over, adrenaline pumping hot currents through Gia's veins as she squirmed and flailed against his iron embrace. "Son of a bitch! Let…me…go!"

Her fingernails dug at the assailant's muscled forearm where his sleeve had ridden up, but his relentless hold never faltered. He lifted her by the waist until her feet kicked aimlessly in the air, and walked for both of them.

She reached back to claw blindly at his face, but he merely ducked his head aside, skirting her attack with quiet patience. She jammed her elbow into his ribs, but it was like punching concrete, and garnered no response, not even an indrawn breath.

Still, Gia struggled. As with the rest of her twenty-six years, the feral instinct to survive gave her no choice.

Only when her abductor hauled her around the side of the house and she spied the white box van waiting in the driveway did the will to fight bleed out of her, replaced by the black, coiling certainty that she was going to die.

Chapter Two

"You're making a huge mistake." Gia coldly regarded the three black-uniformed figures sitting across from her in the back of the box van, her voice high and tight over the rumbling motor. "My husband will send an army to look for me. He never fails in anything he sets his mind to. He'll find me, and when he does, he'll make certain you pay for this."

Only the steady drone of the diesel engine and the hum of the tires on asphalt met her tight declaration.

"You must know whom you're dealing with," she continued, inwardly cursing the quiver that betrayed her fear. "My husband is Vincent Rossi. But then, you probably know that. Why else would you have taken me?"

Three sets of eyes gazed back at her impassively, exposed by the drape of the abductors' black hoods.

Her gaze skirted to the semi-automatic weapon one of them trained on her. She'd seen guns like it before, inside the jackets of the men Vincent had hired to protect her. Men who currently lay unconscious, and maybe even dead, back at the estate.

Defenseless and stolen, she now sat staring at the dark strangers, whose only humanizing features were their bright, watchful gazes. Overhead, a single low-wattage light flickered on and off at the whim of an electrical short, offering eerie, flashing glimpses of her abductors. From the broad shoulders apparent through the material of their uniforms, they were men. Yet none of them eyed the bikini top that clung haplessly to her breasts or the bare, goose-bumped expanse of her stomach and thighs. They only gazed at her face, without respite, until heat seared her cheeks and scalded the tips of her ears. The steady, soul-searching appraisal was nearly worse than being ogled.

"Would someone please tell me what the hell's going on?" she blurted, her body bouncing slightly as the truck rolled over rough terrain. "You can't honestly think you're going to get away with this."

No answer.

Gia nodded at the man on the right, the one with gray eyes and long lashes. Laugh lines etched the outer corners of those eyes. "I can save you a lot of trouble here and now—I don't interfere in my husband's business dealings. I'm no source of information, if that's what you're after."

A fresh wave of heat prickled her neck as she was met with cool silence. Gray Eyes studied her, then looked away.

Exhaustion and desolation slammed into her. With a deep, shaky sigh, Gia leaned her head back against the truck wall and closed her eyes.

Oh, why hadn't she listened to her intuition and demanded some answers from Vincent about his activities? Maybe he would have reacted with outrage. Hell, maybe their marriage would have ended. But anything was better than being held hostage at the mercy of these freaks.

Yes, Vincent could pay for her return. But God help her if this abduction was more than just a bid for ransom money.

She stirred, opened her eyes and again focused on the dark shapes of her captors as the cargo area's light danced on and off. They hadn't moved, hadn't spoken. The interior of the box van was sparse and humid, thick with uncertainty. Hers.

The bulb flashed on and stuck, long enough for her to fix her attention on the man in the middle. Amber eyes. Shaped like almonds and bright, as though lit from behind.

"Just tell me this," she said in a carefully even tone. "What are your demands? You want something, I assume."

The light flickered, went dark, came on again. The assailant to the left moved, drawing her attention. He shifted the pistol from one leather-gloved hand to the other, regarding her through eyes the color of semiprecious aquamarine.

Gia stared at the gun, then at his half-concealed face, while a wild panic seized the last threads of her control. "Does this have something to do with my husband? With Vincent Rossi?"

The silence roared in her ears, pushing her hysteria to an apex. "*What the hell do you want*?"

His dark lashes dropped as he studied her trembling lips.

A scream rose in her throat. Before it could escape and shatter the viscous quiet, the truck bounced over something hard and solid, and with a great, metallic squalling of brakes, lurched to a stop.

Wielding the gun in one hand, Blue Eyes stood and grasped Gia's upper arm to pull her to her feet.

The rolling door screeched up and sunlight poured into the compartment, bringing fresh air and a piercing glare that rendered her momentarily blind. Eyes watering, she felt herself urged toward the open door, the gritty floor of the van abrasive on the soles of her bare feet.

The man holding her arm waited for his cohorts to climb out, then jumped down ahead of Gia and reached up for her.

She shrank back, her sparsely clad body shivering even in the penetrating warmth of the afternoon sun.

"Please don't do this..." A pitiful, ineffectual plea, but she didn't want this. She wanted to be free, not standing on the uncertain end of what could lead to unthinkable torment. What would they do to her once they dragged her to their intended destination? Terror wobbled her knees.

"Come," he said.

She shook her head.

Jamming his gun into his leg holster, he reached up with both hands, clasped her bare waist and lifted her to the ground. The instant her feet hit gravel, she kicked away from him and jerked back with vicious strength.

He let go. She thudded against the unforgiving metal bumper with all her weight, its edges gouging into her naked spine. The toxic combination of physical and mental anguish sent her sliding to the ground, stomach roiling with the urge to vomit.

Blue Eyes glanced back at his cohorts and exchanged some sort of silent communication. Then he stepped forward and squatted in front of her, his gloved hand braced on the bumper by her head. "Mrs. Rossi," he said, a quiet warning.

Gia shuddered at the sound of the truck's front doors slamming closed. More footsteps crunched in the gravel. How many of them were there? Too many to escape. Desperation and pain made her weak, and this time she surrendered when Blue Eyes reached for her.

He helped her stand, nodded at the other men—five of them now—and they began the trek away from the box van toward a sprawling field. Following several yards behind the others, he kept Gia pinned to his side while urging her on, seemingly oblivious to the harsh sobs escaping her with every exhalation.

"You say this happens because of your husband," he finally spoke in husky, broken English without looking at her. "This is true."

Sick relief flooded her chest. "He'll—he'll pay anything to get me back—"

"Mrs. Rossi," the abductor tightened his hold on her arm with renewed conviction, "money will not help you."

They crossed the vast, sun-parched pasture, brittle grass crunching beneath their feet. Gia's soles were scraped and burning, her back gouged and achy, but she hardly felt the pain now. As far as she could discern, there was nothing for miles except windswept grass and barbwire fence. Maybe they meant to execute her, murder her in cold blood out here where there were no eyes or ears to witness it. The thought turned her insides to jelly and drained the strength from her legs. She stumbled, and Blue Eyes had to slow his determined stride to haul her upright.

"Where are we going?" she managed, her lungs burning as he increased his pace and forced her to keep up.

"Soon you see."

He spoke with a heavy accent Gia couldn't quite pinpoint. She fixed her tear-blurred gaze on the four wide-shouldered figures moving ahead of her and trudged along like an errant child, numb to the marrow of her bones.

After a moment she spoke again, her voice high and shaky. "Are you going to kill me?"

One of the men ahead choked back a laugh.

"Do not be afraid," Blue Eyes said in that eerie, impassive tone. "Soon you know."

The first paltry reassurance anyone had offered her. It didn't help.

Their steps slowed, and the man who held her arm glanced up at the sky, head tilted as though listening for something. All Gia heard was the maracas-rattle of insects, the distant cry of a circling hawk.

"*C'est ici,*" he told his companions.

Amber Eyes squatted, removed his glove and ran a naked palm over the thick, matted grass. Crickets leapt out of the way and a swarm of yellow butterflies emerged from the deep overgrowth, hovered and dispersed.

To Gia's amazement, he reached deep into the weeds and grasped what appeared to be an iron handle. He pulled until a rectangular, steel trap door creaked open, then stood and laid it back in the grass. An underground cell?

She'd read horror stories about hostages kept in wooden boxes, deep underground with a single PVC pipe to supply air…for days. Weeks. Until they went mad from claustrophobia and fear and dehydration.

Oh, God! Breaking free from her guardian's grasp, she stumbled backward and hit the ground on her raw, bruised back. The sons of bitches could just kill her right now. Shoot her.

Beat her to dust—anything. But she wasn't going in that hole!

Scrambling away on hands and knees, she ignored the dig of grass and dirt in her tender palms, dark curls slipping free from her ponytail and hindering her sight. Within the space of a breath, steely hands grasped her waist and set her back on her feet, but she wasn't going. She kicked and struggled with ferocious strength, fighting to keep from being *buried alive in that pit*.

The assailant jerked her around to face him and she struck out blindly. "No!" Her fingernails grated across his jaw, tearing free the material covering the lower half of his face and flaying skin with it.

He released her and cursed, a foreign word translatable in its painful vehemence.

One of the others restrained Gia in a vicelike embrace as the man with the snapping blue gaze pulled off a glove, jerked the hood from his head and swiped a hand across his cheek. It came away bloody. For a second his eyes met hers, ire darkening them to nightfall. Then he shook his head and turned away.

But Gia had seen his face, and she would never forget it. Sculpted in stone, fine-featured and darkly sensual. His russet hair, shot through with copper sunlight, was too long, curling around his ears and neck. A fair complexion offset the striking blueness of his cold, emotionless gaze. He was dangerously handsome, and she hated him instantly.

Yet he still hadn't killed her.

"Containment," he muttered, using the discarded hood to wipe the blood from his jaw.

Still transfixed, Gia stared back at him as one of the other men dropped into the burrow and reached to lift her down. Then her feet left the ground and darkness swallowed the sun, the scent of loamy earth filled her nostrils, and all she could see was blackness and the lingering visage of the man who had brought her to this hell.

*****

Joachim paced his office, head bowed and fingers steepled against his brow as he awaited further instructions.

Gia Rossi was contained, sequestered in a sterile, glass-walled cell where she could be closely observed. Even now, he struggled to keep insult from his thoughts as he replayed the moment she'd raked her fingernails across his face. He wasn't sure which hurt more, the furrows she'd dug in his flesh or his pride.

Pride! His brows lowered. Pride was a foreign concept. The frailty of his human form, both mentally and physically, was nearly unbearable. How easily it bled, body and soul!

Despite his chagrin, the objective aspect of his true self, the seraph beneath the mortal disguise, understood her fear. He and Olivier and the others had told her nothing, simply smuggled her from her home and thrown her into a chilled underground world, miles from everything familiar and safe to her.

Joachim had earned the ferocious scrapes in his cheek with his silence, with his iron grip on the compassion that rippled just under his newly acquired human heart. But he'd followed orders, divine orders that had been hatched not only with Gia Rossi's well-being in mind but the safety and welfare of her Earth.

And now he felt…wretched.

The soft fall of footsteps beyond the partially open door caught his attention and he rounded his desk to sit behind it, watching for Nicodemus' appearance. A breath later, the old seraphic counselor appeared at the threshold in a simple cotton robe, his wrinkled features lined with a warring mix of concern and amusement.

Nicodemus cleared his throat, folded his hands serenely in front of him and spoke in French, the native dialect of Joachim's human form. "So. She was less controllable than Intel had indicated."

Joachim cocked a brow and braced his elbows on the

armrests of his chair. “To say the least. What now?”

“We await Rossi’s retaliation, for surely it will come.”

“And the Medallion?”

“The woman will tell us its location.” Nicodemus spoke with a certainty Joachim didn’t feel.

Restless, he sat forward. “The woman will tell us nothing if you ask her now. She wants only to go home. She doesn’t understand why she’s here. How long will we keep the truth from her?”

“She is not ready,” Nicodemus said. “Soleil reports that even now she lies prone on her cot, weeping as though her heart will never mend. We have taken her from all she knows—and from the secrets that would have killed her.”

“It will kill her to think she’s being held captive here indefinitely.”

“She *is* a captive here.” A bushy white eyebrow lifted. “Indefinitely.”

Joachim shook his head. “But if she knew who we are and why we—”

“It is not possible to divulge the truth just now, Joachim,” the old angel said. “You let your human remorse over certain unavoidable issues cloud your senses.”

So he did. He touched his fingertips to the tender scratches on his cheek. “She thought we were going to harm her.”

“Of course.”

“She tried to run.”

“The most basic survival instinct.”

“She clawed the skin from my face,” Joachim added in a desultory tone. “I wanted to throw her back to Rossi, or whatever Therides calls himself these days.”

“She does have spirit.” Nicodemus leaned across the desk and laid a wrinkled hand on Joachim’s sleeve. “And so do you. Too much, perhaps. Vestiges of the self-indulgent soul who inhabited this body before you.”

Joachim blew out an exasperated sigh. "I could have been assigned a more peaceful identity, you know. Tell me, Nicodemus, did you grant your approval to this…this…" He glanced down at himself, at a loss for words. "This body belonged to a violent criminal, I understand."

Nicodemus briefly pressed his lips together as if to withhold a smile. "Yes. Killed in Montreal when a narcotics exchange went unexpectedly sour."

"Montreal, eh?" Joachim shook his head. "You had to pack him on ice and ship him here. Why not just find a local criminal? Any healthy body would do."

"Not necessarily. This one's mental and physical capabilities were the perfect combination for the mission's function. He was the quintessential warrior. A selfish and dangerous individual to be sure, but also tenacious, charismatic and extremely perceptive. Traits you need for this assignment, Joachim."

"I could do without the lack of discipline he suffered." Joachim stared at the computer monitor as he searched the traces of memory left in his physical mind. Sordid images flashed there, of violence, chaos, intoxication, carnality. He glanced down at his hands, turning them over to study the palms. These hands had wielded weapons that took lives, transported narcotics that stole reality, glided over flesh to elicit intense pleasure…and stripped that same flesh from the bone to cause the greatest physical agony. *Man's inhumanity to man.* It had been, and always would be, incomprehensible to Joachim.

He shook off echoes of another man's past and glanced at Nicodemus. "I'd like to speak English more fluently too. I only understood half of what Gia Rossi was saying when we abducted her. I don't know if she understood me either."

"Easily remedied." Nicodemus smiled and passed his fingertips over the other seraph's brow. "Done. You will converse with Mrs. Rossi as easily as if you were a born American." He stepped back and continued in English. "For now, you must debrief. Go to Contact and speak with the

Archangel. Purge your conscience and your worries before you sleep."

It took a moment for the new language to coagulate in Joachim's mind. Then he frowned. "I don't need—"

"But you do." The light humor fled the older angel's expression. "Your emotions run high just now. A dangerous thing for the leader of this operation."

And a mark against Joachim's steadfast record that could remove him from the mission if Nicodemus expressed concern to the Archangel Michael.

No room for mistakes. Joachim's mouth tightened at the thought. The body he inhabited promised all sorts of unwanted challenges this time.

He bolted to his feet and turned toward the window that overlooked the nucleus of the quad-shaped facility. "How do I control it? In a thousand lifetimes, I haven't felt the anger I experienced today when she struck me."

"Then she stirred you, this woman."

Joachim's gaze snapped to the old man's. "Of course not."

Nicodemus regarded him in silence, his pale, watery eyes stripping Joachim's denial, turning and twisting it in meticulous examination.

Joachim hadn't fully understood Archangel Michael's reasoning in sending the old counselor along on such a fierce and dangerous assignment. At the time, he'd worried Nicodemus would only be underfoot. But now he knew. The ancient seraph was a set of watchful eyes for the faction of angels assigned this mission. There would be no secrets between seraphim and Heaven.

"Go to Contact," Nicodemus repeated placidly. "Debrief. Clear your conscience. And then we have work to do."

When the counselor was gone, Joachim turned off the office lights and headed toward Contact as instructed...but the pull in the direction of prisoner accommodations was too great to deny.

He told himself it was curiosity. As a celestial being assigned to this world over and over, he'd often slipped in and out of his wards' surroundings. Ever watchful, of course, ever the guardian angel. But also mesmerized by human emotion, an element that had started out as a pure reflection of Creator and ended up misshapen by the need to survive on this inhospitable planet.

Joachim had always been fascinated by the violence and passion here, the power of the Dark One among these fragile beings. The same sensation now stirred within him as he thought of Rossi's wife. Fascination, plain and simple.

Stopping at a one-way cell window, he found Gia Rossi as Soleil had reported, lying prone on the cot with her face buried in the crook of her arm, sable curls flowing onto the stark linens.

"Tugs at the heartstrings, doesn't she?" a melodic, feminine voice curled against his ear, English words whose meaning came to him without hesitation this time. He shifted to find Soleil standing beside him, and a frown lowered his eyebrows.

Heartstrings. Yes, exactly. A tugging sensation in the chest, almost unpleasant in its persistence. Joachim looked back at their prisoner without responding.

"She'll recover," the other angel continued. "She's stronger than she appears."

He glanced again at Soleil's sculpted profile. Michael had assigned her an appealing human form on this mission. She was slender, tall and lovely. Blonde and smooth, suitable to her celestial persona.

It hadn't been a random choice. The demon Therides liked willowy females. Soleil's position on this mission was well defined without a single word of explanation from above.

"You're concerned," she said without looking at him. "Even the mission leader needs reassurance that his actions are well-founded."

"Mrs. Rossi's despondency bothers me."

"But she's already more comfortable, Joachim, and she no

longer struggles. We have offered her food and drink. She has bathed and accepted a fresh change of attire, all without incident."

Soleil had provided Gia with a white T-shirt and thin cotton pants, and the prisoner did look clean-scrubbed and relatively unharmed beyond her enduring distress. Joachim's gaze lingered on Gia before sweeping the narrow confines of her cell.

Everything in accommodations was colorless except the captive herself. Her figure struck Joachim's human perception with breathless clarity, the fathomless dark of her hair, the sun-golden tone of her skin. Her shoulders heaved once, then again, vestiges of a vicious weeping bout.

"She still grieves," he said.

"But soon she'll rest."

After a moment, Gia's cheek turned against her arm and away from their observation, and she stilled.

Joachim watched the steady rise and fall of her back and knew she slept. He pushed a hand through his hair and sighed. Nicodemus was right. Some of the tightness unfurling in his chest was shame. Another human emotion for which he had no use.

"Stay close to her," he instructed Soleil a little too sharply.

"Of course," she replied with a slight smile.

He left Gia's window without looking back and headed through the bunker toward Contact, formulating in his mind the clearing he would request from the Archangel Warrior Michael. *Cleanse me of shame, anger…and* this.

An unnamed, bittersweet sensation in the vicinity of his human heart he knew better than to examine.

Chapter Three

The soft brush and squeak of a door opening roused Gia from a fitful sleep, and she bolted upright, instantly alert.

The same slender blonde who'd offered her a change of clothing the night before stepped into the cell. The woman's catlike green eyes were dispassionate as they flickered over the tray of food on the corner table, untouched from the previous evening. "You must eat to keep your strength, Mrs. Rossi. Breakfast has been prepared for you."

Gia sat back against the chilled concrete block wall and shook her head. "I'm not hungry."

"Try." With a serene smile, the woman retreated and gestured to an unseen presence in the hallway behind her, then returned with a small bowl of fruit. "Something light, at least."

Sighing, Gia accepted the plastic bowl and settled it in her lap. Her stomach lurched with a mixture of distress and hunger as the sweet scent of berries and sliced apples greeted her. According to the diamond-studded watch on her wrist—the only jewelry her captors had allowed her to keep—twenty-four hours had passed since she'd eaten anything. Fingers shaking, she lifted an apple slice to her lips and gingerly bit into it.

"I'm here to escort you to your meeting," the woman went on, hands clasped behind her back.

Gia froze. "What meeting?"

"You've been brought to this location for a reason, Mrs. Rossi."

"I'm aware of that," Gia snapped. "So what the hell do you people want from me?" When the woman didn't respond, she forced herself to calm. "You know my husband will pay whatever ransom you ask."

"This isn't a financial matter." The blonde blinked, her green gaze searching Gia's face. "In a few minutes you'll be introduced to Joachim. He'll explain as best he can the reason you're here, what you can expect of us—and what we expect of you."

Gia set aside the bowl, her stomach protesting at the fresh wave of rage that shuddered through her. "Joachim—he's the leader of this setup?"

"That's right."

"And who are you? The First Lady?"

The woman's full lips curved upward. "My name is Soleil, Mrs. Rossi. I'm your guardian."

Gia laughed, dry and humorless. "My guardian? You're guarding me?"

"Yes. A protector, if you like."

"I don't *like*. I don't like any of this." She cursed and shook her head. "If you're my protector, who the hell's going to protect me from *you*?"

Soleil approached the cot, retrieved the bowl of fruit and set it on the table, then withdrew a thin plastic band from her white coveralls. Everything in this godforsaken prison was white and emotionless, including the blonde herself.

"Hold up your wrists please, Mrs. Rossi."

Gia stared. "What is that, some sort of…*handcuffs*? Oh, come on. You don't have to do that," she protested as the woman slid the strange plastic band over her hands. "I won't run. I can't. This place is a fortress."

"And you're quite safe here. But for now, we'll follow procedure. If you're cooperative, Joachim may waive the restraints."

Gia allowed Soleil to help her stand, then used her bound hands to push awkwardly at the disheveled curls hanging in her eyes. "I'd like to brush my hair and my teeth and…and wash my face. And I need to use the bathroom."

"You had a shower just a few hours ago."

"I need to pee," Gia retorted.

Surprise flickered across the blonde's beautiful face, as though such a possibility hadn't occurred to her. "We'll make a stop along the way."

They met no one in the steel-walled corridor. An eerie quiet hung heavy in the air, and Gia found herself straining for any sound of life. Even the drift of human voices or laughter would have acted as balm to her raw nerves, but there was nothing. Only mausoleum-like silence, the distant hum of a generator and the soft cadence of Soleil's military boots on the slick linoleum.

When they reached the lavatory, Soleil escorted Gia inside, unfastened the plastic wristbands and stepped out into the corridor, discreetly pulling the door closed behind her.

Alone, Gia stood shivering in the center of the tiny bathroom, the chill of the tile floor soaking through her white socks. God, this place was cold. She rubbed her arms and wandered toward the vanity. A hairbrush wrapped in cellophane awaited her in a small wooden crate by the sink, along with a packaged toothbrush and a tube of toothpaste, a bar of soap and a washcloth rolled neatly with a towel beside the other toiletries. All white.

She took her time with her ablutions, sorely missing her high-dollar facial cleanser and custom-formulated moisturizer. Her eyes still burned from crying, and every muscle in her neck ached with relentless tension. Still, when she was done, the face in the unframed mirror looked fresh-scrubbed and rosy, aside from the gray circles beneath her eyes. She nearly felt human again if she didn't examine her new reality too closely.

Outside the bathroom, she met Soleil and stood in sullen silence as the blonde refastened the band on her wrists. Gia covertly studied the other woman, her fair brow, the angelic perfection of her features, the silky-straight flaxen hair that hung down her back without a strand out of place. What would possess such a beauty to tie herself to a gang of criminals? Money? Power? A misguided need for security, perhaps. Elements not so foreign to Gia's own life, and the irony of it tugged at her conscience.

Hypocrite, a tinny, long-buried voice accused from the back of her mind. *This woman's no different than you, selling your soul to Vincent for love and money.*

But Gia hadn't hurt anyone, damn it.

No one but yourself. The full force of realization hadn't touched her until now. Very possibly she was in this horrible position because she had married a shady businessman named Vincent Rossi.

Soleil glanced up and Gia's gaze darted away, but everything cool and confident in the other woman's manner made Gia feel as though Soleil could read her thoughts and found them utterly amusing.

They continued down the corridor, and this time encountered a sandy-haired man approaching from the opposite direction. He was young, broad-shouldered and handsome, dressed in a white jumpsuit similar to Soleil's. His gray eyes flickered briefly in the women's direction as they passed, and Gia instantly recognized him as one of her abductors.

Funny. Out of his black ninja threads, he looked so…pleasant.

"That's Olivier," Soleil murmured, as though she'd guessed Gia's musings. "And yes, he helped retrieve you."

"The bastard kidnapped me," Gia said flatly. "You people aren't going to get away with this."

The blonde didn't respond. She slowed as they reached a section of corridor lined with doors. "This is Joachim's office," she said, stopping at the first door on the right. "He's expecting you." She tapped lightly. "Joachim?"

"Come," a low male voice replied from within.

Anxiety fisted around Gia's chest as she stared into one of the windows flanking the entry and found her reflection gaping back at her. A two-way mirror. *You can see out, but not in*. She grasped awkwardly at Soleil's arm with bound hands. "You're going to stay with me, aren't you?"

Soleil only smiled and opened the door to usher her inside.

The office was small, steel-paneled walls naked and everything else stripped of décor, save the gray, geometric-print rug beneath Gia's feet. An impressive glass-and-metal desk filled half the tiny chamber, but nothing was as eye-catching as the man sitting behind it.

The cerulean glow from the laptop computer iced his stern features and when he glanced up, his pale eyes reflected the light, two lapis lazuli fringed by thick, dark lashes.

Gia looked away, inexplicably stung.

"Mrs. Rossi," he spoke in an infuriatingly familiar voice. "We meet again."

That accent—she strained to identify it, and it came to her at once. Muted French. The same lilting inflection laced Soleil's velvet tones. This group was some kind of foreign terrorist faction.

She clamped down on that absurd idea. What would a terrorist group want with her? She'd read too many spy novels. They were thugs, maybe from across the Canadian border. A less glamorous scenario, but far likelier.

The door clicked shut behind her and she shot around, horrified by the realization that Soleil—her *guardian*—had left her in the clutches of this animal with no way to protect herself.

She didn't hear his approach, and when his fingers curled around her arm, Gia let out a sharp cry. "Don't touch me!"

He released her. Adrenaline fired through her in electric currents as she backed up against the door, her bound hands curled into fists against her pounding heart. Even shoeless, she wasn't afraid to kick him.

Joachim stopped and studied her with unwavering patience. "I only wish to unfasten the restraints. If you'd rather they remain—"

Clenching her teeth, she thrust her hands toward him.

His placid expression never changed as he approached her again, passed his fingertips over some invisible lock on the plastic bands and drew the cuffs from her hands, his touch a fleeting glide against her skin.

Gia shivered as her gaze followed him back to the desk. Dressed in dove-gray coveralls, he looked like some lonely woman's fantasy, a male model posing as a garage mechanic. His hair, a little too long and richly brown, was swept back from his face, his aristocratic features beautifully offset by a flawless, clean-shaven complexion. Flawless except for the angry red scratches her fingernails had inflicted on his cheek the day before. Painful-looking wounds.

Her lip curled. *Good.*

"I want to go home," she said, rubbing the lingering sensation of his touch from her wrists.

"You can't." He seated himself and nodded at a metal chair on the opposite side of the desk. "Please sit, Mrs. Rossi."

"I'd rather stand."

"All the way over there?"

"As far away from you as I can get."

A polite tilt of his head acknowledged her stubbornness.

"Tell me why I'm here," Gia demanded before he could speak. "You're obviously aware that my husband has more money than God, or you wouldn't have kidnapped me."

For the first time, Joachim's expression shifted…first to surprise, then to amusement. Humor tugged at his full mouth and he propped his elbows on the desk, his blue eyes steady on her face. "Really. I had no idea Vincent Rossi's coffers were so infinite."

Heat climbed her neck and burned her ears. "He'll pay huge amounts for my safe return."

"If we return you, you'll die," he said quietly.

She narrowed her gaze and pressed her spine against the

door. "What do you mean?"

"What do you know about evil?"

"I'm looking at it," she retorted.

His vague smile returned. "Do you have a religion?"

"That's none of your business."

"But it is, more than you know. Come here." When she hesitated, he gestured to his computer screen. "There's something I want to show you."

"Unless it's the exit door, I couldn't care less."

He braced his forearms on the desk and stared at her. "Come here, Mrs. Rossi."

The battle of wills lasted a few slow beats before Gia's curiosity won over suspicion. She crept to his side, folded her arms over her breasts and bent at the waist to study the monitor.

"We'll start with this list Intel has compiled. It's comprised of twenty-three names, individuals you probably know, or have at least come into contact with." Joachim's soft words caressed the curls that hung against her cheek. He smelled clean and warm, like vanilla-scented soap. The pleasant scent caught her off guard and she straightened.

"Beside ten of the names, you will see the word 'terminated'. Do you see it, Mrs. Rossi?"

"I see it," she grated.

"Do you understand what it means?"

Gia's pulse tripled its pace. "I know John Zamora and Mike Francetti were killed in separate freak car accidents this past spring." She peered at the list again, her hammering heartbeat stealing her breath as she recognized two, three, four more names, all employees of Vincent's who had died under mysterious circumstances in the last two years.

Why hadn't she considered their deaths as being related before? It was terribly odd to be just a coincidence. "Joe Alvarez—someone broke into his house. A burglary, the police said. And Wayne Dalton…he just…well, dropped dead." Her voice trailed into uncertainty, then she caught herself and straightened. "But those deaths have nothing to do with each other."

"On the contrary. Those men were under your husband's employ at one time or another, yes? They got in the way with their troubled consciences. Everyone on this list is in Rossi's way, and when he gets what he wants from you, you'll be terminated as well."

"I don't understand." But she did, and automatically she backed away from the desk and bumped into the wall, waves of frigid horror washing through her. "Vincent would never hurt me. This is some kind of bid to turn me against him. I want to know why you're doing this."

Joachim swiveled in his chair to face her. "The man you married is dead, Mrs. Rossi, and a shadow has taken his place."

"You're crazy," she snapped.

"And once you've served your purpose, you'll only be a hindrance to it. The shadow is a malevolent entity. It will kill everyone who interferes with its universal plan. You're slated for termination, and then because you've danced with the devil—albeit blindfolded—the horrible repercussions won't stop there for you. Despite belief to the contrary, life after death is a reality but not a free ticket to paradise."

He hesitated as if measuring his words, then his voice gentled. "You've made some mistakes along the way, out of fear, insecurity, self-loathing. You've chosen the easy route too often, and it has placed you in harm's way. You're an accessory, and I'm afraid your soul is compromised."

Insanity. She stared at him, lips parted, wondering how a man could speak utter mindless nonsense with such calm conviction.

"I see you're skeptical," he went on in that soft, hypnotic tone, his pale gaze searching hers. "Let me throw some terms at you to better clarify. Demonic possession. Spiritual invasion. Definitions for the metamorphosis that has occurred within

Vincent's human form. He's no longer the man you knew, Mrs. Rossi, but a puppet. And the darkness controlling the strings wants you out of the picture once you've served your purpose."

As she stared into his unwavering blue eyes, something in Gia clicked off, like a heavy steel door slamming closed to block out the insidious fear he'd managed to stir. "I saw my husband just yesterday morning before he walked out the door for a business trip," she said, her voice quavering. "We had breakfast together. Omelets and mimosas. Surely a demon doesn't have breakfast, much less omelets and mimosas. I can assure you, *you lunatic,* that Vincent is very much alive and completely himself."

"Did he tell you the destination of his business trip?"

"No," she spat. "And I didn't ask him. I don't care."

"You should care. Not doing so is what got you into trouble in the first place." Joachim's fingertips touched a pen near the desk's edge and rolled it to and fro, a movement as seductive and mindless as the absurd story he wove around her.

"When you play at the edge of darkness, Mrs. Rossi, you welcome it into your soul. Look at Vincent. He made a fortune in his time on Earth. He was an easy mark for demonic possession because he hurt many, many people, swindled them, sometimes killed them. He floated on the rewards, with you at his side. He sold his soul to the devil, as the old saying goes, and invited in the darkness. In accordance with universal law, it swept him out to damnation, and it didn't stop there. Right under your nose, the shadow assumed his identity, all without your knowledge. Now its power is growing, and it will stop at nothing to destroy the world."

She could only shake her head as his quiet assertions echoed in her ears. "I don't know what the hell you're talking about," she said, hysteria tightened her throat, "but you'd better let me out of here *now*."

Joachim's gaze lingered on her, the thoughts behind it imperceptible. Then he reached out and tapped a small black intercom on the desk. "Soleil will take you back to your cell now.

I'll send for you tomorrow, and we'll try again to come to a meeting of minds. You can deny what I've told you here, but the truth is in your heart, and it will clamor and harass you until you give it the attention it deserves. My job is to help you through this difficult process. My job—our job—is to shield and educate you. Not hurt you."

Gia hugged her arms across her galloping heart and stared back at him. "You're keeping me against my will."

"For now."

Before she could respond, the door swung open and Soleil glided into the office. She reached for the plastic restraint, but Joachim shook his head, and she quietly withdrew to wait at the threshold for her prisoner.

As Gia stepped into the hall, a fresh surge of rage burst within her and she glared back at Joachim. "I have something to say after all."

He glanced up from the computer. "What is it?"

Pausing for effect, she clenched her teeth. "*You go to hell.*"

His regard, so blue and untouchable, rested on her face. "Until you embrace the truth, Mrs. Rossi, you're in far greater danger of that than I."

The door closed between them. Tears of frustration stinging her eyes, she let Soleil escort her back to her glass prison, where she could bury her head in the pillow and weep. Where sleep eventually crept over her, seeds of dark, curling fear sprouted and twined around her thoughts…and black, far-flung possibilities loomed ever nearer.

* * * * *

"I didn't tell her much." Joachim leaned his forehead against the heel of his hand, stifled a sigh and glanced at Olivier for his reaction. "She wouldn't listen."

Olivier offered a humorless smile from his indolent position against the office door. "Of course she wouldn't. Nor will she tomorrow, nor the day after that, nor the day after that.

Darkness holds its hands over her eyes. And you, my captain, are the light."

Swiveling restlessly, Joachim fingered his computer keyboard. "It's likely we won't be able to save her if she's as stubborn as she appears." He tapped a few keys. "But alas, we persevere."

"As the Great Warrior orders, brother."

Joachim met the other man's watchful gray eyes. "Sometimes, Olivier, I wonder at the intent behind Michael's strategy, when so often we return from these missions with casualties and unanswered questions. Yes, we are mighty. The Archangel's legions. And yet..." He broke off and shook his head, his fists clenched against the desk. "I've come to this mission with a restlessness unknown to me before now. Is there some kind of test buried in each operation? Is our performance being weighed and measured? If so, for what purpose? Will there be a judgment day for us too, in the end?"

"Hmm." Olivier's smile returned. "And if we fall short, what becomes of us? Where *do* the underachievers go? Have you ever asked, Joachim?"

"No." He cocked a brow at his friend. "You?"

"I've never even wondered."

The men exchanged a long look, and humor bled into uncertainty. As if prodded by the disturbing questions, Olivier straightened away from the door and reached for the knob. "Enough sulking, Joachim. Come to dinner and welcome the new soldiers who arrived this morning. Three of them, all familiar faces and comforting reminders of home. You can practice your English on them."

Despite his frustration, the corners of Joachim's mouth quirked into a smile. "I thought Nicodemus had fixed me."

"Nothing will fix you. Your pronunciation is terrible." Olivier grinned and beckoned to his leader. "Join us and grab a few moments' respite from this stress."

Olivier was right. The chilled steel walls of the cubicle

seemed to close around Joachim more with each passing minute. "Go," he said, snapping shut the notebook computer screen. "I'll be there in a minute."

The other man stepped into the corridor, and then glanced back with a thoughtful frown. "With every mission, my friend, you must tell yourself, on this we will not lose. Even if we protect one soul, one human life, it's a triumph. In the end, even one rescue is victory. Think only on that for now."

Joachim offered a small smile of acknowledgement and watched the door close behind his second-in-command. In the stillness, he inhaled, rolled the tension from his neck and let the breath drift from his chest, only to be refilled by a creeping warmth that both caressed and disconcerted him.

Olivier's words echoed in his mind. *In the end, even one rescue is victory.*

"Very well," he whispered, closing his eyes. "Then let it be her."

Chapter Four

Gia squinted at her reflection in the glass wall opposite her cot. It had to be another two-way mirror. Even if it wasn't, she knew she was under some sort of surveillance. The constant, crawling sensation of being watched kept her muscles tight with awareness and outrage. It stole hours of sleep from her, whittled her nerves to threads.

Her reflection stared back, haunted and hardened. *She wanted out, damn it!* Out of this cage. She stalked across the cool tile floor and pounded a fist against the glass, an ineffective attack against her unseen observers. The hammering sound echoed tiny ripples of pain through her head, and brought no response from the outside. And still she felt their cold appraisal.

Obsessive thoughts rotated in her mind, threatening her sanity. Were the deaths of Vincent's former employees truly related? Unthinkable. It had to be an outlandish and ridiculous attempt at brainwashing her into doubting his integrity.

...He hurt many, many people, swindled them, sometimes killed them. He floated on the rewards, with you at his side.

She buried her face in her hands, banishing the memory of Joachim's assertions. *Focus, Gia. Focus on what's real.*

Vincent. His love for her. Her husband's smooth, easy smile flashed across her mind's eye and soothed her. He would never hurt her. Had he been notified of her abduction? By now the weekend staff would have come into the mansion and discovered the disarray left by the attackers. Frank and the other guards might have survived the assault. If they hadn't, it was still highly likely the police had already launched an investigation, and Vincent would catch the nearest flight home.

Then it would only be a matter of days—or hours, even—

before he sent an army after her. In the meantime, she had to find a way to keep from going stir-crazy, to block out the brainwashing.

Methods of escape crowded her thoughts. Several obstacles stood in her way, not the least of which was Soleil. While Gia was fit from regular exercise, something told her Soleil would flatten her if she tried to overpower the watchful guard. The blonde had delicate-looking features and a slender figure, but the studied calm of her demeanor spoke of highly disciplined mental, and probably physical, training. Martial arts, maybe.

Still, that didn't mean Gia couldn't escape her safeguard. The bunker was apparently a labyrinth of corridors, and the next time Soleil took her out, all Gia had to do was slide from the blonde's grasp, navigate a few hallways, then hide...and in the midst of it, figure out where the exit door was located. And the stairs they'd brought her down. And the cargo elevator.

God. She should have been more alert when they'd first brought her in. After nearly forty-eight hours, she didn't know where the hell she was anymore, only that she was deep in an underground world where no one would know to look.

Discouragement dashed the escape scenario from her mind. She whirled from the wall of glass and collapsed on the edge of the cot, scrubbing her hands over her face in exasperation. Everything in her life seemed to be toppling, and fear simmered beneath her heart.

Who knew the reality of life could be so transient? Gone were the Barrington Hills estate and its cushioned embrace. In her new world, her husband was possessed by a demon, and she, Gia Torio from the slums of Chicago, was number twenty-three on his hit list. *This* was real, though—this cold cell, the invisible watching eyes, the underground bunker and her abductors, frightening, emotionless and otherworldly with their calm, calm voices and icy regard.

Her throat ached. Despair burned her eyes and she rubbed the heels of her hands against them until she saw stars, sucking back the urge to weep. Then her spine straightened and she scowled.

Vincent was *not* possessed.

Only two days ago, his eyes had appeared the same velvet brown as he turned at the limousine to offer her a final wave. Nothing ungodly or demonic about them. Nothing about his persona had truly appeared strange or suspicious besides a general pallor.

The only anomaly he'd displayed in the last few weeks was his sudden proclivity for heat—he'd turned the furnace on in June, for Pete's sake—and an increased appetite for sex. They'd made love in every room of the mansion in the last few weeks. On every desk, in every chair, against every wall and very nearly under the discreet, averted eyes of the house staff, who lately knew to slip out of the room when Vincent entered looking for his wife.

Gia, who'd always had a difficult time attaining orgasm anyway, eventually quit trying to wring any pleasure from these ruttings. She just wanted Vincent to be done with the bizarre phase. He was a man of forty, yet his erection stayed ever present, and he watched her with eyes that seemed hooded and hazy with lust, as though he were on some kind of drug. She'd searched his medicine cabinet in search of the sexual enhancement medication he *must* be taking, but found nothing, only a horny husband waiting for her on the bed when she'd emerged from the bathroom.

And his touch seemed so *cold*, now that she thought about it. Freezing. As though his body was devoid of heat.

She shivered.

Despite her growing dread of his merciless advances, simple guilt was the driving factor in why she hadn't rebuffed him more often. He was so kind, so loving. But it wasn't about sex with Vincent. It never had been. If she looked at him too long or too hard lately, a part of her felt…repulsed. Just vaguely.

And only recently.

None of it mattered now, anyway. She might never see him

again. Might never feel loved or wanted again. For the most part, life with Vincent had always seemed like a dream—and with each passing hour she spent locked in this glass room, the dream appeared to be dissolving, replaced by a chilled, colorless nightmare.

She had to get out.

Joachim had claimed he'd send for her again, for more attempts at brainwashing, no doubt, and this time she was ready for his outrageous suggestions and seductive manner. David Koresh and Jim Jones had nothing on this guy. It made perfect sense that he'd head up a bizarre underground cult. His striking good looks alone would capture a needy soul's attention, and from there he could wield his intense charisma like a lasso, hauling in members left and right.

But not Gia. The doubt he'd stirred in her about Vincent yesterday had been a direct result of her exhaustion and fear, and this time when he came at her, bombarding her with hocus-pocus claims that her husband wasn't her husband but some demon invader, she would deflect it. Turn a deaf ear. Nod politely, tell him what he wanted to hear and make nice. She could be persuasive in her own right. Vincent often said she could seduce the stone off a statue with just her eyes alone.

A sickening idea sprang to life in the back of her mind. This man, Joachim…he seemed impervious, remote, but somewhere under all that cool decorum dwelt a male with desires and needs. And he was isolated down here in this mole hole, surrounded by glass and steel and automaton cult members. Even Soleil, with her feline beauty, lacked the fire of sexual awareness in her green eyes, and from what Gia could tell, no sparks flew between the blonde and her fearless leader.

Maybe Joachim occasionally blew off steam with one of his mindless female minions, but Gia would bet a million bucks he hadn't experienced true seduction in a long, long time. And she was certainly capable of it. Not quite eight years had passed since she'd waitressed at the gentlemen's club in downtown Chicago, and her tips had always been generous proof that she was pleasing to the senses.

She hadn't forgotten how to play the game.

Her gaze flickered toward her reflection again, and with trembling hands she smoothed the unruly dark curls that were still damp from the shower she'd been permitted that morning. She might be sorely lacking in cosmetics and all the expensive toiletries that helped transform her into Vincent's idea of perfection, but she knew how to appeal to a man. Even a man she despised.

And maybe, as she once had with Vincent, she could use her allure to buy freedom from an existence that seemed one step up from hell.

*****

Four seraphs stood outside the glass-and-steel cubicle, watching the restless creature pace its confines.

"She should have fresh air," Dmitri said flatly. "We must let her out."

Mildly surprised, Joachim glanced at the seraph disguised in a lean Eurasian form. Dmitri didn't often voice his opinion, but his sentiments ran deep, and when he spoke, Joachim usually listened.

"She'll go mad in that box if you don't," Dmitri added. "She needs freedom."

Joachim clasped his hands behind his back, returning his attention to the object of their concern. "You'll give it to her yourself, after you've begun her self-defense lessons. Use it as a reward. Once she calms down, you're free to teach her in the field outside the bunker."

"I'm not sure such a reward will prove effective." Nicodemus stepped closer to the glass with his gnarled hands tucked inside the sleeves of his robe. "She's enraged. And she might just be wily enough to use the skills Dmitri teaches her to fight her way out of here."

Like a child at an ice-frosted window, Olivier traced Gia's

figure on the glass with a single fingertip, then let his hand drop. "Perhaps we'll have to break her before we can train her to defend herself."

Joachim paused beside the others, his gaze fixed on Vincent Rossi's wife. She rose abruptly from the edge of the cot, reached lithe arms over her head and twisted her dark hair into a makeshift knot, her brow furrowed with displeasure.

Of its own accord, his regard slid over her gleaming shoulders, bared by the tank top she wore. The long line of her neck granted her swanlike grace. He could make out the rose-colored tips of her breasts through the thin shirt, the sleek curve of her hips through the white drawstring pants. Even clad in the simple attire, she was breathtaking. Slim, high-breasted, golden-skinned—

Lightning heat jolted through him, a galvanized arrow to his groin. He drew in a soft breath and forced the reckless corporeal musings from his mind, but the sensation coiling in his vitals was insistent.

Such stirrings, of course, were merely a physical response whose purpose ultimately lay in the propagation of the species. Purely biological. And poisonously pleasurable, if he gave it any more attention than he already had in this particular body.

Physical desire could easily be a problem on this mission, he'd discovered. Along with money, drugs and drink, the man whose body Joachim now inhabited had undoubtedly worshipped carnal pleasure…maybe more than any other earthly delight. Initially Joachim hadn't been prepared for the vestigial stirrings of lust left behind by the soiled spiritual resident, and when he'd mentioned the problem to Michael during the last debriefing, the Archangel had laughed. *Ah, Joachim. You have fought and won far greater battles.*

End of conversation. The utmost control was expected of Joachim as leader of this operation, and in the past he'd unfailingly risen to the occasion. He'd inhabited all kinds of bodies in past operations—strong, elderly, adolescent, deformed. No weakness had gotten in the way of his mission.

He couldn't—wouldn't—be swayed by carnal need.

"We won't have to break Gia," he told Olivier abruptly. "The truth will do it for us."

Olivier cast a concerned glance at his commander. "And if she won't listen to the truth?"

Joachim forced his attention from the sultry picture of Gia Rossi prowling her cell and met his friend's troubled gaze. "Then we'll show it to her."

* * * * *

She dreamed. Of serpents and demons, of a fiery, brimstone hell.

Of a cool, cerulean Heaven just out of reach, reflected in an angel's eyes.

Gia ran through a cloying fog, lost, dodging ashen, twisted debris and embers that smoldered green with the burning terrain's ferocious heat. Smoke and sulfur choked her; she couldn't draw a breath deep enough to fill her lungs, and suffocation rushed her senses, burned her, blinded her.

From the viscous, nightmarish miasma, a reedy voice threaded around her mind's ear.

Step into my parlor, said the spider to the fly…

"Please no, please no!" Gia heard herself crying in her sleep, but she couldn't quite swim to the surface of consciousness. Couldn't quite reach the pale blue of an angel's eyes hovering above her nightmare.

And then *he* was there, over and around and beneath her, the scent of vanilla soaking the air as his arms and wings surrounded her. Quenching the fires that had scorched her flesh, and igniting a different one within.

Him. The man she most feared and hated. The one who had snatched her from life and buried her in a steely underground grave.

Horrified, Gia tried to run, and when he caught her with

gentle hands, she went lax and seeped back into the shelter of his embrace, not knowing what he was...angel or demon, assailant or savior, enemy or lover. He was all, perhaps, for he terrified and elated her both...stripped her and protected her...captured her body and freed her spirit. The feathery wings closing around her and caressing her naked skin became the soft, chestnut strands of a lover's hair brushing her breasts as his searching mouth nudged beneath her shirt and closed around an aroused nipple.

Je t'aime, Gia... Je te désire trop...

He spoke mindless, passionate words against her breast, his strong hands grasping her waist and holding her still for his caresses, while everything in Gia went wet and wanting, and the burning, hellish world dissolved into cool languor.

Everywhere he touched her soothed and inflamed her. Her traitorous fingers tangled in his hair and guided his hungry mouth to her other breast, and she was floating, floating, as her clothing dissolved beneath his hands and she lay exposed, heart and body, before his burning appraisal.

He...her winged enemy...her abductor...he knelt before her as naked as she, his fair, flawless body luminous with halo and humanly aroused, his heart exposed on his stern, beautiful face. The reverent brush of his feathered wings over her shoulders, her breasts, her belly, belonged to an otherworldly creature, and yet the rawness in his features was that of a man. The big, steely member rising against his stomach was wholly, deliciously corporeal.

Just a dream, she reminded herself. A terrible, beautiful dream. His name rose to her lips, a cry for salvation, and yet it was he from whom she must escape.

Say my name, he ordered, his blue eyes stabbing straight to her soul.

Her resplendent tormentor. To utter his name would be blasphemy.

Gia pressed her lips together against the urge to cry out for him, closed her eyes and rode the waves of exquisite sensation as he bent his head and brushed his lips over her hip, his teeth nipping the soft skin there, his strong hands turning her for his delectation as he delighted in every inch of her.

Who am I, Gia?

She knew him…knew the heat and smoothness of skin over tough sinew; knew the liquid shift of muscle beneath her hands when he stretched fully over her, the long line of his naked back, the hollow and flex of his buttocks as he pushed his rigid cock against the wet, wanting cleft between her legs.

She hated him for stealing her from Vincent. But she loved the feel of him over her, against her, seeking entry into her body, tormenting her, far more than Vincent ever could.

Her pelvis rose of its own accord as he rocked between her thighs, his granite shaft probing and teasing between her legs, coating himself in her silky essence with each slow, tantalizing circle he made. His gentle hands grasped her hips and pulled her up tight as if to thrust into her, but still he didn't enter her. The hot, silken head of him pushed against her slick portal, seared her most tender flesh, wringing a cry from the depths of her soul, protest and ecstasy.

Nightmare and fantasy.

"What do you want?" she cried, hearing herself from a distance, a dreamer observing her own nightmare.

Cry out for me…

The single, cursed name floated on Gia's lips, but she bit it back, shook with the force of her need, every muscle drawn tight in anticipation of release. She was close, so close, tiny, pre-orgasmic quivers shuddering through her as his cock circled through her wetness faster and faster, slid through the soft petals of her flesh, probed and teased. She didn't know such sheer, unadulterated desire could be more intense than any orgasm she'd ever known, but she knew when he finally made her climax, she would come unhinged, her heart jolted loose from its mooring. And she would die from the power of it, the power of their love.

The smoldering burn of arousal was too potent to stay imprisoned in her dream state, and though she slept, her physical body responded. Shuddering on the edge of consciousness now, she twisted her fingers in the sheets of her cot, her legs sliding restlessly against the mattress as he spread her knees wide and his mouth breathed a lover's adulations against her most sensitive flesh, hovering without touching.

His hungry blue eyes stared up her body at her, making promises that dissolved in her fingers like dust.

I've always been with you…you know me, Gia…tell me you know me.

"I can't," she moaned. "Please, please let me go."

Sadness darkened his slumberous gaze, and his voice filled her mind so thickly, she thrashed her head on the pillow. *"Beloved Daughter of Longinus, I'll let you fly."* Then he lowered his head, and his soft, slick tongue parted her folds and speared her deep, his hands cupping her buttocks, lifting her like a chalice from which he would drink.

For an instant she hovered on the edge of war and surrender, wanting him to hold her forever, wanting him to free her…

And then she shrieked under his stroking tongue and came, straddling two worlds as the most powerful climax of her life swept her up, up, away from his hot embrace, into the chill of real life.

"No!" Heart pounding, she shot upright on the cot and stared around the dim cell with wet, blinking eyes. Perspiration trickled between her breasts. Her muscles ached, every nerve raw and aroused, and in the soft, damp place between her legs, the fluttering echoes of her climax still quivered.

Gia lay back on her pillow and wiped the tears from her cheeks with a trembling hand. A nocturnal orgasm, her voice of reason told her. Born of the unbearable stress of the last few days. Her body must have needed the release.

And it had absolutely nothing to do with the insane, beautiful abductor whom she detested with all her heart.

So why had it been his arms around her, his mouth cherishing her?

And why had she, in her crazed, lost nightmare, granted him wings?

* * * * *

"Sleep well?" Soleil inquired as she slipped the plastic handcuffs over Gia's wrists.

"What do you think?" Gia retorted, but swallowed the useless slew of acid insults building in her throat. Nastiness seemed to bounce off these people as though they wore invisible armor.

She shifted tactics and forced her expression to smooth as she nodded at the restraints binding her arms. "If I promise not to run away from you, would you please leave those off?"

The blonde hesitated. "Can I really trust you, Mrs. Rossi?"

"I swear on my husband's pointy little heart."

Soleil's eyes were watchful as she removed the cuffs, opened the cell door and let her prisoner exit before her.

They headed down the corridor in silence, the blonde matching her step for step. Even if Gia had wanted to break away and run for it, Soleil's firm stride and hovering proximity told her it would be futile.

They turned a corner and passed two women in gray jumpsuits, walking side by side without conversing, eyes straight ahead. No one seemed to talk or emote or function like natural human beings in this metal pit. It was worse than a funeral home.

Gia glanced at Soleil, desperate for the sound of another voice. "Where are you taking me?"

"You're meeting with Joachim now, and Dmitri will have you for the afternoon."

"Who's Dmitri?"

"He'll be your self-defense trainer."

Gia shot her a look of astonishment. "I don't get it."

"We can only protect you for so long," the blonde said smoothly. "You must learn to defend yourself."

Gia's pulse quickened. "Does this mean you'll eventually let me go?"

Soleil slowed her pace as they arrived at Joachim's office. "Save your questions for Joachim."

"Why can't you tell me?" she persisted, searching for a flicker of emotion in that smooth, beautiful mask.

"Because he decides what you should know and when." Soleil tapped on the door. "Joachim, Mrs. Rossi is ready to see you."

"Come," his soft reply carried from inside the office, and Gia's heart stuttered at the low, familiar voice from her erotic dream.

The unexpected burn of arousal between her legs mortified and enraged her. When Soleil opened the door, Gia strode right past her and into the room, grabbed the metal chair across from Joachim's desk and whirled it around to straddle it.

"Let's get on with it." *Damn him to hell.* She would be in control this time. Nothing he said was going to bother her. She met his gaze head-on, letting its piercing beauty roll off her. "Forget the niceties, the idle chitchat. What sort of drivel are you going to hammer into me today?"

Unmoved, Joachim glanced at Soleil, who lingered in the doorway with an uncertain expression. "Thank you, Soleil. That's all."

The door promptly and quietly clicked shut. In the silence, he returned his attention to the computer screen, as though he were hardly aware of Gia's presence. After a moment of unbearable quiet, broken only by the soft tap of his fingertips on the keyboard, he spoke. "You look tired, Mrs. Rossi."

Not exactly the response she'd hoped for, after she'd bothered to pinch her cheeks for color and don one of the tighter tank tops that comprised part of her bland new wardrobe. It stretched snugly across her breasts, rode up and exposed a nice slice of tanned tummy above the pajama-like bottoms Soleil had provided her. Vincent, of course, would have loved it. Most men would at least notice. Most men except this one.

Maybe he was gay.

She shifted her attention from Joachim's deadpan features, her bravado bleeding away. "I haven't slept in two days. I laid awake all last night wondering what kind of kooks you people are for trying to convince me that my husband's a demonically possessed killer."

"Good." He closed the laptop. "That means we're getting through to you."

"No, it means I think you're all crazy, but who am I to argue with your cockamamie ideas? It looks to me like you've built yourselves a dandy commune down here. You've certainly made me aware of my husband's more fiendish qualities, and I promise to be careful of him. Why not just let me go and whatever happens will be my problem?"

"You're going to help us detain him," he said in that calm, accented tone that so infuriated her.

"The hell I will."

Joachim's lashes lowered as he glanced down to open a desk drawer. A subtle mechanical humming to Gia's left caught her attention, and she twisted to watch a flat screen descend from the ceiling.

"What's this?"

"A film. Recent footage of Vincent Rossi's activities. Do you ever accompany him on business trips?"

Never. She had no desire to traipse around the world behind Vincent and his goons.

Maybe she should have insisted. Maybe she should have asked more questions. If she had, maybe she wouldn't be here, in this icy prison, with her world in tiny shards at her feet.

Her troubled silence seemed to be the only answer Joachim needed. "A few minutes of your husband's other life, then," he said softly. The recessed lighting around the perimeter of the ceiling dimmed, and a grainy video flashed on the screen. Without rising, Gia scooted her chair around to watch it and immediately recognized Vincent, tall and regal in a black, calf-length leather coat as he climbed out of his limousine. Her heart ached, her eyes stung. *God, she wanted to go home.*

He crossed a cobblestone driveway and headed toward a Palladian-style mansion, two football-player-sized bodyguards on his heels.

"Where was this filmed?" she asked, brow furrowed.

"Michigan. The building he's approaching belongs to the Fellowship of the Fallen Sun. Does that name mean anything to you, Mrs. Rossi?"

It rang a distant bell in the troubled recesses of her mind, but Gia shook her head. Where would she have come across the name before? Curiosity and a creeping uneasiness drew her attention back to the screen.

When the camera focused briefly on a small adornment affixed over the mansion's shadowed entry, her heart tripped. It was the same pendant Vincent wore on a chain around his neck, a partially eclipsed sun with an oddly fashioned, inverted cross carved in its center. He never took it off except to shower, and when she'd inquired about it, he'd mumbled something about it being a trinket he'd picked up during his travels.

"What is that place?" she asked, glancing at Joachim.

He gazed past her at the screen, its glow reflecting silver in his eyes. "You don't know?"

She flashed him a surly look that elicited a slight smile from him.

"The Fellowship of the Fallen Sun is a religious sect, Mrs. Rossi."

She waited for him to explain further, and when he didn't,

she snapped, "Well? What would Vincent want with a bunch of zealots? I'm certain you're dying to tell me."

"The sect was founded by your husband one year ago. There are two hundred fifty-one members currently, all of whom believe Vincent is Ezekiel Rose, a prophet of Yahweh."

Gia's mouth dropped open and she stared numbly at the screen before laughter bubbled to her lips and shattered the surprised silence. "Ezekiel *who*? Oh, this is too much. You are insane."

"The Fellowship is a cult, and Vincent is the leader," Joachim went on as though she hadn't interrupted. "He targets wealthy, love-hungry women and men of all ages, seduces them mentally, spiritually, even physically. They give up everything material to live in hunger and hardship and degradation—what they believe is spiritual grace."

The silence vibrated with her incredulity. So now Vincent was a cult leader? Wasn't *that* the pot calling the kettle black!

Gia dropped her forehead against her arms, weariness pressing down on her with a heaviness that sapped the hysterical laughter roiling in her chest. "The fact that he was filmed at this place doesn't mean he's the leader of some bizarre religious sect."

"What do you think it means, Mrs. Rossi?"

Irritation flared within her and burned away the dismay of a moment before. "I have no idea. It's possible he could be meeting someone there. A business colleague."

The soft squeak of leather indicated Joachim leaned back in his chair. "A business meeting in a religious commune?"

She finally shifted to glare at him in the screen's flickering glow. "Things happen in strange places. Take, for instance, me being imprisoned here under the guise that I'm being protected. This place isn't exactly Candyland, you know."

"You're safe here."

"I'm trapped here. Like some kind of animal."

On the screen, Vincent paused at the mansion's entrance. The massive double doors swung open and a skeletal man in a white tunic appeared, bowing reverently several times as he circled behind Vincent and urged him inside, like a cattle dog rounding up a stray sheep. As Vincent stepped into the shadowed foyer, the little man reached up to remove his coat. The bodyguards flanked the doorway, paused to scan the surroundings, then headed inside behind their client.

The doors closed.

It did seem weird. Swallowing against the tension constricting her throat, Gia looked away from the screen. As if in sympathy, the film dimmed and shut off.

"There's more," Joachim said as the lights came up. "The proof you seek exists when you're ready for it, Mrs. Rossi."

A humorless smile tipped her lips. "Let me guess. A home movie of Vincent drinking goat's blood while dancing naked around a pentagram?"

"We have already infiltrated the cult," Joachim went on, ignoring her sarcasm. "Our contact is transmitting information. You will see it all, and in time, have no doubt that what we say is true. But not now. You're not ready."

"I never will be. How can you expect me to believe one word of what you've told me? Do I look like I just fell off the turnip truck?"

Feeling his appraisal on her profile, she straightened and crossed her arms over the back of the chair. "Supposing any of this *crap* is true, how could a religious sect like the one you claim my husband is spearheading pose a serious threat? So far they have two hundred odd members and a mansion in Michigan. The whole world isn't as gullible as those two hundred odd people. Hell, I'm not. Vincent is my husband and no matter how devoted I am to him, I'd never buy into it. So what's the big danger here?"

"Your husband is not your husband. He is nephilim, Mrs. Rossi." Joachim stood, the tension in his features the only sign of passion behind his words. "Nephilim are the dark angels who leapt with Lucifer in the Great Rebellion. They have the ability—a driving desire—to attain human bodies and walk among men. The one who took Vincent's body is called Therides. He sits at the left hand of Lucifer, more powerful than any evil spirit the human mind can conceive of. He is a principal demon who has come to gain power of this world and the universe beyond—"

"Stop!" Gia turned away from him, too sick and confused to hear another word. "You're out of your mind! And when the authorities find me—and they *will*—you'll go to prison. You and Blondie and all your cronies running around here in coveralls and ski masks—you people are sick in the head, and nothing you show me or tell me will convince me that Vincent is—is—" Tears choked her voice and she couldn't continue.

For a long time Joachim didn't speak. He regained his seat in watchful silence, seemingly waiting for Gia to gather control of her emotions.

Smearing her hands over her tear-streaked cheeks, she squelched the frenzy that had overflowed her nervous system and drew several slow, deep breaths. Then she focused and found a question, a real one, lurking at the edge of her conscience. "I want to know more about the Fellowship of the Fallen Sun. I want proof of your claims that Vincent is bilking and brainwashing people. The only real cultlike behavior I see is right here. You and the people who kidnapped me. Your claims are completely mad, you must know that."

He considered her statement, his blue gaze fixed unwaveringly on her face. "Proof will come. For now, I have more important concerns than convincing you." His fingers skimmed over the computer keyboard, the monitor came to life, and he turned it in her direction so she could study the series of downloaded photographs on the screen. "As of late, the cult has begun to amass an impressive arsenal. The men in these photographs are unloading a van full of weapons into the basement of the mansion you saw in the film. Automatics, explosives, and so forth. Eventually Therides will have all the money, fire and manpower he needs to wreak enormous havoc, and he will slice a path through your world, Mrs. Rossi. Whether or not you believe me, it will happen. But there is one thing he's in search of that he has not yet acquired."

Heaving a tired sigh, Gia looked at him. "What?"

"You have in your possession a religious relic, a medallion. Therides—Rossi—knows you have it, but he doesn't know its location. He needs it to go forward with his plan. And I need it to stop him."

What medallion? She shook her head. "I don't know what you're talking about. I don't have any medallion. Everything I own—jewelry, clothes, the roof over my head—Vincent gave me. I don't have—"

A vague memory flitted across her mind's eye, and the strength left her knees so abruptly, she barely made it back to the chair before she collapsed. She hadn't thought of the necklace in years…wasn't even sure where it was. *How could he know*?

She saw herself as though she were watching another movie on Joachim's screen. A frail, undernourished six-year-old with long black curls, playing in her grandmother's jewelry box, the year before the old woman had died of a stroke. Nonna was the only adult Gia remembered trusting.

"For you, little one," the old woman had told her, draping a chain over the little girl's head as they sat on the edge of her sagging mattress. The chain settled, heavy and cool, around Gia's neck, and Nonna's fingers touched the quarter-sized medallion dangling from its center link as though she could imprint it on her granddaughter's heart. "Nonna Giuseppi gave it to me when I was a girl in Genoa, and now I give it to you."

"It has a picture." Gia lifted the coin to eye level, studying the tarnished image of a man with massive wings who stood with flames licking at the hem of his robe. He held a spear pointed to Heaven. "It's an angel."

"Michael," the old woman said, and lifting the medallion to her lips, she kissed it reverently and let it drop gently against Gia's chest.

"The Great Warrior will protect you from evil, child. All you have to do is ask. Here..." she motioned for Gia to kneel, and awkwardly lowered herself to the floor beside her with the painful creak of arthritic joints. "We will pray together. And the angels will come. Michael, our protector, will come..."

Gia blinked and focused on Joachim, her mind floating in a netherworld between memory, realization and the present.

"She said the angels would come..." Her brows lowered. "Who's *Michael*?"

Chapter Five

The sternness instantly drained from Joachim's face. His throat moved with unspoken words, and Gia felt herself vibrating, aflame, *drawn to him,* as though a chain bound her heart to his, and someone was pulling, and pulling…

The muscles in her thighs contracted as she started to rise, but then he swallowed and closed his eyes, and the spell was broken.

She dropped back to the chair like a puppet with severed strings.

"You're pale, Mrs. Rossi. Overwrought. Enough for now."

"What about the necklace? My necklace? How did you know?"

"Our meeting is over."

Panic reared within her. Her chance for escape was bleeding away. She'd let her imagination be seduced, had lost valuable time and opportunity.

With sudden, icy clarity, the plan she'd devised swept over her anew, fed not by revulsion this time but by desperation. *You can do this. Make him want you. Seduce him if you have to. Anything to get out of here, remember?*

Pushing her hair back with an unsteady hand, she slowly rose from the chair, her gaze fixed on Joachim's face.

He was brutally handsome, and the scratches she'd inflicted on his cheek only added to his appeal in a sickly romantic way. A wild blue fire burned beneath the cool lack of emotion in those eyes, and Gia felt seared by his regard as it narrowed on her.

"We're finished," he repeated sternly, as though reading her unruly thoughts. "You have approximately one hour before your self-defense training begins. Soleil will take you back to accommodations."

Instead of replying, she trailed her fingers along the glass edge of his desk, her other thumb hooked casually in the waistband of her pants as she stalked him. It was damned difficult to hold his icy gaze. Part of her felt stripped by it, the other part overwhelmed by the power he radiated.

He's a man like any other. She could wrap her fingers around him, handle him, stroke him, bring him to his knees.

He reached for the black intercom on his desk, but Gia caught his hand. "Please don't send me back to my cell just yet." The desperation in her voice was real, but she tempered it, even as she spoke the truth. "It's so cold there, and I—I miss my home. Haven't you ever been homesick? You're not from here, I know. You're French. Don't you miss your country? Your home?"

He stilled, his eyes trained on her face. Watching. Waiting. His fingers were unusually warm in hers, as though his skin burned with fever. *So different from Vincent.* She drew them unresisting against her stomach, bare where the hem of her shirt rode above her pants. His palm brushed her skin, his thumb settling in the dip of her navel. To her surprise, a little shudder went through her. He had calloused fingers. They would feel damn good on her body if she closed her eyes, pretended he was someone else, and shut out the reality of letting him inside her.

I can do this.

"I'm hungry for conversation," she continued huskily. "For company. And despite some of the crazy ideas flying around here, I actually like *your* company. You're probably a decent conversationalist when you're not trying to brainwash people." She swallowed and affected a slight smile. "I know a little French, you know. One phrase, anyway. *Faisons l'amour*."

Make love to me.

Joachim glanced down at their entwined hands, at his fingers pressed against her naked, quivering stomach, then back at her face. "What are you doing, Mrs. Rossi?"

"Making friends?" She mustered a smile and with her free hand, brushed an errant curl from his forehead. A tiny white scar bisected the arch of his left eyebrow. Faint crow's feet marked the corners of his eyes, even when he kept his expression so emotionless. Somewhere, sometime, he had smiled enough to create those lines. He had the kind of face that would be beatific in the heat of passion.

Perhaps Gia wouldn't have to close her eyes to lie beneath him and buy her freedom.

She cleared her throat. "We got off to such a bad start, Joachim. Since I'm going to be stuck here, let's be nice to each other. We can start with you dropping the formalities. My name is Gia."

Silence. He stared up at her while her unsteady forefinger trailed down his temple, over the hollow of his cheek and the healing scratches she'd left there, and along his jaw. His skin was smooth and fair, the bone structure beneath it angular and refined. A faint shadow of beard scraped her fingertip. She traced another tiny, crescent-shaped scar beside his mouth, noting more smile lines there. Joachim had a sense of humor.

Her fingertips brushed his full lips. They were softer than she'd imagined. Like satin and beautifully formed. They parted beneath her touch, a sensuous response, and for an instant she felt the sweet, familiar zing of feminine triumph.

Then the world spun. All she saw was a blur of movement before she was whirled around and pressed against the wall, her cheek to its cold expanse, her arm bent firmly and painfully behind her.

The heat from Joachim's body soaked her back, and his voice rushed against her ear, soft but limned with anger. "Listen to me, Gia. I can't be played like the men from your past. You will not touch me. You will not seduce me. I am not your enemy, do you understand?"

Tears of humiliation and frustration scalded her eyes.

"Please! Just let me go. Let me go! I'm going crazy—I have to get out of here!"

"Tell me, where will you go?" His words sounded breathless, the only hint of genuine emotion he'd displayed so far. "Home to Vincent? Home to die?"

"No." She drew a sobbing breath. "He wouldn't hurt me. You're crazy! Please—I just want to be free."

"Gia." His voice went husky as she cried brokenly against the wall. "If I let you go, you'll never be free again. We—seraphim—are your only chance. You must trust."

For a moment, neither of them moved. His body was granite and unyielding against her. She heard his slow inhalation close to her ear, imagined his nose against her hair, felt the soft tickle of his breath as he exhaled.

A spiral of heat shimmied through her insides. Misplaced. *Wrong.*

Abruptly he released her arm and the pressure of his hard body eased, leaving her abandoned and shivering.

Covering her face with her hands, she turned toward him and slouched against the wall, muscles weak with despair. "Seraphim. You're some…some guerilla terrorist group?"

"Seraphim are angels."

Angels. She closed bleary, burning eyes that flooded anew with tears. These people weren't angels. They'd opened the gates of Hell and showed her what awaited her inside. "Just let me go."

"I can't let you die. My orders—" He stopped. "No. It's more than that. I don't want you to die." His tone came quiet and distinct, so close, she knew without opening her eyes that he spoke with his head bowed over hers. "Stop fighting me. Let me protect you, educate you. In time we'll release you, but you mustn't work against us. Gia…"

His fingertips touched her chin, and with gentle insistence, forced her tear-filled gaze to meet his. "You're only as much a prisoner as you make yourself. Help us catch Therides, and you'll be free."

Tears forgotten, she stared back into those enigmatic blue eyes, for the first time reading kindness, perplexity, an urgency she didn't understand. Sensation crept through her belly anew, stronger this time, wound around her insides, made everything feel weak and strange. She could drown in those eyes. This man was twisting her reality…and she was beginning to believe him.

They stared at each other in silence. He was too close, his touch too tender at her jaw. She gulped, watching the breath escape his parted lips. He was breathing as quickly as she. Like the lover in her dream, the one with wings.

Seraphim.

No!

A fresh wave of obstinacy banished the fluid sensation from her limbs and she straightened her shoulders, jerking her chin free from his grasp. "Don't touch me."

The fragile connection between them shattered. Joachim searched her face for a heartbeat longer, and then with a sigh, he withdrew and turned to press the intercom on his desk.

Seconds later Soleil appeared at the door with plastic cuffs in hand, her graceful brows raised as she took in her bemused leader and a tear-stained Gia hugging the wall.

"No restraints," Joachim said, and when Soleil caught Gia's arm and led her from the office, Gia went without another word or look in his direction.

* * * * *

For a self-defense trainer, Dmitri wasn't the massive wall of Slavic muscle Gia had expected. His cultural heritage was indeterminate, but he appeared to be part Asian. Wiry and markedly smaller than the other men she'd seen in the bunker, he stood nearly nose-to-nose with her five feet seven inches and moved with precise, catlike grace, a confidence that suggested unequivocal physical control and conditioning. When he spoke, it was with the same soft, impassive manner as his cohorts. He didn't smile, didn't emote, didn't react. Another robot in this steely underground world.

He was also, Gia realized with a jolt of outrage, the one she'd nicknamed Amber Eyes, one of the men who helped kidnap her.

And now he was going to teach her how to kick ass?

This circus just gets weirder and weirder. She folded her arms over her breasts and hung back against the padded wall in the mini-gymnasium as he stood before her and explained what she would learn in self-defense training.

After a moment of listening to his quiet dissertation without really absorbing its content, she shifted her weight to one foot and said tartly, "So you're going to teach me to kill people?"

"Our goal is to equip you with the skills to defend yourself against an attack, Mrs. Rossi. Not necessarily to kill. We're guardians, after all. Not assassins."

The constant anger simmering just beneath her surface ignited. "And yet you killed my bodyguard Frank, didn't you? He was just doing his job, trying to protect me, and you killed him right in front of me. That makes you assassins in my book."

Dmitri returned her stare without responding, his hands clasped behind his back, legs braced wide on the blue wall-to-wall mat. His expression was a smooth, porcelain mask.

Seconds ticked by, and heat crept up Gia's neck, fueled by ripples of self-doubt. What if she was wrong? What if these people were telling her the truth about…about *everything*?

The sudden dip in her own conviction enraged her.

"How many people died at my home by the time you were done?" she went on, just to spite the nagging uncertainty that festered in the back of her mind. "Three? Four? Ten? They were *my* employees. I have a right to know about them, damn it."

A flicker of emotion—too quicksilver for Gia to identify—flittered across his face. "It appears that your rights are in question, Mrs. Rossi. You relinquished them, remember? One by one, every time you turned your head and denied the impropriety and misdeeds that financed your lifestyle."

"I have no reason to suspect my husband of anything," she snapped.

"You have no *desire* to suspect your husband. There's a difference."

Gia exhaled and looked away from his placid face. "Think what you want. You people are all deluded. I'm not going to debate you."

"Good." He held out his hand to her, a faint smile on his lips. "Then let's begin."

* * * * *

"Her technique is improving." Nicodemus shuffled to a stop beside Joachim at the observation window, his rheumy gaze focused on the slender woman sparring with Dmitri on the other side of the glass. "And with only two days of training under her belt, she's a formidable warrior. Quite impressive."

"Her anger fuels her strength," Joachim said with a wry smile as Gia snarled and delivered a vicious sidekick to her trainer's chest. "Of course such rage will eventually steal her focus. Dmitri will have to teach her to control it. He has his work cut out for him."

Braced to receive the assault, Dmitri caught her foot in mid-kick and, with a slight upward push, sent her crashing to the mat.

Nicodemus chuckled. "No doubt he finds her ferocity a refreshing challenge from the serene beings he's usually assigned to train. A weaker man would have suffered irreparable damage by now."

Inside the room, Dmitri extended a hand to help Gia up. She ignored the offering and rolled to her hands and knees, her breath billowing from her chest in hard gasps of frustration and weariness.

"You parried with a single kick instead of the combination

we've been practicing," he told her as she crawled to rest her forehead against the padded wall. "In this case, you should have used your feet and hands simultaneously. As I shift my weight away from you, both my hands will be utilized as a reflexive cover. You should have continued with the offense one-handed, while the other hand aimed for a vital point where your assailant is most vulnerable. It's *then* that you deliver the kick."

He stopped and seemed to recognize her belligerence in the way she hugged the wall. "Mrs. Rossi, emotion has its place. Fear brings adrenaline, adrenaline is fuel. But if you strike out blindly, acting without focus, your attacker will take advantage of it. He will bring you down and end it."

She swallowed against a dry throat and, without lifting her head from the wall, shifted to glance at him peripherally. "Like you brought down Frank? He was my only friend in the world, damn it. Which one of you killed him? There were two or three of you there, ganging up on him. Was it you, Dmitri?"

He didn't answer right away, but a heartbeat later appeared beside her with a towel, which he held out like a peace offering. "You truly care about the state of your husband's employees?"

Standing, she snatched the towel from his hand and dabbed her burning face with the cool terry cloth. "Of course I care. You people think I'm some kind of mindless bitch, don't you? I want to know what's happened outside of this place. Is there…" An unexpected sob caught in her throat and she clenched her teeth as tears gathered on her lashes. "Is there anything left of my life as I knew it four days ago?"

Dmitri's strange amber gaze studied her with a thoroughness she didn't shy away from. They'd stripped her of everything. Let him see the despair they'd brought her. She had nothing to hide.

"Your bodyguard is not dead," he said finally.

Gia stilled, the towel slipping from her fingers.

"We tranquilized him during the altercation. He was hospitalized for twenty-four hours as a precaution before being released. If he was a smart man, he'd glean knowledge from the experience and move on." His expression hardened. "But Frank is not a smart man, Mrs. Rossi. Nor is he your friend. Like the others employed by your husband, he functions on greed, and despite the occasional warmth and camaraderie he offered you, his true interest is in how well Vincent Rossi can pay him. When your husband summons him again, Frank will go. He is lost to us. We can't help him or the others. But you...*you* are the one who interests us. You have promise." His voice gentled. "You have heart."

Gia absorbed the information with pulse pounding, her thoughts rocketing through her mind like howling banshees. Frank was alive—had been hospitalized—which meant people knew about the attack. *Vincent* knew about the attack. He must be in Chicago by now. Help was on its way. It had to be. Her days in this steel and glass dungeon were numbered.

Bolstered, she drew a steadying breath and straightened her posture. "Thank you for the information, Dmitri. I'm sure you understand it makes me feel less isolated down here."

"You're welcome, Mrs. Rossi. Are you ready to continue your training?"

"Absolutely," she said, and a genuine smile curved her lips, the first one since she'd fallen into this crater in the center of the earth.

* * * * *

"When's my next brainwashing?" Gia asked airily, watching from the far corner of her cell as Soleil stacked a fresh supply of clothing on the foot of the cot. "It's been three days since my last session with Joachim. Has he forgotten about me?"

"Joachim never forgets a guest." The blonde smiled without shifting her attention from her task. "He's been in the field, Mrs. Rossi."

"The field?"

"Gathering intel."

Gia smirked. "Isn't that dangerous, to be out there where demons are running around disguised as my husband? Maybe Vincent will put a curse on your mission. You know, float heavy objects, spin his head around, spew pea soup. Scary stuff."

Soleil finally looked up, her smile fading slightly. "You appear to have some restless energy today, Mrs. Rossi, which works well in accordance with your schedule. Dmitri is going to train you in firearms."

Gia's jaw dropped, then she burst out laughing. "What? You mean he's going to put an actual gun in my hands and trust me with it?"

"That's right. And I'm certain you won't disappoint him." The blonde laid a fresh package of white cotton socks on top of the other garments. "Your cooperation, as I'm sure you've guessed, is tantamount to your comfort here."

A warning. It shivered through Gia and her glee seeped away. Her captors hadn't hurt her or accosted her physically, but if they could control their emotions with such frightening focus, they were more than capable of unknown horrors. Her instincts told her to play nice.

"These are all newly purchased items," Soleil went on, as though the tense moment had never passed between them. "Do you have any other cosmetic or personal needs that haven't been addressed, Mrs. Rossi? Any requests?"

"I'd like to have my wedding rings back."

"I'm afraid that's impossible."

"But they're *mine*."

The blonde just looked at her, her silence a firm refusal.

Gia swallowed, torn between anger and sadness. She was too worn to throw the tantrum building deep in her gut. Her rage had no effect, it seemed, except to exhaust her.

Anyway, in all honesty, her creature comforts had been well met. There was only one thing she missed besides her rings—a bra. It had become painfully obvious yesterday in defense training, when Dmitri's elbow collided with her left breast and brought tears of agony to her eyes.

She uncrossed her arms and straightened her shoulders. "How about a brassiere?"

Soleil hesitated, her clover-green eyes making a quick inventory of the articles at the foot of the cot. "You haven't one?"

"They brought me here in my bikini, remember? And they even took that from me." She glanced down at herself. The curves of her small breasts were only mildly apparent beneath the loose-fitting T-shirt, but she still felt naked. The constant friction of the soft cotton against her sensitive nipples left them blatantly knotted and further fed her self-consciousness, too. "I don't *have* to wear a bra, obviously, but I got elbowed yesterday. It hurt. And I like the coverage for modesty's sake, especially around strange men. Not that anyone here has normal masculine interests...but you never know."

Soleil paused at the door. "What size do you wear?"

"32-B."

She thought for a moment. "We're the same size. I'll loan you a brassiere until I can get lingerie for you. Anything else, Mrs. Rossi?"

Gia sighed. "Since we're going to be swapping undies, you might as well call me Gia."

Soleil smiled. "Dmitri will be here for you shortly, Gia."

* * * * *

The shooting gallery was a long, narrow corridor lined with glass and concrete booths on one side. Beyond the booths, paper silhouette targets hung staggered at varying distances. Gia and Dmitri were the only occupants. The one man who'd been practicing when they entered the range had quietly and quickly packed up and departed as though following silent orders.

"This is a Colt Agent .38 revolver," Dmitri said as he laid the snub-nosed weapon in Gia's trembling hand. "Relax, Mrs. Rossi. It's unloaded for now."

She wondered if he knew she was trembling from the

thought of using the gun as a means to escape. "How's it supposed to help me without bullets?"

"Have you ever discharged a firearm?"

She shook her head, staring at the revolver as though it could rear up and bite her.

"Then first we must acquaint you with its mechanism. We'll do this through dry-fire exercises until you become comfortable with the weapon."

"So I'll be shooting nothing?"

"Dry-fire develops proper trigger control, the most important element to hitting your target." He glanced at the weapon she now held in both hands, then back at her face, and a smile crept into his voice. "How does it feel in your hands? The fit of the gun strongly determines your ability to strike your target under stress."

She considered it, caressing the smooth sections of the pearl grip, her gaze fixed on its snub barrel and on the whiteness of her fingertip as it compressed the trigger. The revolver was feminine, yet powerful. So much power. She'd never realized the invincibility such a small concoction of steel could grant the person who wielded it.

Her lips curved. She felt like a goddess.

Then she remembered the cold, relentless press of Joachim's gun in the small of her back, and her muscles tightened. He could have killed her when she raked her fingernails across his face. He could have shot her, or simply bludgeoned her with his pistol when she tried to scramble away in the field outside the bunker.

Instead he'd wiped the blood from his jaw, his voice low and unshaken as he commanded his men to take her into the bunker. Never raised his voice beyond a knee-jerk expletive of pain. Never showed emotion except for a brief flash of anger and surprise in his eyes. *Damn him.*

What would he do when she aimed this pretty little .38 at his handsome, expressionless face? He'd let her go or he would die.

The trigger released beneath her finger. The hammer clicked, and she jerked in automatic reaction.

Her gaze met Dmitri's amber eyes. "It feels perfect," she said.

Chapter Six

"Vincent Rossi knows we have his wife." Joachim flattened his palms on the conference table, his gaze moving over the operatives gathered for the mission briefing. "In addition, he claims to hold one of our own in retaliation."

Olivier sat forward, a frown darkening his usually amiable features. "Who is it?"

"Intel has lost touch with one of our covert operatives stationed in the sect's compound." Joachim paused, searching the faces of his team. "I'm afraid Gregory didn't get out in time."

Soleil folded her hands against her lips in prayer fashion. "He lives?"

"So Rossi claims." Joachim sighed. "But I must speak the truth. I search my heart and feel no evidence of Gregory's life force."

The seraphs sat in mournful silence for a moment, then Joachim stirred. "I spoke with Rossi personally to arrange an exchange. Mrs. Rossi for Gregory. He agreed to it."

Soleil shook her head. "And you trust him?"

"Of course not. Nor will we relinquish the woman. We will go with proof of Gia's death at her own hand." Joachim glanced at the men sitting to his left. "Tristan, Aristide, Elgin, Xavier, you'll assume perimeter security this time, along with Dmitri. I can assure you Rossi has no intention of allowing us to leave his estate alive, and his guards crawl the acreage like hungry insects. The goal is to regain Gregory, if he lives, convince Rossi of his wife's demise and get the team out without injuring the nephil. It's imperative we catch him alive, but it won't happen on tonight's operation. The time for his retrieval has not yet come."

Olivier glanced up from the map of the estate. "We don't have the Medallion. What of it? Time is short, Joachim. If he gets to it before—"

"He won't. Not even Mrs. Rossi knows its location. She did, however, acknowledge its existence, although it appears she hasn't thought of it for many years."

"So it's not at the Rossi mansion, then," Olivier said.

"We turned the place inside out ourselves, and no doubt Rossi has done the same. I think Gia knows its location, but her memory will have to be stirred. For today, our only goal is to convince Rossi his wife is dead, rescue Gregory and then get out of there with our skin intact."

Joachim's attention darted to Soleil. "You'll run communications from the van, Soleil. Are there any questions?"

The seraph called Xavier shifted, his elbows braced on the table. "Does Gia know of her husband's possession?"

"She knows and yet will not hear," Olivier said.

"I don't think she could bear to believe it," Soleil murmured.

Tension knotted the back of Joachim's neck. Gia was more fragile than he'd first suspected. Like a music box dancer, she had pirouetted precariously through twenty-six years, and now the melody was running down, and the defeat that flavored her rage said she too knew her life was at a treacherous crossroads.

She was both obstinate and desolate. Compassion warred with frustration inside him every time he gazed through the observation window of her cell and recognized her despair. She stalked his thoughts, and at night, his dreams. It was no longer just his human body that had fallen prey to her wild appeal.

"She hasn't yet accepted it." He maintained an even tone, his face carefully impassive as he addressed the team of seraphs. "Only physical proof will sway her."

"She's unbelievably strong-willed," Olivier said, rubbing the space between his brows as though he found the mere thought of Gia Rossi painful.

"But we are stronger," Joachim replied. "We aren't here to save her feelings, but her soul. And with her help, this world. We'll do what's necessary to gain her cooperation."

*****

"The first mistake you made was aiming the gun at the silhouette's head." Dmitri stood beside Gia in the glass booth and reloaded her revolver as he spoke. "The head is an unsteady target. Think of what happens if you miss—which would be easy to do when your attacker is running at you."

He placed the gun in her hands, then moved slightly behind her and repositioned her arms. "Aim for the center of the body's mass, stomach level. A shot fired from this angle will have the greatest chance of hitting the assailant. If he's close to you, aim a little lower."

Gia licked her lips and paused to adjust her safety goggles, stealing a glance at his profile as she did so. There was no wariness in his expression, nothing to indicate he didn't trust her or was on edge with the idea of her firing a loaded revolver while he stood inches away.

A frown creased her brow. *Damn it, he shouldn't trust her.* She was perfectly capable of shifting to the right and blowing out the center of *his* body's mass.

The problem was, she didn't want to shoot him. Nothing about Dmitri made her feel he was the enemy. He wasn't sexy and treacherous like Joachim, or boyishly handsome like Olivier, but more androgynous. While he didn't smile much or laugh or make idle chitchat, he seemed genuinely concerned with the development of her skill and her ability to protect herself. Kindness shone in his almond-shaped eyes too. There was something disconcertingly gentle and patient about him.

She glanced back at the target silhouette, and the random holes she'd managed to pepper like a halo around the figure's head. Dmitri was right. She stood a far better chance of hitting an attacker if she aimed near his crotch.

Directing the gun lower, she squinted, gripped the revolver

more firmly and pulled the trigger.

The recoil popped her arms back and she nearly lost her balance. The acrid smell of cordite filled the air.

"Not bad," Dmitri said. "You hit him in the solar plexus."

Gia peered at the target and grinned her satisfaction. If paper were flesh, this bad guy would be a goner.

"Widen your stance," said another male voice behind her. Lower, huskier than Dmitri's. Heavily accented. Alarms sounded in her head. She lifted one side of her electronic ear protection and looked past Dmitri's shoulder.

Joachim stood at the door, dressed entirely in black. Black ribbed shirt, black cargo pants, black combat boots. The sight of him struck her breathless and she stared for a moment, studying the flash of gold in his left ear. She hadn't noticed an earring on him before. His wavy hair was combed back instead of falling across his forehead, bringing his sculpted features into sharp relief.

He looked like he was headed somewhere clandestine. He looked dangerous.

"The recoil nearly knocked you down," he said. "Your stance is wrong. Widen your legs for balance."

She scowled and turned back to the target, her pulse trip-hammering in her veins. "Ready for me to go again?" she asked Dmitri.

Dmitri nodded, and Gia focused her full attention on the paper silhouette. When she pulled the trigger, the recoil knocked her back again. Hissing out a sigh between clenched teeth, she widened her stance as Joachim had instructed and took aim again.

Before she could fire, warm hands cupped her elbows and urged her arms to bend. Not Dmitri's touch. It was too sensual and light and it shivered across her skin. The scent of soap and vanilla filled her senses and banished the pungent odor of cordite lingering in the air.

"In a real situation," Joachim's voice came at her right ear, its low timbre permeating her headset, "how quickly you recover from the recoil will affect how quickly you get off any follow-up shots. Relax." His palms stroked her upper arms, pebbled her skin with goose bumps. To her horror, her nipples tightened beneath her tank top. "You're tensing before you squeeze the trigger—in anticipation of the recoil, yes? That could send the bullet away from your intended target. Relax, Gia. You're strong. Absorb the kickback."

He spoke her name with a very soft G. Made it sound exotic and beautiful, as though she were someone he knew intimately. That damned French accent made every word that left his lips sound like a nighttime caress.

No wonder she'd been battling crazed sex dreams about him almost since her first night in captivity. Angel or hoodlum, everything about the man screamed sex.

Gia swallowed and fought the urge to look around for Dmitri. Where was he? And why had he allowed Joachim to just…just *take over* like this?

The warmth of Joachim's body seeped into her back and sent a shivery thrill humming through her. Unnerved, she sucked in a breath, settled her weight evenly on both legs and tried to ignore the delicious fragrance that emanated from him as he braced her from behind, his hands extended alongside her wrists, hovering without touching.

For someone so intensely dislikeable, he smelled really, really good.

She turned her head a little and found his cheek nearly on hers, his hard body so close it was as if he embraced her from behind. Misplaced pleasure spilled liquid heat into her belly, into her womb, made her tingle and throb between her thighs.

Never! Clenching her jaw, Gia aimed for the center of the target's body mass, lower than the stomach, and pulled the trigger. Again. Again. Absorbing the recoil, never blinking as she redirected her hyperawareness of the man behind her to the paper silhouette, and pretended it was *he*.

When she stopped and lowered the gun, she'd left a neat spattering of holes in the crotch area. And because she'd kept careful count, she knew there was still one bullet left in the chamber.

"Very good." Joachim sounded mildly impressed. "You are—how do they say it? A crack shot."

She didn't look at him. "Where's Dmitri?"

"He has other duties for now."

With a trembling hand, she removed her ear protection and goggles, let them drop to the floor and turned to face him.

Joachim hadn't moved. This close, she could read the details of his eyes, count the black spokes that shot like brushstrokes through their cerulean blueness.

Her throat tightened, pulse thrashing like a wild thing beneath her breast, in her temples, her wrists, low in her sex. This kind of excitement, shivery and hot, was foreign to her. If they'd met aboveground, under different circumstances, Joachim would be more than irresistible. He could be an obsession. Vincent or no Vincent, it was a damn good thing their paths hadn't crossed in happier times.

But he was her captor, and she was a caged animal. It didn't matter that a part of her, the un-murderous, unsatisfied, aroused part, wanted to strip off that stark black uniform and use her mouth and tongue to find every vulnerable spot on his muscled body.

Instead, carefully and deliberately, she raised the gun between them, nestled the nose against the hard wall of his stomach and cocked the hammer.

Joachim's lashes dropped and he studied the revolver pressed against the front of his shirt. "You're too smart for this, Mrs. Rossi."

"I'm not smart. But I am desperate. There's one bullet left in this gun. I want to go home, and if *you're* smart, you'll let it be my ticket out of here."

"I can't let you go home," he said, raising his gaze to hers again. So calm, so unaffected by the fact that his life was on the line. "I'm afraid you'll have to shoot me first."

Gia's breath came in sporadic pants now, and perspiration misted her hairline as she searched his eyes for conviction. "You think I won't. You think I'm not brave enough."

"You're quite brave," he said. "There's a fine line between courage and foolishness. I see we'll have to work on that with you."

Then, to her wounded amazement, his hand slowly lifted to her face and stole her breath as it hovered near her cheek. He wouldn't—*couldn't*—cup her face in that hand. She'd kill him if he touched her as tenderly as he spoke to her now.

Instead, his fingers brushed a single strand of hair from her brow, a caress that wasn't quite physical contact, solicitude that wasn't quite invasive. Compassion that wasn't quite *personal.* When he lowered his hand, his stare returned to hers.

His expression was empty. No tenderness. Nothing.

Her nostrils flared and tears burned her eyes. "You must know how much I hate you," she whispered.

"You don't know me well enough to mean that." His gaze drifted over her face, then settled on her lips. "Perhaps I've been insensitive, inhospitable. We're in this together, though. You should know me at least as well as I know you."

What did he mean? A fresh wave of heat washed through her insides, born of rage and a sick, wayward thrill. The aching place between her legs throbbed. The mad woman she'd become wanted him to put his hands on her, to silence her with his beautiful mouth, to push her up against the wall and drive himself into her, fuck away this surreal dream…before she pulled the trigger.

She exhaled a shuddering sigh and tightened her grip on the revolver. "I know you're crazy."

"You think I'm crazy. But a part of you isn't quite sure." His throat moved as he spoke. Her attention drifted to the hollow there, noted the minute golden hairs feathering his skin.

A tiny pulse beat beneath his jaw, more rapid than she would have suspected.

"I want you to trust me, Mrs. Rossi."

"Gee," she retorted, "that might be a bit of a stretch for me. You kidnapped me and jammed a semi-automatic in my spine and threw me in the back of a dingy box van with a bunch of your ski-mask buddies." Her voice shook, the sarcasm replaced by anguish. "And here I am, a hundred feet underground in a chrome cage, and I'm so…alone, and I've forgotten what the sunshine feels like on my skin—"

"I'll give you the sunlight, Gia. You can have freedom again, once you understand why you're here. I'd like to show you. Are you ready to learn?"

She studied the stubbornness in his chin, then his full lips. There was no cruelty in his features. It would be so much easier to pull the trigger if there were.

He didn't want from her what men had always wanted. He didn't want to touch her, or taste her, or spar with her in exchange for *anything*. The humiliating realization, and the resulting—*insane!*—disillusionment she felt, made her want to aim the gun at her own fool self.

"Put aside the gun," he whispered, his blue eyes following the single, traitorous tear trickling down her cheek. "You have so much more power without it."

Suddenly she understood. For the first time since this nightmare had begun, she knew the right thing to do, and it wasn't the resolution she'd wanted.

God, she was tired. Two more hot tears slid down her face, and the revolver drooped in her clammy fingers. She closed her eyes, felt him gently remove it from her grasp and waited for the wrenching punishment that would surely follow.

Nothing happened. His fingertips traced the crease between her brows, their soothing touch easing the tension that pounded there.

"No pain," he whispered.

Her knees went watery beneath her. She reached out to steady herself and found her fingers curling into the soft material of his shirt. Found his hands bracing, strong and warm, at her waist to keep her from falling.

Whatever he was, this man was not her enemy.

She tested the realization aloud. "You're not going to hurt me."

"Never, Gia," he said softly. "Never."

The only person who'd promised her thus.

"*Ding-ding-ding,*" she sang in a shaky, choked imitation of a game show bell. "You win. Tell me what you want me to do."

Chapter Seven

An ominous shiver threaded down Gia's spine. Where were they taking her?

To the truth. Part of her—the part that had chosen to stay ignorant of Vincent's life outside their home—still didn't want to know, no matter what she'd agreed to in the face of Joachim's quiet reassurance.

It was a different truck this time. The rickety vehicle used to abduct her was nowhere in sight as they crossed the field toward a black, windowless van. Dmitri's silent presence, along with the four other men behind Gia, told her she couldn't renege on her agreement to cooperate, so she trudged along after Olivier, Soleil and Joachim, her gaze taking in the fiery play of the setting sun on the van's sleek finish.

Her first sunset in days. When it rose again, she would know why she was here, why she was still alive…and what was left of her old life, the one she'd invented and nurtured and polished to a high shine.

Tatters, perhaps.

Only now, after shedding a million tears in a glassed-in cell, could she admit that her former world had been a house of sticks built on a dubious foundation, and the wake-up call at the hands of these strange people, harsh and frightening—maybe some sick blessing in disguise. Even if they let her go, her trust in Vincent had been irretrievably shaken. Right now, she couldn't picture his features, his body—just a flesh-colored blur dressed in expensive clothing. But she remembered the cold touch of his hands…

Sick emotion knotted in her throat and she swallowed, focusing on Joachim's wide shoulders ahead of her.

"How long will we be gone?" she called out in a nervous voice. At the abrupt sound, a flock of birds rose from the overgrown grass and fluttered into the fading cornflower sky.

"As long as it takes." Joachim turned his head to watch the birds take flight. His hand skimmed the tall grass as he walked, passing over the tips so that the blades bowed and swayed in his wake. The breeze fingered through his hair, ruffled it across his forehead. He seemed as much a part of this wide-open sanctuary as the white birds sailing, gentle and graceful, on the sweet tepid wind.

Warm blood rushed to her cheeks, and Gia looked away.

No one conversed until they reached the van. Then Joachim told her, "You will sit in the back with Soleil. You will follow instructions implicitly."

She scowled and moved to follow the others piling into the van, but he grasped her arm and drew her back to stare into her face, the blue of his eyes preternaturally bright in the vanishing light. "You will follow instructions implicitly," he repeated, "*if you want to live*. Do you understand?"

The knot in her throat tightened. "Yes."

His fingers uncurled from her arm and he waited for her to climb into the van, then got in after her and slammed the door on the cool, falling dusk.

They rode for a long time in silence, with the women occupying the rear two seats, five of the men hunkered in the cargo space, Joachim in the front passenger seat and Olivier driving.

Gia studied each face in turn, her memory flipping through their names, which had amazingly stuck in her mind. *Tristan, Aristide, Elgin and Xavier,* Joachim had told her as they climbed into the daylight. *Olivier, Dmitri, Joachim, Soleil.* Strange names, stranger people. All of them beautiful, young, slim and strong, as though they'd sailed from some magical island where the inhabitants had the bodies of gods and demeanors of stone.

Did they ever laugh? Cry? Feel uncertain, afraid, excited,

nervous...*anything*? She tried to picture Joachim losing his cool, and a tiny frisson of electricity went through her. The image was scary and enticing at the same time.

Beside her, Soleil shifted and reached beneath the bucket seat to withdraw a laptop computer and a set of headphones. "You will need these," she said, and handed Gia the headphones.

"Why?" Gia asked, but then the van slowed and pulled to a stop, gravel grinding beneath its tires. It sounded as if they had parked on the shoulder of a road. She started to rise, but Soleil caught her hand.

"Sit down, Mrs. Rossi."

An unidentifiable panic constricted Gia's chest as she watched the men file out of the van and disappear into the descending darkness. "Aren't we going with them?"

"No. We'll stay here and man communications." The blonde's voice was soothing, her grasp on Gia's wrist gentle but firm. "You're safer here. And I promise you won't miss a thing." She turned the laptop computer toward Gia and flipped open the screen. "In a moment, you'll put on your headphones. You'll see and hear everything that they do."

She nodded toward Olivier and Joachim, who were still visible through the van's open door.

Joachim handed his companion a set of keys and a pair of inconspicuous eyeglasses. "The car is through that patch of trees. Start it. I'm right behind you."

With a nod, the other man disappeared into the night.

Alone, Joachim strapped an identical pistol to his ankle and then fastened a small, dime-sized disk on the inside of his own belt. "This is a microphone, Gia," he said without looking up. "Olivier's eyeglasses contain a minute camera. I promised you the truth. Soon you will have no more questions."

"But I have one now." She squinted at him, peered beyond his shoulder to no avail. "Where are we?"

He slid into a black, calf-length duster, straightened his

sleeves and finally met her eyes.

"On the edge of the Rossi estate," he said.

Then he was gone.

*****

A floor lamp's paltry glow was all that illuminated the foyer of the sprawling crimson cavern Vincent Rossi called a home. Somewhere in the bowels of the great house, Luciano Pavarotti thundered through Puccini's ethereal "Nessum Dorma", his tenor adding an element of eeriness to an already tomblike environment.

Joachim's vigilant gaze made a slow sweep of their surroundings as they passed through the ornate foyer. There was no sign of life, save the pair of thick-necked guards who'd greeted them at the mansion's entrance. The two men were zombies, stripped of their souls, bodies occupied by nameless demons that Therides had no doubt recruited from Hell. Their black eyes shone like anthracite, fathomless conduits straight to the fires of damnation.

Nothing human touched this dwelling—hadn't since Gia's departure. With her, all life and light had fled. In her absence the mansion was tainted by specters only a clairvoyant eye could detect.

The henchmen ushered Joachim and Olivier through a set of double doors and into a massive, dimly lit library. The heat that rushed to greet them stole Joachim's breath. It was midsummer, the outside humidity cloying, and yet the faint hum of the great house's furnace was faintly audible. *Yet another symptom of the disease called Therides.* Nephilim-inhabited bodies produced little heat.

"Relinquish your weapons," one of the guards ordered the seraphs, arms folded over his massive chest.

Joachim returned the man's empty stare. "We'll relinquish nothing."

"We are unarmed," the second guard's tone dripped

mockery as he spread his arms wide to prove his assertion. "Mr. Rossi, too, will bear no weapons. He simply wants a nonviolent transaction. His wife in exchange for your associate." His black gaze narrowed as it shifted between Joachim and Olivier. "The woman is nowhere to be seen. I assume she is in a safe place until the exchange is at hand?"

"Score one for the big guy in blue," Olivier said with a wink. "Are all nephilim this bright?"

"Enough." The first guard took a menacing step, his growled words a palpable threat. "Hand over your weapons, seraphs."

Joachim moved to meet him, effectively blocking Olivier, who had an exasperating penchant for aggravating delicate situations. "We will not," he said firmly.

The guard smirked down at him. "You cannot kill Therides with your substandard human weapons."

"But we can send *you* into cycle." Moving to stand beside Joachim, Olivier rested an elbow on his leader's shoulder and reached out to give the henchman's steely chest an affable poke. "Come on, friend. Humor us. We like our feeble little toys."

The guard's features tightened. Danger tainted the air, slightly metallic, like spilled blood. Every muscle in Joachim's body turned to stone.

Then the guard stepped back, glanced at his cohort and motioned to two red velvet chairs positioned in front of a massive, claw-footed desk. "Wait here," he told the seraphs, derision twisting his features. "Mr. Rossi will be with you shortly."

When they were alone, Olivier sank to a chair and offered an arid grin. "Whew. For a moment there I thought I'd gone too far. Those two had no sense of humor."

Joachim cocked a brow and took the seat beside him. "You court danger with your taunts."

"But it's such a small pleasure in the massive scheme of things. How boring would this all be otherwise? Mission after mission with nothing to laugh about."

Joachim resisted a smile, but his humor quickly faded and he lapsed into silence. Amidst the tense anticipation, there was no room for further conversation between the two friends. A Gothic grandfather clock ticked off the passage of time as they waited, and when seconds slid into minutes, he grew too restless to remain seated. Jumping to his feet, he prowled the room's perimeter, studying cabinet after cabinet, which displayed everything from pearl-handled revolvers to machetes to bazookas.

Weapons fascinated the demon. All sorts. Anything that could destroy, maim, create chaos and calamity. Semi-automatics were mere trinkets, the weapons he'd amassed through the Fallen Sun Fellowship a mindless hobby. Death to humans, the ultimate goal. It didn't matter how he achieved it. Bare hands were a most reliable recourse if all else failed. And the strength Therides granted Vincent Rossi's slim, forty-year-old body was formidable…his fabled ability to leap from one body into another even more so.

Joachim was braced for the worst, but they weren't here tonight to grapple the master nephil into his eternal prison. Not without the Sacred Weapon. Not without Gia.

Inside the left pocket of his coat, his fingers caressed the silky spandex material of her bikini top. Her wedding bands were encased in an envelope and tucked in his breast pocket, ready to hand Rossi as proof of his wife's demise. The rings had been out of her possession long enough that the demon couldn't use psychometry to determine whether she still lived. Nephilim, despite their enormous power, weren't infallible.

A smile of irony twisted Joachim's mouth. Gia had wanted the rings back, pleaded for them. After tonight, she would never ask for them again.

Senses acute, he let his gaze skim the endless shelves of books. He couldn't imagine Gia in this dark, musty place, yet it had been her home. The slight, noxious scent of sulfur tinged the air, evidence of the blackness that now dwelled under this roof.

Had she noticed how black and foreboding the house had become in the days since Therides possessed her husband, or noted the change in Vincent, wondered at it, questioned it? Had Therides touched her silken skin with Vincent's cold hands, reveling in Gia's ignorance of the unbearable truth?

A shot of rage fired through Joachim, startling him from his disturbed reverie. He hadn't meant to imagine her long, slender legs wrapped around another man's hips. Hadn't meant to envision her head thrown back, graceful neck arched in ecstasy, all the while mindless of the depraved invasion taking place within her vulnerable body as the demon ground himself into her, spilled his foul seed inside her, stole little pieces of her soul under the guise of a man exercising the rights of a lover and husband.

Swallowing the surge of unexpected and foreign emotion, he paced back to the desk, gave Olivier an annoyed look and glanced at his watch. "Where is he?"

"He comes," Olivier said beneath his breath, and behind Joachim the double doors flew open.

The hair on the back of Joachim's neck stood at attention. He closed his eyes, throat working under the innate desire to whirl around and attack. The Glock in the holster at his ankle seemed miles away. It wouldn't kill Therides, he reminded himself, and dragged in a deep inhalation.

Therides drew closer, and a foul stench singed the air. *Breath of the demon*. Clenching his fists, Joachim turned to face Lucifer's son.

Beside him, Olivier rose to his feet, his somber gaze fixed on the nephil silently crossing the room to greet them.

The demon, disguised as Vincent Rossi, paused in shadow, his features a blurred, indecipherable mask. "Gentlemen. *Quel plaisir*."

"Where's Gregory?" Olivier demanded.

"Where's my wife?" Rossi replied aridly.

"She was no wife of yours, Swamp Thing."

Joachim shot his capricious companion a warning glance and smoothly took over. "We came as agreed, demon. Let's get on with it."

In reply, Rossi stepped into the lamp's dim glow and laid a metal briefcase on the desk.

Joachim stared at him, transfixed by disgust and a new, very human fascination with the macabre image before him. Vincent Rossi's dark hair was thin and oily, swooped back from gaunt, hawklike features, his complexion ivory smooth, bloodless, his thin lips curved into an unreadable smile. He wore wool pants, a turtleneck and a heavy gray cardigan over it, and his fingernails were blue from cold.

Flipping open the locks, he lifted the briefcase lid, then stepped back, clasping his thin hands behind him. The light reflected blood red in his black, pupilless eyes.

"The remains of your friend. I'm sorry to say he didn't survive being transported from the compound."

Joachim clenched his jaw and looked away from the charred bone fragments in the briefcase. They'd incinerated Gregory's human form. *Burned him.*

Behind his leader, Olivier's silence radiated rage.

"So he was called Gregory?" the demon continued lightly, tilting his head in consideration. "Yes. Well. *Gregory* wasn't very cooperative." His expression shifted from contempt to simpering regret. "If only he hadn't tried to escape in such an underhanded manner. I must admit he almost succeeded, your slippery friend. He was quick. But I was quicker. He suffered a regrettably swift and silent departure. A true exemplar of Michael's Holy Legions to the bitter end. How noble. How—" He glanced around, then the pleasure slid from his features and he narrowed his gaze on Joachim. "Enough bullshit. *Where is she*?"

Never before had Joachim taken such human satisfaction in retaliation. His eyebrows lifted. "You're referring to Gia? Of course. The remains of *your wife*," he said, and withdrew her bikini top from his coat pocket.

With solicitous care, he spread the fluorescent green garment on the leather blotter, then reached inside his coat, produced the envelope with the wedding rings and slid it across the desk toward the demon. "Vincent Rossi's wife is dead. Free of his depravity and your malevolence."

The demon quickly recovered from his snarling dismay and propped a hip on the edge of the desk, snatching up the envelope to twirl it between his slim, bloodless fingers. "Playing games with me, seraph?"

"No games," Joachim said, never swaying his attention from the nephil's pallid face. "Unfortunately for everyone who holds a vested interest in the Holy Relics, Gia killed herself shortly after we took her from this estate."

Rossi glared from Joachim to Olivier. "But you are guardians, are you not? How could she possibly perish under your watchful, all-knowing regard?"

"She chose death over coming home to you," Olivier said between clenched teeth. "Not that anyone could blame her."

The demon smirked. "That's one way to look at it. But she also chose death over giving seraphim the Medallion, which takes the sting off this disappointment for me, really." He shrugged. "Her connection to the Medallion was her only worth. If she couldn't produce, she needed to go. Tell me, then, how it happened. Did she hang herself on knotted sheets? Slice her wrists with a pop-top and bleed dry?"

A haze of greed and lust fogged his features, his words quickening to a mutter, as though he spoke to himself. "If this is all the pleasure allowed me, I want details. *I want to know*. How did she die? Was it bloody? Macabre? Obscene?"

Silence.

"Oh, come on, boys. Give me something to chew on."

The grandfather clock chimed out three-quarters of an hour.

Rossi's glee faded, and a shuttered expression cloaked his face again. He glanced down at the envelope containing the rings, as though just realizing he held it. Joachim could almost read his thoughts. *Gia would never willingly give up her precious rings.*

"Where's the body?"

"Cremated," Olivier said, folding his arms over his chest. "We took the liberty of scattering her ashes over Lake Michigan."

"And the angels sang," Rossi snapped.

Joachim's mouth tugged up in a dour smile. "Something like that."

The demon swiped up the forlorn bikini top, wadded it and jammed it in a desk drawer. "So it appears we've reached an impasse, gentlemen. What now?"

Joachim stared at him. "There are many of us assigned this mission, nephil. Michael's Legions will prevail. We'll find the Medallion even without Gia's help, and you will die by the Spear, as Michael ordained."

"In other words, the race is on." Rossi gave an excited little shiver and in a sickening burst of affability, extended his hand to Joachim. "Let us shake on it, then. When I find the Medallion, seraph leader, you'll be the first to know. We'll celebrate. A little fete before I send you and your oh-so-promising career as Michael's pissboy into cycle."

Keeping a placid expression, Joachim bypassed the human gesture of good sportsmanship and snapped shut the briefcase that held Gregory's remains.

Kind, jovial, brave Gregory. He'd been the first to volunteer to infiltrate the Fellowship's compound. He'd undoubtedly suffered a human's agony too under the pitiless torture of the nephil and his minions. And now Gregory's soul had been thrust into cycle by the demon's hand, far, far away from the Archangel's Legions and Creator's Realm. Far away from all he knew and loved. There was no reward for his unfaltering bravery, only the dubious honor of being the first angel on this mission to expire.

Gia's fate might be similar if seraphim didn't tread now with utter care, for while the demon seemed to accept their report, he never trusted seraphim. He would dog their heels at every turn. The race was, indeed, *on*.

"Will you not press my flesh, seraph?" Rossi moved away from the desk, extended fingers shaking with a fury that didn't show on his ivory mask as he drew closer to Joachim.

"In the name of the Dominions, I will rend your flesh and peel it from your soul," Joachim replied calmly.

With a snarl, Rossi shot out a hand and grasped him by the neck, pulling him forward until their noses nearly touched.

Immediately Olivier drew his semi-automatic, but Joachim motioned him back and returned his gaze to his adversary's, never flinching, even as the demon's foul breath chilled his face. "When we are done on this planet, you will be driven to a deeper hell than what Lucifer could ever show you, Therides."

"I'll take you with me, beautiful boy." Fingers digging like talons into the nape of Joachim's neck, Rossi closed the two inches between them and kissed his mouth with foul, clammy lips, sealing the black vow with a single flicker of a viper's tongue between Joachim's teeth.

Joachim shoved away, bile rising in his throat. In an automatic response of revulsion, he snatched his weapon from its holster, thrust it in the demon's direction and cocked the hammer. Before he could act on his own deadly impulse, though, a shaken Olivier surged forward and pressed his own pistol to Rossi's temple.

"I'll pulverize your body where you stand."

"And I'll leap," the demon responded. "Maybe to you, or to your illustrious leader. I can't decide which form is more appealing."

For a thick, endless moment, the three men stood frozen in a tense standoff, each watching for the other to make the move that would launch a bloodbath.

Then, to Joachim's amazement, Rossi gave a weary sigh and

motioned to the foyer. "We could end this here and now, but then none of us would be the winner, hmm? Go. The doors are open, and my guards are without weapons. Get out of my house. And take your hapless 'Gregory' with you."

Joachim nodded at Olivier.

Moving slowly, Olivier stepped away from Rossi, keeping his semi-automatic trained on the demon's forehead with futile stubbornness while Joachim holstered his weapon and slid the briefcase from the desk. Then, with measured movements, the two seraphs backed from the room.

Rossi didn't follow.

They passed the henchmen in the foyer, who stood guard like colossal mannequins over the haunted mansion, but Joachim hardly noticed them, or their peculiar lack of response to Olivier's brandished gun.

The demon's vile kiss had poisoned him, stripped his armor, exposing emotions that coiled and twined within him like a bed of serpents. He had no defenses against his humanity, suddenly. Inexplicable despair twisted his stomach, and with every step in retreat, pictures of Gia assailed him.

For years, from a guardian's distance, he'd witnessed her vulnerability and misplaced innocence and need for love, her intense will to exist, even in the shamefully narrow space misfortune had provided. And this mission could well see her dead, destroyed by the demon's hand, as though she were an inconsequential blink in time. As though, as Therides had proclaimed, her connection to the Medallion was her only worth.

Gia, with the velvet brown eyes, vulnerable mouth and smooth, olive skin. Gia, with the exquisite soul buried beneath a lifetime of damage.

Gia.

Righteous anger consumed him, waves of it, clouding his vision and beading his skin with perspiration. In that moment he lost sight of the mission, seraphim's purpose, the grand battle of light against darkness, everything except Gia Rossi's hapless innocence.

It wasn't until he and Olivier stepped out of the demon's embrace and into the humid, fathomless night that he remembered…and his heart jolted with a shock of sorrow so potent, his pulse stuttered.

Sitting in the mobile communications unit some three miles away, Gia had seen, and heard, it all.

* * * * *

"Mrs. Rossi."

Cool hands closed over hers. Through the wild buzzing in Gia's ears, a matter-of-fact voice rent the clotted silence of the van's interior, an adult speaking to a bewildered child.

"Close the screen, Mrs. Rossi. The meeting is finished. There's nothing left to see."

Wide-eyed, Gia raised her gaze to Soleil, who watched her impassively in the chilled blue glow of the laptop monitor.

"Close the screen," the blonde repeated. "It's over."

It's over. Indeed. Everything. Her life. Her bloated sense of self-righteousness. Any sense of human reality she'd ever known. And most of all, her pathetic, inane belief that she'd always held some kind of worth in the world, that somehow her existence was justified, when really, it was a massive, celestial *mistake*.

Gia blinked. "Yes. It's over. And now I know."

"What do you know, Mrs. Rossi?"

"That God makes mistakes after all," she said.

* * * * *

The two angels drove in heavy silence, scanning the trees that grew like walls of sentries on either side of the road. They were halfway between the highway and Rossi's mansion, still on the estate, still under surveillance via cameras mounted on high metal poles every two hundred feet. Somewhere in the woods surrounding them, Rossi's guards waited, whether human or demon-inhabited, Joachim didn't know, but he prayed for the latter.

Killing a human on these Earthly operations, no matter how necessary to seraphim's safety and the greater good of mankind, stirred an agony in him he could hardly withstand.

The night appeared serene, the summer air drenched with moisture and eerily still. With each passing moment, the atmosphere thickened with unease.

Olivier still clutched his pistol, and at a glance Joachim could see the tightness in his muscles, the wariness that coiled in him as his watchful gaze skimmed the obsidian trees.

"Come, come, little ambushers," Olivier said softly. "Where are you?"

"Waiting." Joachim glanced down at his own pistol resting on his thigh. "We know Rossi's plan. He won't let us leave so easily." He adjusted the comm unit in his ear. "Soleil. Anything?"

"Quiet here," her voice came serene and calm through the unit. "Our Gregory has truly cycled, then?"

Joachim drew a breath, slowly released it. "The nephil speaks the truth."

Her silence radiated grief and dismay.

"How is Gia?" he asked low.

"Quiet." After a pause, she spoke again. "Your location?"

"In retreat. A mile or so from the exit point."

"Outside teams are standing by, east and west."

He signed off and glanced at Olivier, who said, "I don't know what's more disturbing, waiting for the inevitable attack or the thought of actually getting out of here with no trouble."

Before Joachim could respond, a loud pop exploded from the rear left fender well. The BMW swerved and he quickly steadied the steering wheel, his pulse thudding in time to the uneven clack of the busted tire. "It's begun."

"Operatives are in position," Soleil replied, her smooth voice a tiny reassurance in his right ear. "Three hundred feet and approaching."

The car continued to roll, sparks shooting from the crippled tire. "We can make for the gate," Joachim started to say, but another explosion, this time from the back right fender well, proclaimed their escape unlikely.

The stutter and flash of automatic fire came from the forest to the right. Behind Olivier, the passenger window shattered and sprayed the backseat with glass. Both men ducked and Joachim's boot jammed the brakes, sliding the BMW sideways. The rear window was next, glass peppering the car's interior, bullets shredding the leather seats. Metal screeched and the stench of burning rubber and exhaust filled the air.

Then silence.

"You okay?" Joachim whispered. "All parts accounted for?"

"I'm just dandy," Olivier replied, his big body crammed between the passenger seat and floorboard. "Remind me to ask Michael if I can sit out the next mission."

Joachim straightened from his hunched position and shook shards of glass from his hair, his gaze narrowed on the shadowed line of trees some twenty feet from the BMW's final resting place. "I don't see anything." He checked the comm unit in his ear. "Soleil?"

"Teams still approaching," she said, with absolutely no urgency. *Steady as rain*, he thought wryly.

"Do they have the snipers in sight?" he asked her.

"No," Olivier replied in a tight voice, "but I do."

Joachim peered through the windshield at three black-clad Rossi henchmen emerging from the shadows of the trees, their faces white masks in the dark. He glanced at his friend. "Backup or no, we need to go. Head to the east, I'll cover you."

Olivier gave a short nod. "Shoot only to divert," he

muttered, as if to remind himself. Then, moving simultaneously, the seraphs gripped their pistols and kicked the car doors open.

Gunfire exploded around them, silver flashes in the velvet night. Hugging the side of the sedan, Joachim extended his pistol and rained bullets in the guards' direction, distracting them while Olivier escaped into the dark brush. More of Rossi's men materialized from the woods to the right, too many for Joachim to count with a single glance.

A moment later, gunfire blasted from the trees on the opposite side of the road, evidence, he hoped, of seraphim's approach. The Rossi guards were unfazed. They lined up like soldiers along the edge of the trees and faced their still-unseen opponents, firing and reloading like armed robots.

Joachim was about to get caught in the middle. Seraphim operatives sifted through the trees behind him, and he slid around the trunk of the sedan, ducking as bullets whizzed past his head. Jamming another magazine into his pistol, he cocked it, muttered a quick prayer to Creator and threw himself into the perilous space between the car and the woods.

As he ran, he sprayed gunfire to cover his retreat. Despite the uneven ratio between the two groups, the Rossi guards were toppling like dominoes under seraphim's fire.

Creator's power was with them.

It was the last thing he noted before the cool shelter of the woods embraced him, and then he sprinted toward Olivier and safety.

Chapter Eight

"It's so easy to forget about physical pain when we're out of body," Olivier said between gritted teeth as he hobbled through the woods with Joachim's support. "Then I get down here, end up shot or stabbed, and it all comes back to me with refreshing clarity." He swore in French, offered an apologetic look heavenward then added, "It's always in the thigh too. Why the thigh?"

Joachim hitched his friend's arm more firmly around his neck and managed a rueful smile. "Better that than between the eyes. The benefits outweigh the agonies, Liv. Besides, we're good at what we do."

"Did you notice any humans back there?"

"I don't know. I expended all my ammo keeping them at bay. There were so many of them. Pouring out of the trees, materializing from nowhere. Full of hate and murder…as though they were programmed machines."

"Some of them were unquestionably demon flunkies. But I fear some were human cult members, blinded by the light of Ezekiel Rose." Olivier gave a weary sigh. "Creator's light is brighter than the sun, and now they'll never experience it for themselves."

"I know, friend. I know." Joachim nodded toward the clearing ahead. "I see the van. Just a little farther."

The observation seemed to drain the strength from Olivier's body, and he sagged against his leader more with every step. "What about Dmitri? We mustn't lose another. The other ops—"

"Right behind us." Joachim reached the vehicle's back doors and wrenched one open with his free hand.

Immediately Soleil poked her head out and grasped the wounded man's other arm. "How bad is it?"

"A mere scratch," Olivier said aridly, his voice weak with pain. "Bullet grazed my leg. Slap a bandage on it and let's get out of here."

She gingerly lifted the hem of his coat, frowned at the blood-soaked material covering his thigh then glanced at Joachim. "Anyone else down?"

He shook his head, leaning against the bumper to catch his breath. "Not that I could see. Dmitri and the others were on our heels a minute ago." He jerked his chin toward the woods. "There."

The remaining five operatives jogged through the clearing and, one by one, stopped to acknowledge their team leader. None was wounded.

"Several of Rossi's men are dead," Aristide told him, his ebony skin gleaming with perspiration in the glow of the moon. "It couldn't be helped."

Joachim slapped a reassuring hand on his brawny shoulder. "Save it for debriefing. I'm glad you're safe."

"But Michael—"

"—Has never judged our actions unjustly. *Soyez en paix*. Peace of mind, Ari. Trust in the Great Warrior."

Aristide hesitated, his dark eyes shining in the night. "You returned without Gregory. He is lost?"

"He is in cycle. Somewhere in Creator's universe, his life begins anew. We mustn't forget that."

Aristide gave a silent nod and headed for the driver's seat.

Weary, Joachim turned to watch the other operatives climb into the van. Then with a final visual sweep of the silent woods from which they'd all miraculously emerged, he followed his team into the vehicle and slammed the doors.

* * * * *

The drone of the van's tires against the highway drowned out all sound except the dull thud of Gia's heart. She sat like a stone beside Soleil, dry-eyed and shell-shocked, present among the operatives yet somewhere far away, where none of this night could touch her. Where Vincent didn't exist, nor demons inhabiting human bodies, and angels were creatures of love and light, not warrior operatives. A place where her mother had never taken that first taste of whiskey and her grandmother had never died, where Gia Torio had never sold her soul and let the devil twirl her across the dance floor into a nightmare from which she might never awaken.

Where her life was worth something more than some old costume jewelry in her grandmother's music box.

She kept her gaze fixed on her hands, hardly aware of the dark and silent people surrounding her. They were her captors—and now her saviors. As she'd stared at the computer monitor, watching the shadow of her husband speak so matter-of-factly about her death, her worthlessness and his own unique brand of evil, her hatred for the strangers had melted into something unidentifiable and just as discomfiting. Sick gratitude mixed with a wild desire to escape them now more than ever...for they knew what she was. A pathetic woman who'd exchanged morality for a lie.

And Joachim—what was *he*? Salvation or manipulator? He was watching her. She felt his observation across the shadowed cargo area. He'd climbed into the van after his men, closed the doors and found the nearest seat by Olivier, hunkering down next to his wounded friend like the guardian angel he claimed they all were. He hadn't acknowledged Gia or shown a single sign of satisfaction that at last her blinders had been viciously stripped aside. He'd hardly glanced her way, but now his focus on her was steady and pointed, and even without looking at him, she knew he wondered what she was thinking.

She shuddered and clenched her fists, assailed by waves of heat and chill. What she was thinking, quite simply, was that she should have indeed killed herself with twisted sheets or a ragged pop-top, because then she'd be mercifully gone from the ugly world without ever knowing the details leading up to this horrible moment. Without seeing how she really fit into the ultimate scheme of things.

But Joachim had saved her, told her truths she didn't want to hear, supernatural claims of demons and angels locked in a war with her life as the battlefield, and despite what she'd seen on the monitor, she couldn't wrap her mind around any of it, only the wild, heart-shaking idea that those claims might really be true. Anything was possible in this altered existence. Nothing would ever be the same in her comprehension of herself or the world beyond. She didn't know where she was—on Earth, or in Hell.

Tears welled, burned her eyes and spilled down her cheeks, and she wiped at them distractedly, counting the funeral-march cadence of her heartbeat in her ears. She wanted to go home, but there was no home awaiting her. Only a cold cell made of glass and a life without color and hope.

The van lurched and slowed. Beside her, Soleil gathered the electronic equipment. Olivier struggled to sit up, and Joachim spoke gently to him, told him to be still, the others would help him.

The driver, Aristide, parked the vehicle and turned off the engine.

"Go to Contact for debriefing," Joachim told his men as they hopped out of the van. "Don't wait. Tell Michael I'll be there shortly." He followed and paused to glance at Aristide rounding the rear of the van. "Ari, take Olivier to Medical directly."

The giant and another operative braced Olivier's arms around their strong necks and disappeared with him into the dark field.

Gia was the last to disembark. Soleil waited for her, green eyes watchful as Gia climbed awkwardly from the vehicle. They started the trek across the field behind the others, with Soleil offering no comfort, no reassurance, nothing but cool silence.

Gia stumbled, caught herself and took a few more steps, then stopped.

The blonde paused and glanced back. "Mrs. Rossi? What is it?"

"I'm going to—" Gia shook her head, clamped a hand over her mouth and leaned into the tall grass. She retched, everything inside her contracting and twisting, but nothing came up. Her stomach was empty. *She* was empty. Sheer despondency fed a fresh wave of nausea, stole the strength from her legs and dropped her to the ground. Braced on hands and knees, debased, broken, she retched again, wishing she could die right here, that not another minute would pass with her in this world.

"How…how many people did my husband have to hurt and kill to earn the reward of demonic possession?" she demanded, hysteria and tears clogging her voice.

"Many," Soleil said. "As we have told you."

Gia shook her head. "Oh, God, I didn't know—I would have never knowingly let him hurt anyone. He was kind—he—I never suspected—" *But she had.* Deep down, she had always sensed Vincent's immorality and what he did behind the scenes. And had done nothing but aid and abet it with her silence. Anything for a little taste of her own personal happiness.

She might as well have pulled the trigger on Vincent's victims herself.

She stopped, head pounding out realizations. Then the crying started, a torturous mixture of sobbing and coughing. She couldn't breathe. Stars danced before her eyes.

Footsteps crunched through the grass, stopping where she knelt.

"Mrs. Rossi," Soleil's voice floated above her, laced with compassion. "Gia. What can I do?"

Gia shook her head and dug her fingers into the moist earth, a silent wail of despair her only reply. *Please don't touch me,* a disembodied part of her pleaded. *I'm having a nervous breakdown*. A real one. Like her mother had suffered when Gia was eight. She knew the signs. Donna Torio had to be hospitalized for three weeks, and Gia was temporarily sent to a state home. And the world seemed to end that day, when she first realized that nothing in her life had been what it seemed.

Just like now.

Soleil spoke to Gia again, something about getting help, but Gia's overwrought mind couldn't decipher the words. More footsteps, heavier ones, crushing the brittle, overgrown turf. A low, murmuring exchange of French. A gentle hand settled on the crown of her head, and the soft scent of vanilla drifted on the night air. She slid lower in the grass, pressed her forehead against the dew-damp soil. If she curled up tight enough, maybe she could disappear.

The hand that caressed her head slid down her back and around her waist, and then Gia felt herself being lifted, airborne, on the wings of angels and turned toward a warm, solid chest.

"Hold on to me," Joachim whispered against her temple, and her body responded without choice, arms sliding around his neck. She couldn't hate him. At that moment, she couldn't breathe without him. He shifted and settled her more comfortably against him, then the earth moved, and he walked, carrying her, a wounded, abject casualty of her own making.

* * * * *

Soleil followed Joachim, hurrying to keep up with his long strides as they crossed the field toward the bunker. "What's wrong with her, Joachim? Is she ill?"

"In her soul," he said. "But remorse is a cleansing poison."

Gia's arms tightened around his neck, her nose buried against his throat. He could smell her tears on his skin, moist and scented with despair. He felt the heavy drum of her heartbeat through the soft press of her breast against him, and his pulse raced to match it.

Angels weren't so very different from humans in their

emotional makeup, with one exception—they didn't understand or experience instinctive animal fear. The same fear that had driven Gia Rossi to the edge of sanity tonight. For the first time, the bitter emotion burned Joachim, as though it seeped through her skin and into his body. Compassion stung his eyes. He rested his cheek against her soft curls and silently invoked Creator's mercy for an injured creature.

When they reached the bunker, he carefully set her on her feet and, grasping her arms, released the stranglehold embrace she had on his neck. "Gia."

"Just let me stay here," she mumbled, swaying against him like a child caught between consciousness and sleep.

"I'm going to lift you down into the entry chute. You must stand."

She nodded and burrowed tighter against his chest, beneath his coat.

Joachim shot Soleil a rueful look over Gia's head. "Hold her."

While the other seraph stepped forward and supported her with a strong arm, he vaulted down into the chute, then reached up for her. "Gia, come."

Her head lolled against Soleil's shoulder, but gradually she lifted it, opened her eyes and squinted down at his upturned face in the darkness. "Don't put me back in the box," she said, sounding perfectly lucid before the enormity of her situation seemed to hit her all over again, and her shoulders shook with a fresh onslaught of weeping. *"What am I doing here?"*

"Come to me," Joachim repeated gently, and extended his other hand. "No more containment for you. You're not a prisoner."

She rubbed her palms over her face, her dark curls limp, shielding her anguish. "I have no choice, do I?"

"Not tonight," he said.

After a pulsing moment of indecision, she stepped closer to the trapdoor and grasped his hand. Before she could change her mind, Joachim gave her wrist a tug and with a surprised cry, she tumbled into the chute and landed in his embrace.

"No more lock and key," he repeated, staring down into her frightened face. "You're free here. You're safe."

The trembling that shook her limbs vibrated through him. "I have nowhere to go. No home."

"Gia," he said, brushing strands of hair back from her flushed, stark features, "all your life you have walked in Creator's presence, with a hundred guardians surrounding you. Now more than ever, you *are* home."

Chapter Nine

Colors converged and dissipated behind Gia's eyelids as she rose from a dreamless sleep into limpid consciousness.

Her lashes lifted, vision cleared, and she found herself staring at a grid of white ceiling tiles.

It took her a moment to gather her wits and recall where she was. The faint, earthy smell of soil touched her senses, joggled her memory. Not a hospital or a glass cell, but still, some place deep underground. No one on the surface would ever miss her. For all intents and purposes, Gia Rossi was dead…and right now, more comfortable than she'd been in a long time, despite slightly stiff limbs and a full bladder.

The blankets tangled around her bare legs were soft and just heavy enough to block the draft from the air-conditioning duct overhead, and the pillow beneath her head was wonderfully spongy. She shifted and turned her face against it, found the pillowcase scented with detergent and something sultrier, a fragrance she had experienced—and subconsciously savored—before. Vanilla.

Joachim.

With a start, she sat up on the cot and looked around. This could definitely be his room. Sparsely furnished, it was uncluttered, silent and cool. A closet door at the foot of the cot stood ajar, granting a glimpse of hanging garments and boots neatly aligned. Across the floor, a metal-framed dresser held a lamp and a collection of men's toiletries—shaving supplies, deodorant, a small hairbrush. No photographs, no knickknacks.

Gia swung her feet to the floor and shivered as her bare soles touched icy linoleum. A downward glance showed that she'd been divested of every garment except a man's plain white

T-shirt and a pair of cotton panties from the three-pack Soleil had given her.

Her mouth twisted. She didn't remember undressing herself or agreeing to climb into this bed. Her grumbling stomach and mild lightheadedness told her she'd been here a good long while, though, and she felt like she'd awakened from the sleep of the dead.

A cleansing sleep.

Whoever had undressed her apparently felt he knew her well enough to do so, and he was right. She had no secrets left to hide from these people. They'd seen her hit rock bottom.

She rose unsteadily to her feet, tiptoed to the door near the head of the cot and gingerly tried the knob. It was unlocked. The door gave a slight squeak and she peeked out.

And found herself gazing into Joachim's office.

He sat at his desk with his back to her, his fingers moving quietly across the laptop keyboard. After a moment he paused and without looking over his shoulder said, "She has risen."

Aware of her immodest attire, Gia half-retreated behind the protection of the door and cleared her throat. "What am I doing in your room?"

"I wanted you to rest undisturbed."

"How long was I asleep?"

"Two days."

Her mouth dropped open. "Two days?"

"Approximately." He turned his head just enough for her to see the curve of his cheek. "There's a robe hanging behind the door."

Disconcerted, she glanced to her left, grabbed the terry cloth garment from its hook and slid into it. It smelled like him, and the intimacy of wearing the robe—*the robe that had touched his smooth, naked skin*—overwhelmed her and excited her at the same time. A faint memory of being held in his arms flickered through her mind, the scent of his skin, the heat radiating from it, the muscled curve of his neck where she'd buried her face and tried to disappear. The easy rhythm of his gait as he carried her. Strong, certain, protective.

His robe was huge on her. It slid off her shoulder, and she hiked it up again with an impatient shrug, embarrassment burning her cheeks. Her fingers trembled as she knotted the belt around her waist. Now that she didn't hate him anymore, Joachim made her more nervous than ever.

Shoving her hair behind her ears, she stepped into his office. "I'm decent."

He wheeled around in his chair and regarded her with a faint smile. Despite the fact that he'd been exiled from his own bed for the past forty-eight hours, he appeared rested, his handsome face unlined and pleasant. The scratches on his jaw were a fading memory.

"Feel better?" he asked, his blue eyes taking her in, head to foot, with a flash of approval.

She nodded and wrapped her arms around her waist in a fit of self-consciousness, her toes curling against the linoleum. "I'd kill for a shower, though."

His smile deepened, and a crescent-shaped dimple appeared in his right cheek. "Murder isn't necessary. Everything at seraphim headquarters is at your disposal."

She gave a hesitant smile and started past him toward the office door, then stopped with her hand on the knob. "Doesn't Soleil have to walk me to the showers?"

"You're free to roam the bunker as you please." The squeak of caster wheels indicated he'd risen to his feet behind her. "Do you remember what you said two nights ago, after we returned from the Rossi estate?"

A fresh wave of pain seared her at the reminder of that awful night. For a brief few moments, she'd convinced herself it was all a dream.

"I don't remember anything about that." A half-truth. She didn't want to remember. Given enough time, she could forget most of it. The ignoble past. The mistakes she'd made. She wanted to be someone new…the person she'd always hoped she was on the inside. *The person this man believed she could be.*

"You requested not to be contained. I promised you wouldn't be again."

She stared down at her warped reflection in the chrome doorknob. "I know you're keeping me here to protect me, Joachim. I know you told me the truth about my husband's crimes and—and the monster he's become. I'm grateful to you, all of you, for guarding me, even when I gave you every reason to deliver me back into Vincent's hands. But what I don't understand—" She turned to face him and found him watching her with blue eyes so electric and piercing, she averted her gaze in flustered astonishment. "Who are you people?"

"Seraphim," he replied.

The word meant nothing to her. "You said that before, but I mean, where do you come from? You're French, obviously—"

"This body is of Quebecois descent."

She released an impatient breath. "See, I don't understand what you mean by 'this body'. *This body* is you, isn't it?"

"For a little longer, anyway," he said, the corners of his mouth twitching.

She stared at him, trying to read his history in his features, but there was nothing there—beauty, oh, yes, but a slate clean of the wear and tear inherent in the average thirty-something man. He was whole, untouched. Pure.

"Joachim, what…*are* you?" The foggy question slid from her lips before she could examine its meaning herself.

"Seraphim," he repeated.

"Angels?" When his smile warmed, she shook her head. "I thought when you told me that before, you were speaking metaphorically. Or that you were all members of some crazy cult." The irony of her statement rolled through her and arid humor curved her lips. "You're saying, literally, that you're angels? The kind with halos and two wings and harps?"

"No halo," he said. "Six wings. And my musical skills are abysmal."

She wanted to like him. She did like him, despite his craziness and fearful splendor. Too much, perhaps. "None of this is easy to swallow, you know."

"I know."

"You look perfectly human to me."

"This body is human."

"So is this one." She glanced down at herself in disgust. "It doesn't feel human. I'm hitting the showers."

"Go."

She started out the door, then glanced back at him. "You, uh…you eat and sleep, have feelings, all that good stuff, right?"

"Yes."

She paused, searching for the courage to believe in him. He'd saved her life. True angel or not, he was her guardian. "I want to know more about you. When I'm dressed, may I come back?"

"We'll go above," he replied, his regard so intense and earnest, heat flooded her cheeks and her chest filled with a strange, tight ache she couldn't identify. A tugging toward him that started at her heart and branched down her body, making every sensitive place sing with awareness.

Gratitude, she told herself. "Above?"

"To the field outside the bunker. We'll walk. Today, I can give you the sunshine, Gia. And all the answers you seek."

* * * * *

Gia traversed the corridors with careful steps, avoiding the curious gazes of the few people she passed on her way to the bathroom. She might not be a prisoner any longer, but she didn't feel any more at ease in the cold, sterile environment of the bunker than she had when the glass cell was her prison. Without Soleil's careful solicitude at her side or Joachim's quiet reassurance, she wanted to slip her skin and disappear into the steel walls.

The warm pummeling of the shower on her tight shoulders eased some of the tension as she stood with head bowed beneath the spray, letting it rinse away the past and the pain. Her skin tingled and her muscles quaked. A shaky euphoria danced at the edge of her consciousness. Living among this strange faction of self-governed operatives, she could be whoever she wanted. Gia Torio, impoverished wild child, had evaporated as though she'd never existed. The teenaged rebel without a cause waiting tables at the seedy gentlemen's club was gone too, a puff of smoke in some imaginative soul's nightmare. And Gia Rossi, manicured and pedicured and flawlessly clothed and coiffed, the one who'd denied again and again that her opulent life was financed by other people's losses…

"Dead," she whispered, the lone declaration reverberating off the wet tile.

The woman emerging from the shower stall was clean-scrubbed inside and out and ready to embrace a new truth, no matter how farfetched. Joachim claimed he and his team were seraphs, a battalion of angels in human bodies, with killer weaponry skills and poster-boy good looks.

Laughter gathered in her throat, then faded as quickly as it had risen. Ten days ago, she never would have believed Vincent was possessed, either.

Eschewing her usual ponytail, Gia combed the tangles from her hair and left it to dry into its natural state of unruly ringlets. A long glance in the mirror showed a well-rested stranger with bright brown eyes and pink-stained cheeks, a face illuminated by expectancy, as though some grand possibility hovered about her.

The thought was inexplicably unsettling. Moving more briskly, she dabbed lotion on her face, brushed her teeth and dressed in a white tank top and drawstring pants that sagged a little in the rear. She'd lost too much weight, but her appetite was stirring. Maybe she would stop off at the kitchen—if there were one in this place—before she went outside with Joachim.

A walk in the sunshine. She couldn't wait. Pleasant conversation, a discussion of hope and possibilities, glimpses of what came next in her new life. Joachim's low tone in her ears, as easy and soft as the late summer breeze rifling through the grass…

A shiver of anticipation caught her off-guard and she shoved her toiletries back into the basket with unsteady hands.

"Gia?" Soleil's voice floated through the door, followed by a soft rap. "Are you dressed?"

"I'm decent." Gia smoothed the front of her shirt and waited while the blonde stepped into the bathroom.

"I brought you something." Wearing a covert smile, Soleil extended a blessedly familiar pink and white striped shopping bag, and with a yelp of delight, Gia took it and hugged it like a long-lost friend.

"Oh, yes! Thank you so much!" She peeked inside. Three delicate lace brassieres lay nestled in the pink tissue paper, their sweet, powdery scent drifting from the bag.

She looked up at Soleil, her eyes burning with gratitude. "I thought if I were lucky, I might score a garage-sale bra to match my prison-issued cotton undies, but this…hallelujah, this is true lingerie! You actually went shopping for me?"

"Yesterday. Joachim and I."

Gia stopped. "Joachim?"

"We found a collection of merchants selling their wares inside a massive brick edifice," the blonde explained. "Quite amazing, this structure, with many levels, fountains and fauna—"

"A mall," Gia prompted, biting back a smile. Either this woman was truly from another dimension, or she'd fallen off a produce truck in Bumfoozle, USA.

Soleil gave an enthusiastic nod. "Yes, that's right. A mall. The ceiling was made entirely of glass, and the sunlight poured through, reflecting off the marble floor like a million prisms..." She closed her eyes and sighed with pleasure. "It reminded me of home. I could have stayed the entire day, but with Joachim along, of course, it was all business."

Gia rolled her eyes. "Men."

"Seraphs," the blonde corrected, resting her backside against the door. "And in the case of our valiant leader, obviously not immune to a human male's predilections."

The butterflies in Gia's stomach rushed and swarmed. "How so?"

"The first store we came to was stocked entirely with female delicacies. Lacy gowns and nightwear and undergarments. Beautiful things. That's where our adventure ended."

"You took Joachim into a lingerie boutique?" Gia asked, leaning weakly against the sink.

"On the contrary. He took *me*."

Mortification burned through her confusion. "But how? He doesn't know anything about what I—I mean, how would he know—?"

"I told him what we were shopping for, of course." Soleil's smile widened. "The advertisements in this store's windows were very clever. Pictures of beautiful women—slim, like you—wearing brassieres and *angel's wings*! Can you imagine?"

Gia's brows shot up. "Well..."

"As if we run around in undergarments with big white wings made of feathers!"

Gia offered a frail smile. "As if."

"Of course the advertisements caught our attention, Joachim's especially."

"I bet it did."

"Being seraphs, we were naturally curious. A woman inside the store tried to help us, showed us the racks where the brassieres were displayed, but Joachim waved her away as though he'd shopped for a woman's undergarments a million times before." Irrepressible laughter burst from Soleil's lips. "Ah, Joachim. He never ceases to amaze me. He seemed to know just what you should have and went straight for it."

Heat seared Gia's cheeks as she withdrew one of the lacy confections from the shopping bag and held it up from one finger to examine it. The translucent bra was made entirely of sea foam lace, feminine and sexy and scandalous. She imagined Joachim's blue gaze skimming over it, the fragile lace crushed in his strong hands, and swallowed hard.

"Try one on," Soleil said. "I'll wait for you."

Sucking in a shaky breath, Gia ducked inside the shower stall, drew the curtain and slipped off her tank top.

The green bra fit perfectly, like silky hands cupping her breasts. The sensation of something so soft sliding against her nipples made them harden and ache, and she was glad for the barrier the brassiere would provide. The last thing she needed was to walk around the compound another day with hard little knots poking through her shirt.

She drew her tank top down over the bra, then peeked in the bag and pulled out the next two. One was pale peach, demi cups with scalloped edges. The next was baby blue, made of a silky, gauzelike material, with tiny bows on the straps.

And the *piece de resistance*? Lost in the bottom layers of tissue were coordinating silk panties, cut high on the thigh and gossamer soft, one pair matched to each brassiere.

"Wow," she breathed, rubbing one with languorous delight against her cheek. "Coordinating panties too?"

"Like the angels in the advertisements," Soleil said from the other side of the shower curtain. "Are you pleased? Maybe they aren't appropriate for you?"

Reemerging, Gia quickly shoved the garments back into the bag and hugged it to her chest, her face ablaze. "No—they're beautiful. Prettier than anything I could have picked for myself. The one I'm wearing fits perfectly, and I actually feel human again. Thank you. And Joachim," she added with a weak smile. Even his name seemed like an intimate utterance, now that she wore the lingerie he'd picked for her.

"You can tell him yourself." Soleil swung open the door and waited for Gia to pass into the hall before her. "He says you're embarking on a mission today."

"Where?"

"He will explain. But first he wants you to meet the other operatives. There are many more of us at headquarters than you know." Soleil hesitated, offered her an affectionate smile and reached out to brush a wayward curl from her cheek. "You look rested, Gia. I'm so glad you've chosen to live among us for a while. If you need anything, I'm never far."

"Thank you," Gia said, and meant it. Her definitions of kindness and compassion were shifting with each day she spent in this netherworld.

* * * * *

She leaned her shoulder against Joachim's office doorjamb and studied him as he sifted through an endless stack of papers at his desk. Although she wore a cool demeanor, her pulse rapped a wild rhythm in her veins, and inappropriate sensations tickled her in secret places. She wasn't at all sure she wanted to go anywhere alone with this man, and it wasn't entirely due to his bizarre assertions and the crazy events of the last two weeks.

The way he pressed his lips together as he studied a document rendered him irrefutably human. She glanced at his hands, golden against the white paper, and remembered their strength as he lifted her in his arms and carried her, a weeping child, to this place of safety and solace.

Gia had asked him if he ate and slept, if he had emotions, all things human. If he was what he claimed, maybe he'd never touched a woman. She wondered if he wanted to, if he thought about it. She wondered if he thought about her…

Or Soleil, or any of the females in the compound. They all

appeared to have working parts, after all. Beautiful parts. Joachim especially.

He seemed unaware of her presence, so she finally said, "I thought we were going for a walk."

"We are." He spoke without looking up from the file that lay open on his desk. "After the mission briefing."

"Mission briefing? Soleil mentioned something about that. What kind of mission?"

The sharp note of confusion in her voice caught his attention, and he finally glanced up.

For a long moment, he didn't speak. She held her breath under his appraisal as it skimmed her loose curls, her face, the tank top and linen pants, then returned to her breasts.

Gia cast a subtle downward glance. The faint outline of the green brassiere was apparent through the tank's thin material. It fit her perfectly, caressed her skin and gave her the fleeting sense that she wore a lover's gift.

And the way he looked at her, his eyes unusually bright beneath sheltering lashes, was as potently arousing as if he'd put his hands on her.

"The mission," she blurted, snapping awake from the erotic fog her wayward thoughts had wisped around her. "What about it?"

He cleared his throat and looked away. "Today we must locate the Medallion."

"So much for giving me the sunshine." She sauntered a few steps into the office, barging through her shyness. No man had ever made her so self-aware, as though every nerve stood at attention, electrified and raw, beneath the surface of her skin.

Humor curved his mouth as he shuffled a stack of papers and laid them in the file folder. "You will have it today for a brief time, as I promised. The distance from the bunker to the van is half a mile, a healthy hike in the sun."

Ire sizzled through her and tightened her jaw. "Fine."

It wasn't fine. The warm, tender man who had greeted her this morning and made a couple of pretty promises was hidden once again behind a cool, businesslike manner. For a little while she'd forgotten that, not unlike the demon who'd possessed Vincent, these people only wanted her for one reason.

Some glorified necklace she hardly remembered owning.

"If we find what we seek," he continued, "you will live in the sunshine again as you desire, and this time outside of Vincent Rossi's shadow. All you have to do is lead us to the Medallion."

"But, Joachim, you know I have no idea where—"

"I'll help you. We all will. In a few moments you'll become acquainted with the rest of our personnel." He closed the folder and swiveled to tuck it inside a cabinet drawer. "Everyone is anxious to meet you. Seraphim are your friends, Gia, and always have been. Many of them haven't seen you since you were a child. Meeting you as you are now, they will be most pleased."

Her brows drew down and she folded her arms across her breasts. "Oh? And how exactly *am* I?"

"Attractive. Beautiful, in fact."

Gia's heart stumbled, raced to regain its rhythm. There was power in keeping a woman off guard, obviously. He did it so well. Perturbed, she watched him rise, push in his desk chair and approach her. As he passed, he caught her hand and smoothly guided her into the corridor, where he drew the door closed behind them.

"Are you angry with me this morning, Mrs. Rossi?"

She squinted at him, painfully aware of his touch, her pulse shimmying a nervous little dance at his nearness. It took everything in her power not to gulp in the sultry scent of him. "Angry's not the right word, exactly."

"Then maybe you're hungry. Have lunch with me. En route to the briefing."

Lunch? How could she think of food when he'd so artfully tied her stomach in knots with a few offhanded remarks and a sultry visual examination that no true angelic being should be capable of offering? She couldn't read him, she didn't understand him, and although he'd saved her life, she didn't fully trust him.

But he mesmerized her. Angel or lunatic, he was gorgeous and enigmatic, powerful and sexy. Somehow, in the roller coaster turbulence of the last few days, she'd developed a nonsensical attraction to him, and she wasn't ashamed. Maybe Stockholm Syndrome was to blame, where the victim becomes waywardly attached to her tormentor. Utterly sick…and yet a vast improvement over being married to a possessed lunatic.

He hadn't yet released her hand, and she stole a downward peek at his fingers, strong and scarred, laced through hers. Who knew such a simple thing as holding hands could be so arousing?

"Just give me a minute to…to…" She exhaled. "You think I'm beautiful?"

The question rang out in the corridor, mortifying in its clarity, and her gaze shot back to his. He was watching her with an intensity that made her shiver.

"Since the first time I saw you." He smiled. "You were such a thin child, so small, like a waif. I recall being particularly fascinated by the pointedness of your chin. Those huge brown eyes that took up half your face. Then you grew up, and the sharp lines of your hungry features softened, and I thought…" He drew a breath. "I thought I had never seen a creature so lovely."

Gia didn't know how to respond. She was too aware of his hand's gentle pressure around hers. Too aware of how close they stood, of his warm, delicious scent, of the intense heat that radiated through the gray crewneck shirt covering his lean torso. She should have stepped back, steered the conversation elsewhere, left vulnerable questions and long, dangerous looks safely out of the game. Instead she dropped her gaze to his lips and willed him to speak again, to wrap her in more husky confessions.

True to form, Joachim blinked and broke the spell, the softness in his expression replaced by a familiar remoteness. "Our perception goes beyond the body's shell and into the soul, of course. I saw your spirit, a wild spectrum of colors, whirling and magnificent. Now I have the added benefit of seeing you through a man's eyes. Your physical makeup is quite appealing." He stopped and a frown creased his brow. "Tell me, how is mine?"

Another curveball. She glanced around, found the corridor blessedly empty. "You mean your physical appearance?"

A fleeting vulnerability crossed his face and he gave a short nod.

Surprised, she studied his brow, the blueness of his gaze, his full, somber mouth and sharp, clean-shaven jaw. There was no reason to lie. If he were what he claimed, he would probably see right through it.

"You're unbelievable."

"This is a good thing?"

"Too much of a good thing, in your case." She paused, discomfort prompting her at last to withdraw her hand from his grasp. "And you're thoughtful. I meant to thank you for the lingerie before. Soleil said… I mean, she told me you personally picked out—"

"It was my pleasure."

"Was it?" The faltering question, thick with double meaning, slid out before she could stop it and she winced at herself.

"Unquestionably," he said, never missing a beat.

Her eyes darted back to his at the soft response. Gia couldn't possibly read the thoughts behind his blue regard, but wheels definitely turned there, and suddenly she was afraid of him again. She stepped back, putting distance between them. "Let's get on with this mission briefing you're threatening me with."

"But first lunch. I'll take you on a tour of our headquarters as we go."

He strode through the corridor with his hands clasped behind his back, brisk and graceful, a leader with every step. She quickened her pace to keep up with him as they passed several offices and glass cubicles—"Intel," Joachim pointed out. "Medical. Contact. Communications"—then the gymnasium where Dmitri taught her self-defense. The bunker was an industrious underground world. She counted at least fifteen men occupied with various tasks throughout the labyrinth.

"So seraphim are angels," she said conversationally as they passed the shooting range.

"Seraphim are Heavenly attendants to Creator's throne. We hold the highest rank in the celestial hierarchy."

A smile crept across her face. "This is a little hard to swallow, you know."

"It doesn't matter." Joachim shrugged. "You will believe in the end, no matter what I tell you now."

She licked her lips and tried to absorb his claims. "So what are you doing here? Did *God* send you?"

"God?" He considered the moniker as they turned a corner and headed down a new hall. "Yes. God. Yahweh, Allah, The Great Spirit, Universal Consciousness—Creator is known by a million names in a million worlds. And seraphim are angels, protectors, soldiers, spirits. This faction is a retrieval defense force, charged by the Archangel Michael to battle nephilim who have entered the third dimension, or Earth."

"But you're obviously human."

"We can take different forms, depending on the needs and beliefs of those seeking aid. On this mission, we have acquired human bodies whose compromised souls were taken by sudden death. But in true form, we're beings of light energy, not so very different from the makeup of your own soul. The body is just a disposable shell, here and in other worlds."

A disconcerting thought. Gia had grown attached to her disposable shell. Especially lately, when it seemed to be awakening in the most sensuous fashion. Seven years with Vincent had all but buried her sexuality. A mere handful of days in Joachim's presence had undone those ties. Even walking beside him, listening to the accented cadence of his words, set off a sweet throb in parts of her body she'd tried to forget.

Her brows drew down as she ignored the unruly sensations and struggled to wrap her mind around his assertions. "So you're here to battle some kind of evil spirit? Like what you believe has possessed Vincent?"

His pace slowed, and he met her gaze with solemn eyes. "Nephilim are more than just evil spirits. They came forth from Creator as seraphim and were imbued with the same power of light and fire. Once, we were all brethren. But they were seduced by Lucifer and chose to leap with him in the rebellion, and now they feed from iniquity, the flipside of the universe. Darkness is their sustenance."

"Can they kill you?"

"They can send us into cycle."

It sounded like the laundering process on a washing machine. Before she could think of a broad-spectrum response, he stopped at a set of gleaming steel doors and pushed them open, pausing to allow her to enter the dining room ahead of him.

"My team and I have been assigned to track one nephil in particular, called Therides," he said as they rounded a large oval table and approached a kiosk piled high with delectable-looking fare. "The one who possesses your husband. Our mission is to stop him and bring him to judgment before he can destroy this world."

Gia sighed and took the plate he offered her. "You sound like a really bad sci-fi movie."

"Today you and I will find the Medallion, Gia, and complete the second part of this mission. In order to do that, I must have your trust." He reached for his own plate, set a plump pear on it and offered her the same. "It's all I ask."

Taking the fruit from his hand, she searched his features for any sign of insincerity and found only unwavering conviction. "Look—I don't know about all the things you're telling me, Joachim. It's going to take me a while to soak it all in. And I don't know about God. I never have. But I do believe in you." Her throat tightened and she swallowed to stifle her unruly emotions. "You saved my life, a life I didn't believe was worth saving until you convinced me of it. I believe in you, Joachim," she repeated softly. "How could I not?"

"Then we believe in each other," he said, unsmiling. "I'd hoped it might be mutual."

They stood in silence laden with unspoken sentiment, while cool air wafted through the large, empty dining hall, its currents carrying the mouthwatering scents of fresh bread and sweet fruit. Then his expression softened. "Come, Gia of the blinding and magnificent spirit. *Mangeons.*"

* * * * *

He watched her surreptitiously, his quicksilver gaze reading her anxiety as though she'd shouted it through the dining hall. The way she knitted her fingers beneath her chin, white-knuckled, while Nicodemus asked her light, harmless questions in an attempt to draw her out. The tension in her features even as she smiled at an offhanded quip Olivier shot across the table to Dmitri. Her tight nods and furrowed brow—all of it indicated her desire to escape the benevolent energy that must seem so foreign to her.

Around Gia, the seraphs talked and laughed and wove warmth into the atmosphere, but she seemed impervious to the convivial invitation. Compassion gently squeezed Joachim's heart. She didn't know how to be close to anyone. A force field of suspicion and self-doubt spun a web around her, pushing others away. Friend or enemy, it didn't matter. No one was welcome in her space. No one would get in.

Except, perhaps, him.

I do believe in you. You saved my life. How could I not?

Gia's words echoed in his head, chained heavy around his conscience, a dichotomy of pleasure and dread. She was beginning to trust him, to feel comfortable around him. And today…

He pushed aside his plate and rubbed the bridge of his nose with thumb and forefinger. Today, standing at the threshold of his office, she'd looked at him with a woman's eyes instead of a prisoner's. Just a fleeting spark of recognition, but instinct enabled him to recognize its sultry truth, and it discomfited him. He knew how easily a trauma victim could attach to a rescuer, and despite the countless missions where he'd served as a loving guardian, an emotional bond was the last thing he wanted on this assignment.

When it came to Gia, it was the last thing he knew how to handle. Hostility from her, yes. Fear, the desire to escape, hysteria…any of it would be easier to manage than this subtle and rapier-sharp awareness that had sprung between them.

After all, she wasn't alone in her sentiments.

He braced his forearms on the edge of the table and glanced down at his half-empty plate. Foreign emotions he couldn't identify chased round and round in his stomach, killing his hunger. He'd gotten too close to her. It was time to rein in, withdraw. He didn't want to. *Where was his discipline?*

And the cursed male flesh between his legs, the organ that had been the most inconsequential part of every body he'd inhabited for thousands of years, suddenly seemed to hold every key to his agony as it threatened to shift and rise, thus exposing him for what he was fast becoming.

A human wreck.

Last night he'd half-awakened to his own hips grinding a slumberous dance against the makeshift cot on which he slept, while in his sleep his breath caught and exploded, caught and exploded. Pushing that rigid, aching part of him against the mattress, driving hard, every muscle tensed, he'd wanted more.

Of what, he didn't know. But it couldn't happen with Gia

sleeping on the other side of his office wall.

Forcing himself awake, he'd bolted like lightning from the cot, turning it over in his hurry to escape the nocturnal stupor of sensuality that enveloped him. Fortunately Gia had slept through the racket.

A warm shower had only aggravated the problem. Instead of washing away the desire, the spray of water caressed and trickled over his sensitized flesh until it felt as though a massive explosion built in his loins, and it was everything he could do to keep his hands off his own body.

Humans touched themselves for countless reasons, he knew. Everything from boredom to stress could awaken the urge. Joachim couldn't recall even considering it for one second before now. His mouth twisted into a wry smile. Self-gratification had always seemed like a greedy and useless act to him as he perched on high, free of a mortal's physical agonies and delights.

Now, watching the gentle curve of Gia's cheek as she conversed with Olivier, he at last understood. No more warm showers in the middle of the night. If he had to, he could take care of the problem quickly, humanly and with finality. Surely one cleansing ejaculation would resolve the constant sexual stirrings this body seemed to carry in his new charge's presence.

Surely.

Harassment tightened its grip on his mood and he pushed back from the table, hardly aware of his friends' curious regard.

"Leaving already, Captain?" Olivier inquired with an arched brow. "Was it something we said?"

Joachim avoided his gaze and set his plate on a nearby bus tray. "It's time for the briefing. A little less chatter will get you there in good stead." He glanced at Gia, his attention grazing her without settling on her. "I assume you've finished eating, Mrs. Rossi, since you've spent the last ten minutes in conversation. Let's go."

Chapter Ten

"It's been five years since I've even driven in this part of town." Gia's tone was dark with reticence as she peered out the van's windshield from behind Joachim's shoulder. "You can't rely one hundred percent on my directions."

"We aren't," he responded from the passenger seat, shoving a clip into the semi-automatic he held. "But you do remember what the apartment building looks like."

"There's a good chance my mother doesn't even live there anymore. It was falling down a decade ago. Maybe they've torn it down."

"As of two weeks ago, our sources indicated she's still in the area, the building intact."

She released a sigh and a faint rustling told him she'd sat back in her seat behind him. "My mother doesn't trust anyone. What are we going to do if she won't open the door?"

"Let ourselves in," Olivier said with a shrug as he steered the van around a traffic circle.

"You can't just storm into a residential building and break into someone's apartment like that, can you?"

Joachim's brow lifted, but he didn't reply, just caressed the slender barrel of the gun before he leaned to slide it into his leg holster. "This is Newell Street," he murmured to Olivier. "Turn left at the next intersection."

The rutted road narrowed and the desolate cityscape grew more barren, industrial buildings giving way to dilapidated tenements and boarded-up storefronts. So many empty buildings, Joachim mused, and so many people without shelter. Human excess was impossible to comprehend.

Olivier maneuvered the van around double-parked vehicles, jaywalkers and clogged crossroads. At one point, he veered onto a deserted section of sidewalk to avoid a gridlocked intersection. Myriad indignant horns rent the smog-filled afternoon in protest.

"You're going to get pulled over by a cop," Gia pointed out, one elbow braced on the edge of the driver's seat. "What will you do then?"

"It's never happened before," Olivier said thoughtfully. "It'd be an interesting scenario, to say the least."

She released a huff of laughter. "You think I'm hard to convince when it comes to all this angel stuff? Try a Chicago cop on for size." She turned to look at Joachim. "Who taught you people how to drive? Did someone give you lessons?"

"At the next traffic light, take a right," he told Olivier without answering her.

She leaned forward and sought his gaze, insistent. "Do seraphim even have driver's licenses? Do you just march into the DMV and take the test and pose for a picture like everyone else?"

"Documentation is prepared for us prior to the assignment," he said, ignoring the provocation in her voice as he shifted to stare out the passenger window. Somewhere in the last hour, with a little coolness on his part, the distance between them had returned, and it hadn't brought the relief he'd expected. If anything he resented it, and distress layered atop the resentment.

He didn't have to examine the turmoil roiling inside him. It was shamefully obvious. Human emotions, frailties, the chafing conflict of unwanted physical attraction to this woman—he'd somehow fallen prey to all of it, and if he didn't monitor it more carefully, the errant sensations Gia stirred in him could upend today's objective. He was already far too distracted. The sensuous, floral scent of female, of clean silky skin, filled the air inside the van and derailed his focus on what lay ahead.

"So who takes your picture?" She wasn't done. She wanted a fight. The persistent edge to her voice told him so. "Or are you like vampires, with no reflection and no warmth and no heart?"

Joachim met her angry eyes. "Why does it matter?"

"I need some proof here. I thought you wanted me to believe you."

"I want you to trust me. It doesn't matter what you believe. The details you're after—they're inconsequential."

She didn't reply, just set her jaw and stared back at him while tension shimmered between them, thickening the air.

Olivier shattered it when he said, "Oh, just tell her, Joachim. Seraphim are naturally photogenic. We love to have our pictures taken. Of course we have to tuck our wings down the backs of our shirts first."

The light humor in his voice drew Gia's attention, and the rigidity drained from her features.

"We have the halo thing going for us, you know," he went on with a straight face. "Good lighting times ten. Makes the flashbulb obsolete. We never take a bad picture."

Amusement curved her lips and she leaned to regard Olivier's profile with a surprising familiarity that set Joachim's teeth on edge. "Joachim says you don't have halos."

"Maybe *he* doesn't." Olivier glanced at his leader, then back at Gia, his gray eyes sparkling. "Mine is intact and completely untarnished."

"Okay, gorgeous. Let me see your license."

With a scowl, Joachim watched the flirtatious exchange. When had they gotten so friendly? Where was the impenetrable Gia from lunchtime?

He started to intervene, but Olivier had already acquiesced to her demand. Leaning on one hip, the seraph withdrew a leather wallet from the back pocket of his jeans and flipped it open with one hand for her perusal.

She glanced at the ID behind the plastic window and

released a peal of laughter so infectious, it even elicited an answering chuckle from the usually stoic operatives in the back of the van. "Olivier, this picture is awful! Your hair! It looks like a coonskin hat."

Grinning, he snatched the wallet back from her and jammed it into his pocket again. "This body had no style before I came along."

"I do have to admit you look a million times better now that you've gotten 'this body' a haircut." Gia reached out and brushed a wave of sandy hair off his brow. "You have nice eyebrows. Nice eyelashes too. Long." She studied his profile with interest. "You know, you could be a model."

"Enough," Joachim snapped. "Olivier, keep your eyes on the road. And Gia…" He left the sentence unfinished, punctuated by a warning note that silenced her and stole the humor from the air.

They rode in silence. Even Dmitri and Aristide, sitting in the back of the van, seemed to sense the tension now. Their quiet conversation had ceased and they hardly moved a muscle, only sat like black-garbed phantoms in the shadows.

Long moments later, Olivier turned the van onto a side street, and a gray concrete monolith rose before them as though it had sprouted from the ashy slums surrounding it. A giant among sprawling, endless human ruin.

"That's it," Gia whispered, her brown eyes wide and fixed on the high-rise ahead of them. She shivered and hugged herself, running her palms over her bare arms.

Behind the steering wheel, Olivier was forcefully cheerful. "Now, dear Gia, you get to see how well-versed a seraph is in the methods of parallel parking." He braked, considered the one tiny space available on the opposite side of the road, then turned the wheel and eased the van into a shadowed alley across the street from the apartment building. "At the risk of getting a parking violation, I'd rather not embarrass myself. Will this do, Joachim?"

"It's fine." Joachim released his seatbelt and glanced back at the other operatives, a silent order to disembark. He placed a tiny communication fixture in his right ear, then opened the passenger door and hopped out. "Testing."

"Loud and clear," Aristide responded, checking his own comm unit.

Dmitri adjusted the device in his ear, then threw open the van's side door and stepped out, motioning to Gia.

"Who's coming inside with me?" she asked, her dark gaze avoiding Joachim as she climbed out.

"I am." Shielded by the van's breadth, Joachim knelt before her, unceremoniously tugged up her pant leg and strapped a small holster to her calf, his movements brusque. "With any luck, you'll have no reason to use your weapon. But if one arises, you'll know what to do, yes?"

"I think I remember," she said, her gaze fixed on the massive edifice across the street.

"You must not *think*. You must *know*." The sharpness of his words brought her attention to his face, and for a moment he regretted his sternness as he noted the flash of apprehension in her velvet eyes.

Then she nodded, her lips tightened in a downward line. "Fine. I *know* I could blow somebody's head off if I had to."

He rose, handed her a revolver and moved away. After a pause, she slid the gun into its holster and straightened her pants.

"Where's Olivier going to be?"

"Right here, sweetheart," Olivier vowed with a charming smile. "Manning communication and guarding you from afar." And to Joachim's annoyance, he touched a gentle fingertip beneath her chin, eliciting a telltale softening of Gia's features that snapped the last threads of Joachim's patience.

Jaw set, he nodded toward the building. "It's getting late. Let's go."

* * * * *

He took the steps two at a time—quick, graceful strides that hardly seemed to wind him.

Gia raced to keep up with him, breathing through her mouth to avoid inhaling the stale, humid air of the darkened stairwell. The stench of dust and unnamed filth was inescapable when she finally gave up the fight and gulped in oxygen. She'd always prided herself on keeping in shape, but three weekly half-hour sessions in Vincent's private, air-conditioned gym had hardly prepared her to climb the Tower of Babel.

Donna Torio's apartment, the one where Gia had lived for the last five miserable years of her adolescence, was on the eighteenth floor. At the seventh-floor landing, she gripped the rail with a sweaty hand, looked up and swallowed a doleful groan. An infinite optical illusion wound above them as far as the eye could see, flight upon flight of metal stairs wrapped in chain-link fencing and chipped, black lacquered banisters.

"This building has an elevator, you know," she managed to huff, shooting Joachim's muscled backside a leaden glance as he rounded the next flight ahead of her.

"I know," he said, his pace never faltering. "It's not functioning."

"How do you know that? We didn't even—"

"Trust me."

Gia didn't think she could trust someone she wanted to clobber.

When they reached the twelfth-floor landing, she grabbed the back of his shirt to halt him and half-collapsed against the concrete wall by the door. "Wait…" She gasped for oxygen, perspiration trickling down the sides of her face and between her breasts. "Can we…please slow…down? I can't…keep up with you."

He paused with one hand on the banister, his breathing even. "You're tired?"

"Just a little," she snapped, bracing her hands on her knees.

"I'm not like you, remember? I'm not…made of cold, unyielding steel."

The outburst carried a blatant import that exposed her fractured feelings, bruised since earlier that day when his warmth had suddenly reverted to cool, impersonal regard. She stole a look at his impassive face and scowled. How could he seem so caring one minute and so insensitive the next? Not only did it irritate her, it confused her, and it *hurt*. And just when she'd finally decided to like him.

Maybe she'd liked him too much, too quickly.

A fresh wave of heat assailed her face as he studied her, and she averted her eyes, indignation feeding the harsh pants that billowed from her chest.

He didn't speak, but the thud of his boots on the concrete landing came nearer, and when she looked up again, he stood a foot away, watching her with a confused frown.

"I'm sorry," he said finally, sounding—in typical male fashion—as though he had no idea why he was apologizing. "Perhaps I expected too much of you physically."

"You think?"

Sarcasm glanced off him like bullets off a superhero's chest. His gaze scanned her, head to foot, an impersonal examination. "You're overdressed for the temperature of this stairwell. It would benefit you to remove some of your clothing."

She released a wheeze of laughter. "I'm sure it would. What shall I take off first? My shirt?"

"Why not? You're wearing one of the garments we purchased for you beneath it, yes?"

Her mouth dropped open. He was *serious!* "But I can't run around in my bra, half-naked—"

"People on the street are bare-chested. Many people, walking around the city with no shirts at all."

"*Men*, Joachim. Men walking around the city with no shirts. Never women."

Confusion deepened the crease between his brows. "Women can't go bare-chested when clothing is an uncomfortable hindrance?"

"When was the last time you saw a shirtless woman on a Chicago sidewalk?"

To his credit he said nothing, just seemed to mull over this bit of societal hypocrisy. She watched him with a warring sense of frustration and amazement. Despite his obvious power and capability, he harbored almost childlike views about many things. Sometimes—like now—it was easy to believe he truly didn't hail from this world. He seemed so innocent.

She straightened against the wall and sighed. "I take it equal-opportunity nakedness exists where you come from."

His frown eased and the elusive dimple appeared in his right cheek. "We wear nothing."

"Oh?" Her brows shot up at the delicious image that conjured. "Lucky you."

"We have astral bodies. There's no need for clothing."

Gia pushed away from the wall and approached him. "That's too bad. I was really hoping Heaven was a giant shoe store that never ran out of women's size seven."

His smile softened, curiosity reflected in the bold cerulean of his eyes. "You call it 'Heaven'. I've heard you use that term before. When you were a child, during prayer."

"Heaven, paradise, the eye in the sky. What do you call it?"

"Home. And it holds a weight of joy far greater than anything in this earthly dimension." To her utter astonishment, he reached out and brushed away a stray curl clinging to her damp cheek, a seemingly unconscious gesture that fed her sexual awareness of him like liquor to fire. "Better than shoes, in other words."

She ignored the rush of heat spilling through her insides and started up the next flight without him. "Hard to believe anything's better than the right pair of Italian leather pumps."

"There are no words to describe Heaven. I've yet to experience anything in the physical realm that compares in pleasure."

Maybe he hadn't had sex after all.

She paused at the landing to wait for him. "I have a feeling you haven't experienced as much of the physical realm as the average guy."

He conceded with a shrug and continued past her. "Perhaps *I* haven't. But this body has memories."

"Oh, yeah?" She followed him up the next flight at an easier pace, her gaze focused on his back and the shift of muscle visible beneath his ribbed gray shirt. "What kind of memories?"

He was silent, the rhythmic cadence of their footsteps echoing in the narrow stairwell.

"Have you ever tried alcohol?" she prodded, trying to keep her mind off the growing protests of her thigh muscles working against gravity.

"You mean wine and liquor? Of course." He rounded the next flight, his strong, scarred fingers trailing along the metal banister. "Wine has been a dietary staple for many centuries. Some cultures believe it's beneficial to the health. The consequence of ingesting too much is rather unpleasant, though. This body in particular remembers that."

Interesting. "You've been drunk?"

He merely smiled and kept climbing.

Gia raised her brows as she trailed him. A drunken Joachim was definitely something she'd buy a ticket to see. The loss of control, the easing of the concrete command he held over his emotions. He'd be quicker to laugh, more volatile, more passionate.

Despite his apparent lack of emotion, she was positive a hot-blooded creature existed under all that restraint. That potential for passion, combined with the flashes of innate tenderness he'd shown her, and his drop-dead beautiful features—definite crush material for any woman, and Gia wasn't exactly immune.

She tamped down on the realization that despite his erratic behavior, her attraction to him was growing. Maybe the fact that she was in constant physical danger teased the flame. Maybe it was the complete lack of knowledge as to what lay around the next corner.

Maybe it was the way his rich chestnut hair curled against the nape of his neck, soft and inviting, slightly damp with perspiration.

She clenched her fingers into fists and squelched the urge to reach out and touch. Her traitorous attention dropped to his wide shoulders, then to his backside. The man was all muscle, his buttocks nicely curved, the perfect resting place for a woman's hands at the height of pleasure. That ass would undulate beautifully beneath her palms. His hard belly would rub against hers while he pushed inside her, his full mouth hot and open against her neck, exhaling adulations. And all the while, she'd be enchanted by the amazing phenomenon of that beautiful, sculpted backside moving under her hands…

He glanced over his shoulder at her as he reached the next landing, catching her in her illicit thoughts.

Drooling over this guy was about as gratifying as lusting after a priest.

Gia quickened her pace and caught up with him, matching her steps to his. "How about drugs? Did the person who had your body before you do drugs?"

A glance at his profile showed he was searching his memory, his dark brows drawn down in concentration. "Drugs—substances that neurologically alter human reality." He shook his head and resumed a quicker pace of climbing. "With each day, the memory fades more, but drug consumption prior to my occupancy is likely, since he was killed in a narcotics exchange."

An interesting tidbit. Gia tried to picture his face with someone else's persona behind it and found it impossible.

"For thirty-three years, this body belonged to a soul who did everything in its power to destroy itself. There's no doubt in my mind this physical form has experienced a little of everything detrimental to its well-being."

"Sex too?"

As soon as the question was out of her mouth, Gia grimaced. She couldn't keep her mouth shut if her life depended on it. And now she'd probably have to explain what sex was.

Joachim's steps slowed and he looked at her as they rounded to the next flight. "You equate physical love with the recklessness of drugs and alcohol?"

Okay, so he knew about sex. She wiped a trickle of sweat from her temple, equally relieved and disconcerted that he hadn't answered her probing question. "It's not all physical 'love', and it can be very harmful," she pointed out. "Addictive, even. Sex isn't that different from drugs and alcohol." Wry amusement curved her lips. "It can take you out of this world, that's for sure."

Joachim was quiet for a moment. Then, "You, yourself, have used this activity as an escape?"

What a question. Heat seared her cheeks. "Most people have."

"But *you*?"

"Not consciously, but…sometimes. Sure."

"With whom?" he demanded.

Gia scowled. "I don't kiss and tell. Besides, if you really have been my guardian angel all my life, wouldn't you already know all the 'whos'?"

"So there *was* more than one." He seemed to mull this over, then shook his head and glanced at her again. "With Vincent Rossi?"

Her gaze shot to his, found it sharp and unblinking, and she flushed anew, her pulse hammering out a warning drumbeat. The conversation had taken a decisively provocative turn. "He was my husband."

"Did you lose yourself with him in the manner of which you speak?"

The way he worded the question was eloquent and seductive in comparison to the bald reply that played on Gia's lips.

Hell, no. Not even once. Sex had never been a true escape with Vincent, nor anyone. No matter how she tried, Gia had never truly slipped the bonds of reality on the wings of wild, passionate love. Long ago she'd quit believing it was possible. It seemed foolish to even entertain the existence of a love magnificent enough to sweep her beyond the heaviness of her inner unrest.

"I couldn't…it wasn't…*I didn't love him.*" The admission echoed around them, high and vulnerable, an unintentional confession that escaped her amidst the intimacy they shared, there in the dank, sticky stairwell. "I know that now. I was grateful to him for helping me escape a horrible place, and I would've stayed by him forever. But what I felt for him was never love."

"I see," Joachim said simply, and the acknowledgement, the silent acceptance it implied, made Gia feel pardoned for her shallow and needful past.

They passed the fourteenth floor in silence.

"Do angels love?" she asked abruptly.

"Angels *are* love." A smile softened his reply. "You're asking if we experience human emotion?"

She stole a look at him. "It seems like you do."

"In many ways, we do. Seraphim know no fear, however. Fear is an animal instinct that ties humans to the material realm, a necessity for survival on this Earth."

Arid humor tugged at her mouth. "So you're perfect soldiers then. Fearless. In control. No need to escape the pain."

"Not always," he said.

"You make mistakes?"

"The only true perfection lies with Creator."

"What about the way you and the others interact?" Awkwardness stilted her words, and her hands fluttered as she struggled to elaborate. "I mean, do you develop attachments? Do you argue? Hurt each other's feelings? Laugh? Fall in love?"

His blue gaze focused on the steady trod of their feet. "We experience negative emotion as well as positive. We laugh, yes. Often at human folly—and our own. We interact as humans do—not always with the perfect aplomb."

Gia smiled as she thought about Olivier and his lighthearted teasing. Even Joachim wasn't exempt from the occasional ribbing, despite his exalted leadership position. "And what about love, Joachim? You haven't really answered that question."

He turned his head and studied her with such intensity, her heartbeat quickened again. Maybe she'd gone too far, asked too much. She didn't understand the behavioral parameters of these strange people. How could she, without asking a million questions?

"The sensation of being 'in love' is an irregular one for celestial beings," he said at last. "For humans it's biological, a tool of nature. An emotion expressed, at its height, through the act of sexual intercourse, which in turn perpetuates the race. So love, in a remote way, is a means for survival."

Worded like that, it sounded pale and academic.

"You don't fall in love then," she said, deflated.

"I have not."

"But others among you have?"

"It's a human condition," he clipped, and the set of his jaw told her it was a subject he didn't want to pursue.

When they reached the eighteenth floor, the atmosphere seemed to thicken and curdle, a gray dread hovering around the entrance to the corridor. He laid a hand on her arm to detain her, then withdrew his semi-automatic from its ankle holster and cocked it. "Draw your weapon."

The pleasant, fuzzy preoccupation that had blurred her thoughts vanished, replaced by an icy awareness that launched her pulse into a frenetic race. "We need guns already? But why, when we haven't even—"

"Do you know what's on the other side of that door, Gia?"

She frowned. "Of course not."

"Neither do I."

She inhaled, more of an involuntary gasp than a need for oxygen. "Vincent might be here, waiting to spring some kind of ambush?"

"We briefed you before the mission. Have you forgotten?"

No. She'd never absorbed the information in the first place. It had all been hidden in technical mumbo-jumbo. The true danger that lurked here. The potential for horror and death.

"But how could he even know about this place, when I never told him where my mother lived? I told him she was dead! I lied about it constantly, and he believed me. He—"

"—is not Vincent. *It* is a nephil, evil incarnate, and it knows everything we do about you, and perhaps more."

"You told him I killed myself."

"And by now, if he's watching as we believe, he knows it to be an untruth."

Panic seized Gia's heart and clenched. She went cold from head to foot and everything between began to tremble. In the van the possibility of danger had seemed so very far away, fear had only nipped at her conscience. Now it flared in all its blazing glory. "Oh, boy. I don't think I can do this."

"You can."

"Joachim." She stepped back, feeling for the top stair with the tip of her sneaker. "I've never even killed a spider. I'm not cut out for this stuff. I lied when we were downstairs. I don't remember how to use the gun. I don't remember what Dmitri taught me about any of this. I'm not the right person to—"

Joachim caught her chilled fingers and drew her back to him. "Focus."

The abrupt order silenced her stammering diatribe. Her panic attack skidded to a halt, embarrassment diffusing the adrenaline that fired through her nervous system like electric shocks. "I'm focused just fine." *On getting the hell out of Dodge.*

"You're not." His thumb whisked across her knuckles in soft, steady sweeps. "Your thoughts are scattered in a million frightened places."

Her eyes shifted away, burning with sheer trepidation. How could he know her thoughts? He might be some sort of godly being, but they were *her* thoughts, and this was her fear, her right to be scared, damn it. Damn *him*.

"Look at me," he ordered. When she drew a trembling breath and fixed her gaze on his again, he spoke softer. "You're not alone here, are you?"

Swallowing, she gave a half-hearted shrug.

"You never have been, of course, but this time is a little different—a little better. This time we're here in physical form, and this makes our task of protecting you all the easier. *I am here*. You see me standing before you, yes?"

Gia nodded, soothed by his hypnotic tone, his fathomless blue gaze, the utter certainty of his words.

"Listen to me then, and follow my instructions closely, no matter what happens on the other side of that door. You will do this?"

"Yes," she tried to say, but it came out an inaudible wisp of sound.

"Good. Draw your weapon."

With slightly steadier fingers, she leaned and withdrew the revolver from the holster strapped to her calf.

Joachim watched in silence while she checked the chamber.

"I'm ready," she said at last.

But as she moved past him toward the door, he captured her free hand. "Gia."

Heart hammering, she faced him in the small space between the concrete wall and his warm body. "What?"

His fingers slid upward to encircle her wrist, caressing, measuring, while beneath his touch, her pulse went wild with a sensation far headier than fear.

"*Il te faut croire,* Gia. I thought trust was all it took, but I was wrong. You must believe."

"I'm trying, Joachim."

He didn't release her. A wave of hair fell across his forehead, hiding the expression in his eyes as he considered the slender arm in his grasp. He said something else, a whispered chant that sailed past her on the frenetic surge of her emotions, and finally lifted his head to meet her gaze.

Gia's lips fell open. Blue eddies swirled and converged in his eyes, azure swells rising and falling, parting to reveal a blinding cerulean world. Windswept fields of flowers bowed and danced there, waterfalls thundered and exploded into prismatic color. Beyond, the sprawling indigo universe shimmered with a million droplets of light.

His eyes were transoms to another world, *his* world. They spoke the truth. He was a messenger, a guardian, a soldier of Creator.

"Shoot only to divert," he said, his touch slipping away. "Let's go."

Chapter Eleven

Shadows swathed the corridor, broken every few feet by the flicker of dying fluorescent bulbs mounted between apartment doors.

The silence was thick, the musty, humid air even thicker. Somewhere, a baby's faint wail rent the quiet. Beneath Gia's feet, the same threadbare, tropical-print runner from her teenage years spanned the seemingly endless stretch of hall leading to her mother's door.

Her fingers flexed around the revolver she held low at her side. Joachim moved in front of her, soundless and graceful, his wide shoulders a shield between her slight form and any threat ahead of them.

"It's the second to last apartment on the left," Gia whispered, resisting the urge to cling to the back of his shirt like an anxious child.

He slowed and cast a look over his shoulder. "Knock. Call to her through the door."

"And if that doesn't work? We're not exactly buddies, she and I."

"Then we'll break in."

Gia raised her brows. "Quietly, I hope." She paused. "Not that the dregs around here will call the cops. They're too afraid of getting busted themselves, from what I remember."

They reached the apartment. An ancient, faux pine wreath still hung on the door, its red velour bow misshapen and caked with dust. The black lacquer surface of the door was chipped and scratched, revealing blood-crimson paint beneath, the 'eight' missing from the middle of the apartment number '1817'.

"Home sweet home," Gia muttered around the knot that had formed in her throat.

Joachim moved closer. His warm scent engulfed her, soothing and life-affirming. "Knock and call to her," he repeated, the instructions brushing her cheek in a feathery caress.

Raising a trembling fist, she rapped, then cleared her throat. "Donna?"

No reply. Her gaze darted to Joachim's, and he nodded for her to try again.

"Donna? It's Gia. Your daughter." She knocked more forcefully, the hollow thud tinged with desperation. "Could you open the door?"

Silence.

"Maybe she's not home," Gia said, and instantly a surge of hysterical laughter threatened to crawl up her throat. Years ago, alcohol abuse had morphed her mother into a recluse. If Donna Torio was anywhere, she was still holed up in the squalid little apartment with booze for company and sustenance. She didn't need Gia. She'd never wanted Gia, even before the alcohol had replaced all human contact in her life.

"She's not answering, Joachim."

"Step away," he said, his hand reassuring on her back.

Gia moved to the side and watched as he produced a small metal pick and inserted it into the deadbolt. "But there are chains too. Three of them, at least. We'll never get in without scaring the hell out of her."

He said nothing, just continued to gently jiggle the pick. A slight click indicated the lock's surrender, and he glanced at Gia once before turning the knob. "Wait at the threshold until I tell you to move."

The door squeaked open. No chains. No scream of warning from the other side. Holding his semi-automatic against his chest, Joachim stepped into the apartment and slid like a phantom along the wall to the right, scouring the dimness for any sign of movement.

Obediently, Gia hesitated at the threshold. Silence reigned inside the dark apartment. No sign of life—no light, no sound, no smell but dust—greeted her as she peered into the gloom.

Joachim reached a corner and glanced around it into a narrow galley kitchen, then moved quickly, silently, across the diminutive living room, around stacked boxes and piles of magazines and newspapers, to the bedroom Donna Torio had called her own. He disappeared into the shadows, and anxiety tightened Gia's muscles as she stared after him, counting the seconds until he reappeared.

What seemed like a century later, he emerged and nodded toward a closed door on the other side of the living room. "What's in there?"

"My room," she whispered, one hand pressed to her pounding heart, the other gone moist around the revolver's handle.

Stealthily, Joachim maneuvered around more boxes and approached the bedroom door. He paused to try the knob. "Where's the key?"

"I don't know. You'll have to pick the lock."

"There's no time." Stepping back, he studied the door. Then with a lightning-fast movement that startled a squeak from her, he kicked it in. The sound of wood splintering tore through the heavy silence and the door swung open.

Reluctant to lose sight of him again, Gia stepped farther into the apartment as he moved into the bedroom where she once slept. Her eyes adjusted to the dimness, and she held her breath as she examined the shadowed corners of the living room.

Boxes were scattered everywhere, as though someone was moving in…or out. Empty booze bottles sat in tidy groups against every wall, and someone had left debris swept into a neat pile near the kitchen, the broom propped against a nearby table. The place looked abandoned, derelict, and its hollow lifelessness imbedded itself in Gia's chest. Innately she knew her mother wasn't here and hadn't been for some time. But the dingy, floral-print sofa—it was familiar. And the painting hanging haphazardly on the wall beyond—it had belonged to Gia's grandmother. This was still Donna Torio's apartment.

So where was her mother?

A light came on in Gia's old room, flooding the living room with harsh luminosity. Joachim reappeared in the doorway, his gaze fixed on her as he leaned to re-holster his gun. "The apartment is empty. Shut the door and come here."

She pushed it closed, turned the deadbolt, then made her way around the obstacle course of boxes to where he stood. "Where's my mother?" she asked, dread squeezing her chest as she tucked her pistol in its holster.

"I don't know." His lashes lifted and lowered as he searched her face. "I wish I could tell you."

"Do you think she's dead, Joachim?"

"Intel shows she was alive two weeks ago and living in this area. It's all we know."

She nodded and drew a shaky breath, wondering why she should feel like crying when long ago, her mother had died in Gia's heart. "Is it possible that the nephil got to her before we could?"

"It's possible."

"But why? She didn't know anything about the Medallion. She never even knew my grandmother gave it to me."

He lifted a hand to her cheek, and the gentle gesture unleashed her hold on her emotions. "We'll find out what happened," he said softly, his thumb tracking the single tear that slipped down her face. "Maybe it's nothing."

"No. Something's definitely wrong." He felt it too. She saw it in the concern etched on his features.

More tears welled in her eyes, and she dashed them away with a brusque wrist. "I don't know why I'm crying." She moved away from his dangerous compassion and into the bedroom, where she lifted a dusty curtain panel from the window to stare at the grimy play of the sun on the ghetto below. "I hated her for so many years."

The thin carpet failed to muffle the thud of his footsteps behind her. "Hate and love are siblings, Gia. One doesn't exist without the other in the human realm."

"Why?" She let the curtain drop and turned to face him. "Why do we suffer like this? I own up to the mistakes I've made as an adult, and yes, there's a universal price to pay, but what about children? Life was so cruel when I was little, not just for me but for so many other kids."

"It's your path," he said.

The indifference of his words seared her, fed the rage coiling inside her like a noose tightened around her heart. "I want to know something. You say you were here, you and Olivier and the others. Why didn't you stop my mother from getting stinking drunk and hitting me, time after time? What about when my grandmother died, the only person in the world who gave a damn about me?"

She dragged in a breath and launched again, driven by the injustice of it all. "My mother drank up what little cash Nonna left us. She spent it on drugs and good times, and I went hungry. The neighbors fed me once in a blue moon, but mostly I was on my own, and comfort was nowhere in sight. If you were truly here, Joachim, *where were you*?"

"Safeguarding your life."

"What life?"

"It wasn't our place to—"

"Don't! Don't tell me you couldn't interfere."

"We couldn't." He reached for her, but she shoved his hand aside.

"*Why not*?" His face swam before her, blurred by the hot tears that welled on her lashes and spilled down her cheeks. Her nose was running, her face aflame, but she didn't care. "Why protect the hellish life I had when you couldn't make it better?"

He grasped her chin and forced her gaze to his. "For this moment, Gia, when light and dark are made visible to you, and the world's truths are laid before you. For this moment, *now*, when you realize the imperfection of this place and are spurred onward by its disparity."

She tried to free herself, but his hold was firm, his words made breathless by the struggle of wills between them. "For the moment when you hold the Medallion in your hand, feel its weight around your neck and open your eyes to see beyond what any human is capable of seeing. This is why we safeguarded your life, Gia. Like seraphim, you have a job. And no choice. *Do the job*."

She jerked free from him and paced a few feet away, forcing herself to calm, sucking down the sobs that shuddered through her chest in time to her heartbeat. Nothing he said made sense, and yet something deep within her recognized bits and pieces, a subconscious knowing she wanted to deny and couldn't.

Do the job.

She didn't look at him, just walked in circles, sensing—and cursing—his intense, compassionate regard.

After a moment he moved, and she glanced over her shoulder to find him turned toward the window, one hand adjusting the comm unit in his ear. He spoke rapid-fire French to Olivier in a low voice, then faced her, his features like granite. "Time is short. Find the Medallion."

Alarm shoved aside her dying anger as she watched him retrieve his gun from its holster. "Are we in trouble? Has someone tracked us here?"

He didn't reply, just crossed to the bedroom doorway and pressed his back against the doorjamb, his gaze scanning the living room shadows.

Propelled by fear and a strange charge of excitement, Gia wiped the wetness from her cheeks, straightened her shoulders, and headed for the closet. It promised to be a fruitless search.

She'd taken her belongings with her when she left home at eighteen, and ultimately pitched them in a dumpster behind a downtown Italian restaurant. Throwing away her past with a vehemence, everything that reminded her of it. Maybe the Medallion had been among those trashed items.

She turned from the closet door and opened her mouth to voice her concerns, then changed her mind. Joachim's thoughts were somewhere else, every muscle in his body tense as he watched the darkness.

Do the job.

The small walk-in was stacked with her mother's belongings, outdated magazines, boxes of dried-up cosmetics and cheap costume jewelry, moth-eaten clothing. Junk. Balanced on a wooden child's stool, she gave up handling the items with care and threw the boxes to the floor, her palms skimming the shelf's expanse for anything unusual.

Nothing.

Fashion magazines thudded to the closet floor, one stack after another. Clothing, knocked off hangers, added to the pile, sending dust motes migrating toward the bedroom's naked overhead bulb.

"Anything?"

Joachim's voice came from nowhere and startled a curse from her lips. She steadied herself on the wobbly stool and glared down at him. "Believe me, you'll know it when I find it."

His boots thudded a retreat to the bedroom doorway again, and she resumed her search, frustration clenching her stomach. What if the Medallion had gone the way of everything else she'd ever cared about, never to be seen again?

* * * * *

The closet was an irreparable mess by the time she clambered over the debris and out into the bedroom.

Joachim, leaning against the doorjamb, turned to meet her eyes, his features tense with anticipation. "Well?"

"Just this," she said calmly, and from behind her back, produced a small wooden box he seemed to instantly recognize.

Muttering an indecipherable exclamation, he re-holstered his pistol, strode to her and took the box from her hands.

For an instant he hesitated, his thumbs caressing the smooth, ancient grain of the wood. Then he opened the lid and stared. "You found it," he said, breathless. "This is it."

She nodded and heaved a gigantic sigh of relief and exhilaration.

His smile was slow in coming, like the sun's radiant and gradual progression over the darkness of night. He met her gaze, his eyes dancing with a million emotions. Then he released an unexpected whoop of joy and caught her by the waist with one strong arm, swinging her around. "*Gia, ma merveilleuse*! You are amazing. I knew you could do it."

"I'm glad someone thought so," she said, laughing. "I seriously had my doubts."

They were both breathless when he set her down, beaming and elated. Dizzy with joy, Gia clung to his shirt and smiled up into his face. "So now we get the bad guys?"

"That's the objective," he said. "But first…" He gingerly removed the Medallion from its moth-ravaged fabric bed, set aside the box and turned back to her with an expression that had mellowed from wild exultation to tender pleasure. "Do you remember wearing this around your neck as a child?"

"I remember. Nothing strange happened when I put it on."

"That's because you weren't ready."

She reached out a tentative finger and touched the ornate bronzed disc, tested its weight, traced the fiery image of the Archangel Michael in the flames. It was smaller than she remembered, more ornate. "I don't understand how it came to be in my possession. My grandmother gave it to me, of course, but—"

"It happened as Creator planned," he said. "There's much to explain. For now, this is the reward for a job well and courageously done." Lifting the chain over her head, he let it drop around her neck. Then he guided her fingers to the Medallion again, which now rested between her breasts, over her pirouetting heart.

"The mortal one who possesses the Medallion will look upon the world with clarity," he murmured, his eyelids sliding closed, *"and at last beyond it, for in that first moment of tenure, the curtain that divides man and Creator will be torn aside, and the radiance of all the universe – all its entities and nuances-- will be made visible."*

As if he had uttered some magical incantation, rays of light pierced the room, shooting like laser beams from the fast-warming metal in Gia's fingers. With an astonished gasp, she backed up. Goose bumps swept her skin as the lights intensified, curved and swirled inward to encircle Joachim's form. Stars showered the periphery of the room, blazing over the boxes and clutter and manmade squalor, incinerating them, until all she could see was fire and light, the luminosity more searing than a direct look into the sun.

Instead of fear, she was awash in wonder. The light swallowed Joachim, rendering him a transparent silhouette against the blinding glare. His shape lengthened, shards of blue and green and golden flame rushing from his shoulders, his arms, his legs…rushing and meeting and taking shape into…

Wings. Six of them. Three on each side, overlapping, barely visible through the brilliant, shooting radiance that fired the air around him. Magnificent wings that reached beyond the now nonexistent ceiling and spanned the width of the faded room.

Gia was hardly aware of the tears streaming down her face. Shielding her eyes with one hand, she sank to her knees and continued to watch, not breathing, existing only on realization.

This was Joachim, the angel. His true and remarkable form.

Il te faut croire, Gia. She did. At last, she believed.

Against her heart, the Medallion smoldered, branded her through flesh and muscle and bone, burning beyond pain and into her soul.

When she couldn't have borne the heat another second, the angel spoke, saying simply, "Joy."

The emotion took on a physical form and materialized before her, a swarm of butterflies that rose from the seraph's right hand and dispersed toward her, their graceful flutter brushing her face like tiny, delicate kisses, infusing her soul with sheer exaltation.

Gia wept. She laughed. She opened her arms and enfolded the butterflies, and they altered into velvety, fragrant rose petals, floated to the ground and carpeted the spot where she knelt like drops of blood.

He spoke again. "Peace." From his left hand a dove unfolded, whiter than the brightest light piercing her vision. It swept into the air, a lissome harbinger of tranquility, and descended to her shoulder, its weight a blanket of warm comfort that washed through her and filled her with acceptance and understanding. Its feathers tickled her cheek and when she reached to touch it, it dissolved, leaving a scattering of gold dust in her hand.

Shaken, she blindly clutched the Medallion again. Beneath her fingers it vibrated, intensifying until a metallic humming emanated from it, the coarse voice of the Earth and the thrum of its life force.

Overwhelmed by the sight and sound and scent of her Creator, Gia released the disc and closed her eyes, letting the world, as it truly was, spin into nothingness around her.

* * * * *

The hollow thud of footsteps on the rug brought her head up. Blinking, she rubbed the spots from before her eyes and squinted. The light was gone. The tiny room once again enclosed her, its dimness born long ago of a child's grief and unhappiness.

"Can you stand?" Joachim's voice pierced the confusion clouding her mind, and she reached for his hand. His fingers enclosed hers—warmly, deceptively human—and with his help she got to her feet, feeling as though she'd awakened from some bizarre dream.

Part of her hadn't wanted to come back.

"How do you feel?" he asked.

"Alive." Focusing on his face, she squeezed his hand. "For the first time, I feel alive." Despite the magnificence of his true form, she was inexplicably pleased to see his beautiful, familiar features again. "What happened, exactly?"

"You were granted Sight."

Her fingers drifted to the Medallion, now cooling against her shirt. "I saw incredible things."

"Yes."

"I saw *you*."

A soft smile brushed his features. "You saw me." Then his pleasure faded, replaced by a somber frown. "You will see Therides too when the nephil crosses your path."

As if to confirm that black fact, a shadow slid over the afternoon sun and further embedded the room in dimness.

"Great," Gia said, squelching a surge of unease. "I don't suppose someone else could wear the Medallion and see the nephil."

"Only you."

She sighed and glanced down at the silver-dollar-sized disk. "Can I take this off for the time being?"

"Of course." Amusement eased the severity of his expression as he helped her lift the chain over her head. He retrieved the box and laid the necklace gingerly in its bed. "You'll get used to it, Gia."

"Hmm?" She rubbed her palms over her face and struggled to focus on him, weighted by a sudden exhaustion that made her want to curl up and sleep.

"You'll get used to the Medallion's power. Your senses will acclimate." He handed her the box and picked up his pistol. "Ready to go home?"

Home. With this magnificent, winged spirit disguised as a man. She'd never wanted anything more.

"Absolutely. Let's get out of here." She started past him into the living room, then paused, choked by some unnamed emotion, a mixture of gratitude and something deeper, elemental, something…physical. "Joachim?"

He stopped beside her and she turned to him, studied the hollow at the base of his throat while she played words of gratitude in her head. Nothing she could conjure sounded better than touching him would feel.

With a pounding heart, she reached a single arm around his neck, ready to withdraw at the first sign of rejection. He offered none. He stood stock-still, his head bowed over hers, his body radiating unnatural fire.

Rising on tiptoe, she brushed her lips against his beard-shadowed cheek, lingered for an instant, breathing in his scent, vanilla and strength and beauty. Wanting to stay there, to taste him, to know every inch of him.

"Thank you," she whispered. Then without waiting for his response, she withdrew and headed for the apartment door.

Chapter Twelve

"South and east perimeters clear," Aristide's baritone rumbled through the comm unit in Joachim's ear, the third check-in since Joachim and Gia had entered the building.

"North and west clear," Dmitri echoed, the thunder of a passing diesel truck nearly obliterating his report.

Pausing in the hallway, Joachim held Gia back with a protective arm, eased open the metal door leading to the stairwell and stepped onto the landing. All was still, bathed in concrete gloom. A frail fluorescent bulb overhead buzzed and flickered.

"We're in retreat," he told his team, his gaze scanning the shadowed stairs. "Five minutes. We have the Medallion."

A surprised pause greeted his calm declaration. Then Olivier, stranded at the van's mobile comm unit with his wounded leg, let out a delighted chuckle. "Hallelujah, Captain. That was frighteningly uneventful."

"Bravo," Dmitri said, and Aristide echoed the sentiment, careful to keep his enthusiasm low-key as he patrolled the north and west sides of the building.

Joachim smiled and glanced at Gia. She descended the stairs beside him in thoughtful silence, her cheeks flushed, eyes wide. She clutched the Medallion's box to her heart as though she'd die rather than relinquish it.

He liked that about her.

"What are you thinking?" he asked as they reached the fifteenth floor.

"I'm wondering how the little bronze necklace inside this wooden box is going to defeat a demon set on annihilating the world."

"The Medallion alone will not defeat Therides."

She flashed him a doubtful look. "Then what will?"

"The Spear."

"What spear?"

"The Spear of Longinus. It's hidden somewhere on this planet, and we need the Medallion to find it."

"Now you've really lost me," she muttered. "Who's Longinus?"

Before he could respond, the metallic echo of a door squeaking open far below, followed by the thud of footsteps, brought Joachim and Gia to a halt.

"Joachim, who's—"

"Shh." Holding her against the wall with a firm hand, he eased forward and peered through the chain-link barrier above the banister.

A flash of black appeared deep in the bowels of the twenty-story shaft. A hand briefly gripped the rail some ten stories down, ghostly white against the lacquered banister. Muffled footsteps grew louder, the approach of more than one man.

"We have a breach," he whispered into his headset. "Dmitri?"

"North and west still clear," came the soft response.

Joachim drew in a breath and pressed back against the wall beside a wide-eyed Gia. "Aristide?"

No response.

"Aristide, report."

Nothing. Muscles strung with tension, Joachim motioned for Gia to remain where she was and slid down a few steps, his back glued to the wall. "Mobile, check south and east."

"I'm already there," Olivier replied. "Aristide is down."

"Alive?"

"Wounded, but alive. How many are there, Joachim?"

Joachim bowed his head and squeezed his eyes closed, honing in on the steady, menacing thud of approaching boots that echoed through the stairwell. "Maybe five, from the sound of it."

"I'm coming in," Olivier said.

"Right behind you," Dmitri added.

Hugging the concrete wall, her features tight and pale, Gia whispered, "What happens now?"

Joachim returned to her with silent steps and motioned for her to draw her gun. "We're going straight down, very, very quietly. When we get close to the lobby, we'll take a detour. Follow my lead, and—" he paused, reading the conflict of panic and courage playing across her features, and offered her a small smile of encouragement. "Believe, Gia. You must. You hold the whole world in your hands."

She glanced down at the Medallion's box in one hand and the gun in the other and returned his smile with a wry one of her own. "You can say that again."

Perspiration misted Joachim's forehead and trickled down the side of his face as they crept past the next floor, their backs plastered to the wall. His heartbeat kept time with the steady, approaching footsteps of Rossi's men, the rhythm punctuated by Gia's spastic breathing beside him. Halfway to the next landing, the chain-link was torn away, leaving an opportune shooting position. Joachim halted Gia and motioned her back, then aiming his pistol over the banister, caught sight of a black-garbed shoulder and pulled the trigger.

The crack was deafening as it radiated through the stairwell, and a shout of astonished pain told him he'd hit his target. Instantly the pounding footfalls quickened. More than five men, Joachim realized, adrenaline firing in electric jolts through his veins. Bullets ricocheted off the metal banister where he'd stood a moment before, some peppering the wall above Gia's head. Plaster shattered and rained white powder on her dark curls.

She didn't utter a sound, just hunched down on the stair, hugging her weapon and the Medallion's box like helpless babes.

"Get back up to the landing," he whispered, pistol extended in the direction of the approaching threat. "Inside the door. Wait there."

She straightened and shot him a look of pure fear. "But you can't fight these people alone. You'll be—"

"Go."

Biting her lip, she scurried up the flight to the fourteenth-floor landing, where she eased open the door and slipped into the corridor's shelter.

Far below, more gunshots rang out, indicating seraphim's advance.

"Position," Joachim spoke low into the headset.

"Third floor," Dmitri responded. "Olivier's behind me."

"I'm descending, approaching the twelfth story." Breathing hard, Joachim stealthily moved down to the next flight, his attention focused on the banister three feet away. As he slid past the twelfth-floor landing, the door banged open behind him and a crushing weight knocked him face down on the concrete.

His headset skittered across the landing and shattered against the wall. Clinging to his pistol, he tried to roll from beneath his assailant's bulk, but the man pinned him by the neck and jammed a heavy knee into his ribs.

Joachim swallowed an agonized groan and went still as the cold snub of a pistol pressed against his temple. Black-gloved fingers snatched away his gun.

"Where's the girl?" the low, gravelly voice demanded. An inhuman voice. The nephilim invasion had already begun.

"What girl?" The weight on Joachim's spine squeezed the air from his lungs, leaving him gasping. "There's no one but me."

In reward for the unsatisfactory response, the assailant

whipped the butt of the pistol across the side of Joachim's head.

Stars danced before his eyes and bile rose in his throat. Like Olivier, he'd forgotten the experience of physical pain, and now it came rushing back to him with a vehemence that shoved him to the dim edge of consciousness.

"The girl," the voice repeated, and the weight on Joachim's bruised ribs increased.

Light and dark commingled and separated, granting him momentary lucid thought. He had to free himself before the rest of Rossi's men reached the twelfth-floor landing. "Ah, *that* girl. I left her two floors up."

"And the Medallion?"

"She's got what you want."

The assailant grunted in satisfaction and began to rise, lifting his weight just enough for Joachim to tuck in his arms and shove himself, with a single brutal thrust, from the floor. Moving with a speed that gave his attacker no time to respond, he whirled and delivered a sharp roundhouse kick to the man's skull, sending him crashing into the metal door.

Bullets fired from below pinged against the banister, whizzing by Joachim's head as he dropped to a crouch and scrambled to retrieve his gun from the unconscious demon's possession.

He had to get to Gia.

Blood trickled, thick and warm, down the side of his face and through the hair behind his ear. His head throbbed mercilessly, the stairs before him doubling in image and swimming out again with the force of his pain. Grabbing the rail, he pulled himself up a flight, paused to draw a steadying breath, then ascended to the floor where he'd left her.

She met him at the entry, her fawn eyes stark with horror. "My God—what did they do to you?"

He motioned her onto the landing. "You have a weapon," he panted, smearing blood and perspiration across his brow as he wiped it with a weary hand. "Can you use it?"

Her concerned gaze searched his face, taking inventory of the damage. Then her shoulders straightened. "Absolutely."

"Then we'll try again to get out of here."

Only two floors below them now, Rossi's minions rounded the flight, marching up the stairs like a relentless army of insects. With a final burst of clarity, Joachim leaped ahead of Gia down to the next landing, aimed as best he could through the chain-link fence and emptied his clip at the approaching men.

Several fell, he couldn't see well enough to count them. Two did not. They rounded the next flight, their steps thundering their fierce approach. Joachim jammed a fresh clip into his weapon, and with every ounce of strength he owned, he braced his feet wide apart, aligned his pistol with both arms extended and waited for the final confrontation.

* * * * *

All Gia heard was pounding—that of her heart in her ears and the attackers' feet as they approached. Clinging to the Medallion's box and her revolver with equal desperation, all she could think was, *Angel or no angel…Joachim and I are in big trouble.*

Fear reared within her and seized her strength. She slid on the steps and half fell, dropping the Medallion box. She scrambled to retrieve it and forced herself back to her feet, her breath coming in wrenching gasps as she hugged the precious box to her chest.

When the two remaining attackers reached the final flight, one aimed through the chain-link and fired. Bullets zinged around Joachim, plowing into the concrete behind him.

There was nothing to shield him! A scream tore from Gia's throat. Huddling against the wall, she extended her revolver and emptied it with desperate fervor in the assailant's direction. To her utter astonishment, the shooter dropped with a groan, his body slithering halfway down the stairs.

The last remaining attacker let out a shout and charged over the body of his cohort. Without flinching, Joachim discharged his weapon just once, ending the skirmish.

A haze of dust and the pungent scent of cordite filled the dark stairwell. Several floors below, Dmitri's voice called out, "Joachim? Gia?"

"We're here! Thirteenth-floor landing." Gia re-holstered her gun and scrambled down the rest of the flight to where Joachim slumped against the door, his free hand clutching his bloodied head. "You're bleeding so badly—what can I do?"

"You did everything right," he told her, his blue eyes electric and crystal clear behind bloodstained fingers. "Thank you, Gia."

She studied him in silence, unsure of how to respond. She'd killed for this man—this seraph, this magical creature—and knew with utter certainty that she'd do it again when the time arose. In the last few hours, their lives had become inextricably entwined. Before this moment, he was her means for survival. Now he was her friend. *No, he was more*. The sight of him, even bloodied and beaten, fed her soul.

She'd killed, not just for Joachim but for herself, because she didn't want to live without him.

Her gaze drifted toward the body of the assailant she had gunned down. Clad head to toe in black, he lay crumpled like a broken rag doll on the stairs. His face, relaxed in death, was young, his dark hair damp with perspiration. Blood puddled beneath his body and ran in rivulets down to the next step, where it gathered in a crimson pool. His gloved fingers still clutched his gun. He would have used it to kill Joachim and Gia without hesitation if she hadn't fired.

But he was somebody's son. Somebody's brother. Somewhere in the world, his loss might be keenly felt.

Nausea seized Gia's throat and she turned away, drawing in huge, gulping breaths to repress the urge to retch.

"Gia—" Joachim said behind her, but she motioned him away, and before he could finish, Dmitri reached the landing with a rush of exclamatory French.

A quick, urgent exchange between the two men closed the door on Gia's involvement. She moved to the side, watching as Dmitri examined the wound on his mission leader's head.

One flight below, Olivier, hobbling now from too much exertion on his healing leg, maneuvered around the bodies of Rossi's men and gazed up at Joachim with a wry grin. "They're hurt worse than you, Captain. Trust me."

"Are all of them nephilim?"

"Only one or two, I'm afraid." He glanced at the corpses sprawled on the lower landings. "Michael will reassert that this bloodshed couldn't be helped. These humans chose their own damnation, Joachim. You know that."

"It doesn't make taking their lives any easier to bear." Joachim sighed, flinching away from Dmitri's attempt to wipe the blood from his temple. "Tell me about Aristide. He lives?"

"He lives…and joins the ranks of the dreaded thigh wound sufferers. Do you suppose Creator does that on purpose?"

"You'll have to ask Creator. You know how He enjoys being second-guessed by His operatives." Joachim's arid humor faded into a fresh wave of pain, and he drew in an anguished breath, gingerly fingering his bruised ribs. "Is Aristide ambulatory?"

"Enough to get home. The bullet merely grazed him. As soon as he went down, I retrieved him and dragged him to the van. You, on the other hand, look as battered as Rossi's henchmen." Olivier paused and winked at Gia. "Thank you for your skillful and efficient backup, Miss Torio. Without you, our great leader might be floating haplessly through the universe."

Gia tried to muster a smile, but then her attention drifted back to the lifeless form of the man she'd shot. She would see his face in her dreams at night, the way his eyes, wild with murderous intent, had widened with pain and astonishment as the bullet drove home though flesh and muscle and ribs.

Joachim's gaze followed the train of her stare. He studied the body, then regarded Gia for a long moment before he said,

"Now that Aristide is out of commission for a couple of days, we'll be needing an operative replacement, yes?"

"That's right," Olivier said, pocketing the firearms of the downed assailants. "I spoke with Nicodemus this morning on the subject. Jordan awaits an assignment."

Joachim's reply was indecipherable, in French, of course, and obviously not meant for Gia's ears. The other men made comments and a brief conversation ensued, some sort of debate, none of which she could follow.

Annoyed, hovering near tears of exhaustion and trauma, she turned the Medallion's box listlessly in her hands, watching as Joachim made a slow descent to the body of the young attacker. The other operatives followed suit, and all three men crouched on the stairs, laying a hand, one on the other, atop the corpse's heart.

Gia's voice, husky with confusion, broke the quiet. "What are you doing now?"

"One moment," was all Joachim said. The three operatives bowed their heads, and a heavy silence blanketed the stairwell, so complete that even the sound of Gia's own pulse seemed to hush in reverence for the strange ritual taking place before her.

The dead man's limbs jerked once, twice, as if stimulated by an electric surge. Then, to Gia's complete amazement, he sat up and rubbed his hands over his face, awakened from a deep sleep.

"Joachim," he said, smiling at the mission leader who still knelt beside him. "I have been assigned?"

"Welcome to Chicago, Jordan." Joachim glanced up at Gia, his eyes dimmed now with weariness and pain. "Let's get the Medallion—and you, Gia—to a safe place."

Chapter Thirteen

Silence filled the van's interior, broken only by the low conversation shared by Olivier at the steering wheel, Dmitri in the passenger seat and Jordan, who crouched between them with one hand on each man's shoulder, a display of affection Gia found poignant and endearing. The operatives had obviously missed each other. The passage of time, Joachim had explained, was not the same for seraphim as it was for humans. Still, the months that elapsed without Jordan's empathetic presence had seemed lengthy for them all.

Soft laughter drifted back to Gia's ears and she smiled to herself as she stretched to offer Aristide a fresh cup of water. He lay sprawled on the farthest backseat like a lazy ebony giant, his wounded leg bandaged and cushioned. He took the paper cup with a grateful smile, sipped it dry, then crushed it in his big paw and settled down to doze.

In the van's midsection, Joachim sat propped against the wall, his head listing to the side as he drifted in and out of a painkiller-induced sleep. He'd tried to refuse the medication Dmitri offered when they reached the van, but in the end he'd accepted it with a sigh, and gradually his dark lashes drooped until they lay like smudges against his cheeks.

Gia settled beside him with care not to wake him, her gaze fixed on his profile. In the fading daylight seeping through the van's tinted windows, he looked young, vulnerable. A shadow of beard darkened his angular jaw, his complexion nearly as white as the bandage that encircled his head like a rogue's kerchief.

The van bounced slightly, his head bobbed, and his lashes lifted, then slid closed again. He looked so uncomfortable. Gia found a windbreaker behind the driver's seat and folded it into a makeshift pillow. Her hair fell forward and brushed his cheek as she leaned across him to tuck the jacket behind his head, and he stirred when she withdrew.

"I smell flowers," he said without opening his eyes, a lazy smile tugging up one corner of his mouth. "I smell Gia."

She grinned at the drowsy slur of his words. "Right here, Captain."

"Tell me. What did Dmitri give me to make me feel this…this…?"

"Good?" A small burst of laughter escaped her when he rolled his head toward her and opened one eye. "It's a painkiller, a narcotic. Is your headache better?"

"What headache?"

"Mm-hm. That's what I thought."

He braced an elbow on one bent knee and drifted off again, so she said nothing more, just glanced at him intermittently, an anxious compulsion to check and recheck his condition.

Whatever she felt for him, it wasn't like any emotion she'd known before. It made her feel drunk and clumsy and hyperaware of everything she said and did. A glance from those blue eyes sent heat spiraling through her insides, coiling down, down, to the heart of her femininity, turning her soft and shamefully damp, and *that*, she knew, was physical desire. Who could blame her? As a man, he was a beautiful specimen. As an otherworldly being spawned of the highest Intelligence and purity, clothed in the body of Adonis, he was…so…

She couldn't fall in love with him. *Wouldn't*. She refused to be a starry-eyed human groupie grasping at the slightest straw of his affection. He served a purpose, and that was to get her through this nightmare and out the other side, taking the demon down as they went. That was what a guardian angel was supposed to do, and that's how she would look at him from now on. Soon he'd sprout his six magnificent wings and fly off, leaving her on a lonely, scary planet, so falling in love was simply out of the question, and it was definitely something she could control.

She had always been perfectly capable before.

Drawing a deep breath, she shoved the disturbing reverie back to a shadowed place in her mind. It was better to use this time to envision what her life would be like once this was over. A cozy studio apartment in hip South Beach, Miami, maybe…or scenic Carmel by the sea, where there'd be peace, water and silence. The salt wind would cool the air, and she'd sleep on pure linen sheets every night with the windows wide open, and nothing—*nothing*—would scare her ever again.

God, she was tired of being afraid.

Images darted behind her eyelids as she struggled to get comfortable on the turbulent descent from the adrenaline rush that had propelled her through that dank, deadly stairwell. She had shot a man—killed him. Taken a life. Her gaze darted to Jordan's broad shoulders and dark head as he lingered between his fellow operatives in the front seats. He looked perfectly hale and whole, but he wasn't the man whose life she had taken. Where was that man now? His soul—was it damned? Was there a Hell, and would there be a price to pay for having sent someone there?

Her mother's craggy face flashed before her eyes. As much as Gia harbored little tenderness toward the woman, she didn't want to be responsible for her death or suffering. What had happened to her?

The ball of anxiety in her stomach grew, and for a while she forced herself to draw slow, even breaths, warding off a full-fledged panic attack.

Exhaustion won at last. She had just slid into a fitful doze when Joachim stirred again and spoke beside her, as though they'd been carrying on a steady conversation for the last ten minutes.

"Longinus was a Roman centurion."

Gia opened her eyes and turned her head to meet his sleepy

gaze. His nose was two inches from hers, his lashes shading the electric blue of his eyes.

"Longinus? You mean the spear guy you told me about in the stairwell?"

"Yes. Longinus was the guard who drove a spear into Christ's side at the Crucifixion." He paused, searching her face in the shadows. "You know of these things, yes? Christ's Crucifixion?"

"My grandmother pounded the New Testament into my head from the moment I could understand the first word." She slid down against the van wall, bringing them closer, like two children hunched together in the back of a field-trip bus. "When I was seven and she passed away, I tried to read some books about Jesus out of respect for her. But I was angry Nonna had died. Angry at God, angry at anything that had to do with Heaven. I wanted to punish whoever had taken her from me. I never went to church. I never prayed—"

"All children pray," he murmured. "They just don't know it. The line between their souls and Creator has not yet been blurred by fear and pain. Perhaps it was in your sleep, Gia, or maybe in half-conscious thought, but you spoke, and you were heard."

She didn't know if she bought it, but the way his voice caressed her ear, his accent a little foggy and softened, lulled her into peaceful acceptance. "I do know about Christ and some things about his life. I can't say what I believe as far as all that's concerned. But I know what I saw today in my mother's apartment, Joachim." She drew a breath to dispel the tears that instantly gathered in her throat, harbingers of her growing affinity for him. "I saw an angel. A real one. I believe they exist because I saw *you*. And you were beautiful and true."

Joachim didn't reply, just watched her in the purple shadow filling the van's interior. Only the occasional flash of a streetlight illuminated his features now.

"I'll listen to an angel if he wants to tell me about

Longinus," Gia added hesitantly. "I don't know if anyone of lesser stature could make all this crazy stuff believable."

Her forced humor shattered the poignant tension, and Joachim smiled.

Sighing, he shifted against the van's wall. "Longinus was born outside Rome to an impoverished family, and he suffered from near-blindness. He was big for his age, and this fed the clumsiness his handicap caused. Yet as he grew to adulthood, he learned to function as other men, so that eventually no one could tell he was sight-impaired. The army gave him a sense of power he'd never experienced as a child and social outcast. He accepted every assignment, no matter how menial or depredating, to avoid drawing negative attention to his frail eyesight. He was inhumanly strong, loyal and blinded not only by his physical ailment, but also by the regime's provocative glory and power."

He took her hand in his and turned it over, laying it palm-up on his knee to play with her fingers as he spoke.

"At the end of the Crucifixion, the Sabbath was approaching, and it was time to remove the bodies. Longinus was ordered to pierce Christ's body with his spear to ensure he was really dead. The blood and water that spilled forth from the wound spattered into the centurion's eyes. Instantly his sight was restored, and at that moment the blindness also left his heart. He dropped to his knees and proclaimed Christ the Son of God."

"And the spear he used still exists?" Gia asked, trying to ignore the pleasure that pooled low in her belly as Joachim traced the shape of her palm with a languid finger. He couldn't possibly know what the half-conscious caress was doing to her.

"It never left Longinus' possession, through all the years he traveled and served as a devout disciple of Christianity. It was no ordinary weapon, of course. Soaked in Christ's blood, it had been imbued with the magnitude of the universe's forces. The power of the Spear ultimately enabled Longinus to converse with seraphim—it granted him Sight, such as the Medallion gave you in your mother's apartment.

"Under the Archangel Michael's guidance, Longinus learned of the weapon's dual nature. Its power was drawn from the earth and sky and could only be initiated by a human's touch. He who held the Spear held the world's destiny in his hand, and it could be used for good or evil with equal force. Longinus, fortunately, was touched by Creator and pure of spirit. He used the Spear's power to heal and soothe the people of Jerusalem, then Rome and far beyond. But when he was martyred, the relic quickly disappeared."

Gia swallowed an inexplicable, rising dread and looked around for the Medallion's box. It was tucked safely in a niche behind her shoulder, and when Joachim straightened and released her hand, she reached back to touch the lid for comfort. "Who took it?"

"We don't know—and that's how the Medallion came to exist. Michael forged it from the Earth's ore and sent it to the Daughters of Longinus as a tool to call the lost Spear. The Medallion could only be used by a human, and none of the women were willing to risk finding the Spear only to lose it to the wrong hands. As it stood, females were little more than possessions themselves, and it was highly likely a husband or brother could have taken the relic at will. Thus the Medallion was handed down through generations as little more than costume jewelry and eventually possessed no more weight than that of family lore. Its own power was forgotten and lay dormant."

But Nonna had known she possessed something powerful, Gia thought, goose bumps blanketing her skin. Even if she wasn't sure of the extent of its power, the old woman knew the Medallion was a tool of God. She had known to bypass her own daughter as its recipient, a careless and lost soul, and to lay the precious necklace in the hands of her granddaughter—a mere child, in whose innocence there was hope.

"And the Spear?" Gia whispered.

He slid closer to her, his head bowed against hers so that

their foreheads nearly touched. "The Spear, lost somewhere in Christendom, passed from hand to powerful hand. Kings, emperors, dictators were drawn to the superhuman abilities it granted, and they hunted like madmen for the legendary relic. Constantine, Charlemagne, the Hapsburgs, Adolf Hitler—all of these men sought and found it—and ultimately lost their earthly and enigmatic power when it left their possession."

A faint smile curved Joachim's lips as he studied her eyes at close proximity. Gia held her breath, torn between trepidation and a wayward, curling thrill at his closeness.

Three heartbeats passed, a space where anything could have happened between them. A smile, a whispered sentiment, a kiss. All of it out of place in the solemn pause, but all possible.

But then he closed his eyes and winced, the pain of his injuries stealing the moment. After moving to take a sip of water from the paper cup she'd left for him in a nearby holder, he settled beside her again, and when he spoke, his voice was husky from discourse.

"Historians claim to have the Spear displayed in museums all over the world. Rome, Nuremberg, Paris, Vienna. None of these relics are authentic, however. The actual Spear is lost among common humanity, and its power grows with every day that passes."

Gia drew herself up and hugged her knees to her chest. "And no one knows about the Medallion or its ability to locate the Spear?"

"Only you, Gia. And Therides, of course, who has acquired Vincent Rossi's human hands with which to acquire the Medallion—"

"And call the Spear." Gia reached out and clasped his hand again, a half-conscious bid for reassurance. "If he gets it, he'll use it to destroy the world."

"Not just the world. The universe. And all others, if he wishes. Right now, as a demon in human form, he can only stir trouble and unrest in this dimension. But goodness reigns over evil in most men's natures, and many cannot be swayed by the minimal strength he possesses alone. Therides needs the Spear to grant him the power of Lucifer. With your help, we must use the Medallion to call the Spear. Once its location is made known to us, we'll retrieve it and use it to send Therides back from whence he came."

He hesitated, his eyes sparkling in the gloom as his fingers laced through hers. "Then you have the choice, Gia, to utilize the Spear for the good of Man or destroy it. It's your call—and you alone, a distant Daughter of Longinus, must be the bearer."

Gia's sporadic breath played accompaniment to the thunder of her pulse. A million emotions spun in her head. She hadn't asked for this dubious honor. She wasn't sure she wanted to be a Daughter of Longinus. She wasn't sure she wanted to be here in this van, ensconced in this intimate exchange with some phantom figure who drove her to distraction with his charisma and seductive, otherworldly truths.

But it didn't matter what she wanted. It didn't matter if she wanted *him*. He hadn't been sent to keep her company or to fill her with love or teach her the meaning of true pleasure between a man and a woman. He didn't belong here. And soon—as soon as she helped him accomplish what he'd come here to do—he'd vanish from her sight forever, and she'd be instrumental to his leaving.

The faint stirrings of grief tickled her senses, and she scrubbed her free hand over her face to banish the unwelcome emotion.

"Gia," he said.

There it was again, that soft pronunciation that liquefied her bones and made her want to bury her nose in the warm curve of his neck. The simple word laced with a compassion that made her feel like he alone could read her emotions and understood them like no other.

"You doubt what I have told you?"

"No."

"Then what troubles you?"

She turned her head to meet his gaze, her grasp tightening on his. "What troubles me? Where do I begin? Beyond all the usual doubt any normal person would experience, I'm definitely questioning my ability to pull off my part in this."

His sleepy gaze dropped to her lips, then lifted to capture her eyes again. "Why, after all I have told you?"

"Joachim." She couldn't think. He was too close, and it stole her control over her words. "For so many reasons, and you know them all. Except maybe this one."

He watched her in silence, waiting.

"I'm…you see, I'm distracted. Disturbed by these thoughts I'm having." The confession welled within her, and she struggled to tamp it down, but it pushed past her common sense and rushed to her lips. "I can't seem to control—I—my feelings—"

"Your feelings of fear? They're perfectly understandable, and with our help—"

"No. My feelings for *you*. They have nothing to do with fear, but beyond that, I don't understand them. And they distract me. I don't know how to stop them." Then she added low, "I thought I knew what desire was, but I've never felt this way before."

Joachim stilled, searching her face in the darkness.

"You two look like a couple of conspirators, huddled together like that," Olivier said from the front, his smiling gaze meeting Gia's in the rearview mirror. "Joachim, I'm surprised you're awake."

"What's our location?" Joachim released her hand and sat back, his tone remote, withdrawing from Gia not only physically, but mentally and emotionally under the watchful observation of his team.

"Two miles from base. Someone should rouse Aristide," Olivier said with a stretching yawn. "We're almost home."

* * * * *

Joachim lifted his left arm and leaned forward on the chair as Soleil instructed, a sigh of discomfort and impatience hissing through his teeth. She bandaged his ribs with all the gentle care of a tornado wrenching up trees.

"Easy," he muttered, grimacing as she brought a third layer of bandage snugly and efficiently across his bruised side.

"I'm stronger than I look, am I not?" She shot him a smug grin, tucked in the tail of the bandage and straightened. "All done. Would you like a lollipop?"

His brows lowered. "You offer me candy?"

Soleil shrugged, repacking the first-aid kit spread across his desk. "I've seen doctors give squalling children lollipops after inoculation."

"I'm not squalling."

"But you want to." She disappeared into his bedroom and reemerged with a fresh T-shirt. "Here. I won't try to help you dress since you're so edgy. Is there anything else you need?"

"Nothing. Thank you." He took the T-shirt from her, then gritted his teeth and tried to ease it over his head, but even the slight brush of the material against his wounded temple was too much to bear. With a frustrated growl, he tossed the garment on the desk and eased back in his chair. "There are times when this body is more a hindrance than an effective vehicle."

"I think it's a wonderful body. Very pleasurable to look at. I hope you'll keep it for the next mission. Would you like another painkiller?"

He considered it, but then shook his head. "I have to keep a clear mind. I haven't debriefed with Michael yet."

"And after? How will you rest tonight when you're suffering as you are?"

"Your maternal tendencies are showing," he said with a grin, knowing that such an observation would chafe her sensibilities.

"This body hasn't a single maternal bone," she retorted as she snapped the first-aid kit closed. "Get your own painkiller, you stubborn creature."

As she swung open the door, Gia waited on the threshold, fist poised to knock.

Her cheeks heated at the sight of Soleil standing there. "Oh. I was just—" Her gaze shifted to Joachim, who lounged in his desk chair, bare-chested, the alabaster bandage standing in stark contrast against the warm tones of his skin.

The breath rushed from her lungs, and she uttered the only word she could think of. "Hi."

"Hi," he said, his expression inscrutable.

Soleil glanced from Gia's heated face to Joachim's shuttered features, and one tawny eyebrow shot nearly to her hairline. "Everyone is sleepless tonight, I see."

"Yes," Gia said faintly.

"I'll just say goodnight to you both and hope you'll soon rest."

"Goodnight," Gia responded, heart galloping, her attention fixed on the man behind the desk. "Joachim, do you have a moment?"

"For you always," he said.

Gia edged by Soleil, then hesitated in the middle of the room and shot the blonde a restive look over her shoulder. Soleil had paused in the corridor, green eyes wide with curiosity, lingering without even attempting to appear inconspicuous.

"Close the door," Joachim barked.

The click of the latch quickly followed, and then they were alone in the office.

"You should be asleep," Gia said.

"Why are you still awake?" he spoke simultaneously, so their words tumbled together, indecipherable in every way except for the blazing awkwardness they both felt.

They paused, and Gia fought the urge to back up and run.

There were so many reasons sleep evaded her, how could she begin? Starting with concern over her mother's well-being, then the lingering image of the man she'd killed, then the Medallion...the Spear...Longinus. Too much to absorb. And why had she confessed her feelings for Joachim in the van? It was nothing more serious than a juvenile crush, wrought by trauma and gratitude and the extraordinary conditions of the past weeks.

Lying wide-eyed in her glass cell for the last two hours, she had finally determined the true triviality of her attraction to him—but it was too late. She'd gone and blabbed in a moment of runaway emotion and possibly ruined their friendship. The discomfort she felt just from being alone with him in this room was enough to send her fleeing the bunker and all protection, Therides be damned.

"I couldn't sleep," she said finally, forcing herself to approach his desk. "For a lot of reasons. And the only one I can do something about is this one. I need to clear this whole thing up."

He propped his elbow on an armrest, his brows knitted as he rubbed a single finger beneath his bottom lip. "This whole thing?"

"What I said in the van."

"Oh," he said. "*That* whole thing."

She averted her attention from his bare, muscled chest, where it seemed to want to settle again and again, and studied his face, wishing she could read what was happening behind his eyes. They appeared iridescent, a strange light burning behind them. His head was unbandaged, and the blow he'd suffered to his temple had spread vibrant shades of maroon and indigo halfway across his forehead and down to the corner of his left eye.

He was exquisite.

Gia peered at him. "I think you're bleeding again."

Touching fingertips to his temple, he glanced at them and

sighed. "The human head is too—"

"I know. Fragile. Weak. Delicate. It must be so frustrating to be a superhero locked in a mortal shell." She reached for the first-aid kit and opened it, rummaging through it for gauze. "Maybe you need stitches."

"Medical told me no."

Humor curved her mouth and diluted some of the unease between them. "Really? Or was it *you* who told *Medical* no?"

He shrugged. "It all ends the same. No needles."

Gia nearly laughed. Maybe angels didn't experience animal fear, but something about needles definitely made Joachim squirm. She eased around the desk with a wad of gauze in her hand. "Could I…?"

He tilted his head to accommodate her, and she held her breath as she dabbed the slight shine of blood from his temple. His hair was still damp from the shower, and the scent of soap and clean skin had assailed her the minute she walked into the office. The last thing she needed was his unique and delectable fragrance playing on her senses as she tried to explain away her bumbling outburst.

"It's almost dry." She lifted his chin with a single finger to examine the wound, exhilarated at the chance to touch him, even with just one fingertip. "A few centimeters difference, and you could have been killed."

"But here I am, alive and well. Gia…" He caught her finger and swiveled in his desk chair to meet her eyes. "If I've misled you, forgive me."

"You haven't." A fresh wave of humiliation burned her face and she tugged from his gentle grasp. "You haven't misled me at all. Really, you don't have to say anything about this. I just wanted to clear up the fact that I spoke out of turn earlier—that it was simply one of those moments. I lost my head, and truly, I'm just so amazed at how you've protected me, and sometimes I get carried away, you know, by emotion, by gratitude—"

"If I were here to stay, born into a mortal body, this

conversation would be entirely different. Do you understand?"

Did she? Was he saying that if he were here to stay, he might want her? Love her? Touch her the way she so desperately desired?

The distant possibility weakened her knees, and she leaned against the edge of the desk. "How did I get myself in this position? I don't even know what this thing is with you. When I look at you, all I feel is confusion."

"And I the same." He gazed at her for a long moment, his eyes too blue to bear. Then he swiveled slightly away, folding his hands across his bare abdomen. "You're not at fault. From the first moment at the estate when I saw you as a woman, and I, in this impossible body…" He swallowed his words, shook his head. "Let us be friends, Gia. You and I, we are the principal players. There must be peace between us for this mission to move forward."

Releasing a slow breath of disappointment edged with relief, she nodded. "I can do that."

"Good."

"Friends, then?"

"Always, Gia."

Silence hovered between them, galvanized by faint electricity in the air. Reluctant to leave him, she reached for the first-aid kit again. "You should let me at least stick a small bandage on that cut. No needles," she added when he cast her a wary glance.

Joachim sat in obligatory stillness while she tore the tabs off a bandage and covered the abrasion on his temple. The beard shadowing his jaw had grown darker, and the clean scent of his bare skin rose to her nostrils, despite every effort she made not to breathe it in.

She glanced at the muscled curve of his shoulder. Faint freckles spattered a path to his collarbone. His chest was smooth, sculpted from years of weight training and athletics. Golden-brown hair feathered down his abdomen and grew denser around his navel before disappearing behind the waistband of his pajamas. The faint line of a generous male member, resting against his right thigh, was apparent through the soft cotton.

Gia's heart palpitated and her mouth went dry. When she snapped out of her trance, he was staring at her lips, his face upturned in her direction, the sweep of his lashes like feathers on his cheeks.

Waiting for her to make the mistake of all mistakes.

"God—someone—forgive me," she muttered. "I'll probably go to Hell for this."

Then she bent and covered his mouth with hers.

Chapter Fourteen

No one had warned him.

No amount of briefing could have prepared him for the sensations that slammed through his body at the first taste of Gia's lips, as though the soft, hungry kiss had set off a deluge of lava in his veins.

Joachim jolted beneath her, every drop of blood in his body seemingly rushing to his groin, swelling his manhood, tightening his testes, making everything ache and pulse and dance. His fingers gripped the armrests convulsively and he groaned, even as he hovered in an instant of indecision. *Push her away or draw her closer?* The logic of Angel and Man battled.

Man won.

When Gia started to withdraw, he shot forward and recaptured her mouth, a hungry, wordless invitation to stay. And oh, the softness of her lips. The sweet rush of her breath. The skim of teeth and then—tentatively—her tongue. Winding around his. Stroking the roof of his mouth, drawing his own tongue out to play in a thrusting, flickering duel.

She tasted like sugared strawberries and desire. Her sultry floral scent wrapped his senses, rising to greet him from the heat of her breasts. Encouraged, she leaned over him, closer, her fragrant curls falling against her cheek, against his, a curtain to shield this forbidden moment from the world and the Heavens. Her fingertips grazed his jaw, trembling, uncertain. Holding him as though he'd soon slip away, as though to say she too knew that at best this was an ephemeral delight.

Then her tongue slid from his, and their lips parted, a single breath shared between them, a single word hovering that would end it.

Stop.

But Joachim was lost, heart, thoughts and vitals pounding, and instead of speaking he closed that centimeter between them and again silenced the uncertainty with his hungering kiss.

Why, oh why, he thought wildly, as her other hand came up to cradle his jaw, tilted his face and held him like a vessel. *Why was I not prepared for this*?

Should he have been?

Today, this moment, I'm a mortal, am I not? Flesh and blood and want. A man.

Their tongues touched, withdrew, returned to lash and tangle. Bolder now, as his body's memory of another inhabitant's desire pushed aside celestial guilelessness, and erotic sensation detonated in his belly. He was imploding. Exploding. His purpose, his focus, the creature of purity and spiritual ascendancy he was created to be—all of it, shattered and lost. He was beyond damaged, and now beyond control, as a fresh wave of need rushed through his veins and swelled even further the shaft of flesh that determined him male in body as well as life force.

But Gia was there, leaning over him, reaching for him, enfolding him. Her hands in his hair, on the sensitive nape of his neck, tracing his ears from lobe to tip and back again. Making him shiver, wringing mindless sounds from his throat.

Joachim wanted to touch her in return. He didn't know how or where. Everywhere and all at once. They would both be damned.

"Closer," he whispered.

"Yes…" She braced her palms on his thighs, breathing her acquiescence into his mouth, and shifted to kiss his cheek, his jaw, the tip of his nose, his eyelids. He'd never witnessed such tenderness and sensuality coexisting in one embrace.

His hands left the armrests at last and grasped her hips to anchor her, found her body resilient, curvaceous, the lacy texture of her panties enticing through the thin pajama bottoms she wore.

His erection pulsed in reaction as his unsteady fingertips traced the garment's thin lines over her buttocks. How could a simple article of lingerie stir him so intensely? It was cloth…material…solely of the physical plane, just like Gia was flesh and blood and bone.

No, she was more. Heat and softness, wetness and flavor. He wanted all of it. Her body, yes, but her words. Her laughter. Her heart. *He wanted her.* And the danger of her swelled and washed him anew with helpless desire.

The chair squeaked beneath him as he lunged forward and drew her down to her knees, not knowing what he intended—to stop her or to devour her sweet, open mouth.

Grasping her wrists, he wrenched her palms from his face and tried to speak, but her lips were inches away, swollen, moist, waiting, and the words he spoke belonged to a needful stranger. A human. A man.

"This body aches like never before," he nuzzled her cheek with searching lips, heart pummeling his bruised ribs as though it would explode from every pulse point. "What have you done to me, Gia?"

"I'm so sorry," she whispered, even as she turned her head to follow the slippery trail of his mouth. "I never meant this to happen. Tell me to stop, Joachim."

"I can't. I can't. Open your mouth to me again."

With a smothered groan she pressed against him, woman melting into man, their noses colliding in the rush of sexual urgency as they tilted their heads this way and that to find the natural, complementary fit of mouths.

Then they found their places, hands and lips settling in a trembling embrace. Gia's palms curved over his bare biceps. Joachim's fingers eased around her back, arching it to press her small, erect breasts closer to him. Separate of his own driving need, he became aware of the way she quivered in response, the way her lips parted beneath the pressure of his kiss, the way her breath caught and rushed when he dipped his tongue inside her mouth. Delight suffused him, a different satisfaction than any he'd experienced as a Heavenly attendant. Giving physical pleasure was an altogether more provocative and potent joy.

His hands, wildly roaming her back, eased, slowed to a sinuous stroke from nape to buttocks, reading her firm musculature, the graceful length of her spine, then up again, beneath her snug top, high, to burn his palm on the tender, silken flesh between her shoulder blades.

Intent now, he softened the pressure of his mouth, sipped in her gasping breaths, exhaled mindless adulations as his tongue traced a slick path along her bottom lip, then made a gentle, sliding foray into the warm recesses of her mouth. Teasing, probing, a man courting his mate. Seducing her. Making love to her.

He would stop, soon, soon…but he hadn't known that tongues could dance, nor bodies meld and twist as though soldered, nor the physical discomfort of bruises be forgotten beneath waves of pleasure so great, the intensity seared him.

His fingers found her hair, crept through the silken curls, and a murmur of sheer delight rumbled through him. At last he could admit it—he'd thought about touching her hair again and again, always at inappropriate times—during defense training or mission briefings or strategic, covert ventures into Therides' world—always when the impulse couldn't have come at a worse or more inane moment. Rappelling down concrete walls, crawling through sewers and dodging bullets, he'd thought of how those glossy, coiling strands would feel brushing his neck, his chest, his stomach, caressing his aching shaft, how they would feel crushed beneath his fingers in the heat of such a fervent moment as this—and the reality was more exquisite than anything his untried fantasies had conjured.

Their excitement mounted, the only sound in the room the strident rush of their breathing.

Joachim's knees fell open and Gia squirmed between them, twined one arm around his neck, her body undulating against him in a hungering bid for closeness. Her fingers threaded through the hair at the back of his head, her mouth resting against his in an instant of respite before desire took them again, and they rocked together, unconsciously seeking to merge, to absorb into one another.

His hips left the chair, that driven, swollen male part of him seeking succor in the give of her flesh, the pain of his desire far more intense than the screaming protest of bruised muscle and bone as he moved in restless rhythm against her belly. She pushed back, clumsily rose from her kneeling position to fit her pelvis against his and faltered, until he caught her bottom in his hands, hitched her knee against his hip and adjusted her so that the ridge of his manhood slid against hot, damp cotton soaked through from her body's desire.

"You're wet," he whispered, astonished, as he drew back to meet her lambent eyes.

"I know. I—"

Before she could apologize for the slick, delicious acquiescence of her body, Joachim drew her down again to grind her flesh against the pulsing shaft that strained against his stomach now, its swollen tip escaping the drawstring waistband of his pajamas. It was a mindless action, but he couldn't stop. He had to rub against her, to feel her slippery wetness on his engorged, aching flesh, yet it wasn't enough. Not enough pressure. Not enough heat.

"Closer," he whispered harshly. "Move against me."

Awkward, desperate, she straddled him fully, wedged her knees between his hips and the chair arms, and at last found her place. The chair squeaked a discordant rhythm as she pushed down and he thrust up, and they both groaned, foreheads bumping, skin moist with exertion and need.

Gasping now, Gia gripped the back of the chair behind his shoulders and threw back her head. The thin tank top stretched taut across her turgid nipples as she slid against him, grinding, swaying upon his throbbing shaft.

Faster. Faster. A wild, primitive ride. Her back arched like a bow, so that her dark curls swayed down her back and brushed his hands where they relentlessly gripped and guided her bottom.

"Oh, God. *I'm going to come.*"

When Gia's gritted whisper broke the terse silence, Joachim forgot his own driving need and fixed his hazy attention on her rapt, anguished face. He didn't fully understand her phraseology, but his body's memory gave him pause, and he held his breath, watching the tendons in her neck tighten, the flush rise from her breasts and stain her throat and cheeks, until a choked cry shook through her and her frame vibrated with jolting shudders. Waves of them, a magnificent storm battering her slender body in some kind of unearthly paroxysm.

Heat flooded between their bodies, the sweet, earthy scent of female desire filling Joachim's senses as Gia sagged against him and buried her nose in the curve of his neck. Astonished, he slid a hand up her back, twined his fingers in her curls and held her head, counting the little quivers that traveled up her spine like seismic aftershocks.

He, too, trembled, his throat too tight with emotion and untamed need to speak. Closing his eyes, he let his head fall back against the chair and floated to the sound of his own thundering heart, feeling its enormous quake lift his bruised chest, his stomach, the painful, rock-hard erection still pulsing between Gia's body and his belly.

Then the low, throaty sound of her voice caressed his ear.

"Do you know what you just did to me?" Her joyous, disbelieving laughter shivered along his senses. "I'm going to show you. With my mouth, with my hands on you everywhere. I'm going to make you come like I did, Joachim. Harder."

Before he could think, her hot mouth wrenched away to trail a heated, yearning path down his throat.

"Gia," he whispered fervently, letting her curls trickle through his hands as he rubbed his cheek and lips against the top of her head. He couldn't get enough of her. *Of this.* The drunken sensations. Soft. Hard. Wet.

More.

His body pleaded for it. Hers promised it. She slid off his lap and onto her knees again, seared a line of kisses over his hammering heart, over the bandages as though they didn't exist, then lower, to the contracted muscles of his stomach, where she tasted him with lips and tongue and the gentle graze of teeth. And then she blew a warm, moist breath against the exposed tip of his erection peeking from beneath his waistband.

Joachim swallowed a cry.

"Every part of you is beautiful," she whispered, the words brushing his rigid shaft. "Your face, your body, your cock. I want to hold it. I want to hold you…"

Thick anticipation snatched the breath from his chest. He wanted her hungry mouth on his naked flesh, biting him. Licking him. Engulfing the head of his penis and sucking. He wanted to piston himself in quick, oiled motion between her lips, to feel the tug and constriction of her throat. He didn't know how to ask for it. He only knew it was forbidden.

And too late. When her hands slid around his hips and she pressed a scalding kiss on the tip of his turgid flesh, Joachim went still, feeling the first liquid threat of orgasm, the pooling, coiling heat, the rolling fire in his scrotum.

The seraph in him chose that sweet, prime moment to scream awake…

Followed by a chorus of a million shouted warnings.

Joachim! Joachim! Joachim!

Whether they were real or imagined he no longer knew, only that they pulled him back, back to reality, back to the cold veracity of what he was doing with this human woman. He shuddered and caught Gia's wrists, forcing her upright.

"*Arrêt-toi, Gia,* listen to me. We're defying everything. *Le Créateur*—Michael—" he tried to speak lucidly, but his mind was clouded with desire and confusion and distress. "Fundamental law. *Il nous faut ne pas désobéir.*"

He could tell by the frown darkening her brow that she couldn't decipher his words, but his intent sank in immediately. She wrenched from his grasp, lost her balance before him and tumbled backward to land unceremoniously on her bottom.

"Please, let me—" He rose from his chair to help her, but she shook her head and drew her knees up tight to her chest, burying her face against them like a turtle retreating into its shell.

"Gia." The trembling hand he laid on the crown of her head read the answering shudder of her body, the sporadic breaths she sucked in as though she'd been drowning. Her shame seemed to seep through her very flesh and into his. Shame for the pleasure they'd brought each other. Shame for reveling in the beautiful nuances of this physical world.

"Forgive me," he whispered, easing down beside her. "Will you forgive me? My actions—"

"—Were *human*." She raised her dark head at last and looked at him, lashes spiked with tears. Humiliation stained her cheeks, and the bruising effect of his kiss had deepened her lips to crimson velvet. She'd never looked more beautiful than at this raw, unguarded moment. "I have to go."

"Not like this." Anger snapped at the edges of his remorse, shifting him back into military comportment. He straightened, adjusted his traitorous penis back inside his pants and stared down at her, torn between ire and confusion. "You will wait. We'll discuss this first."

"I'm not one of your operatives! I will not wait and listen to your damned voice of reason—which, incidentally, I can't translate!" She found her balance and got to her feet, joints popping in protest of her abrupt movements. She made it three steps before an efficient tap sounded at the door.

"Joachim, I have something for your pain that won't make you sleepy." Soleil didn't wait for an invitation and briskly threw open the door.

Instantly she stopped, her catlike gaze taking in the undisguised moment of anguish and uncensored passion between her leader and the woman they were assigned to shield from all forms of peril.

For a moment, no one spoke or even moved. Then Gia pushed by Soleil, her footsteps echoing her urgency to flee as they faded down the corridor.

In the silence, Joachim sank to the chair, braced his elbows on the armrests and buried his face in his hands. "Thank you, Soleil, for your thoughtfulness," he said numbly, not caring what assumptions she made because nothing could be as shameful as the truth.

He'd wanted to take Gia, drive himself into her soft wet heat, soak in her pleasure and release his own. He still did. A hungry fire simmered in the heart of his manhood, stretching to life like a monster awakened from a deep slumber.

Without looking at Soleil, he said, "Leave me now."

Soleil backed from the room, drawing the door closed behind her. He waited the beat of a minute, and for the first time in any mission, activated his quarters' privacy locks. Then he turned out the lights and headed into the small anteroom beyond his office, where his cot waited.

For a long time he lay in the viscous, velvet darkness, covers kicked to the foot of the mattress, one arm flung above his head, counting the beat of his heart as it echoed in his ears, his throat, his wounded ribs, his still-rigid shaft.

When he couldn't stand the throbbing pressure any more, he pulled the string on his pajama bottoms, slid a hand beneath the loosened waistband and encircled his erection with curious fingers, measuring its heat and breadth. It pulsed and strained in the cradle of his palm, nudging him into action. He shoved the bottoms down far enough to free himself, and this time when his hand returned to grasp his flesh, it was with rhythmic purpose.

Joachim let his mind drift, away from his duties, away from Gia, away from disgrace. The orgasm he'd withheld earlier rushed to the forefront with alarming speed, and he slowed his stroke to savor it, denying himself, building the sweet agony until the need for relief became too great to bear. His free hand clutched the pillow beneath his head, his muscles trembling and going damp as he thrust violently into his own grasp. A ragged groan built in his throat, but he bit it back, refusing to give voice to his pathetic human condition.

He thought of Gia just once, the instant before he ejaculated.

He'd failed her. He'd promised before Creator and seraphim and the Celestial Dominions to guard her very soul, but in the end, he hadn't protected her from the most unforeseen, and therefore insidious, danger.

Him.

*****

You come to Contact with a troubled mind.

Joachim had no response to the Archangel's observation. Six hours after experiencing the most abject frailty of humanity, his body lay supine on the unforgiving concrete, his forehead pressed to the floor, arms outstretched in a position of total humility. His spirit had temporarily left the physical shell to meet Michael, and now stood before the Great Warrior in a nether limbo between realms, transparent in form and emotion.

The Archangel shimmered in iridescent shades of silvered blues and greens. His watchful appraisal penetrated Joachim's conscience, but how much Michael read of his troubled thoughts, Joachim couldn't gauge.

He chose the safe route to begin the debriefing. "We have retrieved the Medallion."

"With physical consequences to you and Aristide," the Archangel noted.

"Minor injuries. The rest of the team was unharmed. Many of the nephil's men—there were casualties. One more notable than the others."

"The Daughter of Longinus protected you," Michael said with a touch of humor. "She's not only fierce of will, but of spirit."

Joachim didn't trust himself to comment on Gia without giving away his inner turbulence. "Out of this defensive, we were able to attain a body for Jordan. He's with us now, another ally to add to the crusade. All we have to do is locate the Spear and contain Therides. Circumstances seem to be falling into place with astonishing ease."

"This, then, is the reason for your disquiet?"

A testing question, perhaps.

Joachim hesitated, watching the waves of spiritual energy that undulated through Michael's form. "It's easy to feel complacent when there seems to be so little resistance from the nephil's side. This sense of success leads me to believe something darker awaits, something perhaps the operatives or Intel have not anticipated."

"There's peril and surprise in every reconnaissance, Joachim. Your anxiety is not unfounded. Be ever watchful." Michael folded his hands behind him and paced a few steps, his aura melding into indigo and lavender. "How soon will we have the Spear?"

"Forthwith. The Daughter of Longinus has tested the Medallion. The gift of Sight is strong within her and needs little nurturing."

"Extraordinary." The Archangel seemed to mull this phenomenon over, a mixture of awe and delight softening his stern, ivory features. "This requires a clear passage between a human soul and celestial energy. Perhaps she is more chaste of heart and mind than Intel indicated."

"Perhaps," Joachim murmured, driving away the decidedly *unchaste* image of Gia kneeling before him, her hands on his naked skin, her soft mouth opening beneath his searching kiss.

Guilt and duty skirmished in his psyche, and he carefully redirected each new erotic memory that battered him, aware of

Michael's astuteness when it came to reading the minds of his militia.

But the Archangel seemed oblivious to the duality of Joachim's thought patterns, a sure sign that the threat of Therides had grown daunting enough to preoccupy his usually incisive perception. "Assemble the team in advance, Joachim. As projected, you will assume field command for the Spear's retrieval."

Joachim nodded. "Any suggestions as to who makes up the team?"

"Olivier's leg is healed?"

"Nearly."

"He'll assume your second-in-command. Aristide and Dmitri as perimeter security leaders, and Jordan in communications. And of course, the Daughter of—"

"Gia," Joachim said softly. "Her name in this lifetime is Gia."

Michael stopped and stared at him. "I discern something in your voice. A heaviness. You are concerned for her safety?"

"Of course."

"She has proven herself capable of defensive action. Set aside your concerns, Joachim. Once you've obtained the Medallion and Spear, you will need to guard them with unwavering focus, thinking of nothing—and no one—else."

Joachim's anxiety leaped, but he kept his voice carefully even. "But surely she isn't dispensable. As a Daughter of Longinus—"

"As a Daughter of Longinus, she alone can wield the Spear. She's indispensable until the demon is destroyed. At that time—" Michael resumed pacing, his chin lifting in his particular imperious fashion. "The end battle will be a daunting one, and some of our soldiers will be lost to Therides' militia. If chance decrees that her body and soul be separated, she'll progress into cycle, as with any mortal death."

"But I promised to protect her to the end."

Michael paused to regard Joachim with a gentle smile. "Certainly we all form attachments to our wards, but this is no different than any of the myriad missions you've undertaken before. As her guardian, you'll do your best to protect her, but you will not interfere when Creator calls her into passage."

Joachim averted his gaze, unable to find the words to reply.

"Joachim?"

Gritting his jaw, he finally looked at the Warrior Archangel. "Will that be all?"

"You are dismissed," Michael said, and the remote note of curiosity in his voice did nothing to delay Joachim's abrupt disconnection.

Returning to his bruised body and icy physical consciousness, Joachim felt the chill of the concrete seep into his troubled mind. Somewhere outside the Contact chamber, a door closed, footsteps passed, voices muffled.

With a jerk, he startled out of his trance and raised his head from the floor. The crucifix etched into the steel wall before him wavered into focus.

And suddenly his isolation seemed crushing.

While he stood guard on this unforgiving and inhospitable planet, who stood guard over *him*? He wasn't supposed to need direction. It was why Michael had chosen him to lead in the first place. All this time he'd proved himself so reliable, so impervious. And now he felt utterly, wholly displaced.

He couldn't turn to the Archangel. He'd be deemed inappropriate to lead this mission and stripped of his duties. Was he alone in his anguish, then? As homeless and disjointed as the emptiness in his chest indicated?

His own words, whispered against Gia's tear-stained cheek as he'd carried her, broken, into the bunker, resounded through his heart. *All your life you have walked in Creator's presence, with a hundred guardians surrounding you. Now more than ever, you are home.*

Crawling painfully to his knees, he buried his face in his hands, mentally closed off the communication channels to all Dominions and spoke directly and confidentially to Creator.

My Father, protect her. I don't know if I can do it alone.

* * * * *

"Very good, Gia. Now take another deep breath and begin the downward count."

Soleil's tranquil tone washed over Gia in silken waves as she lay prone on the blue gymnastics mat, hands resting at her sides, the Medallion a warm, solid weight between her breasts. The blonde seraph sat cross-legged beside her, a wavering mirage in the dim coolness as Gia's eyelids slid closed.

Ten, nine, eight…

"Thinking of nothing but the numbers and the sensation of sinking deep into relaxation…"

Six, five four… Her limbs weighed a hundred pounds each, pressing like dumbbells into the spongy mat.

"Clearing all images and thoughts from your mind, so that it's blank and open to receive."

Two, one…

"Another deep breath. You are not asleep, but completely relaxed, your mind a channel where information will gather freely." A soft rustling indicated Soleil had shifted her weight on the mat by Gia's head. "Soon the first images will come to you. When they do, you may speak."

In her mind's eye, Gia stood in nothingness, her eyes straining for the first sign of the Spear's location. Soleil had guaranteed that under hypnosis, it would come more easily. As promised, a mental screen flashed before her, images of a picturesque village, as quaint and brightly tinted as a postcard.

"There's a town." The words slid from Gia's tongue, leaden, slurred with drowsiness. "Trees. Huge hills and countryside around it. Forest, everywhere."

"Very good." The faint sound of a pen scratching across a notepad served as a faint reminder that Gia existed simultaneously in a physical and deeply subconscious state. "What else do you see?"

"A big…church? No, a cathedral. Cobblestone. Canals."

The writing stopped. "You are in Europe?"

"Western." A triangular object appeared on the screen, like an illuminated map, one corner glowing with golden certainty. "This place sits against two countries. Germany!" At her excited assertion, Soleil's voice swirled around her again, soothing.

"Very good, Gia. Very good. Germany. I'm going to suggest some names to you. You tell me if these ring true." Paper rustled. "Berlin. Bonn. Dresden. Frankfurt—"

"Frankfurt," Gia said quickly, her brow furrowed as she tried to decipher the quickening images that flashed on her mental screen.

"The Spear is in Frankfurt?"

"No." A wry smile touched her mouth at the undeniable clue that appeared before her. "We'll have to take a train from Frankfurt."

A tap at the gymnasium door shattered her concentration, lifting her through layers of hypnotic haze to the surface of consciousness. With a murmured apology, Soleil got to her feet and crossed the mat to speak in low tones with whoever had summoned her.

Groggy, Gia sat up and pushed her curls back from her face. Three figures stood at the glass observation window—Olivier, Nicodemus and off to one side, his expression remote, Joachim.

Their gazes locked through the window, then heat flooded Gia's face and she looked away. She hadn't spoken to him for almost twenty-four hours, but the humiliation of what had happened between them in his office still stung as potently as if he'd rejected her just a moment before.

Their relationship was forever changed, and a knot of

regret tightened her throat at the fresh realization. She blamed herself. He'd given her the kiss-of-death "Let's Be Friends" speech. God, how much more blatant could he have been? He didn't want her, and she'd kissed him anyway.

Open your mouth to me again, Gia.

Okay, maybe he'd wanted her a little bit. At one point in their brief clinch, he'd seemed to want her *a lot*. In fact, the way his hands moved over her body had led her to believe he was as passionate as she. He was a young, healthy man after all, one whose body apparently had missed sex since a new and virginal soul had taken up residence.

It was hardly consolation to the shame curling through her when she recalled how she'd started it so indecorously, kissing him, climbing all over him, and to make matters worse, *having an orgasm* right there in his office, where anyone could have walked in—and *did*. Soleil.

Gia's eyes darted in the blonde's direction as she talked to Dmitri at the door. Soleil hadn't acted any differently to Gia today than any other day, treating her with polite, if distant, solicitude. But surely she wondered about what she'd stumbled upon. There was no question Joachim had broken some sort of rule by consorting physically—*sexually*—with a human woman he was sworn to protect. How loyal was Soleil to her mission leader? Would she turn him in to whoever governed the operatives, and if so, what would the consequences be for Joachim?

Gia swallowed a fresh surge of dismay. This was all her fault. The minute she could get him alone again—if such a miracle were even possible now—she'd apologize. Swear to keep her distance. Convince him that she hadn't meant any of it, that it was a delayed reaction to the adrenaline overload from retrieving the Medallion.

God help her, she wouldn't cause any more trouble for him. He'd done nothing but protect and mentor and support her. The least she could do was keep her greedy hands off him.

When she glanced up again, disappointment sent her

stomach plunging. Joachim was gone, and Jordan stood in his place, conferring with the other two seraphs. Gia didn't wonder what they were discussing. Suddenly she was too weary to care.

Soleil turned to her with a smile. "You've done quite well today, Gia. We'll make another go of it after your defense training with Dmitri. Are you up to it?"

"I'm up for anything," Gia said. Except the spiraling sense that she'd irreparably distanced the one person who mattered most to her in this new life.

Chapter Fifteen

Joachim rubbed the bridge of his nose, drew a deep breath and glanced back at the computer screen. "You're certain you've lost the target?"

"Only temporarily. Joachim..." Aristide's distressed face wavered on the monitor. "I don't know how it happened. We have two shadow teams monitoring him constantly. Is it possible the demon's possession could have granted Rossi supernatural abilities? Enough to slip from our surveillance?"

"Anything is possible when it comes to nephilim. We don't fully understand their abilities in human form, nor how this dimension affects them. All we know is that the Spear will send him back to Hell." Urgency plucked at his nerves. Time was short, and he imagined the nephil's pervasive reach, like an insect's antennae, crawling the Earth in search of the Spear.

"Michael's going to recall me for this, isn't he?" Aristide sighed.

Joachim resisted a humorless smile. If anyone were recalled, it should be *him*. He'd shoved aside every guideline, every celestial law, since the moment he first saw Gia Rossi's lithe, golden body sprawled on that chaise lounge by the pool. His constant state of distraction had affected every part of this mission. Now, even the shadow teams were losing ground.

Aristide's baritone rumbled through the monitor, pulling him from his dark musings. "Has Gia come forth with the Spear's location?"

"Nearly. Soleil is working with her." Joachim paused, searching for the right way to reassure his subordinate. "I'll let Tactical know what's happened, and we'll attempt to rectify this before you debrief with Michael. Continue with the directive, watching all locations Rossi frequents. Things aren't going well for him. I have no doubt he's on a sub-mission to recruit more bodies as vehicles for the nephilim incursion."

"Thank you, Joachim. I blame myself for this snag in the mission's progress."

"No, Ari. We move as one unit. The blame is not yours to shoulder alone." He offered his team member a supportive smile and clicked off communication, only then allowing the tension of this latest development to seep through his muscles.

With a deep sigh, he sat back in his desk chair and rubbed his jaw, his mind bouncing through the methods they could use to extract the Spear's whereabouts more quickly from Gia. If she became stressed or pressured, it would slow the process. But something was blocking her cognitive passages—and he didn't have to search hard for the culprit.

No doubt any attempt to hold a normal conversation with her after the fiasco in his office two nights ago would result in additional tension for her. For them both. He couldn't go on avoiding her though. At some point he had to set her mind at ease, no matter how much his own heart rolled within his chest at the memory of their actions.

Swallowing a rush of unease, Joachim leaned forward and pressed the intercom on his desk. "Soleil, are you there?"

"Of course," came the prompt reply.

"Find Gia for me."

Pause. "All right. And then?"

"Tell her I need to see her."

"You want me to send her to your office…alone?"

Irritation warmed his cheeks. "Just locate her." He stopped, his frown deepening. "Are you questioning my intentions?"

"I hadn't thought so," she said calmly. "But perhaps you know me better than I know myself."

He closed his eyes. A dull pain throbbed in his bruised temple. It kept time with his pulse, which hammered a driving heaviness he didn't understand. "We need to discuss your issues regarding Gia."

"And yours," she replied, succinct and forthright, as was her manner. "Is this a good time for you?"

"No." He bit back his impatience and exhaled through clenched teeth, focusing beyond the personal tension between them. He wouldn't allow his turbulence with Gia to sway his relationship with the rest of his team. "It will have to wait. Locate Gia for me, Soleil. That will do."

"Certainly," she said.

*****

The breeze caressed Gia's skin, scented with the faint smokiness of autumn. In another two weeks the summer would fade into a brisk chill and the dying leaves would infuse the world with color, a change she welcomed every year. She was tired of the stifling heat. Tired of brittle grass and death and danger.

Tired of the emptiness and frustration that nothing but another taste of Joachim could touch.

She plucked a dandelion from the field as she sauntered a few feet—not too far—from the bunker's entry chute, and thought about making a wish and blowing the fluffy seeds to the sky. It used to be so easy to rattle off goals and dreams when there was no guarantee they'd ever come true. Easy when she had nothing but simple poverty surrounding her. Her marriage to Vincent had changed all that, filling the emptiness in her soul with material luxury and false affection.

She shuddered and hugged herself, her gaze scanning the windswept field. How long had her husband been possessed by the nephil? Maybe since before she'd met him. The thought that she'd laughed with him, confided in him, had sex with him—a demon, the basest embodiment of evil—made her want to live permanently beneath the shower spray, scrubbing all memory of his chilled touch from her skin.

She'd noticed how cold his hands were, questioned him about it a million times. He couldn't seem to get warm, no matter how the summer temperatures soared outside.

A sick laugh bubbled up in Gia's throat. She'd constantly worried he was coming down with something. "Nothing a good exorcist couldn't cure," she muttered, flicking a gnat off her arm.

"To whom do you speak?"

The voice behind her sent a jolt of electricity to the tips of her toes, and she whirled around, heart pounding. Joachim stood a few feet away in the tall grass, watching her. She hadn't heard his approach and suddenly she felt sabotaged. By him. By the unwelcome avalanche of desire that rushed through her body with just a look.

Self-consciousness struck her dumb. "I—was I talking?"

"Aloud." He strolled toward her, brushing the waist-high grass with the palm of his hand. In his wake, lemon-winged butterflies fluttered into the sky, roused by his enigmatic presence. "You're preoccupied."

"I needed fresh air. All of Soleil's hypnotic mumbo-jumbo is starting to get to me." A wry smile tilted her lips. "How are *you* feeling? Your bruises have faded."

"This body is nearly healed." He stopped beside her and nodded at the dandelion she held. "I've seen children blow the seeds from the stem."

"You're supposed to make a wish first." She handed him the stem. "Try it."

He twirled it, studying it from all sides. "Seraphim wish for nothing."

Gia rolled her eyes. "How about just this once? For a successful mission?"

His gaze met hers, vibrant in the brilliant sun. "Done."

"Now blow on it."

He brought it nearly to his lips, his lashes shielding his expression as he studied the fluffy head. Then he extended it to her.

Gia's heart, already tripping, performed an impressive somersault. Pursing her lips, she used the last remnants of breath in her lungs and blew the seeds into the air. The fluffy debris drifted like woodland fairies, some striking out on a windy adventure, others sailing into the surrounding grass. A few landed in Gia's curls. She could see them clinging to the strands on her forehead and brushed them aside with a hand.

"You can make that wish come true," Joachim said, letting the forlorn stem fall from his fingers. "Find the Spear, Gia."

"We've narrowed the location." She took a few steps back, a subconscious escape. "We know it's in Bavaria. Every time I close my eyes I see the town, the cathedral and the cobblestone streets, the post-World War II architecture…" Nervousness fueled her words, sped them to a telltale frenzy that he took in with a perplexed frown, the way a customer eyes an overzealous car salesman.

She sounded crazy, but pride propelled her onward. "I've really gotten good at focusing and blocking out all other images and distractions—just the town, and it's getting easier every time." Heat suffused her cheeks, stole her momentum and she finally stopped. "Look, Joachim, I'm doing the best I can."

"I know." After a moment, he slipped his hand into the pocket of his white linen pants and withdrew the Medallion. "Let me help you."

She hesitated, wondering at his intention. "You do realize this is the first time we've spoken to each other since the other night."

"Yes." His attention was focused on the Medallion, his thumb rubbing across the raised figure of the Archangel Michael standing in the flames, Spear of Longinus held aloft. "Tell me, Mrs. Torio, how to close this distance between us."

"I like this distance. I need to not feel anything for you." Her throat tightened and tears stung behind her eyes as if by magic. God, just a sideways look from this man—this angel—

could make her cry. He tormented her simply by *being*, but the terrible pleasure of seeing his face, of hearing his voice this close and intimate, was an undeniable relief.

After forty-eight hours of a Joachim-free existence, she missed him. His charismatic presence, his blue eyes, the cultured, careful way he spoke. The way he said her name in that between-the-sheets, sultry slur. She'd gotten used to him, that was all. It wasn't too late. The damage could be undone.

She motioned to the Medallion with a half-hearted smile. "That thing's supposed to work miracles. Maybe it can wipe out what happened in your office the other night."

"No." His eyes met hers. "What happened in my office is a memory we share. Do you cast aside your portion so easily?"

"No." She sighed. "But it's not for lack of trying. You?"

"I choose to keep every memory of you."

Wayward humor quirked a corner of her mouth, even as her pulse soared. "You couldn't weed out some of the more mortifying moments, I don't suppose."

"No. I haven't a choice." He held out his hand and waited for her to grasp it. "Come with me."

"Why? Where are we going?"

"We're going to call the Spear," he said.

*****

They knelt in the crisp, fragrant grass, half a mile from the bunker and any interruptions. Nearby, in the dappled sunlight, a narrow creek filled the air with the song of trickling water. Birds chirped, cicadas rattled in waves, rising and falling as they called to each other.

His home must be like this, Gia thought, studying the bridge of Joachim's nose as he gently untangled the Medallion's chain in preparation to put it around her neck. No strife, only serene beauty. Even in the midst of danger, tension and darkness, tranquility pervaded his being. He had no fear. He had his Creator. He had faith in himself and in the space around him.

He also believed in her ability to fulfill her part in capturing Therides—or at least appeared to. If not, he was a damned fine actor.

Raising his head, he let his gaze settle on her features. Then he held open the chain, and she ducked her head to receive it around her neck. The Medallion slid inside her tank top and between her breasts, where it rested, a cool weight, until the heat from her skin warmed it.

"Here," he whispered, and taking her hand, drew her closer, so that their knees touched. "Close your eyes."

Nervous tension made her mouth go dry and her heart flop like a netted fish in her chest. "Do I need to count down? Soleil says—"

"Soleil is not here." He passed a hand over her eyelids, and they closed involuntarily. The world spun and dipped and pulsed with light, as it had the day she saw his true angelic form. Then his touch returned, his fingers lacing through hers, first one hand, then the other, anchoring her to the earth.

"Clear your conscience," his voice was as gentle and indigenous as the wind sifting through the tree canopy overhead. "Discard your regret."

Vincent. His touch. Her revulsion and shame.

"What's past is past."

Joachim. His touch. Her shame and desire.

"Look now to the future. To all eyes but Creator's, it is a blank slate. Your free will writes upon it and if you follow your heart, you'll impart a great tale." He paused, and his discerning regard stabbed through her trance. "You're holding your breath, Gia."

She'd been too lulled by his seductive tone to even think about oxygen. Cheeks hot, she sucked in a much-needed breath, then sat back on her heels and gripped his hands against her knees. His palms were dry and warm, while hers had gone utterly damp. He held her fingers loosely, and she clutched his. Didn't he understand how strange this all seemed to her, regular old Gia Torio from the inner-city slums of Chicago? And beyond that—and even worse—what his mere presence did to her?

"Okay, I'm breathing." *With difficulty*. "Now what?"

Dry leaves and debris rustled beneath his weight. He was moving, but she didn't dare open her eyes to track him. It would only make her more nervous. She had to trust him. Trust this man who had returned her kisses and touches with fevered desire, only to withdraw because his sense of spiritual duty was stronger than his physical needs.

Such a man was annoyingly trustworthy.

His right hand disentangled from hers. A second later, it slid around the back of her neck, and his words brushed close to her lips, soft words in French whose chanting rhythm denoted a prayer.

This time Gia did open her eyes and found herself studying the dark sweep of his lashes, blurred at such close range. Her heartbeat jackhammered against her ribs. The space of a single kiss separated their lips, but it never came. Instead, his forehead rested against hers, his fingers warm on the nape of her neck, and the flare of desire that burned through her settled to a low simmer in her womb. Her lashes closed again. He didn't intend to kiss her. This wasn't sexual. It was beyond anything corporeal.

For a moment they remained that way, kneeling in the leaves, foreheads pressed, fingers entwined. Then images began to materialize like a slideshow behind her eyelids, as thin and easily rent as fluttering sheets of rice paper. A cathedral, the cobblestone streets, two canals running side by side.

Her lashes fluttered. Here was something new added to the scene—geese, sailing in a uniform squadron against the cornflower sky. Children's laughter and voices…a school. A morning market erected in the Gothic spire's shadows, fruits and vegetables and flowers splashing color over every kiosk, the scent of delectable foods wafting on the tepid breeze. An accordionist in lederhosen, churning out *Oktoberfest* tunes for the growing pile of euros in his overturned feathered cap. Men laughing at a table inside a fast-food joint.

A fast-food joint?

"What do you see?" Joachim's voice barely brushed her ears.

"A hamburger joint," she said, her brow furrowed with the attempt to make sense of the bizarre details. "They're drinking beer. Eating French fries."

City gates. *Eisenhof* painted across a wooden plaque in faded crimson letters.

"Eisen…hof?" The word slipped from her lips and her eyes popped open, realization churning excitement in her stomach. "Joachim, the town is Eisenhof! Southwestern Germany, near France." She drew back to meet his gaze and pulled the Medallion from beneath her shirt, where it had begun to burn the tender skin between her breasts. "Is that possible? Is there such a town?"

"Eisenhof exists." A slow smile tugged at his lips. "Have you ever been to Germany?"

Gia shook her head, giddy with exhilaration and triumph as she fingered the unnaturally hot metal of the Medallion.

"Tomorrow at this time, you will say differently."

"We're going to Germany?"

"Immediately." He stopped, his blue eyes intent on her face as his smile faded to something softer. "Gia, thank you."

"We did it?"

"We're so very, very close."

And his warm laughter rolled over her as she fell back into the leaves, arms spread wide, the sunlight filling her soul and senses.

* * * * *

"Several elements of tomorrow's operation have yet to be defined." Joachim braced his palms on the conference table, his attention moving from Soleil to Olivier, who had gathered in the conference room for the briefing. To his left, Gia sat in quiet contemplation, absently caressing the wooden box that contained the Medallion.

"Gia has pinpointed the approximate vicinity of the Spear, in southwestern Germany. Eisenhof is a small city, population twenty thousand. It shouldn't be difficult to zero in on the Spear's energy—there will be less mental static than in a larger city. However..." His gaze drifted to Olivier's mild frown, then to Soleil's inscrutable features. "The nephil has temporarily slipped from our surveillance. While I believe it's merely in an attempt to recruit more physical vehicles for the nephilim invasion, it's impossible to predict what obstacles we face when we arrive in Eisenhof."

Olivier sat forward, the usual easy humor in his features sobered by concern. "It seems more likely that he would be on a personal mission to obtain the Spear. Therides himself described it as a race, did he not? No doubt with his resources, he knows we have located the Spear."

"The possibility exists."

"Then shouldn't we take a larger team to Germany?"

Joachim shook his head. "The object is subterfuge. A larger group would draw attention. We must rely on our defensive skills, and even more, on our ability to determine impending conflict. It may be that nothing will happen at all. We'll simply find the Spear, retrieve it and return to the United States with no impediment."

"Or it may be we're walking into a major ambush," Olivier pointed out.

Joachim's brows lifted. "My gut tells me that time has not yet come. But this trip to Germany is no different than any operation we're assigned, Liv. If you're reticent—"

"Reticent? *Restless.*" A twinkle of humor appeared in his gray eyes. "Too long sequestered with this lame leg. I'm ready for action, Boss."

"Good." Joachim's lips twitched before he returned his attention to the file in front of him. "This operation will naturally be undercover. Olivier and Soleil, you'll be sentinels, shadowing Gia and me. We'll travel as separate couples, tourists on vacation. Arrangements have been made for accommodations in Eisenhof. Maybe more than one night, and in separate inns. This is a brief mission, but a dangerous one. Michael has ordered we protect the Spear at all cost. It's our focus, it's why we're here." He paused, a muscle jumping in his jaw as he regarded his companions. "Any questions or concerns?"

Gia straightened and met his eyes. "You're saying I'm going to go along when we do the actual retrieval of the Spear? The whole breaking-and-entering thing, the covert sneaking around someone's property in the dead of night?" At his nod, she grimaced. "I'm not trained in reconnaissance like Soleil or Olivier, Joachim. What kind of partner will I make?"

"We don't know where the Spear is yet, Gia," Soleil said. "Since you are the keeper of the Medallion and Joachim is team leader, it makes sense that you work together in this capacity. Besides…" She stood, tall and icy beneath the piercing track lights overhead. "This is an undercover operation, where we must act as tourist couples on vacation. You two are quite convincing as lovers."

Gia froze.

Awkward silence blanketed the room. For a moment, no one moved. Then Joachim forced himself to act, to suffocate the embarrassment rising to his face in a wave of heat. Gathering the file before him, he gave his team members a tight, cursory smile. "Get some rest. Tomorrow begins the denouement of our mission."

Gia hurried from the conference room without looking at him again. Olivier, eyebrows raised, followed, shooting his leader a questioning glance as he sauntered out the door.

That left Soleil, and if they weren't both celestial beings with purely benevolent hearts, Joachim would have gladly throttled her. When she started out the door, he barked, "*Wait.*"

She paused and half-glanced over her shoulder, her slender fingers on the knob. "Allow me to say—"

"I allow you to say nothing. Shut the door and sit. We're resolving this, here and now. I talk, you listen. And then, if I'm feeling more reasonable, you may explain your thoughtlessness."

"You don't look reasonable," she said impassively, pulling out a chair and seating herself at the table. "You look guilty."

"Of what?" Ire plucked at his nerves despite his determination to keep it restrained. "You accuse me, Soleil. Of what am I culpable?"

"Of harboring inappropriate feelings for Gia Rossi." For the first time, her expression shifted from placidity to pointed dismay. "If Michael knew, he'd…he'd—"

"Revoke my leadership? But surely that's not what concerns you." Bracing his palms on the table, he stared at her across its glossy expanse. "What is it, then?"

"So you do admit to having feelings for her." The tension smoothed from her brow, but his gaze didn't miss the way her fists clenched in her lap.

"We are not perfect, infallible beings, Soleil," he said softly. "We can only aspire to it. Down here in this dimension, battered by temptation and fallacy and dangers from all realms, I've run a million missions. I've guarded a million souls and felt something for each of them. Haven't you?"

"But your eyes follow her every move, Joachim." She sat forward, lips thinned. "You regard her the way a man considers a woman. Celestial law decrees that we mustn't misuse our human vehicles to engage in physical pleasure, and yet I believe I walked into your office two nights ago at the end of something quite physical—and pleasurable—between you and Gia."

Joachim bowed his head, drawing in measured breaths as various responses stuttered through his mind. She was right, but he didn't understand her indignation.

"What do you fear?" he asked, sitting across from her. "You

fear for my well-being? Your own? Is this even about fear?"

In the silence, turmoil and uncertainty volleyed between them. At last, she shifted and looked at him. "We'll lose you, of course. You'll be recalled, stripped of your authority."

"Michael is not a tyrant," he said gently.

"No, but he dislikes secrecy among his operatives, and that's what you're doing. You're secreting feelings for this human woman."

"I'm struggling with feelings for this human woman. I'm fighting them."

"You've acted on them."

"Not to the extent that you imagine."

But so very close.

Soleil got to her feet without waiting for dismissal, her jewel-like green eyes searching his face. "It will happen."

"Then I'll well deserve the consequences. Soleil..." He stood and rounded the table to where she lingered, and found her expression wavering between guarded disapproval and pain. "We are part of each other, you and I. Bound at the heart. Through myriad universes and operations, we have supported one another. Why, now, do you not trust me as your leader and friend?"

"Because," she began, then stopped and looked away, as though she couldn't bear to meet his gaze. "Because this time is different. With every day that passes, you grow more human, more tethered to this Earth, and I feel you slipping away from me."

Tears sparkled on her lashes. "Because Gia Rossi cannot love you through myriad universes and operations as I...as..." She stopped, drew a breath, and the anguish seeped from her features, replaced by waxy composure. "Gia can only offer you fleeting happiness for a matter of years. And for this you will choose cycle? Or even worse, a frail human lifetime on this corrupt planet?"

At last he understood, and warm regret uncurled through his chest, tightening his throat, burning his eyes. This wasn't supposed to happen between seraphs, between *friends*. And yet here she stood, an angel in a human body, full of emotions and yearning she'd brought with her from the skies—not so very different from him. How long had she felt this way? Why hadn't he recognized it before?

"Ah, Soleil," he whispered, and caught her hand, but she tugged free and slipped out the door, leaving him with the echoes of celestial wisdom.

Chapter Sixteen

Olivier shouldered his backpack and leaned to pull Soleil's duffel from her arm as they hiked through the airport terminal, a gesture of tender consideration that made them appear like a real couple traveling together.

"I can manage," she said with a note of surprise in her voice. But she didn't argue further when he winked at her, slung the duffel over his big shoulder and kept on, leaving her burdened only with a small overnight bag.

A few feet behind them, Gia and Joachim walked side by side in silence, their awareness of each other excruciating. They, too, were supposed to be a young married couple.

Right now, their "marriage" seemed in desperate need of counseling. They hadn't spoken since an awkward greeting that morning in the bunker mess hall.

"Maybe we're having a fight," Gia offered aloud, sliding him a sideways glance without further elaboration.

Joachim's profile didn't alter in the slightest. He never even looked at her, but he slowed his pace, and his fingers brushed her elbow. A cursory, husbandly gesture, meant for no one but the public at large. Gia wasn't impressed.

The strain wasn't limited to her and Joachim. Ever since Soleil's snide remark during the briefing last night, the level of tension at seraphim headquarters had permeated every steel- and glass-encased space. Gia and Soleil, Soleil and Joachim, Joachim and Gia…no one was speaking, except, of course, Olivier, who didn't seem to notice anything amiss and would probably talk to a blank wall if one presented itself.

Gia's silence toward Soleil was born of wounded astonishment. She couldn't understand why Soleil—a seraphic guardian of Creator's throne, for Pete's sake!—would show her claws as though she were a common woman with an ulterior motive for stirring trouble.

Joachim was undeniably bothered by the episode, as well. Acrimony chilled the air between him and the cool blonde. Breakfast had been an exercise in icy family dysfunction.

Gia hadn't thought angels fought with each other. Then again, Joachim had told her there was little difference in the emotional makeup of a human and a seraph. Was it possible that he and Soleil shared something that stretched beyond the usual angelic *love-one-another* credo?

Her steps slowed as the ideas began to coagulate in her mind. Why hadn't she seen it before? It was so obvious! Maybe in past missions, Soleil and Joachim hadn't had a *thing*, but this time they had both adopted beautiful and desirable bodies. A healthy, red-blooded man and woman, both with tightly reined self-control, stuck together in close quarters, a hundred feet underground…

She clenched her jaw, shifted her duffel to her other shoulder and resumed speed, this time moving a few steps beyond Joachim, where she remained.

Of its own accord, her attention fixed on the sway of Soleil's slender hips up ahead, the silky brush of her flaxen hair against her back. Male passengers passing in the opposite direction swiveled to look at her, and even some women.

If *Gia* could capture Joachim's affections—although obviously just a fleeting failure in judgment for him—what must the daily sight of such an exquisite fellow seraph do to the male senses he constantly battled?

Realization snagged in her throat, and she recognized the acrid flavor of jealousy.

Snap out of it, Gia!

At last, mercifully, they reached the airline gate and approached the ticket agent. They got in line behind Olivier and Soleil at the check-in counter, and while they waited, Joachim turned to regard Gia.

She ignored him, her thumb absently twirling the simple gold band she wore on her left hand as part of her "disguise". He'd offered it to her that morning as they rode the freight elevator to the bunker's surface.

"What's this?" she'd asked, bemused.

"A wedding ring. Put it on," he'd said tonelessly.

One heck of a romantic proposal.

His band matched it. Both rings plain and significantly… insignificant.

He was still watching her. While the typically gregarious Olivier chatted and laughed with the ticket agent, Joachim stared at Gia, unrelenting, until heat flooded her cheeks. When she couldn't stand another second of his unfaltering scrutiny, she glared at him.

He wore a shuttered expression, but his attention was fixed on her, a silent demand she didn't understand.

She stared back at him, anger stabbing through her consternation. She wanted her distance back, the protective space he had shattered, most recently by kneeling with her in the woods with the Medallion as the only barrier between them. Encouraging her. Touching her. Infusing her with his scent and gentle, enticing presence.

She opened her mouth, prepared to inform him that that it was quite possible to stretch out a crumbling-marriage scenario through the next two days. Anything to regain her precious distance.

And then he set down his bag, reached out to capture her hand and lifted her knuckles to his lips.

Her duffel hit the floor with a dull thud. The breath bled from her lungs. It was such a gentle, repentant gesture for him to make and so…sexy. All for the benefit of appearances, of course. Damn convincing.

Damn *him*.

"Gia." The silent admonishment brushed her fingers, his long-lashed gaze fixed on her face, as though he knew her childish thoughts. She didn't know which stung more, her humiliation or the frisson of galvanized sensation that ran from his soft kiss up her arm and into her bloodstream.

"Enjoy your flight," the airline agent told Olivier and Soleil, and they moved aside, never acknowledging Joachim behind them or his restive companion.

Joachim dropped Gia's hand, stepped forward and handed the neatly coiffed agent the tickets. "*Guten Abend,*" he said, his German accent flawless.

"*Guten Abend*. Flying to Frankfurt with us today, Mr. and Mrs. Armande?" the woman inquired, efficiently tapping information into the terminal.

"That's right." He smiled with a neon friendliness Gia had never seen him display. "For our honeymoon."

Gia's mouth dropped open. *Newlyweds?*

The agent beamed at them. "Congratulations to you both. You make a lovely couple. Do either of you have a seating preference?"

"I'll take the window," Gia said quickly, desperate for a distraction on the lengthy flight ahead, even if it was just a view of the clouds.

"The aisle is fine for me." Joachim cast Gia a surreptitious glance. "I get enough of a bird's-eye view in my work."

"You fly often?" the agent asked with a polite smile.

"You could say that."

Gia cleared her throat and swiped up her bag, unable to bear the tension another minute. "I'm going to find a place to wait." Pressing a hand to her thrashing heart, she headed toward a pair of connected seats overlooking the runway, where she collapsed, duffel resting on her tennis shoes.

How was she going to *pretend* to appear to be in love with him? The ruse was too close to her true chaotic emotions. If she didn't tread carefully, deception would blend with reality, and the mission wasn't the only valuable thing at stake. Her heart couldn't be discounted.

God help her. After only a few minutes of acting the loving wife, Gia wasn't certain she could differentiate between what was theatrical and what was painfully, dangerously true.

* * * * *

Olivier and Soleil were assigned to the front of the massive jetliner's economy class, lost somewhere among the myriad rows of green and aqua-striped seats. Joachim and Gia were seated behind the left wing. Ever aware of the quiet presence beside her, Gia kept her attention fixed on the shrinking landscape, forehead pressed to the chilled glass, until even the major highways looked like strands of fine, wispy hair. Then the plane ascended beyond a tufted layer of clouds, and all she could she see was fluff.

"Gia," Joachim's low voice stabbed through her trance. "Would you like a drink?"

She shifted to find a dark-haired flight attendant with a beverage cart waiting in the aisle.

"White Zinfandel, and lots of it," she said gratefully, eyeing the alcohol selection on the cart's lower portion.

A frown creased Joachim's brow. "That's probably not a good idea."

"Why not?"

"You know how airsick you get when you drink on a flight," he said, and squeezed her hand.

Gia rolled her eyes at the pseudo-husbandly cajoling and sighed. "Fine. Bottled water, please." She offered Joachim a small scowl as he passed her the water bottle and a plastic cup of ice.

They finished their drinks in mild silence. He'd let her have the armrest, but his long, jeans-clad legs inadvertently took up a good quarter of her floor space.

He looked incredible in street clothes, the faded denim hugging his muscled backside just right. He smelled incredible, too, like vanilla soap and sandalwood. She tried not to remember the taste of his hot skin, or his throaty groans of pleasure as she rode his lap. She tried not to picture the way his cock pushed against his sweatpants, or the smooth, perfect, plum-shaped head of his penis when it escaped the drawstring waistband, or the glistening drop of semen that welled on its fiery tip like a single tear.

She had planned to lick it clean, to savor his essence, the very heart of his manhood, then suckle him until he exploded and quaked with ecstasy. To let him be the man he was. Just a man, for one sweet, fleeting moment.

Gia had wanted to give him that gift. Joachim. One of the Archangel Michael's greatest warrior angels.

It shamed her more than she could bear.

She scowled to herself and polished off the water like it was vodka.

"You'll have to verse me on the standard behavior of a husband and wife," Joachim said, studying the ice in the bottom of his cup as his knee brushed hers. "I should have asked you earlier, but I had other issues to contend with."

"To say the least." She rolled her head to meet his gaze. "What specifically do you want to know?"

"How married humans act in public nowadays."

She drew in a deep breath and let it out, releasing some of the lingering tension with it. "It depends. If they're happily married, in love, then they're affectionate. Solicitous of each other."

"I see," he said. "What are we?"

The tension instantly returned to her muscles and her eyes shot back to his. "Well…what does this operation warrant?"

He looked at her a long time without speaking, his lashes rising and falling as he studied her features. "We're on our honeymoon," he said finally, his voice husky. "How do newlyweds behave?"

Gia swallowed, lost in the blue shadows of his eyes. "How do you think?"

"Ah, but you're the human," he pointed out.

"Yeah? And you're becoming more of one every day."

Wry humor lifted a corner of his mouth. "I stand twice accused in the last twenty-four hours. A record."

"Yes, well..." She shoved a curl behind her ear and glanced away from him.

"You haven't told me," he said after a minute. "How do newlyweds behave?"

Gia swallowed, sensing his gaze on her profile. "Like they're in love."

"And this necessitates much physical affection and a general absorption in one another, yes?"

"Yes. I suppose. But Joachim..." She shifted to look at him. Somehow they'd moved closer, sunk down on their seats, shoulders touching, their conversation hushed, as its intimate content merited. "Do you think this is a good idea, considering...?"

"Considering?" he echoed, the single, whispered word a caress.

She licked her lips. "Considering..." *God, his eyes were blue.* She was losing her train of thought. Her common sense. Every faculty except the desire to lean in the single inch separating them and kiss him mindless. "Considering the mutual lack of control we've shown recently?"

A muscle leaped in his jaw as he regarded her eyes, then her lips. "Control is part of the mission. A requirement. There's no room for another slip. It will not happen again."

Clarity washed over her like a bucket of icy water. "Then we're not in love."

His brows lowered. "Aren't we?"

"No." She straightened from her slumped posture beside

him and turned her head to look out the window, heart thudding a dirge-like rhythm behind her breast. "I mean, for this operation, it'll be safer if the characters we're playing are estranged—unaffectionate, distanced. We may be newlyweds, but ours is a doomed marriage. Bound to crash and burn."

Beside her, Joachim gathered their empty cups and bottles, then folded the tray they'd shared into its space in front of him. "What a sad and hopeless scenario," he murmured.

"Yes," Gia said, closing her eyes. "Isn't it?"

* * * * *

Darkness blanketed the sky when the plane touched ground in Frankfurt. Every muscle in Gia's body ached from sitting cramped in the narrow economy-class seat, and it seemed to take forever for the taxiing jet to roll to a halt at the gate.

An endless line of passengers waited ahead of her and Joachim to disembark. Standing in the aisle, first on one foot and then the other, she entertained herself by studying the wide breadth of Joachim's shoulders in front of her, the way gold tipped the chestnut strands of his hair, remnants of another man's summer in the sun. It had that tousled, streaked, roguish look that was so in fashion, but she knew he did nothing to affect his appearance. His beauty came from within, and from God.

Squished between his hard body and a portly woman behind her, Gia stood with her nose an inch from his back. She examined the waffle weave of the gray cotton henley he wore and inhaled his unique scent, secretly thrilling in the fragrance of laundry detergent, vanilla and clean, warm skin. Inane questions filtered through her sleepy thoughts. Where did he shop? What brand of soap did he use?

"Who washes your clothes?" she asked him, curiosity temporarily banishing her weariness. "Who scrubs the bathrooms and replaces dead light bulbs and grocery shops for the supplies you people need to exist?"

He tilted his head to acknowledge her mild explosion of

inquisitiveness, never moving his gaze from the line of passengers ahead, where Olivier and Soleil now approached the hatch. "We have contacts aboveground who see to our supplies. We do our own cleaning, and there are laundry facilities at headquarters."

Though he spoke for Gia's ears only, the man in front of him, a nosy little gnome, turned to gawk at him.

"Hi there," Joachim said cheerfully, staring hard at him until the man shrank back and faced forward again. Then he told Gia in a quieter tone, "No more questions."

Once inside the terminal, they had to contend with Customs. Gia peered around yet another long line at the grim-faced officials checking luggage and identification. Security was intense and thorough, of course. What had Joachim packed in his bag? Nothing that would draw attention to them, and obviously no weapons, so what would they do if they walked out of the airport and were instantly besieged by Therides' henchmen?

Pulse quickened, she set down her bag and stood on her toes to reach Joachim's ear, one hand grasping his arm for balance. "I have another question, but it's a good one."

"Promise?" he murmured.

She ignored the mild provocation. "How are we supposed to defend ourselves on this mission without weapons?"

He turned his head just slightly, his lips so close to hers, the whispered reply brushed her mouth. "We have contacts here, as well. All over the world, in fact. You needn't be afraid, Gia. The rental van will contain everything we need."

"Guns?"

"Everything."

She blinked in astonishment. "I don't know how you manage all this. The arrangements, the covert details…"

"We've been doing it nearly since the beginning of time," he said with a smile. "After a while, it's—what does Olivier say? A bite of cake."

"A piece of cake," she corrected, and burst into helpless laughter.

His smile widened as he studied her face. "You're so easily entertained."

"Yeah? You're funny, and always when I least expect it."

"I like to hear you laugh," he said, his humor fading. "I'll never forget the sound of it, Gia."

Their gazes locked. Suddenly she was aware of their close proximity, of the strength and warmth of his arm beneath her touch, bare where he had pushed his sleeve to his elbow.

Withdrawing, she sobered and folded her arms across her breasts. "I'm sorry."

"For what?"

"For worrying about the weapons in the van. I should just trust you. You can do anything. You're not from this world. Sometimes I forget that."

"I know." He sighed and reached down to scoot their bags forward as the line advanced. "So do I."

* * * * *

They met Olivier and Soleil at the rental van. There was no talking or laughter now, only a terse caginess fed by the shifting shadows of the parking garage.

Joachim climbed behind the steering wheel and started the engine, while Olivier pulled a long box from beneath the middle seat and pried off the lid to examine the weapons it held. Soleil settled in the passenger seat beside Joachim, looking back only once, when Olivier handed her a pistol and a clip.

Gia felt misplaced. Settling on the bench in the rear of the van, she slid down in the darkness until her neck rested against the back of the seat and closed her eyes. She was hungry, shaky, exhausted.

A wild mixture of dread and exhilaration scored her nerves, growing with every mile they swallowed on the Autobahn. If she'd had her say, she would be back in the cool, quiet bunker, where it was safe and mindlessly dull. No end to the mission in sight. She didn't want to think about starting a new life in an unyielding world that broke hearts and promises.

She didn't want to think about never seeing Joachim again.

Eventually she dozed off. An hour passed, maybe two. It was dark and silent in the van when the shifting of gears woke her, indicating Joachim had slowed. The soft, vermilion glow of a traffic light filled the van's interior, and the vehicle eased to a stop.

Clambering to her feet, she maneuvered around a sleeping Olivier, who was sprawled on the midsection settee, and made her way to the front.

Soleil was asleep, too, her head resting against the passenger window, flaxen hair reflecting the crimson light like a veil of mirrored glass.

Bracing a hand on Joachim's seat, Gia knelt beside him and spoke in a quiet tone, so as not to stir her. "Where are we?"

"The outskirts of Eisenhof." He studied her in the red glow, his eyes shining. "Your lashes are heavy."

"Yes." A thread of warmth wound around her insides at his soft observation. "I'll be dead to the world the minute my head hits the pillow."

He didn't reply, just watched her until the traffic light changed. Then he said, "Five more minutes," and returned his attention to the road ahead.

Climbing carefully into the back of the van again, Gia wondered what he was thinking. The sentiments stretching between them had deepened and intensified from the moment they'd boarded the plane, and the last few hours spent traveling as a couple had bound them closer than ever.

So how was she going to survive sharing a hotel room—maybe even a bed—with him, when the sexual tension between them tipped every nerve with a raging flame?

Laughter threatened to slip from her throat. She could

always bunk with Soleil, which would bring its own kind of tension, a decidedly more unpleasant variety.

Whatever happened, this was definitely going to be an interesting night.

Joachim drove through the well-lit city of Eisenhof, maneuvering the narrow deserted roads at a creeping speed. When he slowed and braked to parallel park the van on a cobblestone street, Olivier and Soleil stirred.

"This is it?" Olivier asked in a drowsy voice, peering through the tinted side window at the inn across the road.

"That is where you and Soleil will stay. The four of us won't be seen together. Gia and I have a room at a hotel three buildings down." Joachim turned off the motor, then swung around and climbed back to examine the weapons his second-in-command had assembled. "The artillery will stay here until we evaluate the field. We'll take the pistols." He picked up a smaller gun and shoved a clip into it, handed it to Gia and glanced at each team member. "Stay constantly aware of your surroundings. Every move you make, from the moment you leave this van, could place you in jeopardy."

"Let nothing distract us," Soleil added, her voice a little smoky from sleep.

Maybe it was a jab. Gia didn't care. The gun in her hand made her reality stand out in stark contrast against the night.

Swallowing, she slid the pistol into her ankle holster.

Something told her that the moment she stepped out of the van, the road on this topsy-turvy adventure would take a detour she couldn't predict and wasn't guaranteed to survive.

A wry smile curved her lips as Olivier threw open the sliding door. When had her path ever truly been safe and predictable? Raised in the guts of the Chicago slums by an alcoholic, abusive mother, married to a demon-possessed mobster, kidnapped by a faction of warrior angels—and now head-over-heels for a man with six wings and a time limit on Earth.

Truly, what remained to surprise her?

Chapter Seventeen

The elderly night clerk behind the hotel's front desk wasn't as receptive as most middle-of-the-night motel employees in the good ol' USA. He was sullen and spoke only German, answering with a curt "*Nein*," when Joachim inquired, "*Sprechen Sie Englisch*?"

Standing to the side in silence, Gia recognized the bleariness in the old man's eyes and felt a pang of remorse at having awakened him. Here in this small town, three a.m. arrivals were probably not the norm. He shuffled from the cash register to the key display, his arthritic fingers shaking as he retrieved their key.

"How many keys exist for the room?" Joachim asked in English. He slipped the question in like an afterthought, testing the old guy, his blue gaze assessing the exits and the small room beyond the desk where the man had obviously been dozing.

"One only," the clerk replied in heavily accented English, eyeing him. "One for you. One for me. Do not lose it."

Cocking a brow, Joachim thanked him in German and shouldered his duffel, as well as Gia's. "Time for bed," he told her with a sympathetic smile. "You're asleep on your feet."

They had to climb three flights of stairs as sheer as the face of a cliff to Gia's tired perception. The hotel was clean and silent, almost gravelike, the halls dimly lit.

A single, frosted-glass door stood ajar at the end of their corridor. Joachim set down the bags, withdrew his pistol, and bypassed their room, carefully approaching the lone door.

He pushed it open with a cautious hand, flicked the light on, then off again. "Water closet," he said, and catching her confused expression, added, "Toilet and sink."

The idea of sharing a toilet with twenty rooms full of strangers didn't exactly appeal to Gia, but she was too weary to complain. She waited with heavy eyelids while Joachim unlocked their door and stepped into the room with his gun at the ready.

A moment later a floor lamp flooded the space with a golden glow, and she followed him in, resisting the urge to take a flying leap across the carpet and into the downy cloud that was their bed.

"A duvet," she said with breathless pleasure, sinking into its softness when she perched on the edge of the mattress. "How lavish. And feather pillows? You must have a taste for the high life, seraph."

He set the bags on a nearby dresser and returned her smile. "I didn't make the arrangements, human."

"Oh. Who did? Who are the people aboveground who help you do all this stuff?"

"You ask many, many questions."

Gia was too tired to be sassy, or even nervous about sharing a bed with him anymore. Besides, he didn't look amorous. He was busy checking the extra clips for his pistol.

She kicked off her shoes and socks, then retrieved her toothbrush and paste from her bag. Around the corner in a small alcove, she found a small sink and shower. A half-bath, missing the most important half.

"How much of a stretch would it have been to install a toilet in here, too?" she grumbled, envisioning a sleepy trek to the water closet with little enthusiasm.

"Did you say something?" Joachim's distracted voice floated around the corner.

"No."

How were they going to manage showers? No door separated the tiny alcove from the rest of the hotel room. If she wanted to shower, she'd have to rely on Joachim's sense of decency.

"No problem there," she muttered.

"Are you speaking to me?" Joachim asked from the other side of the wall.

"No. Just myself."

"A strange habit."

"You don't want to get me started on the subject of strange habits, considering yours is possessing bodies that don't belong to you."

He was quiet after that, but she sensed the humor in his retreat.

Half awake, she brushed her teeth and washed the gritty remnants of their travels from her face, then returned to the bed and fell back against the pillows, sleep hovering like a hazy mantle.

Across the room, Joachim tugged his shirt free of his jeans, stepped out of his shoes and unzipped his bag.

It was strangely erotic to observe a man moving about in the dim light, preparing for bed. Gia folded an arm behind her head to get a better view, watching him through half-mast eyelids as she wondered if this was his nightly routine. A naughty little thrill shivered through her. She felt like a voyeur.

He disappeared around the corner, and the sound of running water reached her ears. The brisk, rhythmic bristling of a toothbrush. The tap of plastic against a ceramic sink.

Angels apparently had great hygiene.

Gia dozed, and when she stirred again, he stood at the dresser with his back to her, rummaging through his duffel, clad only in a pair of white jersey shorts. Every muscle in his back moved in beautiful, liquid accord.

A lazy smile tugged at her lips. She could snap a photo of him like this and sell it to a women's magazine for many, many thousands.

"How long are we going to be here?" she asked drowsily, admiring his wide, naked shoulders, the way the shorts rode low at the base of his spine, the smooth curve of his buttocks. He had the best ass on any man she'd ever seen.

"As long as it takes."

"So more than a couple of days, maybe?"

"As long as it takes," he repeated without looking up from his task.

She stretched against the pillows. "Do you snore?"

Joachim paused and flashed her a look of surprise over his shoulder. "I don't think so."

"Good. Then we'll get along just fine." She twirled a finger at him. "Turn your back again."

He did as she instructed. "Why?"

The slide of her Levi's zipper rent the silence and answered his question. With just a tiny sting of self-consciousness, she lifted her hips, eased off her jeans and tossed them at a nearby chair, then slid beneath the cool linen sheets and downy comforter, her eyelids drooping. "I can sleep now, right, Captain? No patrolling the watchtower or manning the look-out with my trusty twelve-shooter at my hip?"

The soft fall of his footsteps approaching her side of the bed brought one eye open again.

"Sleep." Gazing down at her with a tenderness that fed her sweet sense of euphoria, he passed his hand over her forehead in a gentle caress. "Dreamless," he whispered, some kind of magic spell.

It was the last thing she remembered.

* * * * *

Dawn stole between the blackout curtains like a stealthy phantom.

The piercing, repetitive peep of a morning bird brought Joachim's head off the pillow. He squinted at the slice of sunlight that transected the bottom of the bed, then made a quick visual sweep of the room. Silent. Peaceful. The world seemed eons away.

A glance at his watch showed it was only six-thirty. It was so tempting to fall back to the mattress and let sleep claim him again.

Instead, he shifted onto his right hip and propped himself on an elbow, partaking of a guilty pleasure while he had the chance.

Beside him lay the reason he had dozed for a single, paltry hour. She slept facing him, hands curled under her chin as though in contemplation, sable curls a mass of riotous ringlets against the snowy pillow. The T-shirt she wore had slipped off one tanned shoulder, and beneath the sheets her long, silky legs were bare.

They'd tangled with his somewhere in the night, setting off a barrage of forbidden desires that battered him into wide-eyed desperation. He'd gotten up and put on his jeans as armor, then stretched out on top of the feather comforter for the sake of prudence. But sleep had skirted just out of reach like an impish child, and he lay awake, memorizing every shadow and pattern on the ceiling's plaster while the most fallible and male part of his anatomy pressed painfully against his button fly.

"Do you know what you did to me just now?" she'd said, her body still quaking with aftershocks of orgasm. "I'm going to show you. With my mouth, with my hands. I'm going to make you come like I did."

Lying beside her in utter stillness, he'd played and replayed the memory of that fevered night in his office, punishing himself, indulging himself in what he'd given up.

Come. Ejaculate. Spill himself. Convulse through the greatest physical pleasure known to man or beast. Doing it alone in the shadows of his tiny room had been little more than a futile exercise in desperate release. Doing it with Gia—*coming inside her*—would be the greatest pleasure known to this man, this *seraph*.

All through his tortured reverie, Gia's quiet breathing had

caressed the night, and her soft floral scent invaded his senses, until he could taste her on his tongue, feel her lips, her hot, smooth skin, her curls crushed beneath his fingers—

He could have prayed himself through it, evoked Michael or, in extreme desperation, Nicodemus by telepathy. But he didn't. He'd forgotten how. Forgotten where he was, *what* he was, why he was here in the first place, everything except how much he wanted the woman sleeping so innocently beside him.

Wanted. His brows lowered as he twisted and turned the word, examining it from every angle. What did that mean, exactly? Wanted her company? Of course. Her touch, her smile, her tenderness? Most definitely. To possess her? In every way. It was a drive he didn't quite understand, and far beyond the banal remnants of lust he'd experienced as an occupant of this body. It was tied up with the universal heart and mind and soul.

Although he hadn't fully witnessed it, he knew in theory what sexual intercourse was, its nuances, its sensations. Bodies held physical memories, nearly every one he'd possessed in his long history of operative missions. Certain vague recollections were pleasant, to say the least. And the desire he'd felt with Gia was as pleasurable as it was excruciating to recall. But this…*this*…to assuage this new desire, to touch and mesh with her, heart, mind and body…

A slow, painful sigh hissed through his teeth.

How could he mercifully separate himself from Gia, before the mission ended and the space of an entire dimension did it for him in the most wrenching way?

A soft rustling beside him drew him from his pained musings and he found himself staring down into her lambent, chocolate eyes.

"Hi," she said, her voice husky with sleep.

"Hi." He continued to study her unashamed, while his heart hammered a brisk and erratic rhythm in his chest.

She gazed back at him, her eyes moving over his face, left to right and returning, as though she could read his features like text across a screen.

Sexual tension strung a razor wire between them. Man to woman. The Daughter of Longinus and the warrior from the Archangel Michael's legion had vanished in a shock of awareness.

"You slept in your clothes." She shifted to glance at his denim-encased legs. "I thought you were wearing shorts."

He didn't reply, just propped his head on the heel of his hand and slid down a little on the mattress, until a bare three inches separated their noses.

"*Did* you sleep?" she added, uncertainty playing across her softened features.

"Not much."

"Why? Were you guarding me?"

"Something like that, yes." He studied her full, sensitive mouth and thought about kissing her.

"When will you rest?"

"When I leave this body," he said, and lifted his free hand to finger a wayward curl at her temple. Touching her sent an electric current straight to his vitals, and he nearly groaned at the agony of it.

Her brow furrowed, even as she leaned into the caress like a lazy cat. "We're getting close to the end of the mission, aren't we?"

"Yes."

"When it's over, when Therides is gone and you've served your duty, you'll go back to…you'll go back?"

"Yes."

It was as if he'd uttered some magic phrase that instantly brought a gossamer haze of moisture to her eyes. "And your body…will it die?"

He sighed, gently weaving the strand of her hair between his knuckles. It clung to his finger like an infant's grip. "We can't predict what will happen when we attempt to exile Therides.

Our hope is to return every operative to headquarters unscathed. If I am so fortunate, then my body will be reassigned to an operative on another mission, or perhaps placed in cryogenic preservation until it's needed again."

"You'll be frozen?" A single tear, clinging to the bottom lashes of her left eye, lost its mooring and trickled down her cheek.

"It's possible." His voice grew husky as empathy tightened his own throat. "Michael likes to recycle, so to say."

"And what if you're killed during Therides' expulsion?"

"If it is not by the demon's hand, I'll simply go home, and this body will return to the dust."

Her chin trembled. "Ashes to ashes, huh?"

He swallowed thickly as his fingers freed the tendril of hair at her temple and trailed down her cheek, following the damp path of another tear. "You weep?" It was more an observation than a question.

Choked laughter slipped between her lips. "Call me silly. I've always had a hard time when it comes to losing someone I—" she stopped, her lashes sliding closed as his hand cupped her face.

"When it comes to losing someone you…what?" he prompted.

"We've already been through this, Joachim. You know how I feel."

"Do I?" His thumb brushed her bottom lip in feathery sweeps, tested its plump resilience, his stomach leaping in rhythmic opposition to his pulse. Wild things were happening inside him, foreign, intense sensations, and they brought their own sort of nerve-wracking delight.

Lying in this bed, talking to her, listening to her, caressing her, was the single sweetest experience he'd ever known. He didn't want it to stop. He wanted the mission and the world and all the galaxies beyond to go away, leaving just Gia and him in this hazy, languid moment.

Her lashes lifted. "You aren't asking me to explain my feelings for you, are you?"

"I'm a fool," he murmured, reveling in the flawless texture of her cheek under his fingertips, then the side of her neck, where her pulse raced a frantic beat. "A most deficient being, standing on the edge of something more dangerous than any mission I've been assigned…"

"You mean Therides?"

"I mean *you*." Beneath the calmness of his tone, his breath quickened. "Humor me, Gia. Speak the truth that tortures us both, so that I may take it with me when I go."

Her throat moved, but no sound emerged. Only her eyes, coppery with tears, spoke a lover's words. Her fingers crept up to cover his, holding his touch to her face, before she turned her lips into his palm and reverently kissed him.

"You want to know my truth, Joachim? I feel empty," she whispered at last. "When I think about never seeing you again, I feel lost. And every moment I'm close to you is torture because I can't touch you as I want, or kiss you…or desire you, and yet I do. I want you, all the parts of you, seraph and human combined. The way a woman wants a man. Physically. Emotionally. How do I stop?"

Sweet emotion seized his heart. "How do *we* stop?" Slipping from her grasp, his thumb followed the sculpted curve of her chin, then up the sharp line of her jaw to her ear, where its shell-like swirls awaited his exploration. "We fight the same battle, you and I. How do we win?"

"We don't," she said. "This is a mistake, but it's the truth. I love you, Joachim. *I love you*."

Her anguished confession demolished the final barriers between them, even the three inches that separated their lips, and with a suddenness that surprised them both, her soft, hungering mouth swept in and found his.

Light exploded behind Joachim's eyes, brighter than any celestial fire.

"Gia," he whispered against her lips, her name an accolade. "Gia..." The sheets rustled between them as he laid her back against the pillows and shifted over her, their lips fused, their legs twining in a tangle of linens.

His hands cradled her head, thumbs meeting beneath her chin to position her mouth for his delectation. In return her fingers slid over his bare shoulders to his nape, into his hair, and held him captive as she kissed him, sharing the salty sweet flavor of her grief and need.

This time, the shock of desire racing through Joachim was a welcome thing, one he'd craved without surcease since the first taste of her in his office. He'd known this would happen again between them. He'd lived for it...and perhaps, subconsciously, arranged it. What would he do, now that the realization of his soul's dreams lay before him, her heart thrumming against his, her full lips seeking and promising delight?

Bracing on a forearm, he lifted his head to examine her face and found the answer in her heavy-lidded eyes, shimmering with a need more liquid than tears.

Take.

For this you will choose cycle? Soleil's demand filtered through his spinning thoughts. *Or even worse, a frail human lifetime on this corrupt planet?*

"Yes," he whispered as he gazed down at Gia, a defiant reply to the Heavens. "All of it. For this. For *you*."

"Kiss me, Joachim. Put your hands on me." Her fingers sifted through his hair in sensuous strokes, her breath coming in uneven rushes. "Give yourself to me. Let me give myself to you. Time is so short for us..."

Desire lapped at his senses, flooding his belly with a searing heat that spilled into his loins and further swelled the aching tumescence inside his jeans. "I'll give you everything. I want everything," he said, a simple statement of surrender.

Time dissolved. Love and lust combined created a powerful emotion with no name. Lost in its undefined splendor, Joachim lowered his head and took Gia's mouth more gently, sensually, in tiny nips and nuzzles, his tongue slipping along the silken flesh of her lips until she dug her fingers into his hair and strained to capture his kiss more fully.

Something in his very core caught fire and disintegrated as their mouths opened and tongues thrashed together in full, lush greediness. His seraph's conscience perhaps, or his ability to transcend animal need, or maybe his devotion to an existence that had never offered such intoxicating joy as this. Whatever it was, the immaculate guardian was gone, but his spiritual essence—*Joachim, simplified*—stretched and flourished in the luminosity of Gia's love.

Soul and senses raw, he sat back, stripped the sheet from her body with one powerful sweep and splayed his trembling fingers across her breasts, over her hammering heart, reading the urgency of her desire while his own tortured heart bucked wildly in response.

Gia arched into his touch and reached for him again, drawing him down, hands guiding his head so that his lips found the graceful line of her throat and trailed a ravenous path to her breast.

Her nipples were erect beneath the thin T-shirt, her breasts a fascinating combination of resilient and turgid flesh. Shaking with the force of his passion, Joachim gripped her slender waist and let her guide his lips to one of the hardened peaks. He was blind and untried, but instinct nudged him to take her nipple between his lips and wet it, T-shirt and all, with the flickering tip of his tongue.

In response, her ribs lifted from the mattress, following the searching pull of his mouth as he intuited her needs and fulfilled them. First through the cotton, then beneath it, when he dragged up the hem of her shirt to find her flushed, firm nipples.

"Oh..." she whispered as his teeth scissored softly across one erect peak, then the other, tugging and seeking and exploring.

Against the hard expanse of his stomach, her hips initiated a restless dance. A pulse beat there in the warm, feminine juncture that pressed against his abdomen. Joachim felt its fierce flutter through his own skin and muscle, and his heartbeat quickened to match it, throbbing down low in his erection.

Everything about her was silky and tantalizing. Skin, breasts, flat belly, her long, graceful limbs. Her panties, the delicate peach ones he'd so painstakingly selected a forever ago, slid over her supple flesh when he shaped her hips and buttocks with avid hands, lifting her to meet the searching thrust of his pelvis.

Gia lifted and swayed and undulated to accommodate him. The breathless little cries escaping her throat spoke of agony, and yet Joachim understood it was pain wrapped in ecstasy and anticipation, wrought by his caresses. *His* touch. His human ability to give her pleasure, this woman who had known so little of it in her life.

Fading uncertainty gave way to delight. With each sinuous movement and sound she made in response to his gentle exploration, he slipped the bonds of his true existence.

With every day that passes, you grow more human, more tethered to this Earth…

Gladly, his inner voice told the memory of Soleil's accusations. All of his lofty circumstances in trade for a single moment bound, heart and body, to this lovely creature.

He breathed her name against the swell of her breast, hand sliding beneath her panties and between her quivering thighs to find the soft tuft of curls there, then the slick, suppliant flesh it hid, swollen and open to him.

One finger slid easily inside her, and her body closed around his touch like a folding flower. He gave her panties an impatient tug down her legs, then pressed her knees wide and returned his attention to her heated core, shifting his hand experimentally, lowering his head to watch, transfixed, as his finger disappeared inside her velvety wetness. Her moist flesh clung to him as though it would never release his touch.

"Joachim," she said on a sobbing laugh, and instinctively he knew she needed more, something deeper, something more explicit and satisfying than his gently probing finger. *His cock,* she'd called the hard male part of him throbbing for release inside his jeans. Inferring something proud, erect, male. *Something animal.*

Breathing hard, he flattened his hands on the mattress beside her head and stared down at her. "Tell me what you want," he said, but it came out a husky slur of French.

She seemed to understand anyway. Drawing her knees up, she bracketed his hips so that he settled in the vee of her thighs, hardness and softness and searing heat melting together.

"I want you inside me," she whispered. "Rubbing against me like before in your office, but not through clothing. I want to climax with you inside me, and I want to feel you come, deep, deep in me." She grew more breathless as she spoke, and Joachim more desperate. He hadn't known words could arouse like this.

"Do you understand what it means to come? To climax?" she added, watching him from beneath lowered brows.

He bit back a smile. "I have an idea. But you will show me."

"Oh, yes," she whispered. "Yes. Again and again."

"What else?" he prompted, shifting his hips restlessly between her thighs.

Gia licked her swollen lips and closed her eyes, then lifted her mouth to his ear again. "Put your beautiful cock inside me, slide your hands under me and hold me so tight against you, we can barely move. Rock against me, slip-slide inside me, slow and teasing, until I scream."

He brushed his nose against her throat and inhaled the fragrant heat rising off her skin, feeling his penis surge in violent response to her hotly murmured orders. "And then?"

"Then I want you to fuck me."

He stilled, soaking in the bald declaration even as a faded memory of its meaning quickened the throb in his shaft.

Gia sensed his hesitation and kissed his jaw, his ear. "That's what a man does to a woman, Joachim, when he's so desperate to come, he can't hold back anymore. He doesn't worry about hurting her because it feels so good to both of them, the pain mixes with the pleasure. Do you understand this term?"

The word wasn't altogether foreign to him. He knew it as a human expletive. How odd that it could mean an act just as beautiful as the oath was intended to be foul.

"I believe you can show me," he managed. "Tell me more."

She drew a shaky breath, her cocoa eyes nearly black with dusky desire. "Most of all I want you to cry my name when you come, Joachim. I want to be filled with you, and you filled with me. Say my name. Say it now."

"Gia," he breathed.

"Tell me you want to fuck me."

A stranger replied, desperate, husky, foreign. "I want to fuck you, Gia. Show me how."

She groaned and squirmed beneath him. "Move against me first. Please…let me feel you."

Driven by a fresh surge of need, Joachim rocked into her through their garments and dipped his head to recapture her lips, hungry now for more than a lover's gentle exploration. Their bodies lifted and plunged and moved in a sinuous dance of give and take, his growing harder, hers softer, man complementing woman as Creator made them to be.

After a moment Gia urged him to lift up, and he braced himself again on stiffened forearms.

"I want to hold you in my hands," she whispered. Then her hands slipped between them and skimmed down to the buttons on his jeans.

A fresh wave of heat suffused him as he dropped his head to watch her graceful fingers work open his fly. He held himself aloft, muscles shaking. Not thinking. Not remembering. Only feeling.

Gia Rossi cannot love you through myriad universes and operations…

But she would love him now. Here, in this mortal moment. *This* would span infinity, this memory of Gia, of her touch, her kiss, the exalted joy of giving and receiving such staggering pleasure.

"Tu es belle," he murmured, his head bowed over hers as he studied her flushed features and awaited the scorching, intimate touch she promised. "So beautiful."

"You make me feel like I am." Her wide brown eyes glistened with joy as they searched his face. "Let me do the same for you." And her hand delved inside his jeans, freed him, fit itself around his aching member in a hot cocoon of adulation.

The bold contact wrenched a moan from Joachim's throat. His heartbeat skyrocketed, a thundering stampede in his ears as blood rushed and sluiced downward to further swell him within her sensual caress.

"I want you," she whispered through the roar, rising to tease his earlobe with lips, teeth and tongue until he shuddered and chill bumps spread over his naked torso. "I want to touch you. Taste you. *Fuck you*. Again and again."

He closed his eyes, his throat tight with need and emotion.

"I'm going to show you everything," she gritted. "Don't tell me to stop. Give me this one moment…only this one…"

Anything. Anything for her pleasure, for more of this fleeting marriage of want and tenderness. Anything for the silky touch of her hands on his aching flesh.

Joachim didn't protest when Gia reversed their positions and urged him to lie back on the mattress. In the fleeting respite, he freed himself completely from his jeans and shorts, kicked them to the bottom of the bed and then recaptured her fingers, fitting them around his cock with nothing to impede her caress.

This time she stroked him, base to tip, with one hand and cradled his sac with the other, her talented fingers playing a magic little rhythm on the vulnerable flesh there, while lightning streaks of pleasure jolted through him.

He propped himself on one elbow to watch her adulation of his body, the fierce seesaw of his breath catching the rhythm of her stroke. Of its own accord, his trembling hand hovered over hers and tracked its teasing slide on his erection, up, down, without quite touching, wanting a harder grip, a faster pace…wanting the pleasure never to stop, but to drive him ever deeper into the exquisite corporeal prison human sexuality had woven around him.

When he could stand the sweet torment no longer, his fingers closed around hers and he tightened her grip on his shaft to show her what he needed.

Harder. Faster.

The words thundered inside his head. He met her downward strokes with the desperate thrust of his hips, until pleasure weighted his lashes and he closed his eyes to the searing vision of their hands working his engorged flesh in unison. When his fingers at last released hers and gripped the mattress, Gia never faltered, only leaned to kiss his open, panting lips, one lover's acknowledgement of another's surrender.

Only the harsh rasp of their breathing shattered the thick silence. Too quickly the pressure mounted in Joachim's loins, a fire fed by the potent combination of her relentless stroke on his cock and the hungry exploration of her lips at his throat, his chest, his stomach.

Then she gently squeezed the base of his erection, and the wild sensation eased, but only briefly, for she leaned to take the distended tip in her mouth. *Her sweet, hot, wet mouth.* And suckled him while administering quick flicks of her tongue across the swollen, nerve-rich head.

Joachim had never felt anything like it. A half-shout of astonished pleasure tore from him and his neck arched back into the pillow, hands twisting and tugging the flat sheet from its mooring as she took him deep into her throat, and he at last understood the anguish and beauty of sheer physical ecstasy.

He would die from it. He would die without it.

His hips pushed up to meet the plunge of her mouth, the lash of her tongue, the graze of her teeth, and like magic her firm, quickened stroke resumed, up and down his shaft, gliding so easily on the moisture left by her mouth as her palm dragged it down to slick his flesh.

Searing sensation coiled in his vitals, all senses honed down to the dance of Gia's fingers on his erection, the hot suction of her lips, driving him to strain for the approaching explosion.

"*Please…*" His voice, hoarse and breathless, was not his own. His steely control had abandoned him, his body given over to the most primal instincts.

Nothing had ever felt better. Sparks showered behind his eyelids…

Flames licked his being…

Rising…higher…

"Gia." *C'est incroyable.* "Oh, yes, *Gia—*"

The knock on the door came softly.

Gia's head jerked up. A ragged groan rumbled from Joachim's throat. He seized her hand and stilled it on his penis, shuddering violently as every muscle and nerve screamed in indignation.

"Oh, God. *Someone's knocking.*" Color flooded her face as she sat up among the tousled sheets and stared toward the entry. "Who could it be, this early?"

"Don't…move," Joachim grated, and when she cast him a look of regret and reached for him, "Don't touch me, Gia. I'll go off," he added painfully. "Just stay still."

Swallowing the urge to shout, he rolled to his side and lay there for a moment, panting, lost in agony and the relentless throb of his desire. It took every ounce of control to withhold the ejaculate simmering within him.

For a moment, neither of them moved, Gia flushed and

discombobulated, Joachim trembling and willing his body to heed his desperate instruction. *Calm. Calm. Calm.*

The knock came again.

Reality washed over him, chillier this time. His erection eased, painful arousal replaced by instant and acute awareness. Rising, he put a warning finger to his lips and climbed off the bed, head tilted to listen.

Again. The soft but insistent tap of an unexpected visitor.

Stepping into his jeans, he jerked them up around his hips, grabbed the semi-automatic from the night table and approached the door.

Chapter Eighteen

Gia scrambled to pull on her discarded Levi's, her fingers so shaky she could hardly button and zip her jeans. The trembling reaction had nothing to do with fear. Her sexual frustration granted her the strength of a thousand men. Whoever was at that door had a death wish.

A quick glance at the bed showed twisted sheets pulled from the mattress, the duvet a forlorn ball of fluff at the foot. A lovers' bed. They had nearly christened it such.

Nearly.

Humorless irony twisted her lips as she threw the comforter back over the bed and tossed the pillows into place. Creator—or The Dominions, or whoever ruled the roost up there—was doing His damnedest to even the score. *Heaven – one. Gia and Joachim – zero.*

Ardor seemingly forgotten, Joachim flattened himself against the entry wall, tipped his head toward the door and demanded softly, "What do you want?"

A male voice responded. From where she stood, Gia couldn't make out his words, but the tension drained from Joachim's muscles. He lowered the pistol and with an impatient hand, jerked the chain and deadlock open and threw wide the door.

"*Guten Morgen.*" Olivier stepped into the room with a flourish. His bright-eyed smile dimmed a little when his gaze swept from a disheveled Gia to Joachim, surly and bare-chested. "I see you're both up and about and in one piece." He gave Joachim's half-buttoned jeans a dubious glance. "Or somewhat, anyway."

"What is it?" Joachim spoke with quiet intensity as he

motioned his friend into the room. He checked the hall, left to right, before he closed the door and locked it.

"I called to check in with you at dawn and couldn't reach you. Your cell phone is down."

Gia turned to organize a bag that didn't need organizing. Of course they hadn't heard the phone ring. Joachim had been rolling around in the sheets with her, deaf and blind to the world, while poor Olivier was trying to reach him.

"It was working last night." His expression like granite, Joachim strode across the room to his duffel and retrieved the phone in question. He punched a few buttons, then shot a surly glance at Olivier, who maintained a safe distance in the entry. "It's still functioning. There's no problem."

"Then you just slept through the ring?" Olivier folded his arms and cocked a brow, leaning against the entry wall. "How unlike you, Captain."

Oh, God. Gia turned back to the bag and held her breath. Even seraphim had a grapevine. She and Joachim had fooled no one…only themselves.

Joachim said nothing, just set aside the phone and withdrew a fresh change of clothing from his bag, while his second-in-command lingered by the door in uncharacteristic muteness.

Tension choked the air.

Then, mercifully, Olivier seemed to remember his manners. "How are you this morning, Gia?" He shot her a megawatt, morning-person smile as he passed Joachim and perched at the foot of the tousled bed. "Jet-lagged?"

"I'm fine," she said, and stole a glance at Joachim. Not bothering to disguise the heated thoughts that played across his face, he gazed back at her with a concentration that made her shivery and wet all over again. His hand dropped fleetingly to the fly on his jeans, an unconscious gesture that spoke of lingering sexual need.

The new currents of tension didn't escape Olivier's quick

perception. Like a spectator at Wimbledon, he glanced between them in abject silence, eyebrows raised nearly to his hairline.

Anxiety ripped through Gia, but she forced herself to speak to him with impassive airiness. "I thought you weren't supposed to be seen with us, Liv."

"He's not," Joachim snapped, and without waiting for his fellow operative to defend himself, turned on his heel and disappeared into the shower alcove.

Olivier watched him go with wry interest. "Soleil and I were awake with the birds," he explained, his voice loud enough for his mission leader's benefit. "The fact that *Joachim* didn't answer his *cell phone* concerned me. As it should." He paused for a response from the shower area, but Joachim's only answer was to turn on the spray.

"If he weren't in such a foul temper," the seraph finished quietly, "he'd see the sense in me checking on your well-being. *If* he were himself." His eyes met Gia's, all humor gone. "But he isn't."

Hands shaking, she withdrew a bottle of shampoo and fresh clothing from her own bag. "He's tired. We all are. Except you, apparently."

"I don't tire easily."

"Of course you don't." She meant it to sound lighthearted, but it came out terse.

He rose and wandered around the small room, touching, poking and prodding various objects, like a hyperactive child dragged along on his mother's errands. "I slept like a rock, even though Soleil banished me to the floor."

"I'm glad to hear that." She threw open the curtains and dispelled the intimate ambiance of the room, praying Joachim wouldn't be long. She wanted to throttle him for leaving her alone with Olivier and his suspicions.

"It still looks like you two fared better here." Olivier's sandaled foot nudged the undershorts Joachim had kicked to the floor in the heat of passion.

Suppressing a groan, Gia whirled to yank open a bureau drawer under the guise of searching for extra towels. *Change the subject. Now.* "So tell me, what happens today?"

"Now we grid-walk the town center and let the Medallion do its job." He sauntered to the window and stared down at the narrow cobblestone street. In the distance, the Muenster's spire pointed a formidable Gothic finger to the Heavens. "It's a gorgeous day. This isn't such a bad situation as covert operations go, you know. Picturesque European town, good company, a little excitement…" He turned and flashed her a meaningful look. "Maybe a lot of excitement."

Her hands tightened around the towel she'd found, anger and uncertainty warring within her. She didn't know how to respond to the innuendo.

The scent of shampoo and humidity drifted into the room. *Damn Joachim's hide!* There was no recourse but to face this train wreck head-on, alone.

Facing Olivier, she leaned a hip on the dresser, crossed her arms over her breasts and said, "Let's not beat around the bush. I like my friends to be direct, and I consider you a friend. You have something you want to say to me? Say it."

He stared back at the window, one hand braced on the sash, and was silent for so long, Gia wondered if he had an answer. Then he stirred and said, "Seraphim are flawed creatures, you know. We need parameters, much like you. Where we come from, laws create our parameters. Hundreds of laws and guidelines, and addendums to those laws and guidelines, enough to make your head spin. All intended, of course, to protect and lead us in our purpose. When we break those laws, our actions reverberate through the Realm. The celestial balance is swayed. Like a pebble's ripple in water, it spreads and eventually touches each of us."

He faced her and rested his backside against the windowsill. "Seraphim are guardian spirits, Gia. They ascend to that honored rank because of their purity, their capacity for balance, their intelligence. Joachim is a master among Michael's greatest warriors. Many aspire to be like him, to be the Archangel's right-hand man. He's slated for even greater things. He's a rock, immovable, impervious, strong." He paused. "At least, this is what I believed. But now…"

Gia swallowed the lump growing in her throat and lowered herself to the edge of the bed, towel twisted between her hands. "You've been talking to Soleil, haven't you?"

"We've all observed the changes in his behavior. He's distracted, restless." A deep sigh swelled his chest and he flashed her a sad, regretful smile. "He's in love with you. A decidedly human phenomenon. And a mistake."

She shook her head. "I don't understand why it's so terrible! He was created with the capacity to love, to love deeply, to love a woman, or these feelings he's struggling with wouldn't be there in the first place. What kind of God would grant His child such an ability and forbid it to blossom?" Anger coiled and struck deep within her. "I don't understand."

"How can I clarify?" He shoved his hands through his sandy hair, his eyes dimmed to rainwater gray. "If he were simply a guardian—well, these emotional situations between guardians and their mortal wards do arise occasionally, and they're remedied with careful consideration and compassion for both the angel and the human. But Joachim's no regular guardian. He's a covert operative, a highly skilled specialist and even more, a mission leader. He's breaching boundaries that mustn't be considered, much less crossed. Only trouble and regret can come of this, Gia."

She stared at him, tears burning her eyes. "He's in danger of losing his rank?"

"If Michael suspects he's consorting with an assigned ward—you—then yes. He'll be removed from the mission and probably demoted within the legions. Not as punishment, but for the safety of the other operatives who could be endangered by his state of distraction and imbalance. Do you understand?"

"Yes," she said numbly, stung by the morning brightness

pouring through the window behind him. "So what do you want me to do? Because I'm in love with him too, Olivier. And where *I* come from, we don't just flick our feelings on and off like a light switch. We deal with them. That's what Joachim and I are trying to do. Deal with this…this thing between us. Neither of us invited it. It just happened. Like feelings between any other normal man and woman—"

"But he's not a normal man, Gia. He's a celestial being, temporarily housed in a body that will eventually host any number of other operatives in other missions. In time you'll pass him on the street, and it won't even be Joachim anymore. He won't know you, and your heart will shatter."

"Stop," she groaned, putting her head in her hands. "I know all that. I don't want to hear—"

"He's going home after this operation, did you know *that*? The man you're drawn to today will be gone tomorrow, and Joachim won't be assigned to you again, even in spirit. When you say goodbye in a few days, it's forever. Eternity."

Around the corner, the shower shut off, and they both stilled.

Olivier leaned close and hushed his voice. "I don't know, Gia. When you talk to him of love, and you will, because you can't keep your eyes off each other, remind him of who—of what—he is. The leader of this mission. *Our* leader. And desperately needed by the entire Realm. If it weren't for his tactical brilliance and innate sense of leadership, Lucifer would already have—"

He stopped, recognition dawning on his face. "Joachim's a thorn in Lucifer's side and always has been. Long before the Great Rebellion, Joachim used to warn Michael that Lucifer wasn't the loyal and trusty companion he pretended to be." He straightened, his eyes wide with realization. "How do we know Joachim's fixation on you isn't simply the work of the dark forces? If that's the case, this may be easier to resolve than I—"

Gia bit back a cry of insult. "Nothing as deep and beautiful as what we share could be born of darkness!" She struggled to keep her voice down. "Take that back, Olivier. Don't even suggest it. You're wrong. *Wrong!*"

"I'm sorry." After an uncertain pause, he knelt beside her and laid a gentle hand on her shoulder. "I can only stand aside and watch what I believe is a monumental tragedy. This is between you and him. But know, Gia, that as his second-in-command it's my job to reinforce his position. It's my duty to warn him about this for the good of the mission. For the good of all the people Therides could destroy. Beginning with *you*."

She had nothing to say. He was right…and her heart was breaking.

Joachim chose that opportune moment to reappear, clean-shaven and striking in a black turtleneck and pants. His damp hair was swept back from his face, features shuttered as he took in the sight of his second-in-command kneeling by Gia, his hand on her shoulder.

It was impossible to tell if he'd heard any of their hushed exchange. The tender, emotive lover of an hour ago was gone. His face revealed nothing but steely control.

Gia rose from the edge of the bed and started toward the shower without addressing him, but when she tried to pass him, he caught her arm.

"What's wrong?"

"Nothing." She blinked away the moisture gathered in her eyes and forced a smile. "I'm going to get ready."

She knew he didn't buy her cheerfulness, but what could she do? Sob out the whole anguished conversation she'd shared with Olivier? Admit that this romance was more doomed than any dysfunctional scenario she'd waded through in her past? Call it off? She couldn't. *Couldn't!*

Olivier had returned to his perch on the windowsill and was mutely observing them, the wheels turning behind his perceptive gray eyes. It was Joachim's turn to face his friend's version of reality, and Gia wasn't about to hang around and watch.

"Hope you left me some hot water," she said flippantly and tried to tug free, but he held fast.

His penetrating gaze searched her face for a tense moment, then he dropped his hand and moved by her. "Be ready in fifteen minutes," he said over his shoulder. As though she were one of his operatives. As though his lips hadn't caressed her and her mouth hadn't brought him to the brink of ecstasy.

Business as usual.

The beauty of the morning crashed and burned, leaving nothing but the faint, singed essence of something precious destroyed.

* * * * *

With Olivier and Soleil strolling a safe distance behind, Gia and Joachim walked a grid across the center of the town, disguised as newlyweds, smiling and holding hands for the sake of friendly passerby, and then lapsing into silence when they were no longer under observation.

The Medallion pulled at Gia's neck, much like the endless afternoon's tension pulled at her frayed nerves, unraveling them thread-by-thread.

When they turned onto the same street for the third time, Joachim motioned across the road to the shade of a vacant boutique. "We'll take a break."

Across the street, they paused beneath the green and yellow striped awning, where a picture window offered a wide ledge on which to rest. While Gia found a seat, Joachim gave a shuddering stretch, then turned to regard her. At least she thought he looked at her. It was impossible to tell with the black sunglasses covering his eyes.

"Anything?" he asked.

"Not yet."

The lengthiest dialogue they'd shared since leaving the hotel.

He turned his head aside and spoke softly into the minute microphone attached inside his black turtleneck. "Take five minutes."

Two storefronts down, the other operatives stopped in front of a small cafe and seated themselves at a table with a tangerine umbrella.

Gia squinted in their direction. Olivier looked as happy as a clam. He could convince the staunchest skeptic as a cheerful tourist in ragged jeans, a heavy-metal T-shirt and sandals. But the camera around his neck held a tiny microphone, and his obnoxious, lime green fanny-pack contained an intel module that flashed updates on a diskette-sized screen.

Like Joachim, ever the covert shadow, Soleil was dressed entirely in black, her emerald gaze concealed by a pair of black sunglasses. It was impossible to read her expression, but Gia felt her scrutiny like a continuous blast of heat. For the past three hours, it had lasered a hole between her shoulder blades.

"There's something I don't understand," Gia said, watching him as he walked to the edge of the sidewalk. "Maybe you can explain it to me."

He tilted his head toward the Heavens, studying the Muenster's spire looming against a cornflower sky. "What is it?"

"You said seraphim don't harbor inappropriate feelings for each other."

"They don't."

"I think Soleil might be bending that rule." Immediately she wanted to recant, but it was too late. All the pent, unrequited passion and frustration knotting her insides had reached a boiling point.

He returned to the ledge where she perched and found a spot beside her. "With whom?"

"Please, Joachim. I think she has feelings for you, and not in an altogether angelic way."

He sighed, bracing the heels of his hands on the ledge beside him, and finally said, "She accuses you of the same."

Gia opened her mouth to retort, but nothing came to mind. They both knew Soleil wasn't wrong, and just flashing on the memory of his smooth, naked muscles ignited every sensation in Gia's sexual repertoire. Merciful anger quickly came to the rescue, though, and restored her tottering composure. He was as much at fault in this as she. If only for touching her, for smiling at her, for being there in bed beside her when she woke up this morning, watching her with hunger in his blue eyes.

"At some point, we're going to have to speak of what happened this morning," she said quietly.

It took him a long time to answer. He studied the sidewalk, as though the pebbled surface held the key to the universe. "The Spear comes first," he said finally. "The other issues must wait."

He was right, of course. Her timing was awful, but she couldn't stand the tension. She wanted to snatch the dark sunglasses from his eyes and look into his shuttered mind. "Fine. But at least admit that something important happened between us."

He stared ahead in stony silence.

"I had you in my mouth," she added, noting with sick satisfaction the slight tinge of color the seeped into his face. "You had your fingers deep inside me. I loved it."

"Don't." He spoke without looking at her.

"*You* loved it. You can't deny it."

"Gia…"

"Can you?"

"No," he said low. "No, I cannot."

The admission stole her ire and replaced it with shame. What had happened between them was beautiful, pure, and her anger was twisting it.

Biting her lip, she studied his profile, the tiny gold hoop in his ear, his sensitive mouth and stubborn chin. "Will we talk about what happened this morning?"

"Yes." His attention pivoted from left to right as he tracked the pedestrians passing the storefront, the cool breeze fingering through his wavy chestnut hair. "But not now."

Good enough. That was Gia's one attempt at clearing the air, and if he didn't want to talk about it, so be it. She wanted out. Wanted to grab the Spear and climb on a plane and fly home, and start over. Wanted to rewind the past few weeks—no, the past few years—and begin anew.

But most of all, she wanted to forget the man beside her, who wasn't really a man at all, but some kind of phantom. She wanted to forget his touch on her and inside her, to forget what it felt like to kiss his sensuous lips, to caress his hot skin and taste his cock and hear his breathless lover's accolades.

You're beautiful…I'll give you everything…I want everything…

Slapping her hands on her knees, she stood and forced a chipper smile. "Let's get back to it, shall we?"

Rising, Joachim removed his sunglasses, glanced in his team's direction, then back at Gia. "It won't be daylight forever."

"I know," she said, her fire doused by a sudden wave of defeat.

His blue gaze locked on hers, shadowed and full of sentiments neither of them could speak. "Time is running out."

"We're close," she said, and beneath her shirt, the metal disk hummed in warm concurrence.

* * * * *

They passed row houses sagging under the weight of three hundred years, and narrow canals beset by snowy, honking geese, where children ran up and down the wrought iron fencing and pelted the water with bread.

A breeze threaded through the cool afternoon, a languid caress against Joachim's face. The pleasant sensation did little to cool the heat of his thoughts. Gia's lips. Her mouth on his chest, and lower, on the shivering muscles of his stomach, on his aching erection. The sleekness of her skin when he touched her. The tight wet chalice between her legs, its heated silk closing around his probing fingers.

Find the Spear. For so many reasons, it couldn't happen soon enough.

A few steps ahead of him, Gia slowed and glanced up a crooked, shadowy street they hadn't yet explored. She hesitated, uncertainty etched in her profile, then resumed walking, her fingers absently tracing the Medallion through her shirt.

At the next corner, she halted and shook her head. "I'm sorry. I have to go back to that road."

"Don't apologize." He laid a supportive hand on her shoulder. "Follow your instincts."

"It's not my instincts as much as the heat this Medallion is giving off. I assume if it's getting warmer, we must be too." She plucked at it, pulling it away from her skin without withdrawing it from its safe place beneath her shirt.

Backtracking, they turned onto the road. She picked up the pace, her head down, attention fixed on the cobblestones as though she counted each one. The palm of her hand pressed flat on the Medallion through her shirt, sharing some subconscious communication with the blessed pendant.

After a moment, she stopped again. "The Medallion's getting really hot."

"Its metal draws your body heat," Joachim suggested.

"No. It's hotter than that. It's almost uncomfortable."

He took in their surroundings with a single, sweeping glance. They stood on the edge of the town center, directly across from the Eisenhof Muenster, where merchants were disassembling the daily market that had encircled the small cathedral that morning.

"We've passed this church fifty times today," Gia said, the breeze blowing dark curls across her brow. "Why haven't I felt this heat before?"

Joachim studied her face, a twinge of hope sparking within him. She was flushed, despite the late afternoon's brisk temperature. The very air around her pulsated with an invisible current that raised the hair on his arms.

Excitement quickening his pulse, he drew her across the cobblestone and into the blue shadows of the Muenster. "Look around, Gia. Look at each building. Focus on each structure, and inwardly on the Medallion."

Her throat moved as she swallowed. "You think the Spear's in one of these funky little buildings?"

"Only you can know that." He drew a deep breath for patience and leaned against the ancient stone edifice behind them.

Male voices floated on the late afternoon air, a jovial German exchange between two men dismantling a vegetable kiosk a few feet away. Joachim's stomach grumbled as though protesting their actions. He hadn't eaten today, opting instead to study a map while Gia had gulped a hard-crusted roll purchased from a small bakery.

Now his human system felt shaky and strangely light. He looked away from the crates of colorful produce and inwardly cursed himself. More and more, corporal sensation weighted him, chained him to the Earth. He'd never been more physically aware of himself, and when the moment of reckoning came in the Archangel's presence—and it would, without question—Joachim would only be able to blame himself for the consequences of his unruly conduct.

Touching Gia—being touched—had weakened the link that connected him to the higher Realm. To what extent, he would have to examine later because a wild urgency now drew his focus back to the mission and to his true directive. A knowledge that time was running out, that the nephil had grown stronger, that soon it would all be ended, and it was up to him whether triumph would serve as seraphim's reward…or destruction and heartbreak.

His attention drifted to the woman beside him. She was beautiful and fierce in a moment of intense concentration, her brown eyes darting from one building to the next, white-knuckled fingers wadding the material of her shirt over the Medallion.

Muttering a curse, she shook her head and turned to press her flushed face against the cool stone expanse of the cathedral's wall. "I can't see anything. Every building looks alike."

"And the Medallion? Does it still burn?"

"It's hot, all right."

And she was exhausted. The search itself was daunting, but the sacred pendant around her neck no doubt fed itself on her body's energy.

"This isn't working." Stepping away from her, he ducked his head and spoke to the other seraphs through the comm unit. "Do you have us in sight?"

"Yes," Soleil responded. "Ten yards or so. Joachim, look at the sun's position. It's getting late."

He didn't respond to the terse observation. Instead he grasped Gia's arm and turned her to face him. "Gia." His breath came quicker as he cupped his hands around her face. "Gia, where is the Spear?"

Anxiety glazed her brown eyes at the urgent demand. "I don't know! What kind of God would plop the welfare of the universe in my hands like this?"

"No." He slid his fingers into her hair and pressed his lips against her forehead, closing his eyes as he willed her to see beyond her frustration. "We carry the burden as a whole. Let's try again. Do the best you can. Think of nothing but the Spear. Let the Medallion do its work."

"But it's not all up to the Medallion, it's up to *me*. And there's no room for mistakes this time." Her voice choked. "Yet I've made so many. What if this is one of them?"

Gripped by the moment's desperation, he kissed her forehead again, her eyelids, her temple, inhaling the delectable floral scent inherent to her alone. He didn't care if his disapproving team watched the genuine and very public display from afar. In that instant, all he cared about was this human woman.

What must it be like to walk such a formidable planet gripped with doubt and distrust? Then to be given such an assignment as this—*Save the world, Gia, only you can find the Spear*—what had they done to her? And when they returned to Creator and left her behind, what would become of her?

He couldn't think about his own grief at being parted from her when the time came. Just touching on it jolted him more intensely than even his physical desire for her had that morning.

In the end, what would he and Gia glean from each other, besides this hollow pain that seemed to dance around them like a taunting spirit? Would there be anything left of their hearts?

He tried to swallow the lump forming in his throat and failed. He had nothing to offer her now except this moment. This one moment with his hands in her hair, his lips caressing her cheek, his emotions radiating like neon lights around them for all the world and Heavens to see. This single, precious blink in time, whether they could spare it or not. The consequences didn't matter.

Gia's question that day in the stairwell rang through his memory. *Do seraphim love?*

God help me, came his silent, belated answer. *This seraph does.*

Her fingers crept up to grasp his wrists, and she held on tight, her lithe body shivering against his. "Help me, Joachim. I have to succeed. If it's the only thing I ever do right…you know it has to be *this*."

"You will succeed," he whispered, and brushed a lingering kiss against her cheek. "Once I told you that you must do more than have faith in seraphim. You must believe in everything that's happening around us. The Medallion. The Spear. Creator's power. It flows through you, Gia, here—" He touched his fingertips to her temple. "And here—" His fingers glided down her throat to the warm spot between her breasts, where the Medallion radiated heat and her heart thrummed beneath it.

"And now, most importantly, you must believe in yourself. Because I do. I believe in your beautiful, blinding spirit, and I have from the start."

She drew back to look at him, gratitude and amazement reflected in her eyes. "I love you so much," she whispered for the second time that day. And for the second time, his human heart leaped in his chest, grabbed onto her truth and drew it deep inside him to cradle it within his seraph's soul.

As though the Heavens had overheard her forbidden sentiment, a cool northern wind picked up the leaves and skittered them across the cobblestone, scolding Gia's curls and plastering her T-shirt against her body.

Shivering, she withdrew from his embrace and glanced around.

And stilled.

"That building..." Her brown gaze focused on a freestanding contemporary structure twenty yards from the Muenster. "That building, what does its sign say?"

The spire had cast a shadow across the incongruous steel and glass structure, like an arrow pointing to the wellspring of their mission.

They both stared at it in stunned silence. Intel hadn't informed them of this museum's existence. How could their research contacts have missed it in a town this size?

Pulse racing, Joachim stepped closer and squinted at the sign erected by the entrance. "*Das Museum der Kulterell Geschichte*," he read, the words low and breathless. "*Der Bunker von Hitler: Wahnsinn in den Kunsterzeugnissen*."

His gaze met hers. "It's the Museum of Cultural History. And the exhibit—Hitler's Bunker: Insanity in the Artifacts."

Entranced, Gia stood motionless, staring. Then, as though someone had lit a flame beneath her heels, she began walking toward the museum, her stride sure and brisk.

Jogging to catch up to her, Joachim spoke into the comm unit. "Liv, Soleil. Let's go. We found the Spear."

Chapter Nineteen

The museum's interior was cool, sterile and hushed, despite two large groups of schoolchildren being herded through the exhibits by their teachers.

Gia stopped at the reception desk under the guise of gathering brochures while Joachim stood nearby, subtly examining the faces of the people milling about the main hall. No sign of Therides' henchmen, who, despite their best efforts, normally displayed one detail that set them apart from average men—their tendency to lurk in the shadows, as though light would expose them for the automated zombies they had become.

Most of the museum's visitors appeared to be tourists. At the far end of the hall, two men in tailored suits descended an impressive glass-and-steel staircase marked for employee admittance only. That meant the second and third floors held offices—and a choice place to hide until the museum closed for the night.

Pausing beside Joachim, Gia shuffled through the brochures she'd collected. "Look, honey. This is a layout of the bunker exhibit. Let's check it out."

Joachim offered her a vague smile, impressed with her cheerful performance. The woman so beset with self-doubt moments before was gone. In her place stood someone perfectly composed, safely ensconced in the disguise of an enthusiastic tourist.

"Lead the way," he said, and it wasn't until her chilled fingers clasped his that he realized she still trembled.

Behind them, the other seraphs entered the museum and stopped at a small case displaying sixteenth-century artifacts.

"What now?" Olivier's voice came through the speaker in Joachim's ear.

"Stand by," Joachim ordered, his attention on the brochures as though he spoke to Gia about them. "Soleil at the front, you at the rear entrance. Find the security system. Analyze it."

"Everywhere I look I see motion detectors, Joachim."

"Map them between the staircase and the exhibit. We're on our own in this place. Intel doesn't know it exists."

Olivier released a beleaguered sigh. "How did that happen? How could anyone possibly miss this place?"

"I'll be sure to interrogate Intel when we get back to headquarters," Joachim said dryly. "For now, forge ahead."

"Aye-aye, Captain."

The bunker exhibit was housed in a long, narrow room, lit by the harsh glare from naked overhead bulbs, a stage effect intended to color the atmosphere as dim and stark as Hitler's final underground accommodations. The mud-colored walls were broken into erratic spaces by giant newsreel photographs of the maniacal dictator in action.

Gia hesitated just inside the door and glanced around, her eyes wide, clutching Joachim's hand with steely determination. "So how did the Spear fall into Hitler's possession?" she whispered.

Two teenagers passed behind them. Joachim guided Gia to the side, where a case displayed SS uniforms and various articles of Nazi wardrobe. "Our research indicates he searched far and wide for it and had possession of it for a few years before his death. It granted him enormous military strength."

She shot him a look of horror. "But how? I thought it was a holy relic, a—"

"Remember, its power can be utilized for darkness or light. If it hadn't slipped from his grasp, he could have ruled the world. But the Spear became lost when an assassination attempt was made on his life. His guards hurriedly threw his possessions together, and Hitler could never relocate the relic. The moment he lost sight of it…" Leaving the account unfinished, he let his gaze drift over her features. "It belongs to you now, Gia."

"I hope I merit that." Her fingers clutched at the Medallion and a grim smile curved her lips. "This thing's on fire."

"A good sign. Let's end this search."

They moved with studied casualness, like the other visitors wandering through the exhibit. As they approached the rear of the room, Gia grew silent, her features tight with increasing discomfort. "Joachim," she said finally, a little breathless. "It's really burning."

"Try to hold it away from your skin." His hand caressed her elbow. "As soon as we determine which case holds the Spear, we'll find a bathroom and you can remove the Medallion."

They passed two cases filled with spent artillery and debris.

"It's there," Gia whispered, motioning to the final case. Perspiration glinted on her upper lip and dampened the hair at her temples, and her fingers shook as they pulled at the Medallion.

Joachim too was trembling from the excitement and anticipation that swooped through his human system.

They had to wait for a cluster of young scholars to move aside before they could peer into the case. When Gia laid a hand on its glass expanse, sparks arced off the surface and she jolted back with a startled inhalation. A quick glance around showed no one had noticed the phenomenon, and Joachim moved protectively behind her, grasping her shoulders as together they stared down at the display.

"My God," she whispered. "It's nothing. Just an old rusted piece of metal."

The Spear, what was left of it, was hardly recognizable as the formidable weapon that had pierced Christ's side. Along with other charred and decaying artillery, it lay cushioned on a bed of red velvet, its edges corroded and chipped by the passage of two millennia. Just the head remained, its wooden handle long lost to time's decay. Nothing marked it as anything more significant than part of Hitler's personal weaponry collection. The museum curators didn't know what they had.

Time stood still as Joachim studied it, imagining its point gleaming against an overcast Jerusalem sky. Picturing it aimed at the pale, bloodstained flesh of the dead Christ. Then seeing it as a winged blade piercing His ribs and releasing the Sacred Humour, so that the crimson liquid burst forth and rushed down the Spear's handle in an enchanted, healing font, splashing into the stricken eyes of the centurion who'd wielded it…

And Longinus, crying out in agonized rapture as he fell to his knees, blessed with the first silhouette of sight, both physical and spiritual—*Behold the Son!*

Beside Joachim, Gia cleared her throat. "Joachim, I have to get this thing off *now.*"

The urgency in her voice broke his trance and he nodded toward the exhibit's exit. They moved briskly back through the museum, where they found a women's restroom located near the reception area.

Mindless of curious eyes, Gia shoved through the bathroom door. Joachim followed, his gaze sweeping the lavatory for inhabitants while she yanked the chain over her head. It flew from her fingers and hit the tile with a sliding clatter.

"I'm fried," she breathed, slipping a hand beneath her shirt to examine the damage to her seared skin.

Joachim returned from checking the stalls and gently tugged her shirt from the waistband of her jeans. "Take this off. We're alone."

Still shaking, she grasped the hem and drew the garment over her head while he moved to secure the bathroom door.

"Wow." Her astonished exclamation echoed off the tile. When he turned, she was staring into the mirror over the sink at the fiery red tattoo imprinted on the curve of her left breast. "It's etched into my skin!"

He approached her and studied the tender spot. "Even the flames are apparent," he said, tracing the mark with a single fingertip. "Extraordinary." His gaze met hers as he turned the backs of his fingers to the curve of her breast, even now helpless to stop from caressing her silky flesh. "It's the sign of the Archangel. See how it's directly above your heart? You're marked."

Gia offered him a crooked smile. "So now I can leap tall buildings in a single bound?"

"Now you can say you are the true Daughter of Longinus. The only one with the courage and knowledge to utilize the Medallion. This"—he carefully drew a circle around the abrasion—"stands as proof. You are no ordinary woman, but a soldier of seraphim, with whom the Great Warrior is well pleased."

The low intensity of his words doused her wry humor. "And what about you, Joachim? None of this could have fallen into place without your guidance. Won't the Archangel be well pleased with *you*?"

He fingered the delicate lace of her bra that bordered the Medallion's imprint. "I have much to answer for when this mission is ended. To Michael, and to myself."

A faint tinge of color suffused her cheeks. "You're talking about our relationship. Joachim, you're in a human body. It's natural that you have physical feelings, and sexuality is part of humanity. Surely you won't be punished for—"

"I can't explain," he said quietly. "And you can't understand. But thank you for trying."

Her brows drew down. "Because I'm just a human."

"No. You're the Daughter of Longinus."

"So why do I feel so helpless when it comes to you? Angel or human, I love who you are. And I'm sorry for dragging you into this emotional mess. I could have kept my distance, could have stopped myself from kissing you in your office...and this morning, I allowed—"

"We, Gia. *We* allowed it." He laid a finger against her lips, his eyes locked on hers, steady blue to storm-tossed brown.

And while she stood in turmoil, confusion shimmering around her in visible, iridescent currents, Joachim's fascination turned from celestial musings to more sensuous concentration.

His knuckles brushed her cleavage, riding the rise of her right breast as it swelled above her lacy brassiere. Counting the hammers of her heartbeat as it echoed from beneath layers of skin and muscle. Burned by the fragrant heat radiating from her satin skin.

He was the transgressor. He alone. And he couldn't stop.

Simultaneously their breathing quickened, seesawing in harsh rushes between them.

A jolt of pure, misplaced desire shuddered through Joachim, and immediately he opened his mouth to speak. An apology for the untimely return of this physical weakness. A declaration of his confusion and passion and shame.

"Don't say it," Gia whispered. "Damn you. Just kiss me."

Before he could do more than lean toward her, the doorknob behind them rattled, and a woman called out in German, "Hello? Why is this door locked?"

The spell shattered as though someone had ripped aside the curtains of their intimacy and flooded the room with icy awareness.

"Just a minute." In a gesture of painful self-consciousness, Gia crossed her arms over her breasts and turned away.

He handed her the shirt without looking at her. While she pulled it over her head, he retrieved the Medallion, now cooled and dulled, its patina as black as if it had been passed through flame. He carefully wound the chain around the disk and slipped it into his pocket.

Gia unlocked the door, and he followed her past the buxom woman, who eyed them with raised eyebrows and a mouth puckered with disapproval.

"Newlyweds," Joachim offered with a helpless shrug, and sliding his arm around Gia's waist, promptly ushered her from beneath the woman's scrutiny.

The bright light of the lobby, the echo of children's voices, the musty scent of antiquity, snapped his focus back to his directive. He glanced around, spotted the other seraphs across the room and nodded at them. "Have you mapped the security system?"

"It's complete," Soleil replied, stationed at a display across the reception area.

"Good. Retreat to the rendezvous point. Gia will join you in five minutes."

Side by side, Olivier and Soleil strolled past them into the late afternoon without once looking their way.

Overhead, a disembodied voice announced in smooth, robotic German, "Thank you for visiting the Museum of Cultural History. The exhibits will close in fifteen minutes."

Gia shoved her fingers through her curls and sought Joachim's gaze. "What happens now?"

"Now you meet Olivier and Soleil on the north side of the Muenster. Under their protection, you will return to the hotel and gather our things."

"What about you?"

"I take the Spear from the case."

"How will you do it? What if you get caught?"

He grasped her elbow and walked her to the exit, where uniformed school children filed out in an impressive and orderly line. "Go to the rendezvous. Do exactly as the others say. I'll see you soon."

"But, Joachim, what if—"

He pulled her to him and caught her mouth in a quick, searing kiss, silencing her and feeding the hunger that now ran wild and unfettered within him. "Go," he said, and backing away, left her standing at the door, her lips parted in soft amazement.

* * * * *

A chill permeated the curator's office and crept into Joachim's muscles like the shadows that stole across the high ceiling. He rubbed his hands over his arms and paced a path around the desk, his restless gaze taking in the accessories on the leather blotter—a mug of pens, a stack of manuals, the smiling photograph of a pretty young woman—the curator's daughter, perhaps. Or a very youthful wife.

He'd gained entrance to the office shortly before the museum closed, after climbing to the second floor and trying the first door he saw. The room had seemed abandoned for the night, but soon after he let himself into the sparsely decorated space, the curator had made an unexpected return and Joachim dove for a nearby bathroom, where he hid until the man gathered his belongings and finally left, a full hour later.

Now, with the advent of silence that had fallen over the museum, Joachim allowed himself to move about the room. It wasn't yet safe to return to the first floor and retrieve the Spear. Although the museum had been closed for three hours, the janitorial staff was still on the premises, and somewhere, an armed guard patrolled the cavernous rooms with a rhythmic heel-toe gait that signified boredom and a lack of awareness that would hopefully be to Joachim's advantage.

Olivier had also reported that another guard was stationed on the third floor, monitoring the surveillance footage recorded by cameras mounted at every corner in the exhibits. Somehow, Joachim would have to skirt around them.

Outside the building, the small seraphic team patrolled for signs of Therides, sliding through the night like phantoms as they waited for their mission leader to make his escape with the Spear.

"Report," Joachim said into the comm unit.

"All's quiet," Olivier's voice buzzed inside the minute speaker Joachim wore in his ear. "You?"

"Waiting for that magical window of opportunity." He stretched restive muscles and parted the damask curtains to peer out at an ancient township glowing against the night. The seraphim mobile unit was parked two alleys over, tucked between a boutique and a bakery. He couldn't see it from where he stood.

A tiny, indecipherable sound from the hallway jolted his awareness and he let the curtain drop. Approaching the closed door, he leaned close and listened.

The whine of bucket wheels grew louder, then passed, followed by the squeak of a closet door down the corridor. The second-floor janitor was putting away his cleaning supplies. Joachim glanced at his watch. Nearly ten o'clock.

Footsteps approached from both sides of the corridor and converged outside the curator's office. Male voices rose and fell in conversation, idle chitchat between the janitor and the security guard.

Joachim leaned a shoulder against the wall and fought impatience while he waited for them to wind up their dialogue. Did this janitor have no one waiting for him tonight? A warm home, a hot meal, a loving wife?

He shoved aside a floating image of Gia and forced his mind to focus on the operation, replaying Olivier and Soleil's report of where the laser motion detectors were most unfavorably situated.

A virtual laser grid crisscrossed the actual exhibit room where the Spear was displayed. Joachim couldn't disarm the system without alerting the security guard. He would have to hide from the cameras and slide beneath the grid, drill into the display case, and remove the Spear from *beneath*, an awkward scenario at best. And accomplish this in plain sight of anyone passing by the room. If the guard was on his toes…

Fortunately that didn't seem to be the case.

"Two older men exiting the front," Olivier reported.

"The cleaning staff." Joachim eased open the door, peered

left to right and murmured, "I'm moving."

"Good luck."

The descent to the bottom floor was effortless. The roaming security guard had disappeared onto the third floor as Joachim simultaneously slipped down the staircase to the exhibit rooms. He moved quickly past a surveillance camera…too quickly, and nearly ran headlong into a razor-thin crimson beam spanning the reception area that Soleil and Olivier hadn't detected in their earlier examination.

Dropping to his stomach, he dragged himself beneath the laser, his pulse beating an erratic rhythm in his ears. Once clear, he regained his feet and crossed the lobby, slipping in and out of the shadows to avoid being detected by the cameras, his combat boots soundless on the slick tile.

A single light burned in the Bunker Exhibit room, aimed directly over the case that contained the Spear.

Joachim's mouth curved. A beacon. Behind it, Adolf Hitler's mural-sized photograph seemed dim and lost, his fanatical eyes sunken in gloom, Lucifer's fire doused by the cool darkness.

Joachim crouched in the doorway, counting the quickened thud of his pulse as he studied the motion detector grid that tiled the room before him. The lasers hovered over the floor, allowing him a three-foot tunnel in which to crawl to the display case. Cameras were mounted in every corner of the ceiling, but the electronic eye near the door was the only one he had to worry about, since he would be working on the right side of the display case and its bulk would hide him from detection.

Grabbing hold of a thin water pipe that ran from the floor to the ceiling near the camera, he shimmied up ten feet, pressed himself to the wall and pulled a pair of wire cutters from the tool bag at his waist. The camera's wires snapped easily, and he prayed the remaining cameras would offer enough footage to satisfy what was hopefully a sleepy guard watching the surveillance screens on the third floor. There was always the chance the man would radio his wandering colleague about the defunct camera, and Joachim's mission would be thwarted.

He closed his eyes and whispered a brief prayer, his only fortification.

As though in mocking reply, footsteps echoed on the glass-and-steel staircase in the main hall. He slid to the floor and peered around the entrance to see uniformed legs appear as the security guard descended to the first floor.

Dropping to his stomach, Joachim crawled beneath the grid and to the left, into deeper shadows, his nose a centimeter from the waxed tile. French curses danced across his mind. It was impossible to hide completely in this wide-open space if the guard were truly searching the darkness for an intruder.

He shrank into the gloom, away from the door and the cameras, and held his breath, counting off the footsteps as the guard approached, stopped at the exhibition entry a yard away…then continued past.

Joachim's breath slid from his lungs in a shaken rush. Moving stealthily but with new urgency, he crawled on his forearms like a soldier through the swamps, beneath the laser grid to the display case. There, he angled himself half-behind it and paused, listening for the sound of running footsteps, shouts or some indication that the cameras had picked up on his presence.

Nothing.

With a slow exhalation, he withdrew a tiny drill from the tool bag and turned on his side, squinting through the disabling chiaroscuro cast by the single bulb overhead.

The drill hummed a high-pitched whine, loud enough to draw the floor guard's attention if he passed by again…but he didn't. His faint, echoing whistle kept Joachim blessedly apprised of his location. Joachim worked quickly, feeling Michael's reassuring hand on one shoulder and Creator's on the other as he drilled a square through the laminate base, then reached up inside the hollow core of the case to cut a hole beneath the Spear.

One tedious minute bled into several. His arm muscles screamed from his body's twisted position. Perspiration beaded his upper lip, his forehead, trickled into the hair at his temples. He was guessing at the exact arrangement of the Spear. If his hand wasn't true, the drill bit could chip the ancient relic and thwart its capacity to annihilate Therides.

Sawdust and bits of velvet drifted down, sprinkling his cheek. His arms shook with the strain of maintaining the unnatural posture, his gaze honed on the ragged circle opening around the relic's approximate position. In the back of his mind he heard the guard's tuneless whistle coming closer. He released the drill's activation and listened. The man was moving too quickly in this direction.

His gaze refocused on the circle in the display case. Two more inches.

The whine of the drill resumed. *One more inch.*

Joachim shifted and bit back a groan as a cramp seized his ribs. The guard's whistling grew louder, and the sound of his radio crackled with a male voice speaking German.

Michael, guide me. Guide my hand. Guide my heart.

A soft lurch, and the wooden slab came loose in Joachim's hand. With seized breath and trembling hands, he laid down the drill, withdrew from the shallow cave of the case and lowered the slab to examine his cache.

The relic shone dully in the glaring pinpoint of light overhead, unscathed by the invasive drill bit.

Footsteps shuffled to a halt outside the exhibit entry; the whistling went silent as the guard paused in the doorway.

And Joachim, who had rolled with a final burst of strength and preternatural swiftness, huddled unseen in the slim shadows behind the display case, the Spear of Longinus clutched to his thundering heart.

Chapter Twenty

"You're tired." Joachim's quiet observation was nearly lost under the drone of the van's tires on the highway.

"Not as tired as you." Gia smiled at him in the shadows, soaking in the simple pleasure of riding beside him in the back of the van. "You haven't slept in over twenty-four hours."

His incisive gaze moved over her face. "We'll be at headquarters soon. After debriefing, we'll both have some down time."

"You did an amazing job retrieving the Spear," she whispered. "Do you ever fail on these missions?"

"Not yet. But this one…" He sighed and met her eyes. "This one has held challenges of an entirely new variety."

"What do you mean?" she asked, knowing exactly what he meant.

A faint smile tugged at the corners of his mouth as he searched for the right answer. "Let's say that certain circumstances have created an unanticipated diversion. My self-discipline has been sorely tested, and my concentration faulty at times."

"I know that feeling." Her heartbeat hammered a now-familiar, frantic rhythm as she studied his weary face. Even in a state of exhaustion, he was the most beautiful man she'd ever seen.

"Nothing in the Realm is random, however," he went on. "There's a lesson buried somewhere in this for all of us."

"When you figure out what it is, clue me in, will you?"

"You'll be the first."

An electric silence fell between them and they gazed at each other, bodies bouncing slightly as the van traveled the uneven dirt road that led to the bunker. Joachim's elbow, resting on the back of the bench, straightened and his fingers surreptitiously brushed the curls at the back of her head. A private gesture between just the two of them, filled with a rich sentiment that heated the blood in Gia's veins and made her breathless with anticipation…for an intimacy that would never come.

Their time together was achingly short now. She would spend the rest of her existence wondering what it would have been like to love this man fully and without stricture.

Stationed at the computer in the van's midsection, Soleil slipped off the headset and turned to look at her mission leader. "Creator be praised. Aristide's team has locked onto Therides' location—he's back at the compound in Michigan and under surveillance. And our shadow teams have taken out the existing nephilim cell groups in three major cities."

"Yes!" Olivier took his hands off the steering wheel long enough to pump his fists in the air. "Now Therides is a sitting duck."

Joachim moved from the seat beside Gia and climbed to the front of the van. "This is good news. But if we lost him once, it can happen again. I want to move on the nephil in the next twenty-four hours." He glanced over his shoulder at Soleil, then at Gia. "Do you concur?"

"Of course." The blonde seraph closed the laptop computer and smiled. "I'm ready to go home, and I'm sure Gia is ready to make a life among her own kind."

Gia looked away. *What life*? For the millionth time she tried to imagine it without Joachim and failed. He had always been with her, first as a guardian spirit, and now as a man, the one she loved. But her reality would change—even now, the molecules of fate shifted under the weight of approaching circumstance—and she had no choice but to accept it. Once Therides was excised, the seraphs would return to Creator, and she would be forced to return to humankind without Joachim even in angelic form.

Olivier's words resounded in her mind. *Joachim won't be assigned to you, even in spirit. When you say goodbye in a few days, it's forever. Eternity.*

Sadness tightened her throat and she picked at a stray thread on her sleeve. The Daughter of Longinus wouldn't weep. She would embrace every challenge thrown her way, for none would be as great as what she'd already endured.

For the first time, Gia sensed the strength roiling within her, the power Joachim claimed had existed from the first day of her life.

Believe. Through faith in herself, her destiny and the Realm beyond, she would prevail.

Turning her head, she met Soleil's shadowed gaze. "Of course," she said. "I'm ready for anything."

* * * * *

The gathering in the dining hall was a celebration, both triumphant and bittersweet as the operatives discussed the upcoming shift from the physical plane back to the celestial.

Joachim sat in quiet solitude among his team members, studying each face in turn as the seraphs laughed and chatted and shared accounts of past missions. Lately he had come to identify them by their physical features. Everyone, including himself. He liked the face he saw in the mirror. It had become familiar and comfortable. A strange melancholy tugged at his heart as he thought about giving up his body, and all the pleasure and pain that came with dwelling inside the miraculous shell.

Propping his elbows on the table, he laced his fingers across his lips and let his attention drift to Gia. She listened with rapt attentiveness to some wild tale Olivier wove around her, and when the punch line came—there was always a punch line with Olivier's accounts—her brown eyes widened and she burst into laughter.

An involuntary smile tugged at Joachim's mouth. He loved

the sound of her laughter. It was rare, melodic and honest. She had come so far from the frightened, enraged hostage they'd abducted weeks ago. She was part of every day in his existence, both physical and celestial, and had been for so long, he couldn't grasp the inevitability of her absence.

Relinquishing a ward to a new life—and in Gia's case, a fresh start—was supposed to be a guardian's most triumphant moment. Instead Joachim found himself struggling with an insistent pain that brought a lump in his throat and distracted him even more than the constant battle he waged with his desire for her.

Blinking, he looked away from her laughing features and focused on the tabletop in front of him. Every move he'd made since the hotel room in Germany had been tainted by memories of touching Gia, tasting her, absorbing the pleasure of her caresses. The carnality of his recollections seared him, but it was the emotional intimacy they'd shared that haunted him and stole his desire to eat, to sleep, to remain focused on the long-awaited denouement of this mission.

Within twenty-four hours, he would be home, soaring through the Heavens, tied no longer to this Earth or human existence.

And all he felt was emptiness.

"—Do you remember, Captain?" Olivier's mirth-filled voice pulled him from his reverie, and Joachim mustered a smile for the seraphs around the table, who watched him with clairvoyant acuity.

"Do I remember what?"

"The assignment in nineteenth-century Texas when we served as cattle rustlers? The entire mission was a fiasco."

"How so?" Gia asked.

Olivier shook his head dolefully. "For one, imagine me herding longhorn cattle, and attempting such a task while riding a horse—"

"Falling off a horse," Joachim said, his smile widening.

"Again and again, if my memory serves me correctly."

"The body I was assigned held little skill with a saddle."

"You blame the body?" Joachim shot him a chiding look. "Come, come, Liv. Own up to the truth. What is it people say nowadays? You...*sucked*...at horsemanship."

The entire table erupted into laughter. Olivier tried to affect an indignant expression but ended up grinning. "Fine. I have no affinity with animals larger than humans. But that horse—"

"Buttercup," Joachim supplied.

"—That horse *Buttercup* knew I wasn't comfortable and held a vendetta against me. She threw me strictly for the entertainment of it."

"Your poor backside," Gia exclaimed, instigating a fresh surge of amusement in the room.

Olivier winced at the memories. "Exactly. I wasn't sorry to leave all that behind. No pun intended."

Smiling, Joachim sat back and studied the other seraph. Olivier was a fine second-in-command and an even better friend. A deep and abiding affinity bound Joachim to him, a silent recognition of true colleagues. They were brothers of the Realm, had come into existence in a single utterance from Creator's lips, and nothing could rend the mutual affection they held for one another...not even the recent tension among them.

Although Olivier hadn't yet broached the subject with him, Joachim knew his friend had confronted Gia in Germany. But no matter what Olivier had said, he merely meant to guard the mission. Still, unspoken and discomfiting sentiments hovered in the air among Joachim's team, and he would have to address the topic of his behavior with each of them when they returned to the Realm.

He didn't know what he would say. His own confusion soared to fathomless levels. But whatever emerged, Olivier alone would understand and accept without judgment. Of this Joachim was certain. In the end, no matter what his reservations, Olivier would support him. And Joachim loved him for it.

The doors swung open behind him and a somber hush fell over the table. One of the seraphs from Communication entered the dining room and approached the team leader at the head of the table. "The Archangel seeks a private meeting with you before the mission tomorrow."

Thanking him, Joachim scooted back his chair and laid his napkin beside his plate. The respite was over. "We'll meet at dawn for a final briefing regarding the strike against Therides," he told his team as he rose. "Rest tonight, seraphim. Pray. Gather your strength. The moment we've awaited stands before us. With clear hearts and minds, we will prevail."

* * * * *

"Your team is assembled and briefed for the termination of this mission?" Michael asked, strolling back and forth before Joachim's otherworldly vision.

"Yes. We have two operatives infiltrating the end location as we speak. They'll disable much of the security system tonight. Tomorrow morning, a six-man team, including the Daughter of Longinus, will raid the Michigan complex where Therides' army recruits and trains. The rest of the operatives will span the perimeter. It should be a clean sweep, if all goes in accordance with Intel's projections."

The Archangel tucked his hands inside his sleeves and paused to regard Joachim. "And you—all of you—are prepared to give up your physical bodies in battle, if circumstances make it so?"

"As always." Hesitating, Joachim noted the deepening green waves that radiated from Michael's aura. *Troubled misgiving*. He braced himself and met his commander's fathomless silver eyes. "You wish to question me about something."

"A pressing matter, but one you have not hastened to discuss in the last few debriefings."

"I follow your orders, Michael. Ask, and I will answer."

The Archangel studied his subordinate with piercing concentration. "The woman."

"Gia." Her name fell from Joachim's lips as effortlessly as a breath. It hung in the shimmering space between them, an undeniable indication of his turmoil.

"She holds a fascination for you that has distracted you from the mission."

A wave of shame washed through Joachim. No matter how he tried to disguise it, the truth had marked him as a mission leader faltering in his duties and as a man in danger of losing his heart.

"Seraphim will sweep out the nephil and return home, leaving behind our bodies and all the sentiments the human condition carries with it. The matter you speak of will hold no significance for me tomorrow at this time, Michael."

"But it holds significance for you now," the Archangel said, his regard steady on Joachim's face. "Tonight, it monopolizes your concentration. It holds your heart, your thoughts, your emotions."

Joachim closed his eyes, his fists clenching at his sides as his mask of control fell away. "What then do you expect of me? That I should seek your counsel yet again on this issue when so much of the damage is already done?"

"Again? What do you mean?"

"I tried before, Michael. I sought your guidance when I first gained possession of this body and realized its physical predilections could easily present a distraction—"

"That was when the issue was purely physical. But the problem is no longer entirely of a corporeal nature, Joachim. Your sentiments toward this woman are born of the heart and soul. The physical draw you experience is a by-product of—"

Before the Archangel could name it, Joachim dropped to his knees and clasped his hands against his forehead in a posture of desperation. "Deliver me, Michael. I swear to you I'll overcome these invasive feelings and guide the mission to its proper conclusion. But this unnamed turmoil is—is—"

"Joachim." The Archangel's voice came like a distant roll of thunder, filled with concern and compassion.

Joachim hung his head, his celestial manifestation vibrating with shame and confusion. "I beg of you…I beg of our Father…Let me resolve this situation in my own way, Michael. As a seraph. As a man. I won't fail the mission or your confidence. But this—*this*…I cannot define it, but it's mine to deal with. I could not bear to leave it unturned, but I must do it in my own right."

His feelings for Gia were too precious to be stripped and examined with cool, celestial impartiality. They were *his*. Not for Michael's examination. Not even for the Dominions'. At the risk of insubordination, he would follow his heart.

"How do you propose to resolve it, then?" the Archangel asked, astonishment wavering in shades of orange and yellow around his willowy form.

Joachim searched his mind, but his thoughts were too scattered, too diffused with anguish to put it into inarguable terms. "Allow me my solitude tonight. I beseech you, deliver me from assessment. Give me your blessing and let the curtain fall between us for these few remaining hours. I will seek resolution and find it, but I must be alone."

For a long time, the Archangel didn't speak. Then his hand settled on Joachim's head in acquiescence. "You have my blessing. Further, I absolve you from transgressions yet to be committed while still in this body."

"There shall be none," Joachim insisted, but Michael shook his head with a vehemence that silenced all protest.

"A wise being in your position will avow nothing. Go forth and complete the mission, and sweep aside the conflicts your humanity has brought upon you, so that you may return home and proceed unencumbered with your duties. This alone is the directive I issue you."

A cool breeze brushed over Joachim's being, wafting air

from the heavy collapse of a temporary barrier between him and the Celestial Realm. He had his seclusion, the space to resolve his strife without Heavenly supervision.

Gratitude burned his eyes. For the first time since creation, he was as a man. A man with the precious gift of free will.

* * * * *

Gia rolled to her side, her cot giving a restive squeak beneath her. It was no use. Her eyelids wouldn't stay shut. She gazed around the small sterile room, her heart rapping a heavy rhythm against her ribs. Although there were no guarantees, her instincts told her this was the last night she'd spend in the little cell she'd once despised. Now she loathed leaving its tidy familiarity—the cool linoleum floor beneath her feet, the clean white walls, the crisp sheets and slightly lumpy mattress. She'd never felt safer anywhere…except in Joachim's arms.

A mental snapshot of his rare smile flashed across her eyes. The low sound of his voice caressed her ears, and his scent filled her senses. She flung an arm over her eyes and felt his mouth brush hers, felt the slick glide of his tongue between her lips, the quickened rush of his breath against her neck, the way he pulsed in her hands, in her mouth. He'd tasted like clean male and heady desire. So damn human. Just a beautiful, aroused, mortal man.

She loved him. Every inch of him. Every cursed, forbidden caress and kiss and intimacy that had passed between them. *Thou shalt not covet thy Creator's highest-ranking angel*, she thought wryly, and didn't feel one bit guilty for doing so.

With a deep sigh, she sat up on the edge of the cot and reached to turn on the wall-mounted lamp. Sleep would be a stranger tonight. Did Joachim walk his office as restless and unhappy as she?

Blinking in the lamp's harsh glare, she tried to swallow another realization. This was their last night together…spent an entire labyrinth apart.

Don't even think about it, barked the virtuous voice of reason in the back of her mind. Despite its chiding, Gia got to her feet and paced to the door. Her fingers rested on the knob. How easy it would be to open it and sneak down to his room. She wouldn't linger, just knock, say a few heartfelt words, like how much she loved him, how grateful she was for all he'd done to protect and guide her. Then she'd turn and leave. Perhaps it would be their only goodbye. She wasn't certain they'd get another chance. And if either of them was killed in the battle tomorrow…

No. She wouldn't think of that. Still, the anxiety it stirred drove her to open the door and head for Joachim's office, voice of reason be damned.

The steely corridors were deserted, the floor gritty and cold beneath her bare feet. She passed a handful of rooms where seraphs worked at complicated-looking monitors. They were too preoccupied to note her presence, and the rest of the complex was silent, a finely constructed machine at rest. Maybe Joachim was asleep too. She would knock once. If he didn't answer, she'd head back to her cell without hesitation.

When she reached his office, the door was ajar, soft light spilling through the narrow opening.

Swallowing the lump in her throat, she tapped a knuckle against the wood and waited for his familiar, "Come."

No reply.

You said you'd knock once and then go back to your cell, her common sense railed. *No hesitation.*

"I lied," she whispered, and tried to shut out the commonsensical babysitter in the back of her mind.

What are you doing? it needled.

Joachim had asked her that very question the day she tried to seduce him in a bid to escape. She never could have guessed the answer would one day bring her to his office door, her body thrumming with desire and her heart with yearning.

Claiming you, she would tell him. *You're all I want. You're everything.*

If he'd only answer the damn door.

"Gia?"

Startled, she turned to find him approaching from the corridor shadows, bare-chested, towel in hand. He was fresh from the shower, his wet hair combed back from his face, throwing his stern features into sharp relief. His white pajama bottoms hung low on his hips, and she stared, wondering inanely what he wore beneath the thin cotton pants. Last time, he was naked beneath them.

His physique was hard, muscled, flawless. *God, he was desirable.*

"What is it?" He stopped beside her, his blue eyes steady on hers.

"I—" No answer was going to sound even half-sane. Honesty was always the best policy where he was concerned. "I couldn't sleep. I have something to say, but I can't do it out here in the hall. May I come in?"

Acquiescing with a tilt of his head, Joachim pushed open the door and motioned her into the office. When she stepped inside, he followed and closed the door with his back, his gaze never straying from her face.

Gia squelched a rising wave of edginess and wandered toward his desk, where several maps were spread out. "What are these?"

"Diagrams of Rossi's compound." He set aside his towel and approached her. "Remember the Fellowship of the Fallen Sun? The mansion in Michigan?"

"Yes." She studied one painstakingly rendered blueprint, recalling how unruly and offensive she'd acted that day, when he showed her footage of her demon-possessed husband in action. "I didn't believe you, I fought you tooth and nail, and still you were patient and compassionate. I know it's water under the bridge, but I regret the way I acted."

"You were frightened," he said. "And seraphim were to blame. I have learned from the mistakes we made with you. We did make mistakes. If I had it to do over, things would be different."

She fingered the edge of the map, vaguely wondering who had rendered it. "How would things be different?"

In more ways than he would admit. She could see it in his face, and it broke her heart. He had regrets.

She didn't.

"We would befriend you first," he said. "Earn your trust before secreting you away."

Gia nearly laughed. A few weeks ago, she never would have trusted a bunch of soft-spoken beauties like seraphim. Never would have allowed them into her small circle of pseudo-friends. They'd *had* to kidnap her. There was no other recourse.

"Time was short when we abducted you, but we moved too abruptly. We were too distant with you." His quiet voice behind her sent a sweet frisson of sexual awareness through her. "Despite our unintentional errors, you rallied more quickly than any of us had projected. You showed yourself to be a quick learner and someone we could trust. You're a good woman, Gia. Courageous. Strong."

And he was unequivocally empathetic and gentle, no matter the circumstances. He always had been, from the second they locked eyes in the shadows of that rickety van so many weeks ago. *Blue Eyes,* she'd named him, having no comprehension of the beauty behind the ski mask, the seraph behind the man. Every moment she'd kept her distance from him seemed like a foolish waste of precious time.

Lost in a tangle of desire and grief, she stared at the map. "How long has the nephil been recruiting its army?"

"The cult's existed for several years. If you'd stumbled onto it before we took you, you would have died at Rossi's hands."

"I guess it's time I thanked you." She faced him with a rueful smile, which quickly faded when she realized they stood with little distance between them. She could count the drops of moisture that still clung to the thin silver chain around his neck.

"You don't have to thank us." The way his gaze wandered over her features told her that he too was distracted by the heat building between them. "Our job is to protect and guide you."

She couldn't think of a reply, couldn't think of a way to stop the painful conversation from ending. Her attention focused on the small crucifix dangling at the hollow of his throat. "That's beautiful. It looks very old."

"It is very old. A gift, from a long-ago mission in Spain."

"Did a woman give it to you?" As soon as the conspicuous question escaped, her gaze shot guiltily to his.

"As a matter of fact, yes."

"What kind of woman? A friend?"

"A Catholic nun." A hint of humor quirked his mouth, as though he could withhold it no longer. "Feel better?"

"Not much." She lifted her chin. "Nuns can have crushes, you know, even though they're forbidden to act on them. They're human too. Under those habits, they're just the same as most women. Many of them leave the convent for love."

"This one was seventy-five years old and very pious."

"Oh." They stood so close, she wondered if he could hear the trip-hammer of her heartbeat. Wondered if he could see the moisture burning her eyes. Tears seemed to gather between her legs too. Desperate need. Did he know what he did to her? Every cell in her body responded to his nearness, like shards of metal drawn to a magnet. Every emotion she'd never allowed herself to feel knocked at her soul the way her pulse hammered her rib cage, like a wild thing trying to escape.

"Well," she choked, "it's a lovely necklace. I haven't seen it on you before."

"I leave it on Earth and relocate it on every mission, strictly for fortification." His attention dropped to her trembling lips. "For when I'm feeling susceptible."

"Susceptible to what?"

"Well, to…" His throat moved when he swallowed.

"Human emotion."

She drifted closer, helplessly drawn to him, until she had to tilt her head back to meet his gaze. "You're feeling that way now? Susceptible?"

"A little, perhaps." He searched her tear-filled eyes, his own expression melting and reforming in some kind of bid for control over his own response. Then he moved to straighten the maps on the desk, breaking the seductive spell between them. "What did you want to say, Gia Torio, that can't be shouted through the hallways?"

Of course he wouldn't let her beat around the bush. She knew that when she marched her foolish rear end down here in the first place. Now she was trapped, and there was no sweeter prison. But she wouldn't just say goodbye and skip out. Now that she was here with him, their desire a tangible third party, she wanted…more.

Capturing his wrist with an unsteady hand, she opened her mouth to tell him she didn't want to say goodbye without lying beside him again, kissing him, touching him. That she wanted to nurture the fire between them, if only for one night.

Don't leave me, she wanted to plead. *Stay with me. Be my guardian and lover and friend, every day, in body as well as soul.* Faisons l'amour. *Make love to me.*

What emerged was, "What did you mean by 'cycle'?"

A crease appeared between his eyebrows. "Why?"

"I have to know." She swallowed the urge to weep for the hundredth time. "What is cycle?"

He sighed. "You refer to the expulsion that nephilim can impose upon seraphim."

"Yes." She caressed his wrist as though it were a precious object, measuring its strength and breadth. Every part of him fit like a perfect puzzle. Fit *her*. "You told me once that Therides can send a seraph into cycle. What does that entail, exactly? Is it death?"

"No." A distant expression darkened his features. "It's life as you know it, but for seraphim, it's a massive and undesired step backward."

"What happens?"

"Just like seraphim, nephilim have the power to possess human bodies. If a nephil attacks a seraph-inhabited body, it does so spiritually—a battle of souls for possession of that body. If the nephil wins the struggle, the seraph is cast out."

Gia's eyes widened with horror. "To Hell?"

"No such place exists for a pure spirit. Instead the seraph becomes tied to the Earth—or some other physical plane in the universe—and is granted a corporeal body in infancy, with no memory of Creator or the Celestial Realm." His hand covered hers where it clutched his wrist. "Thus the cycle of life begins, and the seraph must exist in this physical way, his status reduced to this position sometimes for many lifetimes."

"Just like me, or any other human here." Her mouth twisted and she withdrew from his grasp, folding her arms across her stinging heart. "Being reduced to a mere mortal must seem like a real kick in the pants to a lofty angel like you, Captain."

He rubbed his wrist where she'd touched him, his lashes like feathers against his cheeks as he considered her veiled accusation. "You must understand, Gia, we weren't made to walk the Earth, but to dwell in the Realm beyond. We're protectors. The worst punishment that can be forced upon a seraph is to deny him or her the ability to serve."

"I know." She strolled around to the other side of the desk, putting distance between them. "So you're pretty anxious to get out of here after all. I thought you might be. Not that I can blame you. I'd like to step off myself, but I don't have the six wings to fly."

The bitterness in her tone wasn't lost on him. "It's not that simple, Gia."

"Tell me something, Joachim," she blurted, damnable sorrow clogging her throat. "What did it mean to you when I told you I loved you?"

His features softened and he reached across the desk for her hand with lightning-quick intent, holding tight when she would have pulled free. "It's a gift. The most precious I have ever received, in this realm or the next."

"But it's not enough to make you stay. It's not as compelling as the desire to serve Creator and Michael and seraphim. I understand that. I've known it since I first felt this attraction to you." She looked down, surrendering to the hot tears that blurred her vision. "It's just so hard to accept."

His thumb swept across her knuckles while she struggled to squelch the sobs building in her chest. "Ah, Gia. Your love, the call to seraphim—the two can't be compared. I was born to the Heavens, and for no other reason than to protect you and others like you. How can I give that up, when it was with this purpose in mind that Creator formed me?"

Ignoring her silent protest, he drew her around the desk to stand before him. "Even still, I look at you now and I wonder the same thing. How can I give you up when the time comes? I'm sleepless, and torn, and confused. For the first time in my existence, I don't know my own heart, my own thoughts. You consume me." He laid his hand against her damp cheek. "How can I want you so much when its impossibility is beyond measure?"

She bit her lip to stop its quivering. "Olivier says that after tomorrow, I'll never see you again. That you'll never see me."

Uttering a sigh, Joachim slid his arms around her waist, and Gia finally moved into his embrace. Her nose found the warm, bare curve of his neck and a shudder of helpless desire vibrated through her when she inhaled the scent of soap and vanilla on his naked skin.

It was so good to hold him with no garment to block his heat and fragrance from her senses. She soaked him up, her hungry hands running over his muscular back. All of Heaven could watch, and they couldn't do a damn thing short of striking her dead. She would give her life rather than relinquish this man's embrace. This *man*. Hers. He would be, for a few more hours, and nothing would change that, not even divine will.

Chapter Twenty-One

Joachim stroked her hair, his lips moving against the crown of her head as he spoke. "The part of me I've held aloft from this mission still imparts common sense, even as I stand here with you in my arms. It tells me that in time, the pain of separation will fade for both of us. You'll go on to—"

"How do you know what I'll do?" She drew back to frown at him. "You may be an angel, but you can't foretell my future. Can you?"

"No," he whispered, fingertips trailing goose bumps down her spine as he rubbed her back in slow, soothing circles.

"So who knows what could happen? After all, I did such a bang-up job of walking into trouble before I ever met you. And look at all the tension I created here, in a place where tension isn't supposed to even exist. Soleil hardly speaks to me, or *you*, and Olivier thinks I'm the devil."

They both hesitated at her choice of words.

"...Metaphorically speaking," she added. "My point is, what makes you think I'm not going to inadvertently leave a wake of destruction behind me once I go back to the real world?"

"Because your eyes have been opened," he said, his gaze caressing her face. "And you have a job. You hold the Spear, for the greater good of this Earth. Do you think you can so easily cast aside your destiny, Daughter of Longinus?"

She had no reply—it was blocked by the decidedly unheroic return of tears. Desperate to preserve her dignity, she withdrew from his arms and rubbed her hands over her face. Later, when Joachim was truly and permanently gone, she would grieve without inhibition. Later, when she no longer walked among angels or stood accountable for the fate of the world. Later, when she was just plain old Gia Torio, alone once again.

Thank God he didn't reach for her. As though he understood the solitude of her struggle, he let her be, his presence a quiet reassurance beside her as she fought to rein in her unruly emotions.

"What else do you want to know?" he spoke at last, the ever-patient angel.

A few gulping breaths, and she regained equilibrium. Wiping the moisture from her lashes, she glanced down at the map of the Brotherhood's compound spread out on the desk. "Tell me, Captain, how will we get into Therides' headquarters?"

"Different ways. I'll show you." He shifted behind her and taking her hand, led her forefinger to a side entry below a portico on the map. "One team will enter here." He moved her finger up a few inches to a second-floor balcony. "And one here. And here." His mint-scented breath caressed her cheek as he guided her touch to the basement. "The initial infiltration will take place through these locations. And seraphim will fill in the perimeter, gradually converging until the invasion is complete."

Gia felt the sweet weight of his chin resting on her shoulder as they leaned together over the map. "I'll be with you?"

"Yes. We'll fight Therides side by side, as a team. And by your hand, the demon will be excised."

"I've never attacked anything in my life," she said solemnly. "Especially a demon I used to be married to. Especially with a flimsy, two-thousand-year-old spearhead. Let's hope I don't blow this."

"Believe in yourself, Gia. You must."

He was so close, all she had to do was turn her head and seek his mouth. "Must I? I can't even think straight. Not when you're this near." Her words faltered as she succumbed to delicious distraction. "Not about decent things, anyway."

In reply, his lips brushed her ear, once, twice, and kissed the tender spot behind it. "When you cry," he whispered, "I feel it in every part of me."

Wayward humor lifted the corners of her mouth. "Really?"

"The scent of your tears…" he nuzzled her cheek, and the soft flick of his tongue stole some of the salty moisture from her skin. "It's like perfume. I should comfort you. The angel in me wants to heal you. But the man in me… Forgive me."

"There's nothing to forgive. Even if you never spoke to me or touched me, Joachim, you would have broken my heart. A mere glimpse of your face, and I would have been undone."

His hand cupped her chin and turned her face so he could meet her eyes, his lashes weighted by desire. Nothing angelic remained in his gaze. The fires of passion burned bright and clear, indigo streaks of searing flame.

"Gia," he murmured. A warning. A promise.

Need battled with grief and won, shooting heat through her veins and curling like a caress down low in her womb. There was no more room for stilted conversation. No place left to stow away forbidden wants.

Her heart leapt and lunged as his hand slid beneath her breasts. The warmth of his palm burned her through her thin T-shirt. She felt the heavy thud of his pulse where his chest pressed against her back, matching hers beat for erratic beat.

"I should go," she said.

"Don't," he replied, and her heart tumbled again at the one-word entreaty.

"This is a mistake, Joachim."

"Yes." His breath came as quickly as hers now. "The voice in my head says the same. *C'est une faute,* over and over." His tongue flicked her earlobe, leaving a trace of dampness and a series of shivers behind.

Oh, God. "What else does it say, this voice in your head?"

"*Tu dois partir.*" He moved aside her hair and kissed her

cheek, then her neck in tiny, gossamer brushes, his hand sliding down her stomach and beneath the hem of her shirt to span her naked ribs.

"What does that mean?" she asked, her head languidly accommodating his lips when they feathered down the side of her neck.

"It means you should go."

Her eyes closed, breath escaping in tiny gasps as his fingers drew erotic designs on her bare stomach. "I will. All you have to do is say you don't want me."

He turned her to face him, trapping her between the desk and his aroused body. *"Je te désire trop,"* he said huskily, his sultry gaze fixed on her mouth.

"And that means…?" She cupped his face with hands that trembled from the force of her desire, reading the carnal intent in his fathomless eyes, the flush of need in his cheeks.

"I want you too much." With that simple assertion, Joachim shoved aside the maps, lifted her onto the desk and stepped forward between her knees.

She tilted her face to him and let her lashes flutter closed, waiting for the ravenous plunder of his mouth. Instead, his lips touched ever so lightly on hers, nudging, brushing, like the slow waver of butterfly wings at rest. And when she thought she'd die for want of a deeper taste, Gia drew back and choked, "Joachim—"

And all pretenses at restraint shattered.

Their open lips met with a hunger unknown to her before, wholly sexual and needful, with thrusting tongues and roaming hands and breathless groans. Sinking her fingers in his damp hair, Gia let go of her pride and trepidation and devoured his beautiful mouth, loving him with the ferocity of a woman too long denied, one whose heart was breaking.

She loved him.

She would lose him.

Fresh tears slipped down her cheeks and pooled between their lips, salty and piquant. Joachim wiped them away with his thumbs as fast as they fell, but when he drew back to look at her with a mixture of compassion and need, an ill-timed sob rose in her throat.

"Shh." He passed a hand over her eyes, and her eyelids closed. "No pain," he whispered, and just like that, her grief subsided, stealing her desperation and replacing it with slow-heating sensuality.

She opened her eyes, found him watching her, his chest heaving, his hands braced on the desk on either side of her. Waiting. They stared at each other in the electric lull, the harsh sound of their breathing tearing the silence.

A certainty possessed Gia then—a woman's knowledge that she could take this man inside her, seduce him, love him, fulfill his every desire and her own, if only the Heavens wouldn't interfere.

Oh, please, don't interfere.

"Touch me," she whispered. "With your mouth, your tongue, your body. *Faisons l'amour,* Joachim."

Make love with me. It was all she wanted in this world. When she saw the answer flare in his eyes, all emotion slid away save the undeniable need for physical passion as powerful as the inner force that bound their hearts. He would take her. She would take him. They would claim each other.

Sliding a trembling arm around his neck, she arched against him and offered her throat to his lips, her body to his exploration. Her knees inched up to bracket his hips, urging him closer as she cradled his head and led his mouth to the hardened nipples beneath her shirt.

"Will you?" she breathed as his soft hair ticked her throat.

"I will." His husky reply was half-lost against the curve of her breast as he tongued and wetted the erect tip through her shirt. "I must."

"Take me all the way."

"Yes," he kissed his way up her neck again, following the sensitive tendon that led to her jaw. "And beyond."

She lifted her chin to oblige his wandering lips. "You'll be breaking all the rules. What if someone comes to stop you?"

"No one will come. The rules…" He paused and shook his head. "*Damn the rules,*" he said fiercely, shuddering as the walls of his celibacy crumbled around him and exposed him as exquisitely human. "Tonight I cannot abide by them, Gia. Tonight I'm just a man, and I need you desperately."

Bittersweet joy stole her words, so her hands spoke for her, caressing his cheeks, his jaw, her tender gaze searching his features in wonder. He was the loveliest, purest creature. No act they committed in this room tonight could be a sin. Nothing could sully this exquisite blink in time—except the inevitability of its end.

He pressed her back on the desk until she lay supine and shivering, her lashes still damp and spiky from forgotten grief. With unsteady fingers he traced her features, lingered at her lips, slipping his thumb between them to meet the tip of her tongue, the even edge of her teeth.

No part of Gia was left untouched, unadored. He kissed her shoulders through her T-shirt, he nipped at the soft skin in the crook of each elbow, where her pulse beat a rapid tattoo. His tongue traced the faint veins in her wrists and tickled her palms, and then he drew each fingertip into his mouth, a hot, suctioning kiss that sent desire rushing to the sacred, feminine place between her legs.

Each caress made her wetter, hotter, more frantic, yet his languid touch demonstrated how he would take his time, how he would love her from head to toe, how nothing stood between them now, not even the brevity of the hours granted them in which to fulfill their explosive yearnings.

Papers rustled beneath her back as he scooted her farther up the desk and leaned over her to align their bodies. A pen rolled across the surface beyond her head and hit the floor, followed by something plastic that rattled and scattered. Paper clips, staples—it didn't matter. All Gia could comprehend was the ache deep within her that only he could fill, and the rigid outline of his shaft rubbing against her very center, a primal, involuntary dance, a delicious measure of his need.

Joachim's palm skimmed the arch of her throat, back down to her left breast, kneading the soft orb, plucking her nipple through her top, enticing it into sweet, piercing erection. Lower, to her belly, where he tugged up her shirt to rub her skin the way a carpenter might stroke a fine polished surface he'd honed with his own hands.

And the look on his face as he touched her…so concentrated, so intense, Gia shuddered.

Her fingers riffled through his hair while his mouth chased the path burned by his hands. Pushing her shirt higher, he opened his lips against her quivering stomach, tongue circling and dipping into the hollow of her navel.

Gia writhed beneath him, exhaling soft, breathy moans. The chain he wore dragged its own enticing caress over her skin, raised goose bumps in its wake as his hips worked restlessly against hers in promise of what was to come.

The only relief she could offer was to slide her knees up high along his sides, bringing their lower bodies into snug contact, and it wasn't enough. She opened her legs wider, squirmed beneath him to better align them, male to female, while he grew harder and she, wetter.

The desk squeaked, its metal frame protesting under their energetic movements. Heat gathered between Gia's legs with every rocking lunge of Joachim's body. In silent demand, she lifted her hips to meet his thrust, damning the garments between them, her fingers digging into the sinewy muscles of his shoulders, his spine, his muscular buttocks.

Despite the barrier of their clothing, the ridge of his erection rubbed her just right. After a moment an errant, unexpected orgasm shimmied through her, little sparkles of delight dancing behind her eyelids. For the second time in a handful of days she climaxed from the mere friction of Joachim's body against hers, and the surprised cry slipped between her lips, renting the hushed air.

They both went still, panting, but Joachim said nothing. He straightened a little and drew a shuddering breath, his fingers resting at her waist. For a heart-stopping instant, Gia thought he meant to halt their lovemaking, and in her heart she knew he would have been wise to do so. She wouldn't have argued. She would have fled to the safety of her cell, fled the threat to their very souls that existed in this room.

But in the end he was no wiser than she, nor any more immune to the power of a desire too long denied.

"I want more with you tonight, do you understand? More than intercourse. More than to taste you, to feel you around me, to come inside you." He stumbled over the words, for they sounded foreign and startling to both of them.

"Then what?" she prompted softly, loving his inexperience, his untried, innate sensuality.

"Lose yourself with me," he said, his ardor written in the stern lines between his brows. "You spoke of such a passion the day we retrieved the Medallion."

A tender smile curved her lips. "That made an impression, huh?"

"It haunts me." He leaned to press a lingering kiss against her belly, then lower, unabashedly, against her mons, his warm exhalation flooding her through her thin cotton pants. When she shuddered and sucked in a sharp breath, he straightened and drew her upright. "I want to take you out of this world."

He'd remembered word for word her description of what lovemaking could do, and she didn't know whether to laugh or dissolve into tears at the magnitude of joy rising within her. For the first time, she felt the potential to fly in a man's arms. This man, with the soul of an angel. *Out of this world.*

"Yes," she whispered, staring into his darkened eyes. "Take

me far, far away."

"To a place where making love is most righteous," he added, his tone husky. "Where we can know each other, body and spirit, and no laws will be broken. Nor vows, nor hearts."

The room spun as he lifted her. Closing her eyes, she wrapped her arms around his neck and her legs around his waist, and he carried her into the tiny room where his cot was located, kicking the door shut behind them.

They sank to their knees on the narrow mattress. Utter darkness engulfed them, but Joachim's mouth unerringly sought and found hers, more ravenous now than tender, his tongue sliding between her lips in rhythmic imitation of what his body wanted.

"Show me how to please you," he whispered against her mouth.

"You do it without even trying." She was crying again, tears of joy, tears of anguish that he kissed away. Her fingers slipped between them and traced his lips in the shadows. "Your smile pleases me. The width of your shoulders and the blue of your eyes, the graceful way you move. The gentle, sexy way you say my name."

Blind in the darkness, Gia slid her hands along his jaw and cupped his face, reveling in a beauty she could only see in her mind. "But most of all, your soul pleases me, Joachim. It's beautiful. You're beautiful. I wish I could look at you when we make love. I want to look into your eyes when you come. I want to see every inch of you."

Abruptly he withdrew and his weight left the cot with a squeak of metal springs. A moment later, dim light flooded the room. Immediately Gia tugged her shirt down over her naked breasts.

"Take it off," he said, his features dark with purpose.

She squinted at him in the lamp's unforgiving glow, heat flooding her cheeks. "But the light…"

"I want to see you as well." Hesitating beside the dresser,

he studied her. "Why do you cover yourself?"

A fresh wave of warmth stung her ears. "I'm not that woman in the lingerie advertisement you loved so much. I'm not perfect."

He took a few steps and stopped, his eyes smoldering with iridescent blue fire as his fingers pulled the string at the waist of his pajamas. "My perception is not the same as yours, Gia. Let me decide for myself. Let me look at you through a man's eyes. Your face. Your skin. Your softness."

She couldn't deny him anything, and he knew it. Still, he moved closer to her in increments, as though she were a skittish fawn and he an observer with hand outstretched. When he was a foot away, he paused. "It pleases you to look at me in this way, yes? As a woman appraises the man she desires."

"Oh, yes." The reply drifted from her lips like a plume of smoke, husky, needful.

"Then look at me now." His thumb slid under the loosened waistband of his bottoms and he eased them over his lean hips, down his strong, sculpted legs, let them fall to a puddle at his ankles.

Gia pressed her lips together to swallow the joyful sob rising in her chest. He was as she'd known he would be—muscled, sleek, his body pieced together in God-like proportion. As magnificent on the outside as the exquisite soul inside.

"I'm yours," he said low. "Every part of this body. Every part of this heart. Look at me…I belong to you." When her gaze skimmed down his torso, his hand followed its path, touching himself lightly, curiously, as though aware of himself for the first time. Guiding her appraisal from his neck, chest and hard, flat stomach, to the generous, demanding shaft of flesh that rose from a dark thatch of hair between his legs. His palm drifted over the engorged head, and it jerked in response, an impatient harbinger of delight, before his fingers closed around it and stroked it from base to tip.

"There have been times," he murmured, his eyes sliding

shut as he caressed himself, "that I couldn't pass the night without relieving the ache you stirred in me. I was ashamed. I thought…I believed it meant weakness."

He opened his eyes, and his electric gaze shot straight through her soul. "And now I know the strength behind a man's desire. The power of a woman's love."

Gia couldn't breathe. She tried to swallow and found her throat dry with desire. "Come to me," she whispered, holding out her hand. "Come."

He took her proffered fingers and knelt on the mattress beside her. "As a man appraises the woman he desires," he prompted, his hand sliding under her shirt.

In wordless acquiescence she held up her arms, and he drew the garment over her head, baring her breasts. One warm hand slipped around to the base of her spine to arch her back just slightly. In this fashion he studied her in the pale light, while Gia squeezed her eyes closed and rode a wave of exquisite self-consciousness, her nipples drawn tight beneath the warmth of his appraisal.

Without warning, he uttered some indecipherable exclamation and then the wet heat of his mouth enclosed her left nipple, and he suckled her as though he could draw her very soul into him.

Galvanic sensation sizzled between her breast and her womb, jolts of fire, every one like a tiny orgasm quaking and searing her body.

"Oh, yes…" she groaned, her fingers seeking and finding the rich softness of his hair. She'd never particularly liked the touch of a man's mouth at her nipple, had found it agitating, unsatisfying in the past. Now, with Joachim, she could climax from it. "Don't stop, Joachim. Don't stop, don't stop, don't stop…"

He smiled and took her other nipple between his lips, pulling it in deep, thirsty tugs.

Whimpers interspersed her quickened breaths. Jolts of

pleasure traveled her nerve paths, dissolving her muscles and replacing them with sheer, straining tension.

He didn't speak, didn't cajole, but encouraged her ever onward with his touch as he palmed one breast and suckled the other, his pelvis shifting a subtle restless dance against hers. Rubbing, *rubbing*, tongue on one nipple, palm on the other, the sleek, steely length of his cock sliding against her naked stomach.

The world tilted backward. Her head sank into a soft, Joachim-scented pillow, which she clutched with both hands as he knelt between her legs, the tip of his swollen member nudging her soft, open folds through the lightweight pants she wore. She could feel its heat soaking her flesh, could imagine its scalding strength pushing into her.

Needful anticipation rode the whimper that escaped her throat. Now he would strip the pajamas from her legs, and nothing would stand between them. He would sink into her body, possess every inch of her, and she would die from the pleasure of it.

But Joachim had other, more provocative plans. He took his penis in hand to tease her core through the damp cotton pajamas, stroking in myriad tiny circles so that she writhed beneath him in delicious agony. The silken head of his cock rubbed and seared her tender, aroused flesh, again, again, until she could no longer lie still, until every breath that escaped her was a half-sob and her pelvis undulated in thrusting invitation.

Then he leaned to recapture her nipple between his lips, simultaneously suckling her and grinding his hips into hers, and a rush of orgasm like Gia had never known washed over her, each frightening, exhilarating wave stronger than the one before, so that her back bowed and paroxysms of delight constricted the cries escaping her throat.

Only when she sagged against the mattress did Joachim relinquish her breast. His hungry lips covered hers again, and he kissed her deeply, thrust into her panting mouth with his tongue, feeding on her languid desire and replacing it with passion all the more potent.

His cock was a fiery brand throbbing against her naked stomach, and Gia knew by the vague trembling of his body that his restraint was waning. "Take off my pants," she breathed. "I can't wait anymore."

Sitting back on his heels, Joachim grasped the waistband of her pajamas and drew them down, taking her panties with them. He tossed the garments aside, never moving his gaze from hers. Then he placed a hand on both her knees and gently but resolutely pressed them apart…and only then did his attention shift from her face.

Cool air whisked across Gia's wet, feminine flesh in the pause that followed, and the heat of his gaze burned her as he examined her, took in every exposed shadow and curve. She had never read such fascination and desire in a lover's regard, and it transformed her into a beautiful, mysterious, powerful creature.

"You're like a flower," he sounded awed, one hand sliding up the inside of her thigh to touch her sex. Only with a single fingertip, but *oh*, it was a potent caress as it drew swirls through her body's moisture. "So wet, so soft. Your flesh is like petals, here, and here, hiding the portal to your body. And this—" His fingertip circled, then brushed her clitoris directly and a new electric jolt shuddered through her. "This is the seat of your pleasure, yes? Or is it—" His finger slid inside her without warning, deep, wrenching a cry of delight from her throat. "—here?"

"Oh, God." She twisted beneath him, and her knees fell wide as her body swallowed the gentle invasion. "All of it. I don't know. That feels so good."

Two fingers slid inside her, then perhaps a third, Gia couldn't tell, but it wasn't enough, she wanted him, his erection, his plunging stroke, the hot pulse of his semen jetting inside her.

"Please," she groaned, throwing one arm over her eyes, half to hide behind and half to shield herself from the blinding pleasure. "Please…I want you inside me so much. I want to come with you."

But Joachim was too mesmerized to withdraw just yet. His fingers played her center, the source of her sexuality, a chalice of moist, delicious heat and invitation. With every gentle thrust of his hand, the tautness in her firm muscles escalated again, a phenomenon of pleasure that filled him with the exquisite certainty he alone could create such an intense reaction in her.

Watching her climax, Joachim had decided, was so pleasurable as to be physical. The sparkle of perspiration on her breasts, the tiny frown lines between her brows, the way her lips fell open to release erratic breaths…the way her thighs fell open to push her harder against his hand…and then the shuddering spasms that rolled through her, one upon the other, moving her again and again. It was some kind of unearthly dance whose sight, scent and sound he would remember for the rest of his existence.

He would have it again, this night. Again and again. As many times as her slender body would surrender. Acting on blind instinct, he slid down between her legs until he found her, sweet and soft and wet like a ripe fruit, with his mouth.

"Yes, *oh yes…*" She thrashed beneath his tongue as he dragged it in quick, hungry strokes through the moist, petal-soft folds of her flesh, piercing and licking and exploring the texture of her, the taste and scent of her. He knew there must be an art to this form of sexual worship, and though he was untried, he was hungry. His fervor drove him to lick and savor every silken drop of her essence, to explore every rise and valley of her succulent, sacred flesh. When he suckled and nibbled the tiny, erect bud at the mouth of her womanhood, Gia came again with a muffled cry and shuddered endlessly around his lapping tongue, bathing it in heat and honeyed moisture.

Propped on his elbows between her thighs, he tongued her until the last quiver had faded away. Then he rose, his cock heavy and aching, and once again knelt on the cot before her.

"Oh," she whispered, shuddering in lax abandon. "I went somewhere just now. Out of body."

"Out of this world?" he demanded.

"And beyond." A smile curved her lips as she lifted her lashes to study his expression. He was so determined, so solemn. So naked and hungry, kneeling on the mattress between her legs.

"Your turn," she said. Still shivering from the delicious aftereffects of orgasm, she sat up and touched the hard wall of his stomach, then lower, where his thick arousal jutted from the thatch of dark hair at his groin. Her fingertips trailed along the fiery head, tracked the pearly moisture glistening there in circles until the tip of his penis was coated in his own essence, until he was slick and hot, pulsing with life, with need, with the promise of a fulfillment neither of them would ever know again.

Joachim sucked in a breath and closed his eyes, his hands fisted at his sides as he bore her lazy exploration. "Guide me," he murmured.

A lover's prayer. Fingers trembling, Gia caressed the throbbing length with both palms, feeling the surge of blood and heat that swelled him, readied him.

The cot squeaked. Joachim shifted his weight and widened his knees to give her better access, one palm braced on the concrete block wall by the bed. While he watched with shuttered eyes, she stroked him, rhythmic and unrelenting, until his hips followed her ministrations of their own accord, thrust and retreat, and oxygen rushed from his lungs faster than he could replenish it.

The sight of his own turgid flesh, crimson-hot, sliding in and out of her cool, slender fingers, shuddered through him, sent perspiration trickling between his shoulder blades and down his spine. Her other hand crept between his thighs and found his sac, cupping, measuring, caressing.

"*Ah.*" His head fell back, eyelids slamming closed as sounds of ecstasy rumbled in his throat. He knew he should stop her, halt her skilled soft hands as they worked him to a rapture greater than any he had ever known. This was making love, and yet it was not, for he hadn't taken her in the way a man possessed a woman, and doing so was a greater need than the urgency that seemed to draw every drop of blood to the shaft she stroked so sinuously.

With a discipline born of sheer determination, he grasped her wrists and halted the inexorable climb to ejaculation. "*Gia,*" he growled, his body shuddering from the shock of denied release.

She grimaced and lay back on the pillow, color staining her cheeks. "I'm sorry."

"No. It's too good. And I'm..." A rueful smile curved his mouth as he followed her down to the mattress and slipped between her open thighs. "Too new, perhaps."

She shifted beneath him, caught his cock against the desire-drenched opening that wept anew for him and undulated her pelvis so that the tip of his penis slid against her. A siren's call. Her lips, lush and damp from his kiss, tickled his ear. "You were going to come just now. In my hand."

"Yes."

"I'd rather you come inside me."

Joachim closed his eyes and struggled against the intrinsic urge to plunge into her softness. "Please. Yes."

Her palm slid down the curve of his spine to caress his buttocks. "Come inside me, Joachim."

It was the attainment of countless, forbidden dreams he'd harbored since the first moment he saw her, graceful and golden in the sun. And like the man he had become, he couldn't deny it.

Bracing his palms on either side of her, he shifted his hips between her legs, positioned his cock at the mouth of her femininity, seeking...probing...sliding forward...

Ah, Gia.

Deep.

So...tight.

Deeper.

So wet.

To the hilt. A million satin fingers enclosed him, beckoned him as her body constricted and pulsed around his shaft.

The lush sensations tore a gasp from his throat. Acting on sheer, desperate instinct, he drew in a drowning breath, pulled back to thrust again, and the second time he pushed to the very core of her.

She cried out, balled a fist against her open lips to staunch the desperate sound from ringing out again.

He didn't want her silence. The sound of her pleasure sang through him, propelled him closer, closer…but they had to be quiet, had to be careful, had to watch the time, for the night was pathetically brief in which to spend a lifetime of passion.

Knowing all this, grieving it, he dropped his head to kiss her and lost himself in her taste, the floral fragrance of her skin and the sultry scent of the liquid silk that drew him deep into her body. She was so *hot.* Her heartbeat surrounded him, massaged his shaft, echoing the rhythmic surge of blood that thundered through it. His lips found the moist curve of her neck, where he could muffle the helpless sounds rising from the center of his own soul.

"Deeper," she whispered. "Oh, deeper, Joachim. Faster." Her fingers gripped his buttocks when he withdrew again, and she led him into another thrust, setting a frantic, rhythmic pace, while fire licked his senses and perspiration slicked his limbs, and his breath pulled from his lungs in haphazard gasps. He didn't need oxygen. Just her kiss…her tongue…her hands on his back, her thighs riding his…the scalding succulence of her femininity as it surrounded him and tugged on an untried place inside him, where the essence of his manhood simmered restlessly.

"Look at me," she ordered against his ear, nudging him to lift his head. "Look at yourself. Look at your cock sinking into me and the way my body takes you. This is the truth of it, Joachim. This is making love."

The thrust and drive between them hardly faltered as Joachim rose up between her legs and grasped her hips, lifting her pelvis to meet his. In the muted shadows cast by their joined bodies, he watched, transfixed, the slow piston of his sex disappearing inside her as he drew her up to meet him, the mesh and separation of their flesh. He heard the soft, wet sounds it made and the harsh rasp of their breathing in rhythm with the ebb and flow of their bodies—all of it a carnal symphony. She was soaked silk engulfing his fevered flesh in more heat. More wetness. More groans and whispers of unintelligible words, the language of lovers.

Memories of another, loftier existence slipped away. Ecstasy swallowed him, rendered him utterly indigenous to the Earth, to this mortal condition, to the exquisite place he now occupied. He was no longer a seraph, but simply a man whose soul soared in a way the celestial guardian had never known.

Fire gathered and coiled in his testes, in his penis, in every muscle. Shaking with the force of his approaching orgasm, Joachim grasped Gia's waist and shifted their positions, rolling beneath her without unseating her.

He lay back against the pillows and settled her astride him to see her more clearly, to revel in her wild rich beauty, to store away an image of this illicit and precious moment, the only possession he would take from the Earth when he departed. "Like this," he gritted. "I've dreamed of it thus."

In a fleeting glimpse of recognition between lovers, she stilled above him, caught his gaze and smiled. "So have I, Joachim. Just like this."

Joy suffused him, sent tears leaking from the corners of his eyes. He tangled shaking hands in her curls, drew her down and kissed her, torn between choked laughter and the anguish of carnal need.

Then exultation slid away, buried under the hot pressure building low in his belly like an explosion. She straightened, braced her hands on his chest and rose and fell on him in a frantic, rhythmic dance that stroked his very heart.

"This," she groaned, "is fucking…you pushing up, me riding you hard, and it doesn't hurt…it's…oh…"

Everything inside him went tight and straining. His legs slid restlessly against the sheets, the muscles in his buttocks and thighs seared by the strain of thrusting so high to meet her. Grasping her hips to further speed her movements, Joachim turned his head against the pillow and squeezed his eyes closed, each labored breath a groan as the tension built in his testes and roiled at the base of his cock, simmering, burning, until there was nothing but sparks and flares behind his eyelids and the relentless pounding of blood in his veins, rushing, rushing…

And at last, with a magnificent, blinding flash, exploding into a million particles of light.

"*My—God—*" He convulsed, cried the mindless human prayer into the night and found the harsh sound muffled against Gia's soft lips, his body bucking and shuddering in her embrace as he shot his seed high and hard within her.

In silent reverence she rode the wave with him, leaning over him to shield his utter vulnerability from the Heavens. She kissed the helpless sounds from his open lips, suckled his tongue, constricted around him to draw every last drop of him within her.

Joachim had never been more naked. Muscles liquefied, he sank into the mattress and shivered once, an aftershock of pleasure, every nerve singing with awareness. Even the brush of her long curls as she rested her forehead against his chest sent a wave of chills over his sensitized skin.

Silence drifted over them, languid and lovely, with only the distant hum of the generator to herald the world outside the tiny room. Joachim's heartbeat slowed, blood flow decelerating through his veins as his body cooled. The sheets beneath him were soft, the room cool and fragranced with the perfume of Gia's skin, crushed flowers and a woman's sultry desire. Beneath it, the vague scent of semen scolded his human condition.

He didn't care. Tiny quakes crept up his spine, echoes of the magnificent climax he'd experienced. His manhood still throbbed inside her. Drowsiness dragged at his eyelids.

After a while, Gia withdrew and curled up beside him, her body tucked against his naked side. Wearily he stroked his palm down her slender ribs and over her hip, half-conscious while he drifted in the wake of supreme fulfillment.

"Joachim," she murmured, calling him back from some unbounded void.

He sighed, remembering at last how to inhale and release oxygen. "Gia."

"I love you. No matter what happens, I always will."

He started to reply. There were so many things he wanted to say. So many promises he wanted to make.

Then, as unexpected and vicious as an unforeseen assailant, sorrow reared up and struck his heart. *What have you done to her*? *Sealing yourself to her in this manner?*

Seared, he sat up and clutched at his neck. The crucifix was gone. Broken. The chain shattered, lost among the pillows.

He braced against the cold concrete wall and rubbed his hands over his face, his own vow to the Archangel seeping through his mind with torturous alacrity. *I will seek resolution and find it.*

But this was no resolution. He'd failed. His heart was inextricably bound to Gia's now. He'd never survive the exodus when the mission ended. He wasn't fit to lead. He was fallen, no better than the nephilim, and perhaps just as cursed.

Gia's gentle fingers caressed his thigh as she sat up and examined his face. "Joachim? What's wrong?"

Laughter burst from him, short and anguished. Despair squeezed his throat and stung his eyes, dissolving, at last, the restraint he held over his emotions. With a quaking sigh, he reached for her and hugged her tightly.

"*Je t'aime aussi,* my Gia," he whispered, rocking her from

side to side. "I love you too."

Chapter Twenty-Two

Gia woke to the soft rasp of a zipper drawn across fabric. She rolled to her side and opened her eyes.

Joachim moved around the room like a pale shadow, dressed only in a pair of white shorts. His closet door stood open, the interior divested of clothing.

"What are you doing?" she asked, bracing on an elbow to see him more clearly.

He paused to look at her, his sculpted body awash in the cool light that spilled from the closet. "It's nearly dawn. I must clear this room before we leave for the final mission."

She sat up, her pulse inexplicably revved. "Why?"

He turned back to place a pile of T-shirts into an open duffel. "In the event I don't come back, these garments can be utilized by someone else."

Alarm snapped her out of her sleepy haze. "If you don't come back? What do you mean?"

"I mean if the raid doesn't proceed as planned and this body is rendered uninhabitable for the next operative." His tone was impassive, steady. The muscles shifted beneath his back as he lifted the duffel to a chair and opened another one. "No matter what happens today, a new team of seraphim will be moving into these headquarters within a matter of weeks, as in every major city. This room will be occupied by the mission leader. He'll bring his own garments."

Gia hugged her knees to her chest, sadness knotting her stomach. "But you do plan to come back tonight, right? Olivier and Soleil and Dmitri? Everyone else?"

"If we survive today's operation."

"Of course you will." When he moved to open another bureau drawer without responding, she prompted, "And then?"

"The exodus begins as soon as we debrief. In the morning, it will be complete."

In other words, tomorrow at this time, the seraphs as she knew them would be no more.

She blinked back the sudden sting behind her eyes. "And how exactly will I be released into the wild?"

"Arrangements have been made for an apartment for you in downtown Chicago. You'll be escorted there safely." He paused to study her, his eyes glinting in the shadows. "Your new home can be as temporary as you like, Gia. You don't have to stay in Chicago, but at least you'll have a roof over your head until you make some decisions. Your life stretches out before you with no parameters—"

Gia held up her hand to stop him. She'd known the end would be this way, abrupt and excruciating. To discuss the cold details now only made it worse.

Climbing from the bed, she gathered her clothing and began to dress, ignoring the sweet ache between her legs and the lingering dampness there, remnants of their utter delight in one another for a few brief hours. Joachim stood in silence as eloquent as the unspoken declarations hovering in the air, and though she sensed his gaze moving over her, she couldn't bring herself to look at him. The time for a lover's dreamy musings had passed, brushed aside by the magnitude of the challenge they faced…and the dangers.

Joachim was considering the possibilities of his own demise today, and that of his colleagues. Gia was more vulnerable than all of them put together. Perhaps he was considering that too.

"I should get out of your office while the going's good," she said, shivering as she pulled her T-shirt over her head. "This place is going to wake up soon."

Joachim set a shaving bag inside the duffel, zipped it, then approached her. "There's a briefing at seven in the conference room. You'll be given your directive for today's maneuver. Afterward, we arm up in the arsenal."

"I'll be ready." She stepped into her panties, heat crawling up her neck and burning her ears as he stood before her and watched. This was a man who knew her body inside and out, had witnessed her at the apex of vulnerability. Why should she be embarrassed to put on underwear in his presence?

It seemed suddenly undignified. They were warriors again, with armored hearts. The lovers had faded with the sweet, sleepy hours of pre-dawn.

Frowning, she drew her pajama bottoms up her legs and tied the string at the waist. Then she straightened, shook her hair back and met his gaze.

And was lost. The detachment she'd heard in his voice—so essential to a merciful parting, she knew—was gone. Joachim's eyes glowed with human passion and preternatural clarity in the gloom. Two semiprecious stones mined from the deepest core of the Earth, still molten. White-hot.

He stepped closer, lifted the backs of his fingers to her cheek. Before he could speak, her gaze darted to his throat. The crucifix was gone.

"Your necklace." She swallowed the urge to weep. "I vaguely remember…I think I broke it."

"Yes," he said.

"I'm so sorry."

"It can be repaired."

"Can it?"

They looked at each other in silence. Then he gently smoothed the curls behind her ear. "Our timing leaves something to be desired, yes? You hardly slept on the night before the most important day of your life."

Gia's mouth quirked, even as a single tear slipped down her face. "Don't blame yourself. I wouldn't have slept if I'd been in my bed, either. There's something a little daunting about holding the world's fate in your hands."

Joachim cupped his palm against her cheek. "For a while last night, we forgot."

"For a while, it was so easy." Her fingers covered his and held them to her face. "You touch me like no one ever has."

"I wonder," he murmured, his other hand gliding down to cradle her breast, "how I ever existed without doing so?"

Her eyes slid closed, tears fading, back arching to follow his caress as the atmosphere shifted from tender to sensual. "What are you doing?"

"Seducing you," he said with that same low-timbre intent, as though they didn't stand at the threshold of death and destruction with the world, like a helpless infant, lying before them. "Touching you."

He slid beneath the hem of her shirt to caress her naked ribs. "Undressing you." He caught the string of her pants and tugged until the bottoms loosened and slipped down around her ankles, then helped her step out of them and backed her toward the nearest wall.

When her back bumped cold concrete, he lifted her as though she weighed nothing, so that her legs encircled his waist. Then his hand slid between them and he freed his erection from his shorts. "Fucking you," he whispered, sounding distinctly, shamelessly un-angelic, and bending his knees, thrust so deeply inside her, she had to bite his naked shoulder to keep from screaming her pleasure.

He held her bottom in firm hands and easily maneuvered her up and down his shaft, his muscles rippling with the effort, his eyes hot and bright in the gloom as he watched the ecstasy roll over her features. "Don't close your eyes," he ordered. "Let me watch you come."

"Oh, yes, oh please yes—" She bucked between his body and the wall as the ferocious orgasm claimed her, pushing down hard on his cock so he could feel the rhythmic pulse of her climax squeezing him. Then the strength left her limbs, and still he held her up, impaled on his pulsing manhood.

Arms shaking now, Joachim shifted her away from the wall and to the mattress, all without slipping out of her. Laying her down on the pillow, he followed and braced on his elbows to stare into her eyes. "God help me, I can't let you go. I'm lost to you. Let me come inside you again and again."

"Joachim..." She enfolded him with arms and legs, taking him deep, worshiping him with every part of her.

"Love me, Gia." The desperation in his voice, in his terse features, offered a fleeting glimpse of his true vulnerability beneath the warrior's armor. "Love me forever."

"I will," she whispered. "I love you now, this moment, and every moment to come. I'll love you always—"

His cock filled her so full and deeply, its tip nudged the mouth of her womb. His fingertips slid between her buttocks, probed and teased while he plunged his tongue into her mouth and silenced her pleasured cries.

This time when she shuddered and writhed and came beneath him, he slowed and went still. Waiting for her to return from sparkling, mindless ecstasy. Waiting with a concentration that said for a few minutes longer, no one, and nothing, existed except them.

When he moved again, with a gentle, sliding thrust of hips, it was with the grace and worldliness of an experienced and knowing lover, not a celestial ingénue. His lips suckled her breasts, his hard, flat belly rubbing hers as his easy movements slid her against the mattress.

Beneath him, she drifted in the wake of release, every nerve vibrating with echoed pleasure while he made love to her with a concentration that spoke of his growing need.

"I adore you," she whispered.

He murmured some unintelligible response, too lost now in ecstasy's miasma to hear her, but Gia didn't mind. Her fingertips glided over his smooth buttocks, reveling in the supple dance of muscle there, then up his sides, counting each perfect rib, each chill bump pebbling his warm skin, gliding around to his nipples, which were drawn as tight and aroused as her own.

His throat was corded, the muscles constricted with exertion. Some sad, sentimental part of her shivered at the memory of his sultry voice when—once upon a time—he'd coolly addressed her as "Mrs. Rossi". Neither of them could have known they'd be here in the dim shelter of this tiny room, in the waning minutes of this, the eleventh hour, struggling to say goodbye while the current of their love swept them back, and back, and back.

There would be no sweet parting, she knew now. Only an excruciating rending of heart, mind and soul.

The realization shattered Gia. Pressing her face to his shoulder, she cried in silence, even as he thrust harder, faster, pushing to climax. She wrapped herself around him and pulled him in tight, holding him inside and out, soaking him into her soul as he pulsed hotly within her and called out his lover's hosanna.

When it was over, he caught her face between his hands and gazed down at her. "Gia?"

She stared back at him in blind anguish, seeing only the aura of celestial light that haloed his head and shoulders, a clear, otherworldly message to the Daughter of Longinus that this seraph didn't belong to her but to the Heavens.

"I'm trying on realization for size," she sobbed. "From angel into man you came to me, and from man into angel you'll leave me."

He kissed her streaming eyes, her damp cheeks, her lips. "So you weep," he whispered thickly. "You weep because your heart is breaking."

"Yes." She nodded, cupping his jaw, loving him. Mourning him. "And I will forever."

"*J'aussi,*" he choked, "forever..."and as he kissed her, she tasted his tears and knew she didn't grieve alone.

* * * * *

Despite the fact that it was standing room only, the conference room was unusually silent during the mission briefing, the atmosphere solemn and electric with anticipation. Joachim's low voice bore a tension and weariness Gia had never noticed before as he addressed the seventeen-man team. The climax of seraphim's mission reared before them, and the weight of their leader's responsibility showed in the slight furrows between his brows as he stood at the head of the table and traced each path the teams would take through the compound.

Sitting between Olivier and Soleil, Gia focused on Joachim's softly worded instructions and struggled to salvage some semblance of concentration.

Her job was to follow him throughout the invasion until they reached Therides. Then her role shifted from shadow to assassin. While the seraphs held him immobile, somehow, with only a crumbling spearhead and one hundred-twenty pounds of angry female to back up her attack, she alone would drive out the demon.

The honor of her position suffused her with shivery exhilaration and pride. She was the Daughter of Longinus. The only woman in two millennia to embrace the title and all that accompanied it. There was no room for fear or self-doubt, and she felt none of the humble emotions that had plagued her for the last twenty-six years. They paled in the light of her newfound identity and in the warmth of Joachim's tenderness.

Because even though his eyes merely skirted over her as he spoke to his team, she felt their touch like the gossamer brush of a sultry breeze.

Whatever happened, Gia would take that warmth with her. It bolstered her. She felt loved for the very first time in her life.

The meeting was short, and immediately after, the operatives headed to the arsenal.

Gia tried not to look at Joachim too long or too hard as they gathered their artillery, but every nerve in her body echoed with the memory of his sensual touch, the feel of him against her, within her. For as long as she'd lived, he'd been her guardian. Last night he was her lover. Today, as they faced down the most horrific evil, he was both.

The operatives moved about the small room in silence, strapping on holsters and artillery belts, stocking up on automatics, tranquilizer guns and the ensuing accessories.

While Gia examined a thigh holster to fit the Glock she'd been assigned, Joachim stopped at the table beside her.

"Need help?"

"I've never worn one of these," she said, her gaze skirting away from his clean-shaven face. Like the others, he was dressed head to toe in black, striking and fair, his eyes piercingly blue against the stark background of his attire.

"It slides around your thigh. You wear it on this one, of course, since you're right-handed." He touched her right leg, his fingers burning her through the thin material of her black leggings as they lingered just a breath too long. He reached past her to retrieve a holster for himself and used the opportunity to speak softly without looking at her. "How are you?"

"I'm okay." She swallowed the knot in her throat and bent to strap the holster around her thigh. "A little tired, maybe. And distracted."

"We both are. But it's imperative to set aside what's happening between us for the duration of this assignment."

"I understand." She straightened, then slid the gun into its holster. "Where will I carry the Spear?"

"Here." He turned to her, reached around her waist and drew a thin leather strap around her midsection, buckling it at her solar plexus. Even this methodical gesture, the efficient movement of his hands so close to her skin, set off flutters of excitement inside her.

He met her eyes finally, as though he couldn't help himself. "Gia."

"Yes?" she whispered, pulse skittering.

"Je t'aime."

I love you. The assertion was so soft, it could have been her imagination. She closed her eyes and struggled to cling to the silken words. When she opened them again, he was across the room, examining a pistol as though no such profound sentiment had passed between them.

* * * * *

They rode in silence, eighteen warriors filling three vans.

Some of them would not come back to headquarters, or even to the Celestial Realm. Therides had been too quiet an opponent, and Joachim knew immeasurable danger loomed ahead, an unspoken promise from the lips of the demon.

Some will go into cycle.

The realization fisted around his heart and released a potent grief within him.

Dmitri and Aristide had infiltrated the compound the night before, disarming the security system and clearing the path for the rest of the operatives, but their last report had come at dawn. Soleil had been unable to reach them by mobile communication, and the few seraphs manning transmissions at headquarters had heard nothing but static on their channel.

The battle had already begun, perhaps with casualties.

Nursing a hollow sense of dread for the two angels, Joachim let his gaze drift to Gia. Bouncing slightly with the movement of the van, she sat in quiet composure beside Soleil, her hands folded in her lap. What were her thoughts as she rode to her destiny? A powerful self-awareness radiated from her soul and intensified her beauty. Strength. Assuredness. The light of Creator moved through her, unimpeded at last.

Joachim wanted to reach for her, enfold her in his arms, kiss her silken skin, feel the warmth of her love bathe him. He dug deep for the guilt he'd suffered after they'd made love and instead found a bittersweet insight. Last night was a gift from the Heavens. His punishment lay not at the hands of the

Celestial Dominions but in the agony he alone would experience upon leaving her.

As though she felt his regard, she raised her head and their gazes locked. Her mouth tugged into a rueful grin that said, *Here we are at last.* The few feet separating them seemed infinite.

"Approaching the compound," Olivier spoke from the driver's seat.

Joachim shifted and glanced through the black-tinted window that diffused the sunlight to an inky, surreal glow. The time for romantic musings was over. Duty stood before him in the shape of the Archangel, flames licking at the hem of his robe, Spear held aloft.

* * * * *

The Fellowship of the Fallen Sun sat nestled among lush, rolling hills and verdant forest. Human hands had built the mansion and its surrounding estate as a place of peace and beauty a century before. Now, malevolent energy radiated from the compound, thickening the air with a humid, sulfuric stench palpable even to Gia.

"How could something so beautiful be so horrible?" she muttered as she climbed from the van, her gaze fixed on the far-off mansion.

Behind her, Soleil distributed comm units. "Funny, that's what Creator said when Lucifer and the nephilim took the plunge."

Joachim slipped a headset over Gia's head and adjusted it. "In case we separate," he explained, then spoke into his own microphone. "Can you hear me?"

"Loud and clear." Her heart thudded a crazy rhythm in her chest, one born of excitement and apprehension. "Think we'll get separated?"

"Not if I can help it." His fingers followed the arm of her mouthpiece and adjusted it along her cheek, his gaze focused on hers. Then he nudged her chin and moved on.

Beyond him, the teams stood assembled, clad in black from head to toe, the same impassive shadows that had swept Gia Rossi into a subterranean world and out of the path of destruction.

A quarter-mile ahead, through a massive hammock of trees, the mansion loomed, a stark white behemoth surrounded by a high wall. The top story windows stared out at the world like soulless eyes. It was impossible to guess what awaited the angels behind those windows, aside from the certainty of a battle they could ill afford to lose.

Nervously fingering the outline of the gun holstered at her thigh, Gia watched Joachim move from one seraph to the next, grasping their hands and speaking words of encouragement and affection. When he reached Olivier, the other seraph grasped Joachim's face and kissed both his cheeks, and the two men shared a smile laden with the tender sentiment of brothers. Perhaps Olivier's perfect image of his leader had been shattered on this particular mission, but his love for Joachim was a tangible force.

Joachim moved on and clasped Jordan's hand, laughed at something he said, then embraced him. Next, he paused before Soleil. "Peace, friend."

"Peace." Soleil's expression didn't relinquish its steely resolve until he clasped her hand in both of his and lifted her knuckles to his lips in a gesture of reverence. Then her chin quivered, and she looked skyward, her tear-filled eyes shimmering like multi-faceted emeralds.

Gia averted her gaze, feeling like an intruder at the brief glimpse of an angel's vulnerability. Whatever tension had distanced Soleil and Joachim these past few days was gone.

He stepped back and swept his gaze over the sea of black-clad operatives. Then, with a nod, he drew his pistol and turned toward the compound. "Let's go."

Chapter Twenty-Three

The seraphs broke into teams of two at the edge of the property line. In silence they slid among the trees, melding with the shadows until Gia lost sight of them.

Joachim moved a few feet ahead of her, his footsteps impossibly quiet in the leaves and debris. It seemed that with every step she took, a twig snapped beneath her tennis shoe. The muscles in her shoulders and neck tightened until a dull ache radiated up through sinew and tendon and formed a crown of tension around her temples.

They reached the high brick wall that surrounded the lawns of the estate. While Gia stared at it in dismay, trying to envision how they would scale its sheer expanse, Joachim withdrew a small grappling hook from his tool belt and tossed it high in the air, where it caught on the lip of the wall. He tugged to test its hold, then handed the line to Gia. "Come."

She glanced up at the looming wall and swallowed. "I'm supposed to scale this thing?"

"You're strong. You can lift your own weight."

"Of course I can." Not that she really knew for sure. But even if she'd never climbed anything more than a Stairmaster, pure determination to succeed would make it possible. "This line is pretty thin, though."

"It will hold you and the weight of five Aristides." He tossed an identical device over the edge of the wall and secured it. "I pray he still lives."

"Me, too," she said softly. Beneath his emotionless features dwelt a deep anxiety for Aristide and Dmitri. Somehow on this mission, the barrier between seraphic certitude and Man's animal fear had blurred for him, although he'd never admit it to her.

"We're at the east barricade," he said low, addressing communications at headquarters through the channel the operatives shared. "What's on the other side?"

Through Gia's headset came a distant, crackling reply, "Security canines. Five of them."

"Lucky you, Joachim," Olivier's amused voice floated over the channel from somewhere on the estate. "This time it's *your* turn to play lion tamer."

"Is that right?" Joachim grasped the line and hoisted himself. "How so?"

"I paid my dues with Butterball."

"Buttercup." Joachim scaled the wall, his feet braced against the brick for propulsion. He moved with an agility that astonished Gia, soundless and graceful, back muscles bulging.

Pausing halfway, he glanced down at her. "Are you coming?"

Wide-eyed, she nodded, grasped her line and began to climb. *Don't look down.*

"Let me handle the dogs," he said as he hauled himself up the line, hand over fist.

"No problem there," she panted. She couldn't think about the threat that lay on the other side of the wall, not when she wasn't positive she would make it *over* the wall. Could one's heart explode from climbing a twenty-foot brick slab? She felt like the poster child for the shamefully unfit twenty-somethings of the world.

"You going to make it?" Joachim stopped to offer her a vague smile.

Heat suffused her cheeks. "Of course. I just didn't know my body weight was so…heavy."

"Perhaps we should have provided more strength training for you at headquarters."

"No," she said quickly. "Believe me, Dmitri ran me through

the wringer. He just didn't have enough time to beat me into shape."

Joachim returned his attention to the climb, not the least bit winded as he reached the top of the wall. "Report," he again ordered the Intel operator.

"Just the dogs," said the voice. "Security agents are clustered on the north side of the house. You have an estimated window of one minute, forty-five seconds."

Bracing his gloved palms on the ledge, he lifted himself with ease, up and over, and disappeared down the other side.

Gia tried not to feel abandoned as she hung a few feet below the ledge. Even through the heavy leather of her gloves, her palms burned against the rope, arm muscles screaming from fatigue. With a final surge of superhuman determination, she reached the top and exhaled in relief…just in time to hear the snarl and thud of stampeding paws as the guard dogs raced toward Joachim.

Dread clumped in her throat. She struggled over the ledge and looked down, expecting to see him immersed in a sea of growling, snapping, salivating beasts.

Five Dobermans had arranged themselves at Joachim's feet in an orderly semi-circle, their obsidian gazes fixed on him as though his pockets were stuffed with juicy T-bones.

"Gia," he murmured without taking his attention off them, "shift your hook on the wall, then descend toward me very slowly. When you reach the ground, don't speak. Cross to the basement window on the southeast corner of the house. Do you see it?"

"I see it."

"Good. And don't be afraid. These animals feed on fear."

Swallowing her trepidation, Gia moved the hook, threw the line over the opposite side of the wall and tugged as she'd seen Joachim do. Then she crawled over the edge and rappelled toward him, every muscle in her torso and limbs shaking with the effort to hold herself steady.

Her feet touched the soft earth, and she resisted the urge to crumble in a pile of exhausted, boneless mush.

"Leave the line," Joachim instructed in an even voice, his gloved hand rhythmically stroking the sleek head of the dog on his left. "We may need it when we retreat."

Avoiding even a mere glance at the dogs, Gia crossed the lawn toward the house. When she reached the window, she peered inside. Dust and filth fogged the two panes, but she could make out massive stockpiles of firearms filling the cavernous sub-floor. She tugged at the sill, but the window was painted shut.

Joachim's footsteps crunched in the grass behind her. A quick, uneasy glimpse over her shoulder showed that since he had moved, the spell he'd cast over the Dobermans was fading. Two of them emitted a low, throaty growl, teeth bared as they stalked him across the yard.

"Joachim..." she whispered.

"I know." Without looking back, he withdrew a cloth from his tool bag, wrapped it around his gloved hand, and with a quick jab, shattered the glass. "Go," he said sharply, kicking away the razor-sharp shards that remained in the panes. "Climb through."

Adrenaline fired through her veins as she dropped through the narrow opening, hit the floor and turned to watch him follow, her heart in her throat. Her hand lingered at the gun holstered on her thigh. She'd never killed a dog. She was an animal lover. But these canines weren't normal. *God, was it possible for dogs to be possessed, too?*

Joachim landed in the cellar with a soft thud as the pack of snarling, snapping Dobermans threw themselves at the window. Snatching a stool from the floor, he blocked their entry and hissed to Gia, "Get to the stairs."

"But—"

"*Quickly.*"

Breath exploding from her lungs, she dashed across the

basement, swerving around crates filled with weapons, an arsenal the likes of which she'd never seen. She ascended the stairs at breakneck speed, but somehow Joachim caught up with her, grabbed her around the waist and pushed her up the last few steps and through the door at the top with the force of ten men.

Gia hit the marble floor, and he followed with the Dobermans mere feet behind him, their snapping jaws eating up the space between them. One hard kick of his foot and the door crashed shut on the ferocious pack.

"Holy Toledo," Gia panted, collapsing back on the tile. "If that doesn't wake the dead, I don't know what will."

Joachim drew his pistol and got to his feet. They'd landed in a deserted corridor, but distant voices echoed from a room somewhere to the left.

After a tense moment in which they froze, listening, they knew they were undetected. Motioning for her to follow, he slid into the shadows and started down the long, dim hall.

* * * * *

"Team leaders, your locations."

"Surrounding the north side of the perimeter," Jordan reported. "Guards have been removed. We're advancing."

"South side," Xavier supplied. "Threshold clear for reinforcements to enter the compound."

Olivier was the last to respond. "Second floor, Captain. We've been detected. Three of Rossi's men are dead."

Joachim eased down behind a large marble console, his hand on Gia's arm to draw her into momentary reprieve. "We heard no gunfire."

"There wasn't time to use my gun," Olivier said. "These weren't average men."

Joachim's eyes met Gia's. "Nephilim?"

"Every one I've seen," Olivier replied.

He exhaled. "As I thought. The incursion must have taken place when we temporarily lost the demon." He glanced at Gia, tension carving lines in his features. "What about Soleil, Liv? She fares well?"

"I'm right here," came the smooth response.

"Deadly with her fists too." Humor laced Olivier's voice. "Remind me never to anger her."

"And the rooms on the second floor?"

"Deserted thus far."

Joachim signed off and told Gia, "Draw your weapon."

She did as she was instructed, holding the Glock down by her side. It was heavier than her revolver had been and seemed to radiate heat and power in her damp fingers. "There's more than one demon here, isn't there?"

"There are many. As we suspected, Therides has surrounded himself with an army."

Gia swallowed. "Do they die if you shoot them?"

"The death of the human body releases most souls, good or evil, into cycle."

"Then why can't we just shoot Therides and send him into cycle?"

"Because he's more powerful than the others," Joachim said, his expression grave as he met her eyes. "A master nephil. Unlike his minions, he has the ability to jump from one body to another when he suffers injury. Only the Spear can impale him to the physical vehicle he occupies and send him back to Hell."

He glanced down the hall. "Intel says this floor is comprised of offices. Rossi's is the last set of doors on the right. We'll look there first."

She peered around the console. "There's no guard."

"There is, somewhere."

Hugging the wall, they slid past three closed doors. The fourth door on the left was ajar, frail amber sunlight filtering through the opening.

Joachim slipped across the hall, plastered himself beside the office and carefully peered through the space, then jerked back, his pistol pressed against his heart. With one hand, he motioned Gia past.

Wide-eyed, she leaped past the doorway and dove behind the protection of a massive concrete urn. Voices grew louder from inside the office as its inhabitants approached the door.

Gia froze. There was nowhere for Joachim to hide.

The first man stepped into the hall, his attention on someone in the office behind him. "Tell Heinrich that despite the setback in Washington, the latest backups arrived yesterday in—"

He never saw the blow from the butt of Joachim's pistol. It dropped him to the floor like an oversized rag doll. A second man dashed into the corridor and threw himself at Joachim with a ferocity that knocked the gun from his hand and wrenched a cry of alarm from Gia's throat. The two men hit the floor, blows and grunts echoing down the high-ceilinged corridor.

Terrified, Gia crawled out from behind the urn, and with shaking hands, tried to aim her gun at the assailant. It was no use. Joachim was too much at risk.

What do I do?

As if he'd heard her panicked plea, he kicked free of his attacker and scrambled backward. "Gia, pull the trigger, *pull the trigger!*"

Gasping, she lifted the gun in both hands and fired. The sound was deafening, her aim dead-on. The nephil dropped to his knees, hand clutching the spreading circle of crimson in the center of his white-robed chest.

Gia bit back a cry of horror. Before her eyes, his features twisted into a nest of writhing serpents, pupilless gaze burning with the fires of Hell. Then the creature collapsed, face first, on the marble tile.

Her entire body shook with revulsion and astonishment. The Spear had granted her sight, just as Joachim had promised.

If this minion of Therides could offer such a horrific glimpse of the underworld, what would the master demon himself show her when they came face to face?

Clutching his side, Joachim knelt to retrieve his gun, his head bowed as he struggled to regain his breath. She started toward him, but he held up a hand to stop her.

"Take cover. The gunfire—others will come." Staggering to his feet, he wiped the blood from his mouth and aimed his pistol at the first man he'd knocked unconscious.

And hesitated.

It took a moment for realization to wrap itself around Gia's mind, and with it came a wave of compassion so powerful it stung her eyes. Joachim was a warrior, but first and foremost, he was a guardian of Life. To kill was against every fiber of his being.

"Joachim," she said softly, "he's a demon."

"He looks like a man." He wiped a hand over his face and shook his head. "I see a living, breathing man lying there. Unconscious and defenseless." He looked at her over his shoulder, anguish darkening his eyes. "I seem to have lost my Sight. What's happening to me?"

"I don't know." She bit her lip, torn between the urge to reassure him and the frantic knowledge that time was short. "Perhaps you're as much human as you are seraph."

Her observation seemed to crash down on him. For a moment his shoulders sagged, and he lowered the pistol.

Then the nephil on the floor stirred. Joachim's spine straightened and the confusion drained from his features, replaced by icy resolve.

"Get back behind the urn," he told her, and she quickly obeyed. Lifting the gun, he took aim again and pulled the trigger.

One shot. The short explosion rang out into the corridor.

Before Gia could speak, Olivier's voice, low and urgent,

filled the comm unit. "Joachim. Are you with us?"

Joachim grabbed his headset from the floor and put it on. "We're okay. First floor." He ducked behind the urn beside Gia, his breath heaving from his chest in labored rushes. "Two men dead. You're right—they're nephilim. I had hoped a few humans remained among them."

Olivier released a wayward chuckle. "Ah, my Captain. Ever the optimist."

Frantic voices echoed through the corridor to Gia's left. "They're coming," she whispered, terror filling her stomach with a floating, sick sensation.

Joachim grasped her face with a trembling hand and pressed his mouth against hers, a brief bid to assure her. "You know how to use your pistol. We're going to fire our way out of this hall and up the staircase behind that door." When she nodded, he flashed her a grim smile. "Let's go."

Before she could comprehend the enormity of what they faced, they were racing toward the exit, charging straight into the hoard of demons now pouring into the corridor.

Gunfire exploded around them, Gia's gun, Joachim's gun. Bodies fell, two, three, ten. The floor grew slick with blood, and still the demons kept coming.

The hair on the back of Gia's neck stood up, and she whirled to see an army of nephilim charging from the opposite direction, some with guns, some with bared claws ready to score flesh from bone. *God, where were the other seraphs? Where was help?*

There was nowhere to run.

Joachim side-kicked a demon, flipped another over his back, whirled and shot the nephil between his yellow, glowing eyes.

"Behind you!" Gia screamed, watching in horror as another demon threw himself at Joachim and slammed him into the wall with a thundering crash.

Joachim slid under the nephil, grabbing at the claws around

his throat, his legs thrashing against the tile as he struggled to throw off the attacker's weight.

Before Gia could raise her pistol and fire, an arm slid around her waist and crushed like a massive boa constrictor. "Hello, Mrs. Rossi."

The voice was sickeningly familiar. *Frank*? Her former bodyguard?

No. Some depraved anomaly of the big Italian. A hot, fetid odor curled around her, a mixture of obscenities and malicious laughter chilling her ear as the demon breathed against her neck. "Miss me?"

Pain filled her chest. She kicked helplessly as his arm tightened in a death grip, the cry strangled in her throat and her lungs burning from lack of oxygen.

With a wrench, he lifted her free of the floor, sent her headset skittering across the marble. Stars danced before her eyes and something in Gia clicked on. Ferocious control. Even as Frank's murderous grip squeezed the breath from her body, she found the ability to lift her pistol directly ahead at Joachim's assailant and fired, killing the demon instantly. Then, squirming with a renewed vigor that could only be Heaven-granted, she drove a vicious elbow into Frank's ribs.

The nephil grunted and loosened his hold enough for her to land on her feet and whirl in his malevolent embrace. In a spontaneous tribute to Dmitri's marital arts training, Gia kicked out with all her might, caught the demon in the gut and sent him stumbling backward. Then she raised the Glock and aimed with cold steadiness. A single bullet from the pistol tore through the nephil's throat and he crashed into the console, dead before his big body hit the floor.

More footsteps pounded from the opposite end of the hall, but this time when she spun in defense, a beautiful vision greeted her—black-garbed seraphim operatives poured into the corridor in a steady stream of reinforcement.

"It's about time!" she muttered through clenched teeth.

Bullets whizzed past her. She dove to the floor and crawled to Joachim, who was reloading his gun behind the urn.

Popping in the clip with the heel of his hand, he shot her an electric smile, clambered to his feet and hauled her up beside him. Triumph and admiration shimmered between them, and Gia had never loved him more than she did at that wild, surreal moment.

The dust of plaster filled the air with a strange, otherworldly haze, and the acrid odor of cordite and the metallic stench of blood hung heavy around them. Nephilim dropped like flies as seraphim advanced, more entering the corridor until, to Gia's aching eyes, an obsidian sea of angels garbed in humanity washed through the hall. The onslaught of nephilim thinned, and within minutes the remaining attackers turned and fled back up the stairs.

At least thirty seraphim operatives filled the corridor behind Gia, males and females alike. All she could do was stare. Many of their faces were unfamiliar, but they were all beautiful and radiant in their crusade for righteousness.

"We heard your transmission," Aristide rumbled, approaching Joachim from the throng with open arms.

They briefly embraced, and Joachim gratefully clasped a hand to the big seraph's cheek. "Ari, you live. We didn't know. Contact said—"

"Dmitri and I got stuck on the fourth floor. It was impossible to transmit our location." His broad, expressive face grew solemn. "Therides can be found there, in an armored room. Although we've taken care of the guards, it will be difficult to gain access."

Olivier, lost somewhere in the mammoth mansion, overheard the conversation on his comm unit and responded, "At last, I get to blow something up. These explosives have been burning a hole in my tool belt this entire mission."

A wave of laughter rippled through the mass of operatives. But then the brief glimpse of light quickly dimmed. Joachim flashed Dmitri a solemn look as he stepped over a dead demon and knelt to examine it for weapons. "Have you any idea how many nephilim remain on the estate?"

"Maybe thirty." The seraph gazed over the corpse-filled corridor. "It appears we took out most of them here."

"These were infantry." Joachim rose and glanced toward the stairwell. "There must be more. Three floors to go, and Therides knows we're here."

"Vincent always loved surprises," Gia said, her anxious gaze seeking Joachim's. "Who knows what he's planned?"

"Nothing we can't handle," he told her, and before an army of his fellow angels, he caught her hand, tugged her to him and kissed her squarely on the mouth. Then he glanced at his team. "Any further questions?"

Silence had fallen over the warriors.

"Good," Joachim said with a decisive tilt of his head. "Onward."

Chapter Twenty-Four

"Olivier." Joachim rounded the staircase, pistol in one hand, Gia's fingers in the other. "Your location?"

"Ascending to the fourth floor via the front staircase."

"How many are with you?"

"Just Soleil."

Premonitory alarm ricocheted through Joachim like a jolt of electricity. "Wait there for backup," he barked. Halting mid-flight, he turned to the small army of seraphs trailing him. "Divide and retreat to the front."

At the foot of the stairs, Dmitri waved agreement and returned to the corridor with at least fifteen seraphs on his heels.

Joachim resumed climbing, his grasp tight on Gia's hand. He glanced up the twisting flights, reminded of the steely, filthy stairwell in the apartment building where she'd spent her childhood. Like the day they retrieved the Medallion, danger lurked at every landing. This time, though, his pulse thudded with a heaviness he couldn't name.

As they reached the third floor, he slowed, keeping her close. A few members of his team moved ahead to secure the corridor. The door slammed shut behind them—and gunfire erupted.

Joachim squelched the urge to tear after his men and forced himself to continue up the final flight. They were trained for head-on defense, yet every cell in his human form longed to shield them. The prayer hovering at the forefront of his mind did little to assuage his anxiety. He didn't know if it was even received, but it was all he could offer.

"They can protect themselves," Gia reassured, reading his

troubled thoughts.

He held her back when they reached the fourth-floor landing. The handful of operatives still following them moved past their leader and slid through the door, into the hall. Aristide, the last one in, beckoned to Joachim once the territory was safeguarded.

"Reporting in," Dmitri's voice sounded through the headset and stopped Joachim at the door. "We're at the fourth floor, front staircase. Joachim, where are Olivier and Soleil?"

Never in his celestial existence had Joachim known the hard, hammering pulse of fear, but it suffused him now like a wave of ice water shot through his veins, tensing every muscle, raising the hair on his arms and revving his heart until it threatened to jump from his chest. "They radioed from the fourth-floor landing," he said numbly. "I instructed them to wait for backup. Do you not see them?"

"The stairwell is empty. And they don't answer on any channel."

Refusing to believe what intuition already screamed through his mind, Joachim switched channels on the comm unit. "Olivier. Report."

Nothing.

"Soleil, report."

Silence.

"Soleil. Olivier...*damn you*..." His eyes closed and he dropped his head.

Gia's hand gently closed around his while Joachim switched his comm unit back to all-access and sucked in a shaken breath. Seraphim entered from both sides of the hall now, but the supreme uncertainty that he could protect them from Therides' malevolent force parched his throat and dried up the tactical orders waiting to be spoken.

Adjusting his grip on his pistol, he drew Gia tightly against his side and moved among his remaining team members. He sensed their trusting regard as they fell into step behind him, the power of their blind faith in Creator and the Great Warrior.

But Joachim could no longer join them in their conviction. Somehow, the lines between him and the Archangel had been severed. The curtain of humanity had fallen between seraph and Heaven.

He had no time to grieve, to feel remorse or pain. As he drew closer to the midpoint of the corridor, Soleil stumbled into the corridor from a sliding door to the left, her green eyes wide with shock.

She wavered on unsteady feet like a sleepy child, unarmed, her headset missing. Blood streaked her cheek and darkened the front of her black jumpsuit. Joachim released Gia and bolted toward his fellow seraph, reaching her just in time to catch her as her knees crumpled.

"We walked into a trap," Soleil whispered, her fingers tightening desperately into the material of his shirt. "Olivier—he—"

Behind them, the door panel again slid open. Immediately Joachim drew back and spun to hand Soleil to one of his men, who caught her limp form and hustled her toward the stairs and safety.

"Come on, then," said a reedy, oddly familiar voice from the bowels of the darkened room.

At Joachim's silent nod, Gia stepped back, and the remaining team took position, flanking the entrance to the armored room. Heart thrashing wildly, he removed his headset, let it drop to the floor, then eased around the doorjamb to face the evil in the space beyond.

Nothing but blackness greeted his darting gaze. The soft click of a desk lamp, and a single light spilled across the stronghold space, divulging the glistening blood that smeared the steel-brushed floor, the footprints and scuffs, Soleil's discarded pistol.

Vincent Rossi sat at a wide steel-and-glass desk, chair swiveled away from the door to face the wall.

"'*Will you walk into my parlor?* said the spider to the fly'," the disembodied whisper threaded into the dimness. "Did you bring the Spear, little flies? At last you play the game by my rules."

Joachim signaled Gia and his team to stay back, noting briefly that despite his silent order, Gia stood at the forefront, the Glock clutched to her chest. He stared hard at her, willing her to obey, and at last she retreated into the corridor, but not far enough for his peace of mind.

Perspiration trickled down the sides of his face as he inched over the threshold, his pistol gripped in both hands, aimed at the back of Rossi's head.

Where was Olivier? His gaze swept the room. Shadow cloaked the four corners, deepened by the pale, stark light radiating from the small lamp on the desktop.

Gather yourself, a sharp, otherworldly voice echoed in his ears. No, not otherworldly. His own human voice. His common sense. For the first time in all the eons he'd served as a seraphic operative, it was the only commanding voice he heard.

Keeping the pistol trained on the nephil's head, he eased farther into the room and forced himself to speak. "We meet again, Therides. Why do you face the wall? Let me look into the eyes of my enemy."

"I hope you like surprises," the demon said, abruptly drawing Joachim's attention to the left. The voice had come not from the figure in the desk chair, but from the gloom lurking on the far side of the room. The darkness cloaked something he couldn't make out, and uncertainty regained its clammy grip on his gut.

"Show yourself," he said hoarsely.

A faint rustling indicated movement in the shadows, then Olivier emerged, and for an instant, Joachim found his breath.

But something wasn't right. He redirected the pistol on his friend, body tensed in creeping alarm. "Liv, get back."

Olivier ignored the order and crossed to the desk, where,

with a single fingertip, he twirled the chair around.

Behind Joachim, Gia bit back a gasp. Vincent Rossi's corpse, riddled with bullets, stared blankly from the chair, his arms crossed in a macabre fashion across his gore-soaked chest.

"Some people are just trigger-happy," the pitch of Olivier's voice climbed with choked laughter as he fingered the bloodied hair at Rossi's temple. "If I remember correctly, Olivier always did have a knack for acting on impulse."

He gestured to himself as though examining his own form for the first time. "Nice accommodations, huh? He did me a favor by riddling Rossi's body with bullets, I must admit."

Joachim swallowed rising nausea and squinted at the demon housed in his best friend's body. "Olivier is indeed impulsive, but he would never shoot unless it was the last resort."

Therides studied his fingernails in the dim light, his tone mildly disinterested. "Well, I suppose he was trying to protect our lovely Soleil. Her name means the sun, you know. She shines so brightly, if I bore the curse of sentimentality your friend did, I might shoot me to pieces too. When I tried to greet her, to embrace her…"

Joachim's finger flexed against the trigger of his pistol. Every ounce of grief and disgust within him drove him to empty the weapon into the demon as the details formed a sickening picture in his mind. Olivier had shot Rossi in a knee-jerk reaction to save Soleil. The demon had then jumped from Rossi's corpse into Olivier…

And sent Olivier into cycle.

Anguish screamed through him.

Swallowing, he adjusted his grip on the pistol and glanced over his shoulder at Gia. She stared back at him with wide eyes, waiting for his word. She would throw herself into battle like the warrior he'd always believed her to be.

But he wouldn't lose her too.

"Your grief over your cohort is aimless." Olivier—no, *it*

wasn't Olivier—crossed his arms and hoisted himself onto the desk, swinging one leg to and fro. "Technically, he's to blame for his own demise. He forced me to jump." His lips curled. "Soleil had no idea what was happening. Her aristocratic cheekbone shattered beautifully under the butt of Olivier's gun." He kicked at the discarded pistol and sent it skittering across the floor, malice radiating from his lean form in ever-growing waves. "Take back your weapon. I have no use for it now, of course. None of us at the Fellowship need armaments to defeat you and your army, seraph."

The Spear. Joachim heard Gia's voice as clearly as if she'd whispered in his ear. He sensed her strength coiling behind him, and beyond her, the reinforcements awaiting the merest gesture of his hand.

Therides' smug expression wavered. "But to up the ante, consider this. The estate is packed with explosives. Even if you best me here today, we'll all go together in a glorious blaze of light. *Cycle, cycle, cycle*. All I have to do is press the button."

Reaching behind the desk, he brought forth a small detonator, held it aloft and poised his thumb above it. "Shall we just end it now? Save ourselves the trouble and bloodshed?"

Joachim didn't move, his gaze darting between the device and the nephil's pupilless eyes.

"Say goodnight," Therides whispered, and Joachim flinched as the demon compressed the button with dramatic aplomb.

Nothing happened. Therides' smile returned. "Just toying with you. A little humor between good and evil, hmm?" He tossed the detonator on the desktop and gave a restless sigh. "I'm tired of this conversation."

"Yes," Joachim gritted. "Enough diabolical monologue."

Therides scowled. "Listen carefully, you duplicitous celestial bastard. I've started the clock just now. Twenty minutes until the compound explodes. I could have arranged for more time, but I anticipated this final battle would be over quickly. I plan to play a bit of leapfrog from this body once I send you into cycle, which will, I promise, be laughably unproblematic."

He slid off the desk and stood. "But I suppose you want your duel of darkness and light after all the trouble you've endured to arrive at this moment. Let's get on with it, then, shall we? And no pistols, since we know what happens when naughty boys play with guns. Besides, I do so relish hand-to-hand combat."

Before Joachim could respond, the soft sound of movement behind him caught his ear.

Therides' gaze fixed beyond his shoulder, and sick humor twisted his lips. "Ah, hold the phone! Gia. My frightened little fawn. Will you face death with any sense of dignity, Daughter of Longinus? You lived with so little for so long."

She stopped beside Joachim. "After I send you back to Hell."

Therides rounded the desk with careful steps. "'*Sweet creature,* said the Spider, *you're witty and you're wise; How handsome are your gauzy wings, how brilliant are your eyes*'!"

"I never did care for poetry," Gia said flatly. "Sick son of a bitch."

The demon's attention shifted back to Joachim. "What a lovely, *eloquent* addition she makes to your team. I had a taste of her while I inhabited Vincent Rossi's body, you know. Quite delectable and uninhibited."

A choked sound of rage escaped Gia's throat, and Joachim's teeth clenched in answering fury.

"Tell me, seraph, does she tempt you with her wild dark curls and those sultry, *brilliant* eyes, trapped in your susceptible human body as you are with all its needs and yearnings?"

A muscle jumped in Joachim's jaw, but he stood in steely silence, pistol trained on the demon, who narrowed his gaze as cruel amusement crept across his lips.

"Hmm. I sense an excruciating awareness between the two of you. Have you shame on your beatific conscience, seraph?

Naughty, naughty angel. What will the Great Warrior think of his right-hand man when he learns of this disgrace? Quick, before you cycle…whisper to me. Who better than a demon to hear your deathbed confessions?"

Without taking his gaze from the nephil, Joachim reached behind him to relinquish his pistol to the closest operative. For a moment, as the demon watched with glittering eyes, no one moved. Then Joachim felt the weapon gently removed from his grasp.

"My tool belt, as well." He unfastened it and extended it behind him, and it too disappeared from his hand, followed by the soft withdrawal of footsteps returning to the corridor. Without turning to address his team, he ordered, "Seraphim, retreat."

Aristide's voice thundered from the door. "I'll not leave you, Joachim."

"You'll leave this compound now, Aristide. Take my men with you." Breathing heavily, he glanced at his watch. "Sixteen minutes."

"I've arranged more surprises for you on your way down," Therides offered with a sneer. "This place is a veritable funhouse. Run along."

Joachim glanced back at his men and gave a short nod. "Make short work of it."

A brief silence told him his men hesitated behind him, loath to abandon him.

Then Aristide muttered, "Retreat." At last, their footfalls echoed through the corridor, growing fainter until the door clanged shut at the end of the hall, and an eerie silence descended.

Joachim's gaze met the demon's. "I stand unarmed, like you. An even battlefield."

"But what of your whore?" Therides hissed.

"She stays," Joachim said, ignoring the slur for Gia's sake.

"How overly sentimental of you." The demon sneered at the woman who stood so staunchly beside her partner. "She's armed."

Joachim glanced at Gia's resolute profile. "Disarm yourself."

She placed her Glock outside the door, smoothly bypassing the small pouch at her waist that held their only true weapon.

Therides glowered. "Rid her of the Spear, seraph."

"And provide you easy access to it? No. She keeps it."

"I'll strip it off her bloodied corpse."

Joachim didn't flinch. "But first you must go through me."

And Creator's protection.

Are You with me still?

He touched Gia's elbow. "Stand aside. No matter what happens, stay clear. You know what to do."

She moved into the shadows, a lethal weapon in her own right. He loved her wildly. Her strength infused him with a strange elation as he moved to the center of the room, circling the demon disguised as his beloved Olivier. All he had to do was injure Therides' host body enough to disable him.

"Shall we begin?" he murmured.

And lunged.

Chapter Twenty-Five

Gia watched from the shadows, her pulse pounding as demon and angel circled the bloodstained floor. Golden light sparked from the tips of Joachim's fingers, haloed his head and radiated an opalescent aura around him, fleeting glimpses of the magnificent celestial being she'd encountered in her mother's apartment.

In contrast, the space around Therides' body swallowed the light, as though a void existed in the field where Life emits energy.

Joachim was the first to strike, snapping Therides' head with a heel palm to the face. The demon reacted with vicious alacrity, throwing rapid blows, but Joachim artfully stayed out of range and kept his opponent on exhaustive and constant defense with a lightning series of jabs that sprayed a geyser of blood from the nephil's nose. At the same time, his other palm blocked Therides' relentless strikes, his hands two independent instruments working as one machine.

Gia was mesmerized by the brutal, choreographed beauty of the dance between good and evil. Joachim moved as though each motion were an automatic reflex, rhythmic and graceful, backing the demon against the far wall with inexorable force.

For an electric moment it seemed Therides had lost ground without having ever held it. Then, as though Olivier's former body had regained memory of its extensive training, the demon crouched and leaped, tackled Joachim and rolled him to the ground.

Grunts of rage and agony bounced off the reinforced walls and blood smeared a grisly composition across the floor as the two men grappled for dominant position.

Shivering with alarm, Gia felt for the small leather pouch at her waist with trembling fingers. When would she step into the violent finale playing before her? Sheer uncertainty drove her to withdraw the Spear, if only to gain strength from its cool weight in her hand. She held it low against her thigh, her wide gaze following the duel as one precious minute slipped into the next.

How many minutes remained?

Joachim slid like an eel beneath the nephil's body lock, rolled free and regained his footing, hauling Therides with him. Twisting, he delivered an explosion of relentless sidekicks that threw his opponent against the desk, overturned it with a resounding crash and tipped Rossi's corpse from the chair.

Therides rebounded as if he'd suffered nary a scratch, even as blood streamed from his nose and bubbled at the corners of his sneering lips.

Their circling resumed, both men panting and battered. To Gia's otherworldly vision, waves of orange and red pulsated from Joachim's aura, brief, white-hot flashes blazing from the six origin points of his wings.

In opposition, translucent ghouls reared and slithered about Therides, coiling around his limbs, guiding his movements and infusing them with black and deadly force.

When Joachim at last maneuvered the nephil close to where Gia stood with Spear in hand, she knew it was time. His gaze pierced hers for a split second, a silent order to strike.

Adrenaline fired through her. She lunged forward to drive the Spear home…

And felt herself lifted free from the earth by invisible claws. She flew. The world shattered into stars and floaters and fireworks. Agony exploded behind her eyes.

"Gia!" Joachim's enraged cry barely penetrated the buzzing that filled her ears. The floor rushed to greet her and waves of nausea poured over her. She'd hit her head somehow. And the Spear…her hand was empty. She ordered herself to rise, to move, but her body wouldn't obey. It had somehow disconnected itself from her will.

She had failed.

From a great, black distance, Therides' low laughter vibrated the air. "Oh, seraph. Why would you lay the keys to the kingdom in the hands of a child?"

And then the nightmare drifted into black, hollow silence.

* * * * *

A few seconds passed. Or maybe hours. Gia stirred, lifted her throbbing head and found herself sprawled near Rossi's corpse, its empty gaze gaping into hers.

She jolted awake. *Joachim. The Spear*! Urgency slammed into her and pushed her through the pain and nausea to crawl out from behind the desk.

Her vision swam and the room made a crazy rotation. When she focused, she stared in disbelief and screamed.

Joachim lay crumpled against the far wall like a lifeless puppet. One look and she knew he was dead. "*No*!"

"Oh, but yes." Emerging from the shadows, Therides glowered at her with yellowed, swollen eyes, his ridicule still recognizable beneath the abrasions and bruising that obliterated Olivier's once-beautiful features. "'The way into my parlor is up a winding stair, and I have many curious things to show you when you are there'."

"No," she whispered, crawling backward. Her spine collided with the cold, hard wall, and hollow grief dislodged her heart from its tenuous mooring.

"Lose something?" Therides straightened and produced the Spear from behind his back. "I searched far and wide for this, and here it is, just a rusted little thing. But so powerful."

He caressed the relic, examining it with vague curiosity. "Thank you for giving it over to my keeping, Daughter of Longinus. On to Creator. I'll dethrone Him and crush the Dominions with my bare hands."

The only sound was her gasping sobs as he raised the Spear to his lips to kiss it reverently…and licked its corroded edge instead, his tongue a forked, two-headed serpent that desecrated the blessed relic with its vile caress.

Then, unexpectedly, he gasped and dropped to one knee, his hand clutching at his side in a paroxysm of agony. "Damn damn *damn*! Your human bodies are…so badly…put together. Shabby…workmanship." He opened one eye and peeked at her, offered her a frail smile before another spasm hit him and crimson bubbles frothed at his mouth.

The Spear dangled from his grasp.

He was bleeding internally. He was dying.

Realization surged through Gia and froze her tears. *Her job wasn't done*. She had another chance. Grief and gratitude and determination rolled through her like a ball of lightning from God's hand.

Move. Eyeing the sacred relic sagging in the demon's hand, she slid closer, her breath shuddering from her lungs in shallow, erratic pants.

Blood trickled down Therides' chin and he sank close to the floor, his reptilian eyes flipping open to watch her approach.

"Sneaky little fly," he panted, and half-brandished the Spear in her direction. "Get back….you stupid, stupid…bitch."

Gia swallowed and scooted closer.

This time Therides swung at her with the relic, but she jerked back out of range and stared him down, gauging his vulnerability and the increasing rivulets of blood slicing a vermilion path down his chin and neck. For a moment, neither of them moved. Then Gia threw herself into him, tackling him to the floor.

She managed to straddle him beneath her, but he wasn't as weak as she'd thought. His hand, a vicious claw, flew to her throat and squeezed hard enough to choke away her breath, but her wrath was stronger. Shoving at his grip, she dislodged it long enough to inhale and dug a free hand beneath his body, where his left arm had trapped itself. Her fingers brushed metal and closed around it, and she shot upright.

Electricity crackled around them in brief, flashing forks, raising the strands of Gia's hair. Brown eyes locked on yellow, and a faint smile crossed his features. Then his face dissolved into a swarm of insects and pestilence, Gia's final sight into the true evil of the demon before she drove the Spear with all her strength into his heaving gut. Again. *Again.* Exorcising her rage as she sent the demon back to Hell in splatters of blood and gore, until all that remained within her was sickness of the soul.

Gagging, Gia dropped the Spear, scrambled back from Olivier's body and stared at the lifeless heap. It looked as though the demon had stepped out of a suit made of flesh and bone and simply discarded it.

It wasn't Olivier. He was gone.

And Joachim too.

Her only company now was the sound of her own weeping, the dirge-like thud of her pulse in her ears, and the relentless passage of time that counted off the seconds to the compound's explosion.

Move, Gia. You have to get out of here!

Her tear-filled gaze darted from the motionless bodies around her to the deserted corridor. Trembling, she shifted to her hands and knees in an attempt to rise, but then stopped.

Across the room, Joachim stirred and sat up, one hand rubbing his head as though he'd merely bumped it.

Hope soared through her and sent a fresh deluge of tears streaming down her cheeks. "Joachim—"

He squinted at her, then a smile of recognition slashed a path across his face. "'*Come hither, hither, pretty fly,*'" he hissed, the singsong verse sliding out on a serpent's tongue.

In that second of renewed, blinding despair, Gia gleaned the truth, but horror stole her ability to accept it. Smearing the tears away from her eyes, she struggled to her feet and took a tentative step toward him. "Joachim?"

"'...How very soon this silly little Fly, hearing his wily, flattering words, came slowly flitting by.'" He rose with sublime grace and moved toward her, a ghastly phantom of the man she loved, more horrible than any demon she'd encountered in this nightmare labyrinth. "Time to sleep, little fly. Come let me turn out the lights."

A sob shook her to her core. "Oh, no."

"This body holds fond memories of you, Gia," the nephil said, a harbinger of death disguised in Joachim's lithe, black-garbed form. "Erotic. Delicious."

"Go to hell," she ground out.

"I like it here much better."

Her gaze darted around for a weapon, anything to fight off the inevitable attack. Her Glock was hopelessly out of reach. The Spear was lost somewhere near Olivier's crumpled body. "Don't come any closer."

"Just a little closer." The demon's smile broadened, his pupilless eyes blazing a fire stoked with a thousand writhing, twisting, naked souls. "We're about to be blown into oblivion, my little concubine. You will die and I will leap."

"To the devil." Her back hit the wall and she hugged it, ready to strike out with the sidekicks Dmitri had taught her.

"No, to the Middle East. I have my eye on a particularly unhinged terrorist this time, a religious zealot." His head cocked at an unnatural angle. "One last touch of your sweet lips for nostalgia's sake? And maybe a little tongue, just to humor me?"

Gia glanced at Olivier's corpse, at the black, viscous puddle of blood beneath him. The Spear called to her, its voice a dim metallic ring only she could sense. She had to reach it.

Help me, God, Creator, whoever you are. I'm not just the Daughter of Longinus. I'm your *daughter.*

"Don't be a prude," Therides went on, drawing closer. "Give us a kiss. You can pretend I'm your angel lover." He looked down at himself. "All the yummy parts are the same, after all."

She felt the heat radiating from his body long before he reached her. A blast from a foul furnace, stoked with brimstone and screaming, tortured spirits.

An unholy weight pinned her limbs to the wall, Therides' gleeful expression boasting that he controlled her like a maniacal puppet master. She couldn't reach the Spear.

Gia closed her eyes. There was no God in this nightmare. No escape from it. No hope. She held her breath and turned her head aside, waiting for the fetid, clammy touch of the nephil's lips.

Nothing happened.

The supernatural bindings that held her motionless slid from her arms and legs, and her eyes shot open.

Therides clutched his head and staggered back a step, the tendons in his neck bulging with some tormented, invisible struggle she didn't understand.

Dropping to his knees, he reached out and wrapped his fingers around her ankle. "Gia…the Spear…get the Spear."

Her eyes widened and flooded anew. God, it sounded like Joachim. It looked like Joachim. Was this a trick?

She jerked free from his desperate grasp and backed toward the desk. "Who are you?"

"Please," he groaned. "Release me and send the nephil back to Hell. The Spear…send the…"

It was Joachim! "Oh, God—" she hunched down beside him and her fingers hovered over his head, shaking with fear and joy. "We have to get you out of here. This place is about to—"

"No." His blue eyes, filled with anguish, pleaded with hers. "The nephil is still in me! We fight for this body. The cycle opens—" He cried out and clutched his chest with a bloodied hand. "Get the Spear! End this!"

Terror sent her scrambling on hands and knees to Olivier's corpse. With a grunt of exertion, she rolled him to his side and frantically searched around the body, blood sticky and still warm as it oozed between her fingers. Then she touched something hot, and drew back with the Spear in her grasp, vibrating with the sheer power it granted.

"I've got it." She swiveled and reached for Joachim, then hesitated as realization shoved an ugly path through her relief. He meant for her to impale him.

Never.

A slew of incoherent words and low, deathly moans tore from Joachim's chest as he crouched on his knees and pressed his forehead to the floor.

Gia laid a hand on his back, but a new wave of pain rolled through him in a massive spasm, contorting his body until he thrashed backward and twisted. He clutched at thin air, tears washing the blood from his face in clean rivulets. "Deliver me from this suffering, Gia—do it!"

"You want me to stab you?" Dropping to her knees beside him, she wept openly, rocked by disbelief. "How can I do this, Joachim? How can I hurt you? *How?*"

"Longinus…your destiny…help me!" His plea slid into an inhuman growl and he rolled to his back, body arched in a convulsion of agony.

She heard his words from so long ago as though he whispered them now into her ear. *This is why we safeguarded your life, Gia. Like seraphim, you have a job. And no choice. Do the job.*

The Spear pulsated in her hands, a live thing. An instrument of death and liberation.

Do the job.

Quaking with the force of her grief, Gia raised the holy relic high and trembling over Joachim's heart. "I love you, Joachim. *I love you*. Do you hear me?"

His lashes lifted. Their gazes locked.

And with a fierce, downward swing, the Daughter of Longinus drove the Spear home.

Chapter Twenty-Six

The world was an arid void, its stillness echoing, tomblike, around Gia's senses. She sat with her back against the steel wall, Joachim's body sprawled beside her. Cradling his head in her arms, she squeezed her eyes shut and listened to the hollow silence of a life without joy or meaning.

A life that was about to blow apart.

She couldn't find the strength to move, to crawl out of the armored room. Pain hammered a relentless drum behind her eyes. Serpentine voices whispered in her head. All she had to do was sit in this heavy, black quiet, and it would soon be over.

Somewhere, a door squeaked open. The urgent thud of boots approached, but she didn't stir. Rescue her or kill her, it didn't matter. They couldn't strip away her soul—it had already been flayed. Nor could they heal her. Like the body clutched in her arms, she was a shell.

"Gia." Aristide's rumbling voice washed over her from above, and his electric life force invaded the numbness that cocooned her. "Come, we must leave here."

A strong hand closed gently around her arm, but she didn't respond. Didn't move. Didn't open her eyes.

More footsteps pounded from the corridor. "Gia, it's time to go." Dmitri's voice, softer and filled with compassion, permeated her oblivion. "The nephil spoke the truth. Explosives pack the compound. Our time has nearly run out. Let us help you."

She stirred and glanced up at him with blurry eyes. Joachim's head was a precious weight in her lap, one she couldn't relinquish. *Good night, sweet prince,* Shakespeare's timeless farewell echoed in her aching brain as she stroked the still-damp hair at his temples. *And flights of angels sing thee to thy rest.*

"He's gone," Dmitri said quietly.

"Back to Creator. His mission has ended." Aristide bent to retrieve the Spear. It lay in a spattering of blood, where Gia had discarded it seconds after stabbing Joachim.

"Leave it!" she cried.

He quickly withdrew. "It still holds power—"

"It holds *death*. I am its keeper, and I say *leave it in this hellhole*." Her eyes wandered back to Joachim's face, her hands aimlessly caressing his lifeless features. "It took him from me."

Dmitri crouched in front of her. "Listen to me, Gia. You would have had to say goodbye to him, whether now or upon seraphim's exodus. It would have ended the same way. And because of you, Joachim is home, where he belongs."

"I killed him."

"No, you saved him from cycle." He extended his hand to her. "And now you must save yourself."

A fluttering of awareness roused her a little more. The seraphs had made a dangerous trek back into the mansion to rescue her, and their own well-being grew more endangered as each second slid by.

Fresh tears filled her eyes. "We'll take Joachim out of here with us?"

Aristide shook his head. "It's not Joachim. It's a shell, a corpse—"

"Of course we'll take him with us," Dmitri interrupted, rising to his feet. "Ari, will you carry our leader?"

Instant comprehension softened the giant seraph's features. "If it's all right with Gia." Kneeling in front of her, he sought her gaze. "I'll take him from you now."

At her silent nod, he slid an arm under Joachim's head and one under his knees. Then with tender care he lifted the body of his commander and bore him toward the door.

Using Dmitri's hands as support, Gia rose on unsteady feet. She stopped once, before the Spear, and with every ounce of strength in her battered body, kicked it across the room. "It's my choice," she told Dmitri. "I choose its destruction."

They made it as far as the corridor before her legs gave out.

"You're too weak to walk out of here," the seraph said calmly when her panicked eyes sought his. "May I carry you?"

"Absolutely." Gratitude and exhaustion washed over her as he hoisted her into his arms. "Please carry me out of this hell."

The operatives descended the stairs with determined speed, maneuvering around the dead bodies of nephilim and seraphim alike that littered their path. Dmitri's breath burst in ragged rushes against Gia's hair by the time they hurtled out the front door and into the blinding sunlight.

In their wake, explosions detonated in quick succession, glass shattered, thousands of panes at once, and the mansion behind them shuddered on its foundation.

Beyond the gates, the surviving seraphim operatives had gathered to receive them, and now their urgent shouts of encouragement rose into the air.

Dmitri raced on Aristide's heels as if Gia were weightless, but they couldn't gain the distance they needed before the compound blew apart. "Down!" he yelled.

Gia's battered body slammed into the hard earth and he dove to cover her, his weight knocking the scream from her chest.

A wave of heat rolled over them like the breath of a hundred dragons. Debris rained down in a shower of flaming rubble across the enclosed yard, the stench of black smoke and sulfur filling their noses and choking their lungs.

To Gia's overwrought mind, the very wrath of the demon had descended upon them, consuming Vincent Rossi's deluded world and everything in its vicinity like a hungry beast. All she could do was huddle beneath Dmitri's protective shield and wait for surcease…or darkness.

Gradually, the rumbling explosions settled into the crackling roar of fire, and the air grew opaque with smoke and dust.

"Gia?" Dmitri shifted over her, the slight movement sprinkling glass and fragments around them. "Are you hurt?"

Coughing, she shook her head, even though her very bones felt jarred and bruised. "I'm—I'm okay. Are you?"

A wry grin tipped his lips as he brushed glass shards from her hair. "We're resilient creatures." Then he sobered and glanced through the haze at the operatives jogging toward them. "The others are coming. You'll get medical attention now, and soon, rest."

Gia sat up to cast a frightened glance at the compound. The fire's heat swirled a wild wind about them, whipping through her hair, warming her cheeks. Greedy flames licked at the ruins, detonating mini-explosions in the bowels of the inferno and sending billows of noxious smoke into the cloudless, cerulean sky.

A few feet away, Aristide straightened from his hunkered position and shook himself like a big dog shedding dust from its coat.

The seraphs approached him too. Six of them. Pallbearers. Joachim's lifeless form lay at his feet.

Numb, Gia watched the operatives descend to retrieve their leader's body. A running reel of images flashed before her weary mind. Joachim's features relaxed in slumber. In repose. In joy and sorrow. In ecstasy.

And now, bloodied and deathly still.

A new surge of grief clogged her throat. "He sleeps," she whispered to herself. "He sleeps."

"Come, Gia," Dmitri gingerly helped her stand. "The worst is over."

She leaned against him and let him lead her across the lawn, away from Therides' Armageddon and the stench of Hell.

Her story was indeed over. She'd made it out alive, swept to safety on the protective wings of guardian angels. The only part they couldn't rescue was her heart.

*****

The sun balanced precariously on the horizon, an orange orb that shivered in the chilled wind sweeping across the field.

Two women faced each other in the low-bowing grass, one with duffel bag in hand, the other holding nothing, her left arm bandaged from shoulder to wrist.

"Well, then, Gia," the blonde seraph said, her tone impassive and efficient as always. "This is goodbye. Franco and Phillip will escort you to your new home, and then you will be free." A faint smile curved her perfect mouth. "A day I'm sure you often doubted would come."

Gia didn't know how to respond. Once upon a time, she would have sold her soul to face freedom without the hot breath of danger searing her back. Now she stood before the simplicity of a life unhampered by demons, subterfuge and magic and found its taste mildly bitter, tinged with loneliness.

The knot in her stomach tightened as she gazed past Soleil to the dying vermilion sky. "When do you depart?"

"Tonight. Part of my duties is to ensure the new team has settled and that headquarters are functioning smoothly under the new directive." She glanced down at her bandaged arm. "I won't be sorry to leave this physical discomfort behind, that's certain."

"You took quite a beating." Gia studied the fading abrasions that still colored the side of Soleil's face. Even bruised, the seraph was the most striking woman she'd ever seen. "Your body will recover, right?"

"Straight away, when the next operative takes it. Seraphim bring with them healing power when they possess their assigned bodies."

Gia didn't ask for further elaboration. She'd seen Joachim's broken body sealed in the cryogenic cylinder, had watched Dmitri, Aristide, Jordan and the other operatives who had survived the mission happily strip off their humanity and climb into their icy steel coffins. Even old Nicodemus held a designated chamber when the time for his departure came. As a counselor who embarked on myriad missions, he'd developed a funny attachment to the old body he was assigned. He too would return to the celestial kingdom tonight via the cryogenic chamber, and then the seraphs Gia had known would be gone.

The two women strolled toward the waiting van, their steps slow and measured. Gia opened her mouth to speak, closed it, then tried again. "I'm glad you're one of the last seraphs to leave, Soleil. I have a few things I want to—"

"Please, allow me to speak." Desperation flooded Soleil's eyes, turning them a shimmering green as she swung around to face Gia. "I must ask your forgiveness. I have behaved badly to you. Your interactions with Joachim shouldn't have been my concern, and yet I judged—"

"It's okay, Soleil." Empathy stung Gia's eyes, and she laid a gentle hand on the seraph's shoulder. "Like the others, you only had your leader's best interest at heart, and my track record coming into this mission wasn't anything to be proud of. Why should you have trusted me? Especially when the mission was compromised because of…because of what he and I became to each other?" She couldn't bring herself to utter Joachim's name. It was like a magic password to open the floodgates of grief.

Soleil covered Gia's hand with her own. "Your heart is true and righteous, Gia, and I knew it from the start. I don't understand human emotions, not even the few I experience on missions, and when I began to see the little ways he changed in your presence…the brightness of his mood, his attentiveness to you, the softness in the way he regarded you, I felt…a tightness in my chest, right over my heart. A rending of sorts."

A rueful laugh slipped from Soleil's lips. "His eyes followed you everywhere you went, as though you carried his heart in your pocket. And now I know…" She bowed her head, the wind whipping flaxen strands of hair across her grief-crumpled features. "Now I know, he carried yours too. He loved you as a man and as a guardian. He'll love you in the Realm, on every mission, in every dimension. Joachim will love you forever."

Gia couldn't reply. She swallowed repeatedly to clear away the tears gathered in her throat, to no avail. When Soleil reached out and tentatively embraced her, Gia dropped her duffel and clung to her, shoulders shaking under the weight of emotion.

In consolation, Soleil's embrace tightened, and the two stood in the healing silence of forgiveness and genuine affection.

After a moment, the seraph stepped back and placed her fingertips against Gia's furrowed forehead. "Close your eyes."

Gia's lashes fluttered closed.

"No pain," Soleil whispered.

Gia's pulse slowed. The tensions drained from her facial muscles, her shoulders. Even the wind settled, threading gently through her hair, its own turmoil appeased by the advent of night.

"Breathe please, Gia."

Gia inhaled peace, exhaled sorrow.

"Very good, Miss Torio." The seraph's touch slid away.

When Gia opened her eyes, Soleil was gone.

Chapter Twenty-Seven

Six Months Later

Gia shot a dismal glance at the overcast sky and switched her backpack to the opposite shoulder, her breath puffing soft clouds into the afternoon air. Washington, D.C. in February wasn't the most hospitable environment, but at least the shearing wind that had blown off Lake Michigan wasn't an ever-present companion to her five-block walk from school to the Metro.

Chicago, of course, had held nothing for her in the end. The seraphs were long gone, replaced by a new team of operatives who'd delivered her back to the real world with polite impassivity. And when, in desperation, she'd searched for ties to bind her to her previous life, all she found were tenants in her mother's old apartment. Donna Torio had died of a stroke, old at the age of fifty, mere days before Gia and Joachim had found the Medallion.

Washington offered a new start. Despite the weather, Gia's step was a little lighter today. Time had worked its magic on her wounds, and with every passing week, her grief became more bearable. But a part of her loathed to let it go, for it meant surrendering her belief in happy endings. The child in her clung to the fantasy that Joachim wasn't separated from her forever, as Olivier had warned. That one day, when her existence on this Earth was done, she'd see him again. Feel him again. Hear the sound of his voice and be the recipient of his beautiful smile.

Until then, she would live this earthly life, touch as many people as she could, offering comfort and compassion to anyone in need who crossed her path. Though she no longer held the Spear, she was still the Daughter of Longinus, in word *and* deed.

Three more years of nonstop semesters, and she'd have her bachelor's degree in family counseling. The classes kept her distracted, excited, half-overwhelmed.

Sometimes, though, if the wind blew just right and carried a vague scent of vanilla and wildflowers, she still cried.

It was getting late. The daylight faded fast into wintry dusk, and minute flurries floated on the air. Tomorrow, according to the forecast, the city would be blanketed by snow.

Gia paused at a newsstand and bought a magazine to read on the Metro ride home. As she turned toward the sidewalk, a tiny, skyward fluttering of yellow caught her peripheral vision.

A butterfly! Transfixed, she stood and watched it dance and dart in the cold. An incongruous harbinger of spring, sadly premature.

"There's a butterfly," she told the magazine vendor, who eyed her with curiosity.

His craggy eyebrows shot up. "No kiddin'? In the dead of winter?"

"And in the heart of the city too." Her gaze followed the ethereal insect until it caught a breeze and sailed out of sight. "Strange, huh?"

"I've seen stranger," he said with a shrug.

"Me too." She offered him a wry smile and headed toward the Metro, her heart inexplicably lightened.

The steep, lengthy escalator leading into the underground station was sparsely populated, a window of quiet before the rush-hour storm. Gia rode down on a single step, leaning against the moving rail to peruse the magazine.

The escalator bringing passengers up from the subterranean station was more crowded. Her gaze drifted from the article in her hand to the people moving past. Old women in wool coats, teenagers with skullcaps and facial piercings. Pretty girls in Greek-lettered sorority jackets, mothers with firm grips on their children's hands.

A handsome, immaculately groomed man in a suit and trench coat, his attention fixed on a newspaper he held folded in one hand.

Gia focused on his bowed head as the escalators pulled them closer, and her heart skipped a beat. He looked like…

Ridiculous.

She glanced away, then back again. The daylight behind her caught the chestnut highlights of his neatly shorn hair. And when he straightened a little, the cool glow slid across his features like a celestial spotlight, exposing each exquisite detail.

The magazine slipped from her fingers.

Joachim.

Gia was paralyzed. Gripping the rail, she stared as he approached from the opposite direction, tried to choke out a word, something, anything. How could he be here? In the same body? *Alive?*

Hysterical joy reared within her, but a bitter memory quickly brought it crashing down. Olivier's prophecy echoed in her ears.

He's a celestial being, temporarily housed in a body that will eventually host any number of other operatives in other missions.

The man passed her a mere three feet away. He drew a breath and flipped the paper to the reverse side, utterly unaware of the wild-eyed woman staring at him.

Gia's throat worked, but the memory of Olivier's warning parried every word that rose to her lips.

In time, you'll pass him on the street, and it won't even be Joachim anymore. He won't know you, and your heart will shatter.

"No," she whispered, a flat refusal. But it was too late. The man had already stepped off at the street level.

Heart pounding, Gia swung forward for the rest of the ride down, her face burning, her fingers digging into the rubberized handrail. *Breathe.* She shook from head to toe. What did it matter if she had just passed Joachim? If Olivier had spoken the truth, it wasn't truly Joachim. Whoever was in his body wouldn't know her, anyway. Why bother to give chase?

Why bother to even breathe anymore?

Stepping off the escalator at its termination, she hesitated, then with quivering legs, got on the opposite escalator and began to climb.

I can't lose him again.

But Gia, said the voice of reason, *you never had him.*

Even though she knew in her gut that heartbreak waited at the end of this chase, she quickened her steps on the moving stairs, pushing past people who blocked her path, muttering "excuse me" as she plowed through the scattering of pedestrians.

She reached the street, gasping, trembling with urgency, and half-stumbled into the chill air. Rush hour traffic congested Connecticut Avenue, and the sidewalk was crowded with pedestrians heading home. Which way should she go?

Alternately freezing and feverish, Gia jogged a few blocks, her muscles tight with sick anticipation and spiraling hopelessness.

Grim-faced businessmen in suits and trench coats were out in droves, but none of them were Joachim.

She'd lost him.

Despair drove her onward. Her mindless journey took her past an apartment complex where she sometimes stopped on warmer days to watch children play in the small park tucked between the two high-rise buildings.

Today, a bevy of kids, bundled in thick winter coats and toboggans, scampered around the playground. Their schoolbooks and backpacks were scattered on the curb, and they raced and frolicked with the pent-up energy resulting from an eight-hour day stuck in a stuffy classroom.

Numb with anguish, Gia paused to watch them, marveling at the display of joy and laughter, when within her soul dwelt such incongruous grief and frustration. Wandering into the park, she chose a bench at the perimeter, dropped her backpack and sat. There was no hurry to get home. All that awaited her in the small efficiency was hollow solitude.

Nearby, a boy in a plaid coat plucked the striped stocking cap off a smaller boy's head and tossed it to a leggy girl.

"Keep away!" he shrieked, while the victim scurried between them, half-laughing and half-pleading for mercy, his chestnut curls damp with exertion and the trickling snow.

The forlorn hat arced through the air and landed on the bench beside Gia, and she reached for it before the two older kids could retrieve it.

"What'll you give me for it?" she asked, squinting at the tall girl when she jogged over. "Ten bucks?"

The girl's wide features broke into a grin. "Aw, we don't got money."

"It's mine, anyway," the injured party declared, stalking to take it from Gia's outstretched hand. "Thanks, lady." He stopped in front of her and pulled the cap over his brown curls, his somber blue eyes studying her face.

Gia stared back in breathless amazement. The child could be Joachim at age seven or eight, a premature vision of the tall, handsome warrior to come.

He could be the child she would never have with the man she loved, the man she would never see again.

As if reading her sadness, the boy half-shrugged and smiled a little at her, a wordless reassurance, then turned to rejoin the game.

The fun didn't last long. Soon a hefty, dark-haired woman appeared from one of the apartment buildings and approached the playground, hollering with little aplomb, "Kids! Get in here! It's late!"

Gia watched the beautiful boy and his companions dive for their schoolbooks and scramble across the playground. She watched until they disappeared inside the warmly lit lobby of the building, until their laughing chatter faded to silence, until the wan sunlight slid further into the purple glow of dusk.

Then Gia Torio, Daughter of Longinus, who'd thought she had not a single tear left to shed, buried her face in her hands and cried.

* * * * *

Awareness of life returned to her with the metallic screech of a truck's brakes as it pulled to a stop nearby. Horns honked. Someone shouted.

There was no romance in sobbing one's heart out on a park bench. Gia's crying jag was over. It hadn't done her any good. Grieving like this, when she already felt so alone in the world, only worsened her despondency, and she vowed it would be the last time.

She straightened her spine and glanced around. No one had noticed her. The people cutting through the playground half-ran toward the apartment buildings, anxious to get out of the cold and falling darkness. Anxious to get home to their families and a warm meal.

Gia, too, had obligations— a paper to write, an apartment to clean. *Up and at 'em, girl.* Unzipping her backpack, she rummaged for a tissue, to no avail. At this rate, the tears would freeze on her cheeks.

As though she'd spoken her need aloud, a neatly folded handkerchief floated into view.

"Oh…thanks." She hadn't heard anyone approach her bench. Embarrassment flooded her face as she took the hankie without meeting the gaze of the Good Samaritan who'd offered it. Even in big cities, people were mostly kind, especially when they saw a decently dressed, middle-America woman blubbering on a park bench.

If they only knew.

Self-conscious, she wiped her eyes, her nose. This guy definitely wouldn't want his handkerchief back after she was through with it. Crumpling the cotton square in her lap, she glanced up to offer him an apologetic smile and froze.

Joachim stood before her, shoulders hunched against the cold, breath coming in quick, billowing clouds.

Gia hiccupped on a fresh sob and clasped a hand over her heart, an unconscious attempt to protect it from this piquant, electric moment. "Who are you?"

His expression softened. "Have you forgotten so quickly?"

That accent. The low timbre of his voice. The blue, blue eyes so full of tenderness.

The angel of her heart.

Her backpack slid from her lap as she rose to her feet, her gaze wide and unblinking on his beautiful, beloved face.

He smiled.

Her knees crumpled beneath her.

"Gia—" Joachim caught her and drew her against his chest, at last, at last, tightening strong, loving arms around her, whispering words against her temple, her cheek, her hair, impassioned words she'd dreamed of but never thought she'd hear again.

"Gia, my Gia..." His lips brushed her brow, her lashes, following the fresh flood of tears down her cheek. For a moment he lifted his head to look into her eyes, and she cupped a trembling hand to his cheek, sobbing, laughing her joy because no words could express what surpassed the boundaries of the human heart.

Then she lifted her other hand to his jaw and led his lips down to hers.

Like new lovers, their mouths brushed, caught and clung, Joachim's gentle with restrained hunger, Gia's trembling with delight. The world with all its trivial activity spun around them unheeded, for they only heard the hammer of their own hearts and felt the sweet warmth of each other's bodies seeping through cloth and flesh and bone.

"You came back to me," she whispered, too afraid to close her eyes even as he kissed her, lest he slip away from her like the dream he appeared to be.

Too soon, he withdrew to rest his forehead against hers, his breath rushing quick and unsteady against her lips. "They sent me back. With no wings, no halo, no Medallion or Spear. Just a mortal body and a love for you more eternal than all the Heavens combined. Will you have me then? As a man?"

"Joachim. Oh, Joachim." She couldn't speak whole sentences, couldn't think, couldn't breathe. She didn't need to. She hung suspended in the magnificent disbelief of the moment, in the sweet anticipation of what would happen next.

Grasping his warm hand in hers, she lifted it to her lips and kissed his fingers, remembering all at once how they had touched her in comfort, in tenderness, in passion, and how lifeless and pale they'd appeared in death as his body lay cradled in her lap.

And now he was here, looking at her, holding her, loving her, as though time hadn't passed, as though he hadn't left this body and returned to a glorious realm far beyond her frail human perception.

It was impossible.

It was *real*. Divine comprehension poured through her like warm, sweet honey. The loving and benevolent Creator, of whom Joachim had so often spoken, existed after all. How could she have ever doubted it? How could she have questioned what her heart had always known to be true?

"How?" she demanded, her voice throaty with shock and emotion. "How in God's name did you ever find me?"

Choked laughter shuddered through him. "It helps that I live in that building." He nodded toward the one behind them, and then looked back at her, his too-bright gaze drinking in her features as though starved for the sight of her. "But only Creator could have placed you in my path this way, after I've waited, and suffered, and searched for you."

Gia kissed him again. "You've been looking for me?"

"From the moment I returned to this Earth I've been preparing, readying a life for both of us, all without knowing how to find you or where to even begin. The frustration—the human helplessness I felt—sometimes I thought I would die from it. And here you are, as though Creator sat you on this bench with His bare hands for me to find."

Uttering a silent prayer of thanks, Gia parted the lapels of his trench coat and slid beneath it to embrace him, hungry to feel the heat and strength of his lean body after so many months of yearning and grief.

Joachim's eyelids slid closed at the contact, all the tension draining from him as she reached up again to touch his face. "I thought there was no greater pain than being parted from you. But this happiness, it overwhelms me. I don't know where to start." He opened his eyes, their azure brilliance magnified a million times by joy. "We have much to talk about."

"Yes." She shivered, a combination of lingering shock and the swiftly plummeting temperature, and he rubbed his hands briskly over her arms to warm her.

"It's getting dark and cold," he said, drawing her toward the building to the west. "Come inside with me and I'll tell you everything."

The elevator was deserted, and once the doors slid closed, they turned toward each other again, kissing, touching, hands roaming to soak in the feel of each other, to fill themselves with the reassurance that this blessed moment had actually come to pass.

"Don't let me go," she whispered against his neck, breathing in his beloved scent and the wooly fragrance of his damp coat. "Don't let me go."

"Never again, my love. My Gia."

When they reached his apartment, he slid the key in the lock and glanced at her. "Be prepared."

"Prepared?" She smiled at him, dazed with happiness. "For

what?"

"My apartment—it's empty. I have a mattress, some cooking utensils, but I haven't been a resident of this Earth long enough to acquire real material items."

"Have any of your neighbors heard you talk like that?" she said, laughing.

Humor curved his lips. "I hardly think I'm the most unusual conversationalist in this neighborhood." He brushed a strand of hair from her eyes. "My home needs your touch, Gia. And so do I."

Her hand slipped beneath his suit lapel and caressed his chest, settling where his human heart beat a strong assurance that this night was sweet reality. "We have some catching up to do, Joachim."

His expression intensified as his gaze skimmed her face, a visual caress that weakened Gia's trembling limbs. Then he unlocked the door, and they made it as far as the parquet foyer before Joachim pulled her into his embrace and backed her up against the bare wall, kissing her open mouth with hungry fervor.

"I have so many questions." Breathless, she tilted her head to accommodate his lips as they skimmed her throat. "How long have you been here? In this apartment? In this city?" She pushed the coat off his arms as she spoke, exposing the charcoal suit beneath. "Why are you dressed in this gorgeous suit?"

Bracing a hand on the wall above her head, he smiled down into her eyes and withdrew a wallet from inside his jacket for her perusal. "I was returned to this body fourteen days ago. This is my identity in this life."

"Agent Joachim Armande," she read, "Federal Bureau of Investigations, Criminal Tactics Division." Her gaze returned to his, wide with disbelief. "You're working for the government? How the heck did you arrange such a thing from…from up there?"

He cocked a brow. "I was qualified for the job, was I not?"

"Overqualified, I'd say." Delighted, Gia wrapped her arms around his neck again and watched him return his wallet to his jacket. "Did you even know I was in Washington when they sent you back?"

Joachim sighed, his humor fading. "They told me little. In accordance with the human experience, I was dropped into this body and forced to make my way, with the exception of a little guidance from Michael. He aimed me in the right direction for the first few days, and then all of a sudden, nothing." He swallowed, fingering a stray curl against her cheek. "I suppose the Dominions put an end to our communication. It wouldn't have been fair for Michael to guide me further. Not after I'd been discharged from his legions."

At the sadness that dimmed his expression, Gia pressed a kiss of comfort against his lips. "Oh, Joachim. I never would have wanted you to give up your position, your—"

"I was dying for want of you," he said fiercely. "Do you understand? The Dominions had no choice. I tried to get on with things. I tried to forget, to return to who I was before, but..."

He fidgeted with the zipper tab on her coat, the tears on his lashes turning his eyes aquamarine. "I felt as though my heart had been stripped from me. They had to send me back to you, out of mercy. Out of compassion. And now, yes, I mourn what I was, but it's bearable, and with you I will heal."

She murmured a wordless response and drew his cheek down to hers, and they stood like that, braced against the cool, unadorned wall, breathing each other, reveling in the silky desire that shimmered between them.

"So this is what it is to be wholly human," Joachim whispered at last, his fingers sifting through her hair and grazing her neck until she shivered. "There is so much to say after all the time we've been apart. Yet all I can do is touch you, kiss you, and having done so, ask for more."

"Oh, yes." She sighed and opened her lips beneath his, welcoming the languid slide of his tongue, the warm cupping sensation of his strong hands claiming her breasts. "But I do have a thousand questions..."

Laughter rumbled in his chest. "Ah, my wonderful Gia. I'd hoped you hadn't changed."

"They're good questions," she protested with a grin. "For example, what happens now?" Her hands slid over his broad shoulders, exulting in the steely muscles there and remembering them bare and damp under her palms. Beneath his impeccably tailored charcoal suit, his exquisite body awaited her exploration, and Gia shivered with anticipation as she thought about the nights to come. The *life* to come, with him at her side.

"Now we address this human need we share." Joachim's sensuous fingers traced her wrists as his husky words slid through her senses. "How shall we go about it?"

"Don't you remember?" She unzipped her coat and shrugged out of it, let it join his jacket on the floor. "The delicious give and take? The unbearable buildup? All those dirty words I taught you?"

"I haven't forgotten," his voice was thick with both laughter and desire as he tugged at his tie. "This body remembers everything."

"Then take me out of this world, my love."

Lifting her into his arms, he buried his face in her hair and carried her like a child through the dark, empty apartment.

When they reached his bedroom, she stopped him in the doorway and met his eyes. "Tell me, Joachim, because you know Creator's mind more than I ever could. How have I come to this place of happiness when it all started so badly?"

He pressed his lips to her forehead. "Your choices, Gia."

"I made terrible ones for so long."

"And then you made the right ones. To be honest. To be courageous. To be giving and selfless when the time came to serve your Creator and your human brothers and sisters. As His child, and as a proven warrior of His legions, you inherit all the riches of the Earth, and one day the Realm beyond."

"With you?"

He paused, smiling down at her in the dim light. "With me. Here in this physical form, and then in the spiritual one when we go into cycle. We'll never be parted, Gia. Never. *Il te faut croire.*"

"Yes," she whispered, her heart aching with joy. "I believe."

They moved into the bedroom, where the blue haze of moonlight through snow clouds pierced the blinds in opalescent slivers and they could melt into each other's arms, no longer the seraphic guardian and the Daughter of Longinus, but simply Joachim and Gia. A man and a woman. Fallible, mortal, and at last, the recipients of Creator's greatest and most abiding gift.

Epilogue

"You *didn't*." Soleil cast Nicodemus a half-shocked, half-amused glance as they studied the sunny scene through the transom.

"I did. With Creator's blessing. Even the Dominions saw no reason why old friends should be separated."

"Joachim will be overjoyed," she murmured.

"When he figures it out, yes, I believe he will."

"And what will they call the babe when he arrives?"

"I imagine by his name," the old seraph said with a chuckle.

Soleil was silent. Then she turned to frown at him. "But Gia is the Daughter of Longinus. In accordance with her legacy, won't she bear a girl?"

Nicodemus regarded her bla

nkly, then a look of startled dismay seeped into his wrinkled features. "Oh, dear. I hadn't thought of that."

"Oh, dear," she echoed, staring back at the window with wide eyes.

Neither spoke for a long time. Then the seraphic counselor rubbed his chin and sighed. "Well, well. Maybe it's a prudent change for our friend. Olivier won't be happy about it at first, but it's long past time he cycled into human life."

Soleil nodded. "Yes. He's been floating around in the abyss too long. And once settled, he'll soon forget he was ever a..." She cleared her throat. "A *he*."

"Besides," Nicodemus straightened his shoulders, "there's nothing we can do about this little miscalculation now. The die has been cast."

"It most definitely has." Soleil bit back a smile and returned her attention to the transom, where Joachim and a very pregnant Gia walked hand-in-hand in a city park. "Well, then. They'll just have to call him Olivia."

Enjoy this excerpt from

A Fine Work of Art

Who would think a single red hair could end a marriage?

Elizabeth rubbed a hand against the throbbing pain behind her left temple and tried to force her attention back to the half-graded term paper in front of her, but it was no use.

The culprit had been an auburn hair actually, glinting in the sun that streamed through the door behind Stuart as he'd set his briefcase and coat on the kitchen counter and leaned to offer Elizabeth's cheek a perfunctory kiss. That was when she saw it on his lapel, the red, silky remnant of his infidelity.

She closed her eyes and fought down a wave of nausea born of grief and exhaustion. Somewhere out there, Stuart was frolicking with Cecilia Aldorf like a sex-crazed teenager instead of the highly accomplished, forty-five-year-old neurosurgeon he was.

The hair was unquestionably Cecilia's. No one had tresses, long and wavy and clingy, quite like Stuart's surgical assistant. Elizabeth's own hair, cut in a conservative, shoulder-length style, was unarguably brown. Naturally so. Apparently Stuart's taste ran the gamut of artificial, because the redhead's breasts were round and perky and as utterly questionable in their authenticity as her hair color.

Months ago Stuart had sworn to end the affair. Anything to save the marriage, he'd said. Elizabeth meant everything to him, he'd said.

Liar. Last night he'd even smelled like his lover; floral and cloying and sexy-sweet. Elizabeth had nearly choked on the scent, half-blinded by the flash of setting sun on the evidence of Stuart's guilt. A single hair, and he hadn't bothered to deny her shriek of accusation.

The urge to laugh now bubbled in her throat, followed by an unexpected sob that rose so fiercely, she clapped her hands over her mouth and sat back in the chair, her welling eyes fixed on the beige, concrete-block wall above her desk.

A mere twenty-four hours had passed since the denouement of her ten-year marriage, and in that time she'd managed to give two art history lectures, counsel three freshmen on the upcoming semester schedules, and grade an impressive stack of term papers, all without shedding a single tear. She couldn't keep a husband's attention, but she made one hell of a college professor.

"Dr. Gilstrom?" The male voice, followed by a soft rap at the door, drew her attention from the concrete wall.

Immediately Elizabeth straightened at the sight of the young man standing at her office threshold. He was a student in the graduate art history class she taught three times a week. Although they'd never formally spoken, she knew his face intimately. Too intimately. For the first weeks of the fall semester, even in the midst of slide shows and lectures, her gaze had strayed to him of its own accord. He was, quite simply, one of the most attractive men she'd ever seen. A work of art that stirred something within her most creative—and feminine—core.

And right now she couldn't remember his name.

"I know you're probably trying to get out of here for the night," he said, a smile curving his full, sensuous mouth, "but could you spare a moment?"

The castors on her desk chair squeaked as she pushed back and turned toward him, motioning to the folding metal chair a foot away. "Of course. Have a seat…"

"Boone," he offered, and sat, filling the six-by-eight office with the scent of autumn, faded shampoo and healthy, warm male. "Boone McCrea. I'm in your 506 art history class."

"Yes, I know." Elizabeth could think of nothing clever to say. She certainly wasn't a flirt, and had always worn her marital status as protective armor against temptation. Now, stripped of it, she found herself the object of the young man's intense contemplation, and she felt…naked.

He was too young to look at her with such solemn fascination. Perhaps twenty-three or twenty-four, with sculpted features, a golden complexion and wonderful, expressive lips. A face from a dream.

She studied the wave of rich, dark hair that fell across his brow and experienced a fleeting sting of satisfaction. She'd actually managed to forget about Stuart for all of two minutes, thanks to Boone McCrea's extraordinary beauty.

"I need to ask you about tomorrow's field trip to the Binoche Gallery," he said finally. "I know you gave the pertinent information yesterday in class, but I had to leave early."

She squelched the indignant urge to demand *why* he'd left her class in the middle of lecture, and lifted the pile of papers on her desk to withdraw a photocopy of the trip's itinerary. "Did you get one of these?"

"No. Thank you." He took it from her, folded it and slipped it into the pocket of his navy windbreaker. He had strong-looking fingers. Paint-stained. The hands of an artist. Elizabeth felt her own fingers tremble slightly and crossed her arms over her breasts to hide the reaction.

"We're meeting in Georgetown, in front of the gallery," she said, forcing her attention back to his face. "But some of the class is gathering at the Tenley Metro station around three o'clock to ride together."

His dark lashes lifted and he met her gaze with clear, clover green eyes. "What about you? How are you getting there?"

She hesitated, surprised at the question. "I hadn't thought about it. I suppose I'll drive."

"Does your husband like art?"

Again, she was struck by his directness and the wayward direction in which their conversation seemed headed. "I...yes." She noticed his gaze linger on her naked ring finger, where the pale circle of skin spoke of her wedding band's recent removal. Its absence hadn't felt so obvious before now. Hurriedly she tucked her hand beneath her other arm and added, "But he doesn't have time to attend galleries often."

"That's too bad," he said softly. "He's missing out."

Silence crashed between them, and all Elizabeth could hear was the inexplicable thunder of her heartbeat. She had to think of something to say, because Boone McCrea gave her the feeling he'd sit across from her all evening, perusing her every feature if she allowed it. Maybe she'd given him the wrong idea. Had he noticed her attention lingering on him in class?

That's what you get for playing with fire, Professor.

Straightening her spine, she swiveled back toward her desk and said in a cool, clipped tone, "I have work to do, Mr. McCrea. Is there anything else?"

"Nothing." The rustle of his jacket as he stood to leave told her he'd gotten the message. "I'll see you tomorrow at the gallery. I'm looking forward to hearing what you have to say about the Fielding exhibit."

"I have plenty to say about the exhibit," she said, and used her red pen to vehemently circle an abysmal misspelling of Michelangelo's name on the term paper in front of her.

"But not so much about the artist?" The smile in his voice brought her gaze back to his face. "People say he's a real piece of work."

That was putting it mildly. Ferber Fielding was a brash, disagreeable old man who had a way of showing up in Elizabeth's world whenever she turned around, armed with a sarcastic barb or a disheartening scowl. Even a simple greeting stuck in her throat when they came face-to-face, whether at a gallery opening or the nearby Seven-Eleven. But Fielding had more talent than any artist Elizabeth had encountered since moving to Washington a decade before, and despite his surly demeanor, she held a grudging respect for him. At least enough to haul thirty art history students to view his work.

"He's scheduled to lecture here before Christmas," she told Boone. "I'll make it a point to introduce you to him."

"That should be interesting." He studied her a moment, his humor fading to just a slight, curious tug on the corners of his mouth. "I'm sorry to interrupt your work."

She shook her head. "You didn't interrupt my work. I was daydreaming."

"About something sad."

Elizabeth blinked at him. How could he know that about her? Her own husband hadn't been able to read her emotions in a decade of marriage. Hell, until this moment, *she* hadn't even known that her sadness was as great as her rage over Stuart's betrayal. Maybe Boone was young, but his perception probably ran circles around most of the men she knew.

She heaved a sigh and glanced back at her work. "Yes. Something sad."

He paused in the doorway. "It'll fade, you know," he said, in a voice that made her feel oddly comforted. "Nothing lasts forever, Dr. Gilstrom."

Not love, nor marriage. Not even life in general, she thought, staring at the empty space he left behind as his footsteps disappeared down the hall. No promise was truly kept.

For the first time since realizing her marriage to Stuart was over, Elizabeth put her head down on her desk and cried.

* * * * *

It looked like bloody handprints smeared on canvas.

Thirty-one pairs of eyes fixed on the chaotic abstract mounted on the gallery wall while disconcerted silence stole the soft, good-natured chatter of the group.

"How awful," muttered one female student.

Elizabeth glanced back at her pupils and smiled. "Just the reaction I'm sure Mr. Fielding would relish."

"So much of his work seems to be about death and violence," the girl continued, sidling through the spectators to take a closer look over her Coke-bottle eyeglasses. "Is there something wrong with him?"

"I'd say there's something right," a familiar male voice spoke behind them, and Elizabeth turned to find Boone McCrea at her side, his hands clasped behind his back as he studied the painting.

She was surprised to see him. He hadn't shown up at the Metro station when the group convened to ride to the gallery together, and Elizabeth had tried not to feel disappointed. In her shadow-swathed existence of the previous few hours, he was a tiny, guilty pleasure, a pinpoint of light. Their brief encounter in her office last night had piqued her interest further. Earlier at the subway station, she'd been so busy staring up the escalator for a sign of him, she'd nearly missed the train's arrival. A silly, broken woman, in love with youth, with the past, searching for…for what? She couldn't explain her odd preoccupation with the young graduate student. It was too ridiculous.

When he hadn't appeared at the Metro, she'd assumed he would miss the field trip, and silently, firmly, she closed him out of her thoughts…leaving only the bitter remnants of Stuart, and the sharp return of depression.

Now Boone McCrea had materialized before her like a sweet, silky breeze across her skin, and she shivered with misplaced delight. His dark hair was windblown and curly, his lean cheeks ruddy from the autumn afternoon. The maroon Henley he wore beneath his denim jacket set off the crystal clarity of his gaze, like red velvet behind emeralds in a jeweler's showcase. He was…how could one adequately describe such balanced, sensual features? Or do justice to the shine of intelligence and humor in his green eyes?

Elizabeth stifled the urge to laugh. He was a distraction, a means of frivolous relief sent from heaven to offset the pain of her pending divorce. There was no other explanation.

Abruptly she realized she was staring and quickly regained her composure. "What do you think the artist intended with this particular piece, Mr. McCrea?"

He lowered his gaze to hers and smiled, an odd, secretive smile, before turning to address the chubby student who found the painting so disconcerting. "Manipulation of the masses. He knows how to flip the switch on the public's emotions. Most people who look at this painting will automatically see violence."

"And yet the painting is entitled 'The Patisserie's Hands'." Elizabeth's own mouth curved into an ironic smile. "It's not blood that makes the handprints. It's chocolate."

Wry laughter and murmurs floated through the group as they shuffled on to the next canvas.

While they examined the smaller, more traditional landscape, she glanced back to locate Boone. He still lingered at 'The Patisserie's Hands', but his attention wasn't on the painting. He was quietly chatting with another student, a blonde girl, his dark head inclined toward her as they spoke. His gaze focused on her as though she were the only other soul on Earth. Either he found her honey-skinned beauty totally entrancing, or Boone McCrea was a damned good listener.

Elizabeth tried to look away, but found herself mesmerized. Despite the unseasonably cool weather, the girl wore a cropped T-shirt and low-slung, bell-bottom jeans that bared her flat tummy. Her silver navel ring caught the light and glistened like a droplet of water, ready to drizzle into the waistband of her Levi's. But Boone wasn't gobbling her up with a hungry, sweeping gaze, the way Elizabeth had seen a thousand other men his age regard such a beautiful girl. His eyes were locked on the blonde's as she gestured to the painting. He was listening, with what appeared to be genuine interest, to what she had to say.

Elizabeth swallowed her resentment, returned her attention to the smaller painting before her, and flipped through her notes to find information on the landscape. "This is one of Fielding's earlier works. Note the tighter brushstrokes, the realistic color and rather unimaginative subject matter. It's amazing how twenty years of living can change an artist's style."

* * * * *

It's amazing how ten years of living in a loveless marriage can change a woman's sense of self.

The screech of the Metro's brakes and the train's accompanying lurch brought Elizabeth out of her maudlin reverie. She gathered her briefcase, tugged the lapels of her trench coat across her breasts, and stepped out onto the platform to bid her students goodnight. Boone McCrea wasn't among them. Suspiciously enough, neither was the blonde with the navel ring, whose name Elizabeth couldn't remember. They'd simultaneously disappeared as the students filed out of the gallery, and she wasn't exactly surprised. Resigned was more like it.

"If you come up with any further questions about the exhibit at The Binoche, bring them to class with you on Monday," Elizabeth told the remaining students as they rode the escalator to the darkened city street above.

Her gray Mercedes sedan sat in the deserted Kiss-and-Ride Metro lot near the college campus. Juggling her briefcase and purse, she activated the keyless entry, slid inside the chilled leather interior, and drew the seatbelt across her lap. God, it was cold for a late September night. But it was the thought of returning to a silent, empty house that chilled her to the bone.

She slipped the key into the ignition, turned it, and...nothing. Frowning, she tried again. Only a single click. The battery light came on.

"Damn..." She let her forehead thud against the steering wheel. "Damn!"

The five-minute walk across campus to her office left her trembling with cold beneath the thin trench coat. To make matters worse, it had begun to rain; a soft, misting drizzle that made the grass glisten in the streetlights like a field of diamonds.

"Forty-five minutes," the tow company told her when she called from her office in the eerily silent art building. "Stay at your car, miss."

"By myself, for almost an hour in a deserted parking lot?" Astonishment curdled her tone, and she immediately clenched her jaw and breathed patience. "I'm sorry—cancel the tow. I'll think of something."

Setting down the phone, Elizabeth rubbed her hands over her face and squelched the urge to cry. A dead battery. Big deal. A dead marriage; a dead life.

"Damn," she whispered again, and with a slow, deep inhalation, banished the self-pity that circled her soul like hawks over carrion. Then she called a cab.

Outside, the crystalline mist had turned to a steady rain. Bracing herself against the cold night, she tucked her chin into the collar of her coat, stepped out of the art building…and abruptly collided with a warm, hard body.

"Whoa." Two strong hands encircled her arms and steadied her. "Dr. Gilstrom, this is a surprise."

Elizabeth looked up, faltered, sputtered.

And found herself smiling into clear, green eyes...

About the author:

Writing romance comes naturally to Shelby Reed and has flavored most of her work since she first fell in love with Jane Austen's stories years ago. She strives to write about real women with contemporary issues, who manage to find love despite the trials and tribulations of today's single female. When not churning out fiction, Shelby utilizes her B.A. in Art as a portraitist, works part-time as an editor, and considers herself a full-time author since she recently quit her day job to throw herself headlong into writing. She lives in the flavorful deep south with her husband, two rambunctious dogs, and a house full of manuscripts and artwork in various stages of completion.

Shelby welcomes mail from readers. You can write to her c/o Ellora's Cave Publishing at 1056 Home Avenue, Akron OH 44310-3502.

Why an electronic book?

We live in the Information Age—an exciting time in the history of human civilization in which technology rules supreme and continues to progress in leaps and bounds every minute of every hour of every day. For a multitude of reasons, more and more avid literary fans are opting to purchase e-books instead of paperbacks. The question to those not yet initiated to the world of electronic reading is simply: *why?*

1. *Price.* An electronic title at Ellora's Cave Publishing and Cerridwen Press runs anywhere from 40-75% less than the cover price of the exact same title in paperback format. Why? Cold mathematics. It is less expensive to publish an e-book than it is to publish a paperback, so the savings are passed along to the consumer.
2. *Space.* Running out of room to house your paperback books? That is one worry you will never have with electronic novels. For a low one-time cost, you can purchase a handheld computer designed specifically for e-reading purposes. Many e-readers are larger than the average handheld, giving you plenty of screen room. Better yet, hundreds of titles can be stored within your new library—a single microchip. (Please note that Ellora's Cave and Cerridwen Press does not endorse any specific brands. You can check our website at www.ellorascave.com or

www.cerridwenpress.com for customer recommendations we make available to new consumers.)

3. *Mobility.* Because your new library now consists of only a microchip, your entire cache of books can be taken with you wherever you go.
4. *Personal preferences are accounted for.* Are the words you are currently reading too small? Too large? Too...**ANNOYING**? Paperback books cannot be modified according to personal preferences, but e-books can.
5. *Instant gratification.* Is it the middle of the night and all the bookstores are closed? Are you tired of waiting days—sometimes weeks—for online and offline bookstores to ship the novels you bought? Ellora's Cave Publishing sells instantaneous downloads 24 hours a day, 7 days a week, 365 days a year. Our e-book delivery system is 100% automated, meaning your order is filled as soon as you pay for it.

Those are a few of the top reasons why electronic novels are displacing paperbacks for many an avid reader. As always, Ellora's Cave and Cerridwen Press welcomes your questions and comments. We invite you to email us at service@ellorascave.com, service@cerridwenpress.com or write to us directly at: 1056 Home Ave. Akron OH 44310-3502.

Cerridwen, the Celtic Goddess of wisdom, was the muse who brought inspiration to storytellers and those in the creative arts. Cerridwen Press encompasses the best and most innovative stories in all genres of today's fiction. Visit our site and discover the newest titles by talented authors who still get inspired - much like the ancient storytellers did, once upon a time.

ELLORA'S CAVE
ROMANTICA PUBLISHING